Now she was si...
forever, stay t...
Our love...
that mean... ...end.

Sunny stared straight ahead and didn't even glance at her. After a beat Sunny snubbed out the most recently lit cigarette in the ashtray next to her chair and looked at Dahlia with a raised eyebrow. "Gotta go now," she said, and Dahlia wasn't sure if she was saying Dahlia had to go or Sunny had to leave the porch until Sunny stood, turned, and walked into the house. Her exit was so abrupt that Dahlia let out an outraged laugh. She was being dismissed. She'd come all this way to offer this woman a deal that could provide her with enough money to get her the hell out of this beat-up little rest home for fruitcakes, and the woman was walking away.

"Sunny," Dahlia said, following behind her, "I haven't seen you in so long. You can't walk away. I need to tell you about this offer."

Sunny didn't look back, just headed right up the staircase. *I can't let her out of my sight,* Dahlia thought. "Sunny!" she called, moving toward the steps. But before she could get to them, she was blocked by a large man dressed in a white jacket. He had a crew cut and a big round face, and he was smiling, a forced smile.

"We don't like guests upstairs," he said.

"Entertaining . . .
Dart keeps the story moving at a fast clip."
Publishers Weekly

By Iris Rainer Dart

SOME KIND OF MIRACLE
WHEN I FALL IN LOVE
BEACHES

IRIS RAINER DART

SOME KIND OF MIRACLE

AVON BOOKS

An Imprint of HarperCollins*Publishers*

Grateful acknowledgment is made to the Volunteers in Medicine for permission to reprint from its mission statement, copyright © 2002 by the Volunteers in Medicine.

AVON BOOKS
An Imprint of HarperCollins*Publishers*
10 East 53rd Street
New York, New York 10022-5299

Copyright © 2003 by Iris Rainer Dart
ISBN: 0-06-103177-1
www.avonbooks.com

First Avon Books paperback printing: January 2005
First William Morrow hardcover printing: December 2003

Avon Trademark Reg. U.S. Pat. Off. and in Other Countries, Marca Registrada, Hecho en U.S.A.
HarperCollins® is a registered trademark of HarperCollins Publishers Inc.

Printed in the U.S.A.

10 9 8 7 6 5 4 3

*This book is dedicated to
the memory of Marly Stone,
the newest and brightest voice
in the heavenly choir.
I miss you.*

The two children loved each other so dearly that they always walked about hand in hand, whenever they went out together. And when Snow White said, "We will never desert each other," Rose Red answered, "No, not as long as we live," and the mother added: "Whatever one gets, she shall share with the other."

—"Snow White and Rose Red"

May we have eyes to see those who are rendered invisible and excluded, open arms and hearts to reach out and include them, healing hands to touch their lives with love . . . and in the process heal ourselves.

—from the mission statement of
the Volunteers in Medicine

thank you

Dr. Murray Brown
Dr. Jeffrey Galpin
Dr. Joseph Snyder
Michelle Brourman
Elizabeth Mello
Lynn Marta
Harriet Shock
Artie Butler
Susan Dempsey *and the folks at* Step Up on Second
Rabbi Norman Mendel
Betty Kelly
Elaine Markson
Carrie Feron
Alice and Cliff Cohen

As always, for Stevie, Rachel, Greg, Lydia, and Stuart

ost of the guests arrived at about four, parking their cars up and down Moorpark Street, slowly trailing in, carrying bouquets of flowers or white bakery boxes tied with string. Dahlia looked at the clock on the mantel again, relieved that it was already five-thirty and there hadn't been even the tiniest incident yet. She was sure the success of the day was thanks to the fact that all the fingers on both her hands were tightly crossed. For an hour and a half, she'd kept her hands in her pockets so nobody could see them, because her mother always laughed when she did superstitious things like that. But this time it was actually working.

Thanks to her crossed fingers, any outsider who happened to look in the window might think this was an ordinary family gathering. No Sunny locking herself in the bathroom screaming out death threats to everyone at the party by name, no Sunny keening and wailing about how some unidentified "they" were after her. No Sunny frantically rushing around the house destroying every breakable item in her path. Today there was just the music.

Just Dahlia and Sunny sitting at the baby grand piano singing their best songs, surrounded by friends and family. Everyone seemed to love the new one they'd finished writing just that morning as Sunny belted out each verse in her big, husky voice. And every time she came to the chorus, Dahlia chimed in, harmonizing in her pure, childlike voice, their sound enchanting the friends and family who swayed to the music, smiling.

Most of them were gazing at Sunny, probably wondering how a pink-skinned, blue-eyed blonde like her could have been born into this olive-skinned, dark-haired family.

"Recessive genes," Uncle Max said with a shrug when anyone asked him.

"The milkman," Aunt Ruthie joked with a grin when anyone asked her. Dahlia didn't get why everyone always laughed at that.

Sunny was seventeen and curvy, and her long, wavy hair was as white as the piano keys she stroked and pressed and cajoled until glorious tunes rose from them. Tunes she fashioned from her tormented psyche. And always, from the moment her graceful fingers began to play until the last song was over, nobody who was listening ever yawned or stole a glance at the clock, wondering when she would finish. They were much too caught up in the spell of the songs, the way she delivered them and the way their melodies transported her. But Sunny never saw their awestruck gazes, because she was far away in what she sometimes called the "secret garden" of her songs.

"Music isn't just something I play or write," she told

Dahlia many times. "It's a place where I get to go." And it was clear when the others watched the way she threw back her head and closed her eyes as she played and sang that she was unquestionably elsewhere, gone into some parallel world where none of the rest of them could travel, including the twelve-year-old Dahlia singing along, pale and dark and looking particularly frail because of the inevitable comparison to the dazzling Sunny.

Usually when the song was over and Sunny turned to discover the relatives fishing in their pockets and purses for handkerchiefs to wipe their teary eyes, she laughed an embarrassed laugh at their emotional reaction and told them they were "too cute." Today while the girls were singing their original "Stay by My Side," Dahlia spotted Aunt Ruthie making an O with her thumb and forefinger and holding it up to Uncle Max to say, "So far so good," and she was sure everyone else in the room was thinking that same thought.

Unfortunately, it was only a few minutes after the performance, while Dahlia stood at the buffet table hoping nobody noticed she was sneaking slices of corned beef from her own plate and feeding them to Arthur the dog, that the shrill cry went up from Aunt Ethel warning the others that they were on the brink of another Sunny emergency. And Dahlia hated herself for uncrossing her fingers so she could eat.

"Maxieeeee!" Aunt Ethel squealed, causing everyone in the room to look up from his or her sandwich. "Naked" was the only word Dahlia's mother's sister could get out as she dropped her paper plate on an end table and headed for the screen door to the front porch.

All the family members left their own plates behind, rushing outside to look west toward Coldwater Canyon, *where Sunny was now sprinting away from the house wearing only the red rubber band that held her white-blond hair in a ponytail. All of them lined up on the porch looking down the wide street after her except Sunny's older brother, Louie, who could chronicle his entire life, after the age of five, around landmark Sunny emergencies and was no longer fazed by them. Louie stayed inside, filled his plate from the tray of sweets, and turned on the TV to watch a baseball game.*

Now Sunny was halfway down the block dodging traffic, and Dahlia was relieved that the most anyone in the family could see of her was her very white back and her pretty white tush bouncing along as she moved down Moorpark Street, the long ponytail swaying from side to side against her white shoulders. Many of the astonished drivers who had just passed Sunny now drove by the family, red-faced and tugging at their rearview mirrors to get another look.

Dahlia saw Uncle Max hurry back inside the house, letting the screen door slam behind him. An instant later the door flew open and he bolted out onto the porch, now hanging on to the floral-print throw Aunt Ruthie always flung over the couch when company came, in case anyone spilled food from the buffet. Uncle Max was big and athletic and fast, and as he leaped off the porch and sprinted down the street after Sunny, it was easy to see he wasn't going to have any trouble catching up with her.

Dahlia saw Sunny dart between a red pickup truck and a silver convertible to get across the intersection, and the driver of the convertible slammed on the brakes and veered left and right as he spotted her. That was when Uncle Max, close enough to overtake her, in one acrobatic move managed to toss the floral-print throw over her. As he reeled her in, the others cheered as if they were at a sporting event. But Sunny fought off the throw with flailing arms and spun quickly to face her father, raising what the others could now see was the flashing blade of a meat cleaver as it caught the sun.

Then, letting out a throaty cry that the others could hear all the way back at the house, Sunny wielded the cleaver at her father, who didn't move out of the way fast enough. Even from that distance, the family could hear both of them screaming, Sunny in outrage and Uncle Max in pain, until, with a loud grunt, he seized his beautiful, tormented child and lifted her into his arms, their cries and screams commingling indistinguishably now. Dahlia heard doors slam, and she looked around to see the neighbors hurrying from their houses to see what was causing the commotion.

The blood was pouring out of the gash on Uncle Max's face onto the throw and onto Sunny as he trudged back toward the house, holding tightly to his daughter, who kicked and shrieked for him to let her go. The family stood quiet and somber-faced, except for the occasional cluck of a tongue or an "Ay, ay, ay" of sadness as they watched the bloody Uncle Max trying to contain the irrational outburst of the hysterical Sunny.

Dahlia noticed that there was not a trace of surprise on the faces of anyone in the family, all of whom had seen Sunny meltdowns like this many times before. Once at a picnic, when Sunny threw handfuls of food at all of them, then sawed at her wrists with a bread knife and bled over what was left of the potato salad and coleslaw. Then there was the time they all met at Disneyland and Sunny stood up on the Matterhorn and removed her blouse and, when the ride was through, ran through the park screaming obscenities.

Dahlia would never forget when the ambulance came to take Sunny away from Disneyland that day, how embarrassed she'd felt when the other families stood gawking, watching Sunny being strapped down as if she were another park attraction, some of them snickering, one woman actually letting out a big laugh. Dahlia wanted to run around and pummel them all and scream at them to stop staring. Especially when Sunny caught Dahlia's eye and begged, "Don't let them do this to me," and Dahlia had been helpless. Too young and too afraid to do anything.

Now Aunt Ruthie sat on the curb moaning. The party was over. Louie came out of the house as if nothing had happened. He was eating a brownie, and the crumbs were all over his chin and falling on to the front of his shirt.

"Hey, Ma, I'm going over to Richie's house to watch the game."

Aunt Ruthie didn't even look at him as she hurried inside. Dahlia's parents gathered their things to leave as Sunny's agonized wails filled the house. Aunt Ruthie hurried upstairs, and in a minute Dahlia could hear her aunt's muffled attempts to calm Sunny, which were doing no good. Soon the high scream of an ambulance heading toward them grew louder. Dahlia looked through the living room window and saw it pull up, the flashing light on the top continuing to blink even after the two men got out and walked, in perfectly matched steps, toward the house.

When Aunt Ruthie opened the front door and saw the serious-faced men, she let out a little grunt of surprise, as if she hadn't been the one to call them, as if she hadn't already known they were the ones who had rung the bell. Then she gestured for them to follow her up the stairs. Dahlia was sure she recognized one of the men from another time

Sunny had been taken away in an ambulance. After a moment Dahlia heard what had to be the instant Sunny laid eyes on the men, because her poor cousin cried out in protest, "Nooooo! Nooooo!" And then there was the sound of a struggle and finally only the sound of Aunt Ruthie crying quietly and repeating, "My baby. She's my baby."

Dahlia heard the men's voices at the top of the steps as they tried to decide how to get the stretcher to turn the corner on the tiny landing, and Dahlia suddenly felt as if she shouldn't be there when Sunny went by. She felt sure she couldn't stand to see that helpless, panicked look in Sunny's eyes one more time. Maybe, she thought, she should go out to the backyard and stay there until she heard the ambulance pull away.

But she stood right where she was, mesmerized with sadness, as one of the men walked backward, guiding the head of the stretcher down the narrow staircase. And when the men got to where she was standing, Dahlia held the screen door open wide for them. As they moved past her, she saw Sunny strapped down to the stretcher, her hair wildly askew, but this time she didn't look helplessly at Dahlia the way she had in the past. This time her face looked dramatically changed. She was slack-jawed, wearing a vacant, far-off stare, probably induced by the drugs one of the white-coated men had given her. How scary, Dahlia thought, that those drugs they forced on her poor cousin transformed her into someone that she, Dahlia, the closest person to her in the world, was barely able to recognize.

At the curb two little boys from across the street peered into the open doors of the ambulance and watched as the men slid the stretcher holding Sunny, the beautiful Sunny, into the back. Then a solemn Uncle Max hoisted himself up *and in to sit beside her. Dahlia always remembered that, even though the scream of the ambulance's siren was ear-piercingly loud, it couldn't drown out the screams of Aunt Ruthie, her face clouded with a black and terrible despair, as the rest of the family circled her protectively and moved her back toward the house.*

❧

one

ere's how it feels to massage Marty Melman:
like making a pizza, Dahlia thought. His
white, hairless body looked like pre-rolled-out pizza
dough and felt like it, too. In fact, she had a recipe
she'd cut out of *Los Angeles* magazine years ago, for
Wolfgang Puck's Pizza, and every time she took the
homemade dough out from under the dish towel
where it had been rising and moved it around between
her floured hands, she thought about Marty Melman.

Massaging Helene Shephard was like massaging a
Cornish hen. The old woman had bumpy skin and a
body that was bony and fragile and felt eminently
breakable in Dahlia's strong hands. And the funny
thing was that Helene was so ticklish that when
Dahlia worked on her feet, she always let out a cackle
that sounded like something right out of the barnyard.

Massaging Leroy Berk was like washing a car. He

was big and black and shiny and just as silent as a parked car, at least to Dahlia. He was always lying facedown on the table when she got there and never even acknowledged her arrival. The room in which she massaged the handsome basketball player was lined with awards and trophies Leroy had won over the years, and if Leroy happened to be asleep when she finished, Dahlia took the opportunity to look at them.

Helene always offered her a cup of tea afterward, and even when Dahlia had a lot of errands to do that day and knew if she said yes she'd have to hear the same stories repeated again and again, the hopeful look in Helene's eyes when she asked made Dahlia agree to stay. To stop for a while in the kitchen where Helene, still in her robe, brewed what she called "a proper pot of tea" and put out a plate of home-baked cookies, one of which she would dip into the tea and munch as she complained about her adult children and how they never came to visit. Sometimes Dahlia worried that she was the only person the poor old woman talked to at all, so she had to stay.

Tonight she was working for Marty, that hunk of pizza dough, who invariably tried to do what he laughingly called "cop a feel."

"Couple of extra bucks in it if you massage me under the towel," he liked to say to Dahlia.

"I don't do that, Marty. You can look in the Yellow Pages under 'Hookers' for that," she said to him the last time.

"Tootsie, I don't need the Yellow Pages."

He was right. He didn't. Marty's white, doughy

body and obnoxious personality aside, his house was invariably populated with young, tall, skinny, bright-eyed girls, who answered the door, talked on the phone, gabbed on the tennis court. Usually there were at least two of them standing in the kitchen preparing dinner when Dahlia picked up her check from the houseman and left through the back door. Tonight Marty was in his bedroom, dressed in a white terry-cloth robe, sitting on the bed talking on the phone. The robe was hanging open, and Dahlia could see the flash of his bright yellow bikini underwear, most of which was covered with the roll of his white belly.

He waved her in, and she moved past him to the grand marble master bathroom, which was mirrored everywhere so she could see her tired self reflected on all sides. Above the sink, where she washed her hands with Dove soap from the crystal soap dish, she caught a closer look at her own exhausted face. Only one more today, she told herself. You can make it through one more. This was the sixth massage she'd given to-day. Her only break had been to sit in the van and wolf down a sandwich she packed herself that morn-ing, and her back and shoulders ached.

Now she heard Marty say into the phone, "Gotta run. Gonna have a good-lookin' woman beat me now. Check in with you later, babe." Then he marched into the bathroom while Dahlia's hands were still covered in soap, pulled off his yellow bikinis, kicked them across the marble floor so they slid to a stop near her, and then waddled to the toilet and peed. Dahlia rinsed her hands and, still carrying the towel, hurried out of the room to set up Marty's massage table. She could hear the water go on in Marty's shower stall, which was bigger than her entire bathroom, as she struggled to pull the heavy massage table out of his huge bedroom storage closet. It was filled with Tumi luggage, and there was an exercise bike and a Stair-Master, too, both of which, from the shape of Marty, she knew he never used.

The table felt heavier than usual, and it seemed to be stuck between the gym equipment in such a way that no amount of Dahlia's tugging could release it. The tears rose behind her eyes, and she was afraid she wouldn't be able to hold them back. She couldn't do this anymore. It was ruining her hands. There wasn't one day when she was driving home from giving her last massage that they didn't throb in pain. She really should be home at the piano working on her songs, not having some obnoxious Hollywood producer think it was okay to pee in front of her because she was less than human—just another servingperson who came in the back door.

Okay. No more complaining, she thought, taking a deep breath. Her mother would have told her she was lucky to have a talent to fall back on when nobody wanted to buy her songs. Besides, she had only one more hour to go, she repeated to herself, pulling again with no success as she tried to free Marty's massage table from whatever was stopping it from moving. In one more hour she'd be out of here, and then she could go home. And do what? she asked herself. Sit and pay bills? Worry and panic over which ones she could avoid this month so she could pay the ones that were the most pressing? That was the story of her life these days.

She could hear Marty singing in the shower in a booming, off-key voice. That old Dean Martin song called "That's Amore." I can't do this to myself anymore, she thought, clenching her aching hands and pulling harder on the table. When I get home, I swear I will work on my songs, she vowed just as her hardest tug at the table brought it crashing toward her. Hang in, she told herself. Just one more hour.

West Los Angeles was her territory, Beverly Hills, Westwood, and Brentwood—all fancy neighborhoods so she was able to charge seventy-five bucks each for these house calls, but Marty's butler, Victor, always handed her a check for a hundred. The extra twenty-five was a tip, and nobody else tipped her. Marty was turning off the shower, and she rushed to get the table made up so that when he emerged, clean and glowing and talcumed like a baby, she'd be ready for him.

Marty marched into the bedroom wrapped in a huge bath sheet that he held at his shoulder like an actor in an amateur play wearing a bad toga. The table usually creaked, begging for mercy, when he climbed aboard, but tonight the creak was so loud that Dahlia was afraid this time it might really buckle while he wriggled into place. But soon he was lying still, face-down and ready for her as she sighed and poured oil into her left hand with the bottle in her right, rubbed her hands together, then placed them on Marty's naked back. As she began to work, Marty let out a happy groan of pleasure.

"God, did I need this," he said, his head down in the face cradle. "Insane week. One picture supposed to start next week. No cast. Another one in post. Supposed to open next month. Music got all fucked up. We've got no song for the credits. We've got no score. Three new projects in development— Ouch! Shit! That's the spot that always kills me. What *is* that?"

"Muscle spasm," Dahlia said, working the big knot with the heel of her right hand.

"Ouch. Oh, yeah. Dig in there," Marty said. "What muscle is that?"

"Your trapezius."

"Fucking trapezius always goes on the fritz," Marty said.

"So what's the name of the new picture?" Dahlia said, not really caring but making her usual friendly-masseuse small talk.

"*Stay by My Side*," Marty said.

"No kidding?" Dahlia said, laughing a genuinely surprised laugh. "*Stay by my side forever. Stay by my side, my friend.*" The tune was being played in her head now by what she called her inner DJ. That lyric was one she'd written at age twelve and set to Sunny's tune. The girls wrote dozens of original songs together, and that was the title of one that had been the all-time favorite of each of them. Probably because it was about the two of them and their close friendship.

"That's funny. When I was about twelve," Dahlia said as her hands moved down to Marty's chubby legs and she pressed hard against his calf with her thumbs, "my cousin and I wrote songs together, and one of them was called 'Stay by My Side.' It was good, too. I don't know if I could find an old tape of it somewhere, but that's a funny coincidence, isn't it? That you need a song with that title and I wrote one?"

Dahlia dug deeper into Marty's calves, and her mind searched her little house in Laurel Canyon, wondering what she could have done with the old tapes of the songs she wrote with Sunny twenty-five years ago. She hadn't heard them since then, and they were probably dopey and immature, but they were worth a listen, if only she could find the damned things. "I mean, you know I'm really a songwriter. Right? That I only do this as a side business. Right?" Marty didn't answer.

Those old tapes were probably crumbled and destroyed by now. "Well, you know what? I'm going to look for them tonight, and if I find that one, I'll get it over to you. Is the best place to send it your office? It's on Beverly Drive, right? I massaged you there one time after you got hurt playing tennis. I can bring it there."

What a funny coincidence. Now as she worked on Marty, she tried to remember the exact tune of "Stay by My Side." In those days Sunny never bothered to write down the tunes on music paper, and Dahlia never saved the little pieces of notebook paper with the lyrics scrawled on them. The two of them were the only ones who sang them, so why take the time? Every so often they recorded them in Sunny's living room on Dahlia's funny old reel-to-reel tape recorder, and maybe she could find some of the tapes. No doubt the song would sound laughably bad all these years later. But what if it held up and was good and Marty actually went for it? Having a song in a movie was a very big deal, so she wasn't going to be shy.

After all, everyone knew the story of how Mariah

Carey had been a backup singer and then got herself invited to a party so she could push a demo of hers into the hands of Tommy Mottola. That story was a legend in the music business. After that night Tommy Mottola made Mariah Carey into a big star. Of course, Tommy Mottola also married Mariah Carey, and Dahlia could barely stand to look at Marty Melman . . . but never mind.

The lesson in the story was that it pays off big time to be aggressive. Mariah Carey went from being a backup singer to a star. Hey, maybe it was true that God moved in mysterious ways and that in the grand scheme of things Dahlia had become a masseuse because of this very moment. Maybe she'd become the masseuse to Marty Melman—referred to him by Cathy Slavin, a cousin of his—so someday she could sell him a song. Oh, God, she thought, if Marty Melman bought her song, wouldn't she laugh about how it had been worth all the crude behavior she put up with from him all the time? The song was dancing through her brain, and she was remembering the way she and Sunny used to sing it in close harmony. The friends and relatives ate it up at parties.

"Stay by my side forever. Stay by my side, my friend," Dahlia sang softly to Marty's back. "Is it a kind of pop feel you're looking for?" she asked hopefully, but there was no answer. "I mean, is the film a comedy? 'Cause if it's a comedy, the song probably doesn't have to be something real serious like one of those Céline Dion anthems or anything? Right?"

Marty's reply was the low growl of a snore. He hadn't heard one word she'd said about the song.

Well, so what? She'd go home tonight and find the tape and pray that the old song was as good as she remembered. Somewhere in the back of her storage bin, she probably still had that old tape player, too, so she could listen to it and then figure out how to transfer it to a CD, and then she would get in Marty's face with it now, when he was desperate for a song with that title.

Somehow, after a while, she persuaded the sleeping Marty to turn over. She watched him shudder happily from somewhere deep in a dream when she rubbed the front of his thighs, and she hurried to finish at the bottom of his pudgy feet. Maybe, she thought, this day was a turning point for her. Maybe this was the day she'd look back on and remember as that low point in the trough period when she didn't think things could get worse—and then her songwriting was rediscovered. One of these days she'd tell that story to Larry King and all the other talk-show hosts when she was a guest on their TV shows, and they'd shake their heads in amazement.

At the end of every massage session, Dahlia always did something she learned in massage school. It was one of those techniques she used not because she believed it worked but because it was the kind of touchy-feely, New Age–y thing some of her clients were convinced contained some magic. She would place her hands gently on the client's face, her thumbs on their forehead and her fingers resting on their cheeks, and then slowly she would take in and release long breaths, as if she were summoning some divine spiritual energy into herself and then transmitting it to the client. People like Helene Shephard, lonely little old women who believed in all that way-out stuff, ate it up.

Marty was still asleep, and his snore was coming out in little popping spurts, but she decided to do the face thing to him anyway. After all, if there was ever a time to transmit something to a client, this was it. Now she stood behind him and placed her thumbs on his forehead and her fingers on his pudgy cheeks that pulsated with each emerging snore. Then she closed her own eyes tightly and took a deep breath. Buy my song, she thought. Oh, please, oh, please, oh, please. Buy my goddamned song!

A song in a movie could turn her life around. She'd move out of that little house she had mistakenly bought and watched fall apart because she couldn't afford to keep it up, and instead she'd find a condo with a new bathroom and windows that didn't leak. Or maybe she'd completely redo the house, add a second floor and a music room. She still had big dreams, and the way to make them happen was definitely through her songs.

In Marty's bathroom, the bright yellow bikini undershorts still near the sink where he'd kicked them, Dahlia washed her hands, passed back through the bedroom, Marty's snores now rattling through the whole space, and down the hall to the kitchen.

"Snoring away?" Victor asked her.

"A regular Texas chain-saw massacre," she joked. He laughed, then handed her the check on her way out the back door. The back frigging door. The service entrance for people who weren't big enough hotshots to use the front.

Out in the driveway, she climbed into her beat-up Toyota van and closed the door, then sat for a while looking at Marty's palatial Bel Air home. The sun was beginning to set, and as it glanced off the huge front windows, it made the whole house look as if it glowed. She had to sell her songs. She had to get out of her own pitiful little life. She started the van and had a surge of wanting to drive back and forth over the perfect lawn shrieking, "Buy my song!" But instead she drove quietly into the night, determined to make it happen.

two

*D*ahlia pushed the play button, and the tape lurched, stopped, and stuck for an instant, looking as if it might split. Then the two plastic wheels began to creak and turn, and the first thing that came out of the speaker was a loud blast of static. The tape had been in a mildewed cardboard box for twenty-five years, on which the twelve-year-old Dahlia had written in pencil: ME AND SUNNY SINGING "STAY BY MY SIDE" AND "GIRLS ARE BETTER."

Where in the hell would she find a studio that would have the equipment to let her listen to this thing and then transfer it to a CD? Why hadn't she and Sunny ever made a lead sheet for the song? Maybe they had and she didn't remember. Well, there was certainly no shot that this old fossil of a tape recorder was ever going to be able to deliver whatever had once been on that tape.

The minute she got home from Marty's, she'd dragged a ladder into the storage room and pulled the big, heavy machine down from the dusty shelf and cleaned it up enough so that she would be able to pry the lid off. As she dusted it and hauled it into the kitchen, she had to laugh at the fact that she was such a pack rat she'd never been able to part with even something as obsolete as this machine. Somehow she had talked herself into the idea that one day she might need it. And here was the day!

But now it looked as if there were no shot that the big dinosaur was going to work. Another loud buzz of static made her wince, convincing her she was never going to hear the tape. Just as she was about to push the stop button, she was startled when the next sound she heard was her own voice at age twelve.

"Move it over," she heard herself say, and she knew that at that moment she must have been climbing onto the piano bench next to her cousin in preparation to sing. Now the sound was clear enough for her to hear the scraping noise the piano bench made on Aunt Ruthie's floor as Sunny pushed it back to welcome her. A jolt ran through Dahlia's whole body when Sunny's voice filled the air. A voice she hadn't heard in twenty-five years.

"Ooookay," Sunny said. "Here goes nothing." That was what she used to say when she was about to perform one of their songs. Dahlia felt as if she could close her eyes and be transported back to that day. Her father had bought the tape recorder and brought it over to Aunt Ruthie and Uncle Max's to show it off. It was on a night when all of the relatives were there, and they stood around it and looked at it as if it had just landed from outer space. Even Arthur the dog sniffed it and walked away.

The clarity of the sound was eerie now, and as the plastic wheels squeaked around, Dahlia watched them, remembering how funny it was that everyone got very quiet and nobody wanted to say anything into it. Not even Sunny. So finally Louie, nasty little creep that he was, kicked Arthur the dog, making poor Arthur yelp, so the first tape they made was of that sound and the sound of Louie laughing in the background.

Now Dahlia could hear Sunny noodling on the keys, trying out the melody with her right hand and saying aloud to herself, "Let's see if I can get this one under my fingers." Then there she was, playing the intro in that bouncy style of hers and segueing into the wonderful melody she'd composed. After a few bars, Dahlia heard her own voice from more than twenty-five years earlier, chiming in with the words about a friend who swears to be there no matter how, no matter when. And Sunny joined her in close harmony. Hearing the two of them delivering their song together in those long-ago days made Dahlia need to lean against the kitchen counter as the memories swept over her.

She wrote those lyrics the morning of the day Sunny was forced to stay locked in her room for being out too late with a boy the night before. Dahlia knew Sunny would be depressed and unhappy with the punishment, and she wanted to cheer Sunny up, so she crept into Aunt Ruthie and Uncle Max's house and slid the sheet of paper with the song lyrics under her cousin's door, then slipped away. Now she remembered hearing from her mother later that day, when Aunt Ruthie told Sunny she wouldn't allow her to see that boy anymore, Sunny opened the china closet, took her mother's best china out piece by piece, and, screaming obscenities, threw each dish at the wall until she had broken the entire set.

The next morning while Dahlia was eating breakfast, the phone rang, and when she answered it, there was no voice on the other end, just Sunny at the piano playing the perfect tune she had composed for Dahlia's words. After school Dahlia rushed over to Sunny's to hear it again. She loved sitting next to Sunny on the bench of the Steinway baby grand that Aunt Ruthie originally bought for Louie because she wanted him to play on TV like Liberace. Even though Louie never touched the shiny black piano except to take one disastrous lesson, Sunny fell instantly and desperately in love with it. Magically, from the first time she sat in front of the keyboard and her little fingers touched the keys, somehow, with no lessons, no music books, perfect tunes came out.

As time went along, the tunes became sophisticated and melodic. Tunes she made up in that other world into which she disappeared, tunes that stayed with anyone who heard them, so people found themselves humming them every day for weeks. Tunes that, as a teenager, Sunny created with the urgency of someone who was playing to save her own life, because she was. Later the others all learned that from the time she turned thirteen, terrible demons had filled her head, and the music was her only defense against them.

"It's a fight to the finish," she confessed to Dahlia. "I'm never sure if the music will block out my voices or if the voices will win and overpower the music." Songs became Sunny's life. She never stopped talking about them—how they were written, who wrote them—and she obsessed about how much she admired her favorite songwriters.

"Leiber and Stoller, Dahl. Listen to their songs. Every one of them can be sung by anybody after the first time they hear it. They write songs that feel as if they've been living inside you all along and they just brought them out. Direct, sexy, coming-at-you songs that make you want to move, make you *need* to move. 'Searchin'.' What a tune. You have to rock out when you hear it. When the Beatles were trying to get jobs, they auditioned with it. They wanted to get gigs, and their audition song was 'Searchin'.' What does that tell you? 'Little Egypt.' Put it on and then don't dance? It's impossible. I want to write songs like that."

And, amazingly, she did. Sunny's music had that unforgettable drive, a freewheeling, irreverent, low-down heat, backed by memorable tunes. Of course, Dahlia's lyrics were okay, too, but not extraordinary like those melodies Sunny found somewhere in the far reaches of her overactive, complicated brain. And throughout all those years, very few people ever heard them, except for Dahlia and a few family members and friends, because finally, much too early on in her life, Sunny's demons won the battle and got the better of her. And soon she was spending more time inside the lockup wards of hospitals than anywhere else.

Now, through the living room window, Dahlia saw the lights of Seth's Jeep approaching as he pulled it into the carport next to her van, and after a minute she watched him come through the door carrying a grocery bag. God, he was delicious-looking, she thought. She loved his thick, warm-brown hair, that boyishly handsome face, and the big brown eyes that lit up when he saw her.

"Whatcha up to?" he asked, seeing how excited she was watching the wobbly plastic wheels move in reverse as she rewound the tape.

"You won't believe this," she said. "Listen to this song my cousin Sunny and I wrote when we were teenagers."

"You mean during the Civil War?" he joked. Seth loved to tease her about their seven-year age difference, kidded her all the time about being the older woman. As he wrapped an arm around her, she could smell the fresh baguette that jutted out of the top of the bag.

"Sorry I'm late," he said. "Stopped to see Lolly for an hour and give her a bath." Lolly was Seth's four-year-old daughter from a marriage that had gone bad when he found his wife in bed with the pediatrician. The wife was now the ex-wife, and she and the pediatrician and Lolly were all living together, and Seth's visits to his daughter were painful and awkward.

"I'm gonna sell this song to Marty Melman and

take you to Hawaii with my first big check," Dahlia said, standing on her tiptoes to kiss his sweet face.

"Better transfer it to a CD before that old clunker machine eats the tape." Seth winced at the loud blast of static.

Then the sound was clear again. "Here goes nothing," Seth heard Sunny say, and he laughed when he heard the two girls' voices singing their song in close harmony. Dahlia was taken by surprise by the wave of sadness that passed through her chest as she heard the song this time. Once she and Sunny promised, swore to each other in the passionate way young girls do, that they would sing the song at each other's weddings. Vowed to perform the song they had written to honor what would be their lifelong friendship. And now it had been so many years, and she didn't even know where Sunny was or how she was.

"So that was Sunny the cousin in the lockup?" Seth asked her as he put away the groceries. Years ago, not long after she and Seth met, Dahlia had shown him old photos of herself as the skinny little tagalong of the beautiful older, magical, musical cousin who had taught her how to play the piano, who had told her the facts of life in more detail than she ever should have, who had been her songwriting partner and idol. Dahlia had wanted to explain to him how close they were before Sunny's voices convinced her she was better off in the world of the insane with them and she had to be put away.

After that, Sunny's once fun-loving parents had become morose, Dahlia's parents tried hard to be solicitous and sympathetic, and Dahlia was devastated, lost without the friend she'd relied on every day of her life. Somehow, over all those subsequent years, she'd never bothered to cultivate any other close friends, just stayed in the pattern she and Sunny had created. Every weekend she had gone to Aunt Ruthie and Uncle Max's house to make music with Sunny, and after Sunny was put away, she continued to go to Aunt Ruthie and Uncle Max's house and play the piano by herself for hours. The music was her only friend.

Everyone in her high school class knew that Dahlia was a loner. When she graduated and went to college for two years, she sat dreaming in every class, unless it had something to do with music. She was a late-in-life only child of parents whose years of hard work made them old before their time. Her soft-spoken father, who should never have become a salesman because he was not confident with people, knew he would never have enough money to pay for four years of college. That was probably why he didn't argue with Dahlia when she told him she had decided to drop out and spend her days creating songs she would try to sell.

But nobody was buying. Everyone in the music business greeted her songs with lukewarm reactions. She made dozens of demo tapes and dozens of phone calls trying to get her songs to this artist or set up a meeting with that record company, but there was no interest. And when she did get a return call from an agent's assistant or someone who was the assistant to the assistant at a record company, the critique was invariably the same: Her lyrics were solid, from the heart, and moving. One record-company executive even used the word "poetic." But they all let her know they thought her tunes were derivative, repetitive, and it seemed as if "dull" was the word they were dancing around but not uttering in order to spare her feelings.

"Ever think of working with someone else?" Howie Penn asked her one day, forever ago, when she cornered him as he was leaving his office at Artists Inc. The agency offices filled a four-story building in Beverly Hills, and Dahlia had waited for an hour in the parking lot, standing near what she knew was his car with the personalized plate STRMAKR so she could ask him what he thought of her songs.

When he finally came down, it was about six o'clock, and when she saw him heading toward the car, she panicked, afraid he'd think she was a stalker and call security. But she took a deep breath and convinced herself she was doing the right thing. He had some overprotective assistant who always said to Dahlia on the phone, "Oops, you just missed him." But now, at last, she had him cornered, and he was actually talking to her as he leaned up against his Mercedes.

"What kind of someone else?" she asked while Howie clicked the remote in his hand to open the trunk of the glistening black convertible, then moseyed over and tossed his black leather briefcase inside.

"A composer. You need a composer. I mean, your words are cool, but your melodies are . . ." He screwed up his face, then extended his hand and moved it back and forth in a gesture that meant "not so hot." Then he pushed a button on the remote that made the parking lights flash and unlocked the doors with a click, and he slid into the Mercedes CLK430 convertible. Dahlia could smell the new-car smell. It was her favorite car on the road.

She watched as Howie turned on the ignition and opened the windows, then reached up and released a handle, pushed a button. A lid opened in the back, and the top lifted and rolled slowly into the compartment revealed by the open lid.

"I *have* thought about finding a partner," she said, realizing that now that the top was down, she only had seconds left until Howie Penn would be on his way out of the parking lot. "I mean, it crosses my mind now and then. . . ." That was a lie. She'd always been sure she could write both the words *and* the music. She knew she played the piano well, she knew she had ideas for songs. What made her ideas good were the stories of the songs, and those came easily to her. But the truth was, she always struggled over how to make the story sing. She hated to admit to herself that she was the word person and not the music person as well.

"Let me give you the number of a guy I know who's looking for a lyricist. Name's Jamie Reiss. His tunes might be a little down-home for your lyrics. But he writes a nice melody and . . ."

The end of the sentence hung in the air. *"And you don't."* Maybe Howie Penn was just trying to get rid of her and hoped that giving her this guy's number would get her to quit bugging him with her bad songs all the time. He found Jamie Reiss's phone number in his organizer and wrote it on the back of one of his own business cards with a Mont Blanc pen. Then he backed the Mercedes out of the spot, and the tires squealed as he pulled away.

Dahlia resisted calling the composer Howie Penn suggested for a week. Instead she continued to sit at the piano, trying to squeeze out a tune that had some kind of magic in it. But nothing worked. It all felt forced. She drove over to Sunset Plaza and parked in the lot behind the fancy shops and restaurants and walked up and down Sunset, hoping a tune would come to her.

The smell of food coming from the line of restaurants made her stomach rumble, so she stopped for lunch at Chin Chin even though she couldn't afford it, and at the next table she saw a woman in her fifties pull out a plastic accordion of pictures and show them to a woman across the table. The woman who looked at the pictures was not interested but polite. When the older woman said what she said next, Dahlia wrote it on a napkin: "My kids are my life." Then, while she waited for her moo shu vegetables to arrive, she wrote the lyrics on a napkin. The next day she called the composer and asked if she could bring them to him.

Jamie Reiss was tall and lanky and handsome enough to be a country-western star. He'd had his own radio show in Nashville for years and had recently moved to L.A. to act in a TV pilot for a show that never made it past the pilot stage. He had always made music and wanted to write songs but didn't have a lyric idea in the world.

"Ah lahk this one," he drawled as he looked at one of the pages of lyrics Dahlia handed him.

"Great," Dahlia said, then watched him as he casually picked up a guitar and strummed out a tune at the same time he looked at the paper on which she had transcribed the lyrics to "My Kids Are My Life" from the napkin.

The pictures she showed were of faces that glowed,
One was Matt, one was Josh, one was Jenny.
I asked her to tell me what work she was doing,
But she told me she didn't have any.
"MY KIDS ARE MY LIFE, I keep busy with them,
And the grandchildren love when I visit.
My kids are my world, and they need me so much.
Now, that's not so terrible, is it?"
I remember I thought, What a sad life she lives.
There's no man, there's no job, there's no money.
But twenty years later I pull out my wallet,
Show pictures, and think, Gee, it's funny.
MY KIDS ARE MY LIFE, I keep busy with them,
And the grandchildren love when I visit,
My kids are my world, and they need me so much.
Now, that's not so terrible, is it?

Jamie Reiss's tune for her words was tender and understated, and the melody was simple and easy to remember. It was a tune Dahlia never would have thought of for those words. But best of all, Jamie knew Naomi Judd's manager, and in a few weeks Naomi was recording it and singing it with so much heart that Dahlia wept the first time she heard it.

Dahlia lived on the money from that song for a long time, and she'd never sold another since. But tomorrow she was going to. Marty Melman needed her song, and she had found the tape, and pretty soon he'd be begging her for it. Tonight, eight years after the one time she'd had a song recorded, she couldn't stop talking about what she was going to do after Marty Melman wrote her a big fat check for her second one, babbling to Seth as they made dinner together.

"Once my song's recorded, I'll have money coming at me from two directions, like I did with my last one. A check for record sales from the publisher and another from ASCAP for airplay. It's going to be rolling in, and then I'll be set. Then I can get a publishing deal where they give me money every month, and I'll sit here and turn out the hits. We can move into a better place. We can go on vacations. When was the last time we went on a trip?"

Seth washed the lettuce and wrapped it in a dishcloth, letting her ramble. Then he chopped a tomato, peeled a cucumber and diced it, and poured some olive oil into a mixing bottle.

"Why are you frowning?" Dahlia asked as she turned over the chicken breasts in the broiler.

"Because you're too psyched. Marty Melman isn't going to buy a song from his masseuse."

Dahlia bit the inside of her lip to stop herself from saying something mean. But it occurred to her that this was why she and Seth had no future. He was a small-time thinker.

"I wrote a hit once," she said, unable to keep the anger out of her voice.

"You wrote a nice song. Naomi Judd put it on a C&W album. It did nicely. The Marty Melmans of the world are looking for huge songs by happening rock groups for their movies. Not a sweet little song by two women in their late thirties and early forties, one who's in a nuthouse somewhere and the other one who's his masseuse." Seth caught sight of her tight jaw. He knew that the reality check would annoy her, but he also knew how she could spin out on fantasies and then get hurt. "Sorry, honey, for the cold light of day. But somebody has to tell you the truth, and I hate to see you do what you always do. You start tripping about how you're going to sell something, and the next thing you know, you start spending the money on vacations and clothes—and then you get slapped in the face."

Dahlia turned away and opened the refrigerator, pretending to be looking for something. What she needed was the blast of cold air on her flushed cheeks. Seth was the one who was slapping her in the face. Why did she stay with a man who had a glass-is-half-empty mentality? Maybe when she sold the song, she'd have the confidence to end it with him and start dating some more upbeat, upscale men.

three

Dahlia was disappointed when Jamie Reiss decided to go back to Nashville to work in his wife's father's car dealership. He told Dahlia it had been his dream to have a song recorded and now that he'd done it, he was moving on. But the taste of success had made Dahlia determined to sell more. She went out into the world with some of her old songs and some new ones. She spent endless hours in reception room after reception room with her tapes, until some sympathetic receptionist took them and said, "We'll get back to you," with a look in her eyes that made Dahlia know they wouldn't. Nobody ever did get back to her, no matter how hard she pushed.

Once or twice someone looked at her résumé and asked, "On that song 'My Kids Are My Life,' are you words and music?"

"Just words," she said and watched them nod disappointedly.

"Mmm. We'll get back to you."

Okay, she said to herself. I get it. I hear them. I need a composer. She went to songwriting workshops so she could network, a word she hated when it was used as a verb. She even sat in dingy clubs at open-mike nights listening for composers who had lousy lyrics, hoping they would realize they needed someone like her. But none of them had the kind of tunes she thought were right for her, so she didn't even bother to approach them.

She met Derek at a workshop, and his tunes had promise. One evening, after she'd read some of her lyrics out loud to the enthusiastic applause of the group, he said he'd like to try to work with her. He drove up to her house in a Mustang convertible, bringing a tape recorder to their meeting, "In case," he said, "I come up with some brilliant idea and you try to steal it." Then he laughed as though the laugh was supposed to mean he was kidding, even though he wasn't. Dahlia listed some of her ideas, and Derek shook his head disapprovingly the entire time. "We're never going to work," he said. "Maybe it's generational."

She met Carol at Genghis Cohen, a Chinese restaurant in Beverly Hills where they held open-mike nights, but Carol canceled their first work session when she decided to move to Santa Fe with her artist boyfriend before she and Dahlia even tried to work together. That week Dahlia signed up for massage school. Massage seemed to fit the bill in so many ways for her. Her time would be her own, she would meet unique people, and there was something appealing about the intimacy that developed between masseuse and clients that she felt she needed in her lonely life.

Besides, her hands were strong and she was a good listener, and soon she built up a solid client list. Eventually it was just easier to admit to herself that writing songs was the hobby and massaging was the job. But even after she hadn't written a song in nearly a year, and she had her massage license and a number of clients, any time she filled out any kind of form that asked for her occupation, she always wrote "songwriter." And when someone asked her at a party, "What do you do?" she would never dream of answering, "I'm a masseuse."

Maybe it was embarrassing to say that massage was her career because rubbing people's naked bodies wasn't the high-line life she'd always imagined for herself, just the backup job she was doing temporarily. Or maybe in some secret, hopeful place inside her, she knew that one day in the future she would come back and break through again with another song. And this was that day, and now was her chance to do it, no matter what Seth thought.

"Marty Melman Productions" was what the pretty redheaded receptionist said when she answered the phone. And then the person who was calling in must have made a joke, because the receptionist threw her head back so that her gorgeous red hair splashed around her shoulders. "I'll connect you," she said, still grinning, but her smile faded when she looked at Dahlia standing in front of her.

"Yes?" she said coldly, as if she were waiting for Dahlia to try to sell her something and she was prepared to call security to throw her out of the building.

"Hi, I'm Dahlia Gordon, and last night I was at Mr. Melman's house."

"You were?" the redhead, one eyebrow raised, asked in surprise.

Dahlia promised herself she wasn't going to say why she was at Marty's house, hoping the receptionist would think she had been a dinner guest or—yech—Marty's latest girlfriend. There was already an undisguised sneer on this woman's face. All Dahlia had to do was say she was a masseuse, which would conjure up pictures of naked Marty and his oily body, to make this bitchy woman smirk knowingly.

"See, I'm a songwriter, and last night, when we were talking, he asked me to drop off a CD for him of a song called 'Stay by My Side.'" Okay, so he didn't ask. He snored. But Dahlia wasn't going to get bogged down in details. She had spent the whole morning running from studio to studio until she'd found one that could knock off a CD from a reel-to-reel tape, and now she had the CD in her hand, and she wasn't going to let some more-important-than-thou receptionist stand in the way of her getting it to Marty. If the redhead didn't take it right now, Dahlia would stop by Marty's house, buzz from the gate at the driveway, pray that Victor the houseman would let her in, and then beg him to get it to Marty for her.

The redhead took the CD and looked at it dubiously. Okay, so it probably looked amateurish. Dahlia didn't have time to start printing a label for it. So what if she had neatly printed the songwriters' names and her phone number in marker on the disc? It wasn't exactly a great presentation. But she and Sunny singing the song sounded so cute, and the song was really good, so she didn't want to waste another day worrying about labels.

"I'll get it to him," the redhead said.

"He told me he needs it right away," Dahlia said. Nothing to lose by being aggressive, she thought.

"It's done," said the redhead, dismissing her by taking a call and not only averting her eyes but rotating her chair so her back was to Dahlia, making it clear that their transaction was over.

"Why does Sunny act like that?" As a child Dahlia asked her mother that question at least once a week, but Rose Gordon always got that look in her eyes when her daughter asked. It was a look that said, Poor baby, there are no answers. Most of the time she would pull Dahlia onto her lap and envelop her in a big Shalimar-scented hug.

"How come she can't stop being that way? Does it just happen to her? Could it happen to other people?"

"You mean 'other people' as in you? Is that what you mean? I told you it isn't contagious. You're not gonna wake up one day and want to rip your clothes off in the shopping center. I promise."

"She did that? In a shopping center?"

"That kind of thing. You know what I mean. You can't get it by taking a bite out of her sandwich," Rose said, running a brush through her daughter's thick black hair.

"You sure?" Dahlia asked, hoping her mother would offer her a promise, but none was forthcoming. Dahlia could never shake the fear that somehow it would creep up on her, that she would be the next one in the family to get that horrible disease that made her cousin take an ax to the television screen, bite the dentist until he bled, run hysterically around the amusement park at the Santa Monica Pier knocking over trash cans, turning over baby strollers with the babies still in them, destroying the dressing room in a department store where she'd gone to buy a prom dress.

Every headache, every loss of equilibrium, every sad feeling Dahlia had made her worry that it was the onset of "the flying crazies," as Louie called his sister's disease, which always made Aunt Ruthie tell him to shut his big dumb face.

Dahlia remembered the morning she was wearing the pretty sapphire ring her mother gave her, an antique that had once been worn by her grandmother on her mother's side of the family, and Sunny spotted it on her hand.

"Oooh, great ring!" she said. "Such a gorgeous color. Can I try it on?" Sunny took Dahlia's hand and looked closely at the stone.

Dahlia felt panicky. What if she let Sunny try it on and the craziness was in her hands and she passed it along to Dahlia? Dahlia hesitated and couldn't look at her cousin, convinced at that moment that it had to be bad luck to let a crazy person wear your jewelry. Maybe the craziness could be transmitted from skin to skin. What if the instant Sunny gave her back the ring and she slid it on, she became the *other* crazy Gordon girl? Fast, she said to herself that day, think of an excuse.

"It's too tight to get off," she lied, praying Sunny couldn't see how guilty she felt immediately after she said it.

The phone rang, and Dahlia grabbed it on the first ring.

"Ms. Gordon?" the woman's voice on the phone sounded vaguely familiar, but who in the hell called her "Ms. Gordon"? It had to have something to do with a bill she'd forgotten to pay.

"Yeah. This is Dahlia Gordon."

"I have Marty Melman for you." Then there was a long silence, and then there was Marty's voice.

"Dahlia Gordon?" he said in a formal, businesslike way he'd never used with her before.

"Yeah. Hi, Marty," she said, wondering why he'd called her by her first and last names. "How're things going with the three projects?" There was a long silence.

"Wait a second. You *know* me?" Marty asked in an oddly detached voice for a guy she'd been massaging for years.

"Marty. It's Dahlia, your masseuse."

Marty was quiet, trying to figure out what was going on. "Did that dumb bitch secretary dial wrong?" he asked. "I didn't ask her to call my masseuse. She is so fucking dim-witted sometimes. Pepper! I thought I was calling some songwriter, and she called *you*?"

"I *am* a songwriter," Dahlia said.

Marty laughed. "Yeah, funny. Pepper!" he called out again.

"I left you the CD of a song I wrote," Dahlia said.

Another silence. Then Marty asked, "With two kids singing?"

"Yeah."

"*You* wrote *that* song?"

"With my cousin. That's the two of us singing."

Marty's voice was giddy now. "I'm using it in my new picture! I love it! It rocks! It's the title song. I'm sending it out to J.Lo today." He guffawed. "This is a killer. Dahlia the masseuse wrote a great fuckin' song for my picture. Did I know you write songs?"

"I mentioned it many times."

"Ha!" he laughed again. "This is too much. Maybe my pool man has a screenplay! Ha! And my gardener probably has a three-picture deal at Fox." That idea really made him laugh, and Dahlia stopped herself from shrieking into his ear that she'd sold a song to a star long ago, way before she started rubbing his marshmallow of a body, but she kept her mouth shut.

"Well," Marty said, his laughter subsiding, "let's see. What has to happen next? The studio is gonna want to own the publishing, so I'll get the paperwork all together, and you can come over here and sign off on it, and then we'll give you a nice little check, and you can quit oiling up oversexed fat guys for a while and take a vacation. Okay, doll?"

"Uh . . . okay," she said, still lost in the unreality of this turn of events.

"I can't believe this," Marty said. "Pepper walks in here with this CD, and a little while later I'm on hold with my doctor's office, so I stick it in the machine, and out come these voices, and they're singing a song with the title of my movie in it. And it's good. So I pick up this CD case, and I see 'written by Dahlia Gordon and—'" Marty was quiet for a second, then he asked, "Hey, hold it. Who the hell is Sunny Gordon?"

"My cousin. She was the composer."

"You mean you only wrote the words?" Marty said, with more than a little disappointment in his voice. "Well, then she has to sign off on this, too," he said. "So I'll have the paperwork done by tomorrow, and you gals can come on in."

Sunny. Come in? No chance. "Oh . . . that won't work, because I'm not even sure where she is," Dahlia blurted out.

"Better find her, tootsie. Or no deal. No way we can take a chance she'll surface later lookin' to screw us. Bring me two signatures or I'm usin' some Randy Newman song I heard him do a couple of weeks ago. Talk on ya tomorrow." Marty clicked off.

Dahlia put the phone down. Shit! Shit! Shit! Okay, it was a stupid idea. Sunny was off in some lockup wacko ward where she'd been for years. Aunt Ruthie and Uncle Max were dead. Louie, Sunny's son-of-a-bitch brother, was around, but years ago he had stopped going to see Sunny. Probably because he was scared she'd rub off on his kids or something like that.

"Lost cause," Louie told Dahlia the one time she'd asked him about it. And that was years ago, when she bumped into him at Gelson's Market in Sherman Oaks. He kept clucking his tongue and shaking his head. "She's not even really alive. Just existing. What's the point of going to see her? She doesn't know me.

She wouldn't know you. My parents used to go all the time. She didn't even know *them*. I'm sure it's why the two of them died so young. They couldn't bear to go there one more time."

When Uncle Max died in the eighties, Louie, who had been his father's business partner, took over their hardware store on Moorpark Street. Somehow, in spite of his abrasive personality and the big discount retailers opening all around him, Louie managed to stay in business with that little firetrap of a store all these years. God, what a schmuck he'd always been to both Dahlia and Sunny. He had been fiercely jealous of their relationship and tortured them because he felt so left out when they didn't want to play games with him, just wanted to be left alone to work on their songs.

"Who cares about lousy songs from two unpopular scags?" he'd say, passing through the living room on his way to work at the store.

"You're supposed to be an adult," Aunt Ruthie would yell. "Leave them alone."

Once, when they were kids, he put a mouse in the piano while they were rehearsing, and it skittered onto the keyboard and made both girls scream. Dahlia remembered how the screaming had triggered a bad episode for Sunny that day. Another time Louie had smeared oil all over the keys, ruining the mechanism so a specialist had to be called in to clean it, and then he lied about it. And now the nasty bozo was her only source of information on Sunny's whereabouts.

Bad idea. There was no way she was going to go begging Louie. If she told him she had to get through to Sunny, he'd laugh at her. He'd definitely want to take Sunny's share of any money for himself. Somehow, just because he was Louie, he'd figure out a way to screw it up. Shit! Why had she written Sunny's name on the CD? That was really stupid. Maybe she could just tell Marty that Sunny was a fictitious person she made up. Yeah, sure. He'd really believe that. Maybe she could get him to send the contract over and she could forge a signature. Sunny would never know about it. According to Louie, Sunny would never know about anything again.

four

"Thank you for calling Bank of America's twenty-four-hour banking service. For account balances or to stop payment on a check, please press one."

Maybe it was the stock market's being so iffy that made people cut back on their luxuries, or maybe it was just the fact that it was summer and people were traveling, but the massage business was going into the toilet. Dahlia still had her few regulars, but they weren't enough to pay her bills. At least Seth split the mortgage payment with her, and that helped a lot, but her cash-flow situation was getting desperate. Tomorrow she'd deposit about two hundred and fifty dollars, but her balance had to be precariously low.

"Please enter your ten-digit account number.

"Please enter the last four digits of your Social Security number.

"Your current balance is seven dollars and twenty-three cents."

After her mother died, her father had been in such bad shape that Dahlia had moved him into a convalescent home where they provided assisted living. He had no health insurance, so all the proceeds from the sale of her parents' house had gone into keeping him in the tiny, shared room where Dahlia went to visit him nearly every day, though he barely knew she was there. Then, as if her father had been keeping daily track of what was in the bank, he died on the day the balance in his account was down to twenty-seven dollars.

The truth was that this little massage business of hers wasn't going to keep her afloat. She had to do something about her life. She was too young to be a has-been and too good to be a one-trick pony with only one idea. She had lots of ideas. Unfortunately, nobody thought they were good but her. Today there were very few publishing deals like there used to be for songwriters. Once she thought her future was going to be turning out hit song after hit song and living a life of luxury. Tonight she put the heels of her hands against her eyes, trying to ward off the headache that was coming on. She had to do the math and figure out how long it was going to take her to come up with the cash for her half of the mortgage payment.

The familiar smell of Uncle Max's hardware store engulfed her the instant she walked in the front door. She used to come here as a little girl and be fascinated with the seed packets and their flowery designs, and she used to love the colorful plastic kiddie pools that

Uncle Max always displayed outside every morning to attract the commuters who drove by on Moorpark Street. Louie still put the same racks of merchandise outside that she remembered from her childhood.

Maybe seeing her face would bring back some warm feelings and Louie would drop his usual hard-ass defensiveness that used to make everyone in the family refer to him behind his back as King Kong. After all, even King Kong had his tender moments, Dahlia told herself as she wandered through the aisle of hose nozzles. When a punk-haired young clerk asked if he could help her, she said, "I'm Louie's cousin Dahlia, and I just dropped by to say hello." She smiled and hoped she sounded casual and sincere.

"He's takin' a break out back," the clerk said. "I'll go find him."

Charm, charm, Dahlia said to herself, watching the punk kid head for the back of the store. Don't bring up old family stuff. Just charm the little creep into giving you the address. After a minute she heard Louie's voice.

"Hey, it's my famous cousin Dahlia! You must be slumming to come down here. You still writing those bad songs that nobody wants? Maybe you stopped by to hit your old cuz for some dough?" Louie had some gray in what was left of his hair, and he was considerably rounder in the waistline than the time she'd seen him in Gelson's.

"Whaddya say, Louie?" Dahlia said, offering him a hand to shake, since she knew a hug was out of the question. Louie shook her hand with his meaty paw. He was her father's brother's son, and now in middle age he looked remarkably the way she remembered her father looking. Only he didn't have her father's gentle nature. At the moment he had a crossed-arm stance and a sneer of distaste on his face.

"So I know you're not here to buy a wrench," he said. "And you can't be here to tell me somebody in the family died, 'cause all those poor schmucks croaked a long time ago, leaving only you and me behind."

"And Sunny," she reminded him.

"Yeah. Sunny. She's not exactly what you call alive," he said.

Dahlia shrugged, trying to look nonchalant. "So how's it going, Louie? I was just in the neighborhood, and thought I'd pop in."

"Still single, I see," he said, looking at her left hand. "I'm still with Penny, and I've got three kids. Maniacs. They keep me working night and day in this place. No men in your life? You gay? You're not gay."

"Not gay. Have a boyfriend," Dahlia said, trying to remember if she needed anything from a hardware store. Maybe she could pretend she was there because she needed something for her house. How the hell was she going to ask a question that she was certain would piss Louie off? Oh, well, screw the niceties. She'd go right for it.

"So exactly how *is* Sunny?" she tried, steeling herself. And she was right about his reaction. His eyes hardened instantly, and his mouth turned into a tight-lipped slit.

"How's Sunny?" he said in that way that meant, I can't believe you're asking me that. "Sunny's a vegetable. Just like always. Why do you want to hear about Sunny all of a sudden? She's been in and out of funny farms for the last twenty-five years. How do you *think* she is? Not waiting around for the Pulitzer Prize committee to call, *that* I can promise you. Not exactly at the top of her game."

Dahlia knew this was going to be hard, but she forged ahead. "Yeah, but isn't she out of lockup and in some halfway house now?" She remembered hearing something like that from her mother about eight years earlier. Eight years ago when her own career was flying high and she was way too busy to think about Sunny except in passing now and then.

"Some of the time, yeah. When she isn't regressing and refusing to take the medication and talking to demons who want her to saw off pieces of her body and feed them to the neighborhood dogs. What's it to you?"

Dahlia hesitated. She hadn't really thought through what she was and wasn't going to tell this nasty little beast. Certainly not that she wanted to go by the nuthouse and get Sunny to sign off on their potentially moneymaking song. That would be the kiss of death. He'd want to screw it up somehow. He'd probably say that as her brother he controlled everything that belonged to Sunny because she couldn't be responsible for anything anymore.

"She's in some shitty dive in San Diego," Louie went on, "and believe me, you don't want to go there. It would scare the crap out of you. I made the mistake of going about three years ago. Trust me, she doesn't look like anyone you remember. And worse yet, she doesn't have any idea who you are or what you were to her or even where she is."

Louie pulled a feather duster out of his back pocket, and then, as if he wanted her to be sure the discussion was over, he turned, taking his eyes from Dahlia's, and silently dusted items on nearby shelves.

No, Louie, she thought. I came here to get the address, and I am not going to budge until I get it. "Will you give me the address?" she tried. The direct approach was a good start.

Louie looked surprised. "What the hell do you want the address for? You all of a sudden got some do-gooder impulse or something? Go adopt a pet."

A young couple was wandering through the store, and she could see that Louie's attention was about to shift. She had to go for it immediately.

"Please, Louie. I was looking through some old photos, and I found that locket, the one that she and I exchanged years ago, and I had this rush of feeling to see her."

Louie whirled on her now. "She's not her. I took my kids with me last time. Why I did that, I don't know, but it scared the livin' shit out of them. They had seen all those gorgeous pictures of her when she was younger, and they couldn't believe what she was like now or how she could live in that place. Kassie threw up in my car on the way home from going there! Can I find something for you?" he said, suddenly turning into Mr. Nice Store Owner, as a tall thin man in a Hawaiian shirt rounded the corner into the aisle where Louie and Dahlia stood. The man wanted a hasp, and it was obvious that Louie was happy to have a reason to leave Dahlia so he could find it for him.

"*Go adopt a pet*," he'd said to her. Well, a song in a

movie was worth too goddamned much to her to let that little dork get in the way of her having it. Why would he take kids to a board-and-care for schizophrenics anyway? The guy was a moron. But she was going to get the address out of him somehow, and then she'd go there and find Sunny. Marty's secretary had called that morning to say she was sending over the paperwork for the release of the song. Dahlia had to get to Sunny soon, or Marty could change his mind.

God, would it be great when the song was up there in a hot new movie. Sung by Jennifer López or somebody big like that. It could win an Oscar, for God's sake. There was no way she was leaving here without the information she needed. She'd be patient with Louie. Kiss his ass even. Whatever it took to get to Sunny, get the papers signed, and get the song sold. The customer was paying for the hasp, whatever the hell a hasp was, and some shaggy-haired young clerk wearing a Cordon Hardware T-shirt was helping a lady choose which combination lock she wanted, and Louie would be free again. Dahlia searched her brain for a way to get through to him.

The hasp-buying guy walked past her and out the door, and she approached Louie again. "So fill me in on your kids," she said, slapping on a smile and hoping to sound as if she actually cared about his three little children whom she'd seen only once, when the third one was born and Louie and Penny had invited her to the bris.

"Ahh," Louie said, lighting up, "they're stars."

It worked, Dahlia thought as a grinning Louie rattled on for a long time about the kids and their school and their big parts in plays and their sports activities and Dahlia nodded, pretending she knew what AYSO meant and other kid stuff, and when Louie laughed while he told her about all the adorable things they said to him, Dahlia laughed, too, hoping he couldn't tell she was faking it.

"My girls both play the piano also," he said. "And they're great at it. My Kassie has white-blond hair, too. Now, my Michael . . . he's a demon," Louie went on, and her forced smile made Dahlia's face ache. In Louie's endless stories, his son sounded as if he were the same kind of monster Louie had been at his age, and when Dahlia mentioned that, Louie seemed to soften a bit, and then he must have drifted off into the past for a minute, because eventually he said, "You and Sunny always got all the attention. I was just the little troublemaker in the background. You girls would sing and everybody was hooked. I remember how you used to climb up on the bench next to Sun and put your arm around her and then you'd start singing."

Dahlia nodded and kept on smiling, as if she and Louie were old buddies reminiscing. Louie had a big grin on his face when he reached into a bin of hose nozzles, then held the nozzle vertically in front of his mouth as if it were a microphone. And of all the songs he could have chosen, the one that came out of his mouth gave Dahlia a stomachache.

"Stay by my side forever. Stay by my side, my friend." He was singing it in a mock-nightclub-singer voice, enjoying his own performance, remembering every word of the song the girls had written more than twenty-five years ago. Dahlia was queasy. It was a damned good thing she hadn't tried to promote the idea that she'd written the song alone, because if she had and Louie saw the movie, there was no doubt he would come after her.

"My mother actually got that piano for *me*, you know," he said. "Not Sunny. But I thought only sissies played the piano. I mean, you probably don't remember Liberace, but my mother loved him and wished I could be just like him." Dahlia was trying not to show her surprise at Louie's picking that song and then belting out every word and getting it right.

A fat couple was coming in the door of the store, and Dahlia knew she was about to lose Louie to them, so she forged ahead. "So sad they're all gone and nobody's left but you and me and Sunny," she tried, hoping she sounded appropriately sentimental. The couple was wandering over to look at garden tools, and Dahlia watched Louie watching them. "Maybe that's why I thought I ought to go see her to find out if I could help her."

"Yeah," Louie said, sighing absently.

Gimme the address, gimme the address, she thought. That goddamned address could change my life.

"Just a sec," Louie said. "I'll go get the address. But, Dahl, I gotta warn you—she's pretty bad."

She smiled what she hoped looked like a gentle smile of understanding, and Louie went into the back room while a clerk walked over to help the shoppers. In her head she could hear her song being sung by Jennifer Lopez. "Stay by my side forever. . . ." Dahlia would be watching from the audience at the Oscars in a long sequined dress, looking hot as hell. The camera would find her and linger on her because she was the songwriter and she looked so great. Maybe she'd even tell the story on the stage of the Oscars, about the way she and her cousin were so close that they wrote this song as a paean to their friendship. The audience would eat that up.

"Here you go," Louie said. "No point in calling ahead. They never answer the phone."

"Why not?" Dahlia asked.

"Why not?" Louie laughed. "Because they're all in a mini–funny farm, zonked out on drugs. They all think they're Napoleon. You expect them to take a message? They can't even string two thoughts together. Believe me, if I thought my sister could have even one human interaction, I'd bring her back here and give her a job in the store."

Louie waved the piece of paper bearing Sunny's address in the air as he spoke. Dahlia nodded in agreement until she had the address in her hand. "Louie," she said the minute she did, "I can't tell you how much it means to me to see you again." And she breezed out the door.

In the silence of her van, she took a deep breath and, still parked in the small Gordon Hardware parking lot, looked at the address and wanted to kiss the scrap of paper. The name of the halfway house was the Sea View. It was in San Diego. Not too bad. For a while, she remembered, Sunny had been in some place up near Oakland. Oakland was far. San Diego was a couple of hours' drive from L.A. No big deal.

She'd pack a few things and head down there to-morrow with Seth. They'd stay overnight somewhere. Make it a romantic outing. She'd enjoy spending some of the money she'd have by next week. Just the begin-ning, she thought. She was back in show business. Marty Melman would never dream of dropping his pants to pee in front of a songwriter.

Seth watched her pile her clothes into an old suitcase that smelled musty because she'd just dug it out of the same storage area where she'd found the tape recorder and the tape.

"Think they'll let me into the hotel with this shabby suitcase?" she asked.

"As long as you pay the bill, they don't care about the suitcase," he said.

Dahlia held up a black T-shirt with the signs of the Zodiac on it, but it was tired-looking, and she threw it back in the drawer.

"There must be some kind of legal issue here," Seth said. "Maybe she's incapable of signing anything, and her brother has to sign for her."

"Get ahold of yourself," Dahlia said. "I mention a big deal to Louie, and the next thing you know he'll get greedy ideas and try to call Marty Melman. He could blow the whole thing right out of the water. I'd forge her signature before I'd do business with Louie."

She stopped folding an olive green T-shirt she liked to wear with her camouflage jeans and looked at Seth. "Believe me, I thought about putting two signatures on the thing, telling Marty that Sunny signed it, and that's it. The problem is, that little monster Louie not only remembers the song, he remembers it better than I do. He sang every word of it to me using a hose nozzle as a microphone. He's not going to hear that song in the movie and say, 'Isn't that nice?' He's going to say, 'Where's my sister's piece of the action?' And the only way his sister is going to get her share is if she signs the contract. So I'm going to San Diego to get her to do it."

Dahlia placed the T-shirt on top of the camouflage pants and stood gazing absently into the suitcase. "I can't believe I'm standing here wondering what I'm going to wear. If Louie's description of Sunny was accurate, she's probably not going to notice my outfit."

"Dahl," Seth said, sitting on the bed, "this has fiasco written all over it. Let's talk it through for a minute. Okay?" "

Oh, no. Here we go, she thought. Her face flushed, and she tried not to flare. He's going to try to talk me out of this. Either by making me feel guilty for doing something bad to my "poor crazy cousin" or by starting in again about how it's only money and he doesn't care about money. This is what happens when you're with a man who has no ambition. He was satisfied doing what he was doing and earning his meager salary doing it. She was someone who worked all day and night standing over people's bodies, kneading their flesh with aching hands and arms, only half listening to their stories, wanting to say to them, "Could you just go to sleep? I don't care about your dog's asthma or your sister's diabetes," and this little talk Seth wanted to have was going to be designed to make her think that the way her life was now should be good enough for her forever. What was that quote he always ran by her? "Stop living the life you planned and live the life you were given."

"Tell you what," she said, closing the suitcase. "I'll just go down there and feel it out. I'll leave you at the hotel pool and go over there by myself. Worst case? The whole thing inspires a song or two."

"But maybe she's in such bad shape that it's a real bad idea?" he tried.

"Or maybe it's the best idea anyone ever had," she said.

"My Jeep's got a real bad leak, and I can't drive it that far. Think the junk heap can make it?" Seth asked, putting an arm around her. It was his way of telling her he wouldn't fight her. He'd go with her even if it was a fool's errand. Dahlia nuzzled her face into his hair.

"Guess it'll have to," she answered. He smelled so good, and she loved him in her bed, but she wasn't going to give up this sliver of a possibility that she could have the life she'd planned, not this floundering-around life she'd been given.

In the morning it was still dark, four-something on the blue digital numbers on the clock, when she woke up with Seth wrapped around her and the possibility that something good was about to happen filling her. I might have a song in a movie, was her first thought. I might be able to dig myself out and write songs again. Slowly she extracted herself from Seth's arms, padded into the living room, and sat at the piano.

After a few minutes of noodling, she had an idea for a verse, but it wasn't very catchy. She played out some chords, but none of what she was coming up with was terribly inspired. Dahlia stood and looked inside the piano bench because she remembered she'd put a few lead sheets in there from the times she'd made passes at songs over the last year. At least one of them must have potential. But as she leafed through them, she was more and more disappointed when she realized that her memory of them was a lot better than the actual songs. One had an unwieldy bridge that sounded as if it were from a different song than the refrain, and another one had an uninspired melody that was as dull as dirt.

As the sun came up, she reworked a ballad idea she'd started a few months earlier, called "Don't Make Me Laugh," but halfway through it she decided that the tune was only fair and not worth the work. Besides, the thunk on her front porch signaled the *L.A. Times* delivery and that was a good excuse to stop working. She left the piano bench and went to the door.

It was still dark outside. The black sky was filled with morning stars, and she wanted to wish on one, remembering how she and Sunny always used to wish on stars together. She remembered that her own wish always had something to do with becoming famous and Sunny's wish was always about being "wildly in love" with someone who felt the same way about her. Dahlia told her that was dumb, that she should wish for being both famous and loved, pointing out that there were plenty of stars and plenty of nights to wish on them, so why always wish for a man? But that was all Sunny wanted.

Shivering from the cold morning air, Dahlia came inside and sat on the living room floor with the paper spread out in front of her. Page by page she riffled past all the bad news and stopped to look longingly at the ads from Saks Fifth Avenue in Beverly Hills for clothes she couldn't afford, then on to the Calendar Section to see the show-business news, even though it never failed to depress her.

On page two her eye caught an item that said Jane Myron and Roger Mark were writing the score for a Disney animated feature. Now, how did they get that? She remembered meeting the young songwriting team at a party, where Jane Myron said to her, "I love your songs. 'My Kids Are My Life' is one of my favorite lyrics ever." Dahlia put the newspaper into the trash can. She couldn't waste any more time. She had to go back to the piano and sit there until she thought of something to write. "Don't Make Me Laugh" had sort of a nice verse, but it wasn't drop-dead good, just pleasant, and nobody was paying big bucks for pleasant. Maybe she'd crawl back into bed next to Seth and think about what she would say to Sunny when she got to San Diego.

five

Dahlia remembered the way Sunny used to love to get dressed to go on a date. Sometimes it seemed that her cousin's primping and preparation, her love affair with her own skin as she slowly worked the moisturizing cream into her face and throat and down each arm, was such a production it was almost as if she were doing it in a show on TV where she was demonstrating the products.

The care she took in the application of each step of her makeup was exquisite, and Dahlia loved to watch and imitate the faces she made while drawing and painting and dabbing and brushing and tweezing. First she smiled that big forced smile to create the apple cheeks on which she feathered the pink color with a big bushy brush; then she stretched her eyelids for the liner that she put on with a very sharp pencil; then she made that stretched-down face to allow for the mascara on the lower lids that she put on with a brush on a wand; and then she pulled her lips very taut for the lipstick she put on with a stiff retractable brush. And she would talk while she was doing it, truly as if she were on television giving a makeup lesson.

"You need to keep the eye pencil very sharp," she would say, "and then come up like this from under the lashes, and that way the line stays very thin and very close to the top of the lashes. Then I like to put a little bit of loose powder on both the upper and the lower lashes, too, because it gives the mascara something to grab on to and makes it hold better."

Dahlia sat on the floor marveling as she watched, and soon the finished product of all that perfectly done makeup was as glamorous as any movie star. *More* glamorous and more wonderful than any movie star, because this one hugged her little cousin and teased her and wanted to play duets with her and write songs with her to bide her time while they waited for Sunny's various dates to arrive.

Dahlia would hear a car door slam and run to the window to watch the nervous dates get out of their cars and approach the house.

"Another victim is about to fall into the clutches of my baby sis," Louie would yell from the kitchen, and Dahlia would be embarrassed for Sunny because her brother was such a jerk that he was calling her dates victims, right in front of them. Sometimes the date would be carrying flowers. One of them, who wore a tweed jacket in the summer, lifted his arm over his head on the way to the door and sniffed his armpits, not knowing Dahlia and Sunny were watching through the window.

"He's poor," Sunny explained, "so he only has that one heavy wool jacket."

And all of the dates looked at Sunny with that same hungry look in their eyes. Boys that Dahlia found stupefyingly handsome would seem to go weak at the sight of Sunny, and Dahlia wondered if any boy would ever look at her that way. But after a while some of the boys would be scared off when the incidents began happening too frequently. Like the time Sunny deliberately drove one of their cars into a telephone pole. A week later she shaved the head of another when he fell asleep at a romantic picnic they'd been having at the beach. Not long after that, she stood on the lawn of another one's family home naked, hollering for his parents to come out and meet the girl their son was "boffing." It was a word Sunny often used that sounded to Dahlia like a game you played in gym.

It didn't take long for Sunny's reputation as a nutcase to get around, and there would be extended periods where no boys called or came to take her out. A lot of the time her behavior at home was lethargic and insolent, and soon her parents started having her put away in a hospital or "a home" for a little while here and a little while there, hoping at the end of each limited stay that this time she'd improve and be well. But she never was.

Dahlia remembered how in the early years, in between the hospitalizations, Sunny would come home and, in spite of whatever she'd gone through in her treatment, still look gorgeous. And within a few days, a new boyfriend would surface, because her beauty was such a magnet that everywhere she went, young men fell all over themselves to talk to her. For a while "the boyfriend of the month," as Louie called them, was Bob Hirsch, the son of the pharmacist on the corner, even though he had to know better than anyone about all the drugs Sunny was taking for her mental-health problems, because she refilled her prescriptions at his dad's drugstore.

And then she was back at the makeup table, first applying the creams, then the colors, then the scents, able to make herself as beautiful as ever. All right, Dahlia admitted to herself, so the last few times she had started to look a little worse from the wear and tear of whatever they did to her in those hospitals. And what they did must have been bad because Dahlia's parents would shoo Dahlia out of the room when they talked about it. But in her little cousin's mind Sunny always had the radiance of an angel.

Unfortunately, the Sea View didn't have a view of the sea or anything else besides another run-down building across the way. It was a two-story wooden house on a side street in a downscale residential neighborhood. The railing on the big front porch that ran the length of the house was sagging. The house next door had a side yard that was adjacent to the Sea View, and on the patchy grass were a dilapidated set of swings and a slide. Dahlia wondered how the parents of young children must feel having a board-and-care for schizophrenics overlooking their children's play yard.

"Wish me luck," Dahlia said as she and Seth stared up at the people sitting on the porch. All of them were lined up on rocking chairs gazing quietly out over the railing as if there actually were a sea view to look at, except for one white-haired black woman, who was perched on the railing looking at the wall and talking. All of them were smoking cigarettes.

"I'm scared," Dahlia said softly.

"You don't have to do this," Seth said in a voice that made her know he was wishing she'd turn to him and say, "You're right. Let's get out of here."

"Yeah, I do. I have to do this," she snapped. "This is a big chance for me, and I'm not gonna blow it."

"You realize that I don't care if you write hit songs or massage people or wait tables," Seth said.

"Seth, my honey," she said, trying not to turn this into an argument, but her face was hot and she was trying to keep the irritation out of her voice. "You *should* care. Because if I get Sunny to do what I'm asking, my present life of walking in the servants' entrance of rich people's houses is over. I didn't drive all the way down here to turn around and go back to that. Last week my ancient client Helene asked me if I wanted some of her old sweaters because she felt sorry for how shabby I always look. I nearly cried. She actually used the word 'shabby.'"

"I'll buy you all the sweaters you want," Seth said, and she saw the adoration in his eyes, but even the tentative way he said it reminded her of her late father. The kind of man who was too nice to be aggressive in business and never destined to be a worldbeater. After her father died, people came up to her at the funeral and told her stories about the times he'd graciously let them skip a few payments on furniture they'd bought because they couldn't come up with the money. "He got in trouble with his uncle," they said, "but he understood that some people struggled more than others."

Seth worked hard in a publicist's office, but he couldn't have chosen a career that was more wrong for somebody with his too-nice personality. Publicists had to be killers, pushy and aggressive never-take-no-for-an-answer types who beat down people's doors in service of their clients. Seth could never do that very well. That's why he was still working at a so-so firm in a low-level position and living on a meager budget. And yet he didn't seem to care. That was the part that bugged Dahlia so much, that he was content with so little.

"I'm going up," she said.

Sunny. Is it possible that she could look so bad that even *I* couldn't recognize her? Dahlia wondered, opening the door of the van and climbing out. As she walked up the steps, the foul air blowing at her was thick with the stink of cigarette smoke. Not one of the four men or the woman even looked at her as she walked past them into the house. The kitchen was to her right, but it was barricaded with half a dozen piled-up kitchen chairs on which someone had taped a handwritten sign that said OFF-LIMITS. Maybe kitchens were too dangerous for the Sea View denizens to handle. The fire, the use of knives and other tools—it was all probably more than they were able to negotiate safely. There was a dreary living room to the left, with two threadbare sofas and a chair against the wall and a large TV in a corner, which a dozen metal folding chairs were facing.

At the farthest window, there was an old upright piano. Nobody was in either of these rooms, and though the stairwell was right in front of Dahlia, she thought that going up might be a mistake, so she went back out to the porch. The white-haired woman was talking to herself earnestly with her brow furrowed. "And you know what I told him? I said, 'Baby, I'm not gonna do that,'" Dahlia heard her say.

One of the men looked like Santa Claus—he was round and large, with a white beard—but he certainly wasn't jovial. His beard rested on his chest as he stared straight ahead. Dahlia cleared her throat loudly, thinking one of them might look up at her, but not one of them even blinked.

"Uh, hi. I'm looking for Sunny Gordon." No response. "I'm her cousin. I was wondering if she was around? Anybody know?"

Finally Santa Claus looked up and turned slowly toward her. He was dead-eyed and sleepy-looking.

"Field trip. Couple of 'em went to the mall to get cigarettes and that kinda thing," he said, then went back to his reverie.

"I'll wait," Dahlia said. "Thanks." And she walked back down the steps.

Seth was reading a newspaper in the van when she got in again.

"Did they say she lives here?" he asked.

"Not exactly. But one of the men seemed to know who I meant."

"Maybe we ought to go to the zoo for a couple of hours and come back later and try again—"

"Look."

There was a faded brown Oldsmobile rattling up the street. Even before it turned into the driveway, Dahlia was sure it had to be the car returning from the mall. The car with Sunny in it. The car stopped, and she was surprised to hear her heart pounding too fast in her ears. She put her hand nervously on Seth's arm as the doors to the car opened and they watched each of the passengers climb out.

There were two women. One was a short, stocky woman who was jabbering to the one who was still in the car and waving an angry finger as she did. The other one had flaming wild and frizzy orange hair, wore too much makeup, had long blue fingernails, and was dressed in a bright red parachute jogging suit that clashed with her hair color. A burly black man with a big belly and a very bushy Afro was the driver, and he locked the car doors, then took the steps two at a time and went inside.

Behind him the short woman rushed up the steps and into the house while the orange-haired one walked more slowly. She stopped to talk as she got to the top of the steps, and now Dahlia saw she was chatting with Santa Claus, who stood and pointed down to Dahlia's van. The shocking orange hair shimmered halolike around her beaten and tired face, and she squinted hard as she peered at the van where Dahlia leaned out the window to look back at her. The color of the woman's hair was a blindingly bright Day-Glo fluorescent that practically pulsed. Dahlia got out of the van, and when she did, the woman walked down a few of the steps to look more closely at her. Dahlia felt panicky, but she moved forward to return the woman's gaze.

"That her?" Dahlia heard Seth ask. His voice sounded very far away.

A clammy feeling crept into the back of Dahlia's neck as she began to make out the woman's facial features clearly—the flat nose, the prominent ears, the almond eyes, the turned-down mouth of her father's family. There was no mistake. Under the haggard face and baggy eyes and blazing hair was the result of twenty-five years of God only knew how many electroconvulsive shock therapies and probably every kind of mind-altering drug. Sunny. Nicknamed that instead of called her proper name, Sandra, because she was born to brighten all of their lives. That's what Uncle Max always said.

"That's her," Dahlia replied as a slide show of the times they'd spent together rushed through her mind. Sunny, Sunny, my God, it's you, Dahlia thought, wanting to run to her and shake her and shriek. You have to remember me. You were the one who taught me to play the piano and write songs and love music. You were the one who adored my lyrics and sang them until you broke people's hearts. You were the one who told me the facts of life. You told me about boys and how dumb they all are, you taught me how to dance and put on lipstick and practice kissing my pillow so

I'd be ready for kissing boys. But by the time I was ready to put it all to use, you were gone. And "gone" was definitely the word to describe the vacant look in this woman's eyes as she walked down a few more steps, staring fearfully at Dahlia.

This is a mistake, Dahlia thought. In spite of what Louie had told her, the Sunny in her dreams was the one she'd been certain she was going to find here today. The Marilyn Monroe Sunny of the poofy bosom poking out of a sundress and the raucous, contagious giggle that would always get Dahlia giggling, too, and the pretty hands that used to take Dahlia's tiny fingers and place them on the proper piano keys to teach her how to play each tune. I will get back in the van and leave right now, Dahlia thought, fearing there was a real chance she was going to get physically ill. This woman doesn't know it's me anyway, she rationalized, so her feelings won't be hurt if I leave.

But she didn't. In fact, something made her move toward the odd woman in the red jogging suit, and the closer she walked, the more she was able to sort out the Sunny she knew somewhere in among those weary and distorted features.

"Hello, Sunny," she said, still not believing that this bizarre person could really be Sunny. "I'm your cousin Dahlia." Then she stopped a few steps down from where Sunny stood. There was nothing in the woman's eyes that remotely resembled recognition. Of course, the last time they'd seen each other, Dahlia had been twelve. Twenty-five years ago. Maybe Dahlia was supposed to explain to her now how, in the beginning, in those early years after Sunny was first put away, if she'd even mentioned the idea to her parents that she wanted to go and visit her, her mother would immediately say, "Let's not talk about it," and shake her head nervously. Even at Aunt Ruthie's house, all the pictures of Sunny, the ones that had been on the piano and on the mantelpiece, were taken down, because except for Aunt Ruthie and Uncle Max's weekly visits to her, and Dahlia's parents' perfunctory visits to the mental wards to see their pitiful niece, Sunny's illness had been treated like a death.

Maybe that was why Dahlia was feeling so uneasy and weird. It felt as if someone she'd thought of as dead had suddenly come alive. Like Jimmy Stewart finding Kim Novak in *Vertigo*. A distorted version of the person he once loved. Was this the time to say to Sunny, "I'm so sorry. I was too selfish to try to see you all these years? Or too afraid?" Sunny's shocks of hair stuck out in bunches at the top of her head, reminding Dahlia of Bozo the Clown. And now she moved down another step.

"I'm Dahlia. Benny's daughter. Our fathers were brothers. Do you remember that we gave each other lockets?"

Sunny blinked, and her jaw moved back and forth repeatedly.

"I drove down here from L.A. because I thought maybe we could spend a little time talking." Dahlia heard the shakiness in her own voice. "Do you remember me at all?" A seagull shrieked loudly overhead, and Dahlia wanted to let out the same high-pitched sound, jump into her van, and leave.

Sunny dug in her purse and pulled out a pack of

Marlboros, which she flipped open in Dahlia's direction.

"You shouldn't smoke," Dahlia heard herself say. "It'll kill you."

In a series of swift moves, Sunny turned the pack toward her own face, opened her mouth, sucked three of the cigarettes between her lips, pulled a lighter out of a pocket in the jacket of her red jogging suit, snapped it open, and flicked up a flame. Then, in a cloud of smoke, she lit all three, her eyes never leaving Dahlia's. When her mouth was filled with smoke, she blew it at Dahlia.

"This way I can die three times as fast," she said. Then she laughed at her own joke and turned and walked up the steps, and a chill swept through Dahlia at the familiarity of the raspy family voice. It was the way Aunt Ruthie sounded when she used to holler upstairs at midnight to tell them to stop singing and go to sleep.

Dahlia sighed. Oh, my God. I've got to get out of here, she thought, hating to admit to herself that Louie the weasel had been right. This woman was too far gone to remember a thing. There was probably no point in staying here one more minute. She clearly didn't know Dahlia. This was a colossal waste of time. Dahlia's mouth felt dry, and when she reached into her purse to look for a piece of gum, she saw the contract Marty Melman had sent over from the studio sitting there as a reminder of the reason she'd come, and she sighed. Don't be a jerk, she said to herself. At least give it a try.

After all, if Sunny would sign the paper, who cared

if she remembered Dahlia or didn't remember her? This person didn't have to like her or want be taken to lunch by her. This was not some sentimental trip down memory lane. This was a business transaction, and Dahlia would have to treat it as one. To hell with feeling nostalgic. That wasn't going to get her anywhere. She was talking to a woman who was smoking three frigging cigarettes at a time, for God's sake, so how much sense did she have to make? Okay, she told herself, deep breath. Jump right in.

"Sunny," Dahlia said, following her up the steps. This has to work, she thought, or I'll be back watching Marty Melman pee. "I'm your cousin Dahlia. When I was born, you stood outside the nursery and told everyone they had to wash their hands before they came in to touch the baby. Remember? Everyone said I was your little doll."

She could hear the television blasting inside. A doctor was talking to Oprah and the women in the audience about rescuing their relationships. It would be so easy to run down the steps, get back in the van, and admit this was a mistake.

But she couldn't take her eyes from this woman's face. It was so eerie to look at her and see Uncle Max's eyes and Aunt Ruthie's nose and her own mother's pout. A blend of her entire family was in this face, her long-gone family. This person, this poor specimen of a person—unless you counted that monster Louie— was all she had left of that family, and look at her. She was a beaten shell of a human being, with eyes that didn't seem to be able to focus when she looked at Dahlia. Unblinking, glazed-over eyes that made

Dahlia certain she didn't connect her in any way to her past. It was a past that for Sunny had been blown away years ago.

As a child Dahlia had asked, she had tried, sometimes forcing herself to ask the questions even though she was afraid of what the answers might be.

"Mom, where is Sunny?"

"Sunny is in as good a place as she can be under the circumstances, but don't worry, you won't ever have to go there," Rose would tell her.

"But I want to go there. To see her."

"No," Dahlia's father would say, wearing an expression that meant, When you're old and wise like we are, you'll understand.

Well, it didn't do her any good to feel guilty about all those years of staying away from Sunny. That's what happened to everybody, wasn't it? They got caught up in the minutiae of their own days and didn't spend time thinking about anyone else's. Unless the "anyone else" was their kids or their husband. Cousins didn't fall into that category. Dahlia wondered if Sunny had any idea how many of the others in the family were gone. Her parents and Dahlia's and all of the Gordon aunts and uncles.

Sunny was still holding those three cigarettes between yellow fingers, and now she took a deep puff, shaped her lips into a tight circle, and blew out a large O of a smoke ring. Then she leaned over and stubbed out all three in a very full ashtray on the railing. This is a lost cause, Dahlia thought. I should really just get back on the road to L.A. and take it like a grown-up when Seth tells me how he knew all along this wasn't going to work. You do things for bad reasons, you get bad results. Everyone knows that.

"Want to sit down?" Sunny asked, but when Dahlia looked at her face, Sunny looked past her, never making eye contact. For an instant Dahlia thought Sunny might have been talking to someone else on the porch. But there wasn't anybody else on the porch. She could hear Oprah's theme music coming from inside as the show broke for a commercial, and Sunny walked away and slid into a rocking chair.

Okay. Sunny asked her to sit down. That was a good start. Maybe after a while they'd chat, and she could take out the contract and deliver the speech she'd worked on last night.

"Sure, I'll sit down," Dahlia said, following Sunny and slipping into a rocking chair next to hers. Sunny rocked in the chair the way a child would, moving it vigorously back and forth, making her feet land hard on the wood porch, then lifting them as the chair moved back.

"Do you remember my mother? Aunt Rose?" Dahlia tried. "She loved you. You sometimes wore her jewelry when you went out on a date."

But Sunny stared straight ahead and didn't answer. Maybe talking about her dating was a bad idea. Aunt Ethel used to go on and on with her theory that it was while she was on a date that Sunny cracked, flipped, blew her cork, all those phrases they used behind Aunt Ruthie's back to describe Sunny's condition. Yes, Dahlia remembered how they all had tossed around the idea that Sunny probably lost control after being raped by some unnamed boy. The rape was a popular family theory, because it placed the blame on an out-side force instead of on the possibility that the genes all of them had in common with her might be faulty.

For a long time now, the only sounds were the creak of the rocking chairs and Sunny's stomping feet, the crying out of seagulls, and the occasional rise in the voices of Oprah's guests.

"Do you remember that we wrote songs together?" Dahlia asked. The only answer was the flick of the lighter as Sunny lit yet another cigarette. "One of them was called 'Stay by My Side.' " A puff of another smoke ring came out of Sunny's rounded lips, then another, but still her eyes never met Dahlia's. "Well, I've become a professional songwriter, and I can tell you it's a tough-ass profession. Sometimes you sell one song, and then you can wait years to sell another one. So you can imagine how thrilled I was to find out that somebody, I mean somebody really big, wants to buy that song from us. The one we wrote in your mother's house when we were kids. Isn't that wild?"

Sunny puffed hard on the cigarette. All right, Dahlia thought. Let's cut the warm, fuzzy family stuff and move in for the kill. "You see, this is really a big deal in the music business. Someone actually wants to give us money for a song we wrote and use it as the title song for a movie. Millions of people could be lis-tening to a song that we wrote. And at the end of the movie, our names will actually be on the screen. We'll get a credit saying we wrote the song." Now she was singing, "Stay by my side forever, stay by my side, my friend. Our love's a perfect circle. That means it cannot end." Sunny stared straight ahead and didn't even glance at her.

After a beat Sunny stubbed out the most recently lit cigarette in the ashtray next to her chair and looked at Dahlia with a raised eyebrow. "Gotta go now," she said, and Dahlia wasn't sure if she was saying Dahlia had to go or Sunny had to leave the porch until Sunny stood, turned, and walked into the house. Her exit was so abrupt that Dahlia let out an outraged laugh. She was being dismissed. She'd come all this way to offer this woman a deal that could provide her with enough money to get her the hell out of this beat-up little rest home for fruitcakes, and the woman was walking away.

"Sunny," Dahlia said, following behind her, "I haven't seen you in so long. You can't walk away. I need to tell you about this offer."

Sunny didn't look back, just headed right up the staircase. I can't let her out of my sight, Dahlia thought. "Sunny!" she called, moving toward the steps. But before she could get to them, she was blocked by a large man dressed in a white jacket. He had a crew cut and a big round face, and he was smiling, a forced smile.

"We don't like guests upstairs," he said. She escaped, Dahlia thought. Before I could even get through to her. The man in the white coat didn't budge from the bottom of the steps, as if he expected Dahlia to try to bolt past him. He was standing in a position that said he wasn't going to move until she walked away.

Dahlia, go home, she told herself. You came here to take advantage of a mentally ill woman, which was a lousy idea, and not just *any* mentally ill woman—your own flesh and blood. The same Gordon family blood that's in your veins is in hers. Go away and leave her in peace. You'd be better off robbing a liquor store for the money. Without turning around, she backed up toward the front door.

"Medications!" she heard the man in the white jacket call out as he lifted a small bell that he shook, and the shrill ring seemed to get everyone's attention. Now she noticed there was a cart next to him with little cups of medication on it, and various members of the Oprah group were standing and heading in his direction.

Dahlia turned and walked out of the house, down the steps, and opened the passenger door of the van. Seth was napping, and the sound of the door woke him.

"How did it go?" he asked groggily.

Dahlia climbed into the passenger seat and shook her head. "It *didn't* go," she said. "Let's just hit it and get out of here. I was wrong. You called it. It's a fiasco. She has no clue who I am. She has no clue who *she* is. She just walked away from me. God, they must have burned her brain out."

"Wouldn't it be simpler just to write another song by yourself and use the same title?" Seth asked. "Maybe Melman would like it as well."

Dahlia put her face in her hands. "Do you have any idea what it means for someone as big as Marty Melman to like a song and want it to be in his big-time Hollywood picture? You don't just call a guy like that and say, 'Oh, hi. I decided I don't want to give you that one. I have another one with the same title instead.' Seth, he said he loved this song. He said it rocks. He was calling Jennifer Lopez to record it."

Seth was quiet as he started the car. "Do you even want to bother going to that hotel?" he asked. "They said we could cancel up until four o'clock, and it's only three," he said, looking at his watch.

"And drive all the way back to L.A.?" Dahlia watched as the guy in the white coat came bounding out the door of the Sea View, slid into a battered station wagon with a bumper sticker that said PLANNED PARENTHOOD, and drove off.

"I guess you're right," she said, trying to keep back the tears of frustration. "No point in spending money I can't even dream about getting." Seth pulled out his cell phone and a card with the hotel's phone number on it.

"Dumb idea. Poor Sunny," Dahlia continued, picking up her appointment book from the floor of the van where she always kept it and flicking through the pages to see how many massages she was scheduled to do this week, wondering how she could get a few more clients so she could increase her monthly income. She felt sick about the idea that she had to tell Marty Melman she couldn't sell him the song.

"Yeah, we had a reservation to check in this afternoon and stay tonight," she heard Seth say into the phone. "And we're going to have to cancel—"

But then Dahlia clutched his arm and stopped him from saying another word, because at that moment, filling the air and wafting down through the open living room window of the Sea View, came a familiar refrain, and Dahlia strained to hear if it actually was what she thought it was or if her wishful thinking was making her hallucinate. Just a few more bars and it was unmistakable. She seized the phone out of Seth's hand and spoke into it. "Never mind," she blurted out. "We're staying!" Because she could hear that on the falling-down upright piano in the living room of the board-and-care, Sunny was playing "Stay by My Side."

Dahlia pushed open the door of the van and gestured for Seth to follow. Together they ran up the steps of the Sea View and through the door. All the other residents were gathered around the piano, rapt as Sunny sang. Dahlia stood at the back of the group between Santa Claus and the black woman who was no longer talking to herself but listening to the song written so long ago.

"Our love's a perfect circle. That means it cannot end," Sunny wailed in what was now a big, gravelly, funky voice.

"Didn't take her meddies again," Santa Claus said softly to Dahlia. "Stuffs 'em in her bra when Grover's not watching, even though he knows she's doing it. Then he leaves, and she sits down and plays her songs. She says the music blocks out the voices better than any pills."

Santa Claus's face was lit up proudly as he swayed to Sunny's music.

"She plays a lot of songs?" Dahlia whispered in return.

He nodded. "We call her the Goddess of Music. She

makes 'em all up, too. This one's nothing compared to the ones she usually plays of her own stuff. Most of 'em are better than the Beatles."

Dahlia made her way through the group, which was now swaying with arms around one another, grinning and tapping and rocking back and forth on their heels, and when she got to the piano, she sat next to Sunny on the bench where she always sat when they performed as children.

Sunny used her right foot on the pedal and had her left foot sitting on the bench with her left knee turned out, and Dahlia, taking a chance, slid her arm around her cousin's waist and sang the words with her. Sunny's big voice was still so much louder than Dahlia's soft one, just the way it had been when they were kids. And somehow, after all Sunny's brain had endured, she still remembered the childish lyrics of the song Dahlia had written at age eleven.

The song was unquestionably catchy. As the two cousins launched into a repeat of the refrain for the third time around, some of the people in the group sang along. "When you are by my side, my life is worthwhile." Seth laughed at himself for singing along and feeling so moved, but watching these people come alive with the music was heartrending, even though he knew that Dahlia was only thinking about this as a business opportunity. He was sure that her sliding her arm around the waist of the woman in the parachute jumpsuit was just her first step to pulling out the contract and a pen.

Maybe it was because he knew so much about the two cousins' history that he had to hold back the tears.

Tears that if Dahlia spotted she would ridicule, so he was relieved when the song ended in a big musical flourish and everyone was cheering and hollering for an encore. At that point he could escape out onto the porch and wipe his eyes. But he did stay long enough to see Sunny rise in the midst of the ovation and, without even turning toward Dahlia, lumber through the group and make her way up the stairs.

six

"Now, this is the life," Dahlia said. She was curled up next to Seth on a lounge chair by the pool of the elegant Del Coronado hotel. Once, about ten years ago, a concert promoter she was dating brought her to this hotel for a night, but then the schmuck spent the whole evening on the phone talking to his ex-wife. Dahlia had sworn to herself that night, hating the date and hating her life, that she would come back to this beautiful spot when she had money. Okay, so she still couldn't afford it, but now that Sunny obviously remembered the song, things were moving along in that direction. Sunny remembered it. That clownish-looking woman who seemed to be completely blotto actually remembered their song from twenty-five years ago.

"The Santa Claus guy told me she always plays the piano," Dahlia said. "That she has tunes, other tunes that she wrote, and they're great. Tomorrow I'm going back there, and I'm going to worm my way into her brain and get her to remember me. And then she'll sign the contract. And when the movie comes out and the song's a hit, she can go buy herself a whole new wardrobe of straitjackets."

Seth didn't laugh, and Dahlia poked him. "Lighten up. I'm kidding. Hey, she's my cousin. You can't seriously think I'm that mean. Can you?"

Seth frowned.

"Okay, it was a bad joke. But you have to laugh. That Sea View place was horror-movie time. Weren't you freaked out?" Dahlia asked. "I mean, that group made me queasy. The one guy never stopped tapping his index finger so hard on the rail of his chair I thought he was going to hurt himself. And one of the women was moaning to the music. In the right key."

A peal of laughter made them both turn toward the gate to the pool. They watched as a pretty, dark-haired woman who was probably in her fifties pushed a wheelchair carrying a bearded man who sat chatting amiably with her, despite an oxygen tube in his nose. The man said something that must have been funny, because the woman laughed again and pushed the chair to a stop near the edge of the pool. Then she took off her shoes, sat on the edge of the pool, slid her skirt above her knees, and dipped her feet into the water.

"Ooooh!" the woman exclaimed. "Been wantin' to do this all day."

Seth put his face against Dahlia's and whispered into her ear. "Would you push my chair around if that were me?" he asked softly.

"I would," she said. "And then I'd tip you right into the pool and find me a dude who could take me dancing!" She laughed, but when she looked into his face, there was something serious about his expression that bothered her. "Why are you asking me that? Don't you think I would?"

Seth didn't answer.

"You don't!" she said quietly. "You think I'm too selfish. You think if we were married and you got hit by a car, I'd say, 'I'm out of here,' and leave you helpless. Don't you?"

"Can you imagine how hard that woman's life is?" Seth mused quietly, but Dahlia was sitting up now, her feet tapping around on the ground feeling for her sandals.

"Dahl, cut it out. I'm not going to get into a big harangue with you about some imaginary situation. Let's go get dinner and call it a night."

"I'm not hungry," Dahlia said.

"Well, I am. I'll eat something and be up later."

"Why won't you discuss this?" she asked. Her face was dark with anger.

"Discuss what?"

A bubble of laughter erupted from the couple at the edge of the pool.

"The idea that you think I'm a greedy flake."

"You *are* a flake! Look what you're doing. Look why we're here. Look at the money we're spending in this overpriced place so you can get that poor, drugged-to-the-teeth woman—"

"So I can get her to make a ton of money. Money she can use, keep, roll around in. She may even come up onstage at the Grammys—where, the way she looks, she'll fit in better than I do. Why is this a sin? I'm doing her a favor. Maybe if she had tons of money, she could find herself better doctors, better care, a better lifestyle. Not to mention what it would give you and me. So how about having positive fantasies about how we're going to be flush with dough? Think about a life for us that's full of prosperity, instead of 'poor me' scenarios where I'm going to have to take care of you when you're disabled. You are the most negative person on the planet, and if you hate what I'm doing, then just go home. There's a train or a bus or a flight between here and L.A. every hour."

Seth shook his head at her tirade, then stood and left her sitting at the pool.

When Dahlia was eleven and her parents told Aunt Ruthie and Uncle Max how much they wanted her to learn to play the piano, even though they couldn't afford to buy one, Aunt Ruthie volunteered the Steinway and her living room to Dahlia once a week for her lesson and any other time she wanted to come over to practice. Aunt Ruthie and Uncle Max only lived a few blocks down the street on Dahlia's way home from school, so it was easy for her to walk there, and Dahlia couldn't wait to get started with Mr. Hughes, who had been Sunny's teacher when Sunny was Dahlia's age.

Luckily, Sunny had already taught Dahlia some of the basics, so Dahlia was able to skip the first few *Teaching Little Fingers to Play* beginners' books and start playing songs right away. Andrew Hughes had a long, thin face and very short hair. He always wore a coat and tie no matter what the weather, and he carried a brown leather briefcase with his initials, AH, embossed on it in gold. He smiled a smile that showed protruding front teeth, and he blushed uncomfortably when he talked, as if he'd rather not have to say anything, just come in, put music in front of you, have you play it, give you some more pieces to work on for next week, and then leave.

"What an odd bird," Sunny said, remembering when she studied with him and warning Dahlia. "He never tried anything with me, but he's a bizarre one." Dahlia, who was shy with everyone, felt especially shy with Mr. Hughes, as she called him, because he had this way of sitting too close to her on the piano bench, and she could feel his warm thigh pressing into her. And when he moved her hand off the keys so he could put his own hand on, in order to demonstrate something to her, he placed her hand on his lap.

But what bothered her most was the way he would show her how to play certain difficult passages in a new song. He'd have her stay where she sat at the keyboard, then get behind her and lean above her, his arms over her shoulders, his face close to hers, the back of his arms grazing her chest, and he would play the piece. After he'd done that the first time, Dahlia dreaded the next one, and soon he was doing it at every lesson, so when she'd see him stand and move behind her, she'd feel fluttery and sick, but she was too afraid to say a word. She would try to focus on what he was playing, but his closeness and the way his arms casually brushed her budding new breasts made her dizzy.

"So how was the lesson?" her mother would ask when she came home at night from her job at Dr. Raphael's office.

"Good," Dahlia would reply quietly, not looking at her mother, ashamed that she was letting the intimacy continue without reporting it, but afraid that if she told her parents, they would cancel the lessons. She was learning so much so fast, playing so many new and difficult pieces that even Sunny was impressed. And she wanted to tell Sunny what Mr. Hughes was doing, wishing she could ask her what to do about it, but she didn't have to. One day just after Mr. Hughes put his arms over Dahlia's shoulders and began to play a passage of "Für Elise," leaning so close that Dahlia could smell the soap he used, she heard Sunny's voice penetrate the air.

"What in the hell do you think you're doing?" Sunny roared into the room and grabbed Dahlia's arm, pushing Dahlia behind her and standing face-to-face with Mr. Hughes, who flushed fuchsia.

"Showing her how to play this passage?" he tried, but the question mark in his voice gave him away. Sunny sat at the bench and played the passage perfectly. "That's how you play the fucking passage, Dahl. And you get up when he wants to show you how to do anything." Then she turned to Mr. Hughes. "If I ever see you touch her in that way again, I'll break your fucking head, and that'll be the nicest thing I do to you, before I go to the newspaper, the cops, and the Music Teachers of America Union, if there is such a thing. Got me?"

Dahlia remembered how Mr. Hughes pushed the

sheet music into his briefcase and hurried out the door, and she was sure he wouldn't be back there on the next Wednesday after school, but he was. And when he wanted to show her how to play a new passage, he asked her to excuse him, she got up, and he played it for her, and then she sat down and played it for him. Sunny had saved her, not just that once but time and time again when Dahlia was a kid. Now she was returning the favor and saving Sunny. That's what this was all about, she told herself as she dozed off that night in the hotel room. Saving her. Not taking advantage of her.

Seth was showered, dressed, and playing solitaire on the laptop when Dahlia opened her eyes the next day and realized she'd slept away a lot of the morning.

"I'm sorry," she said quietly.

"So much for romantic nights in San Diego," he said.

"I said I'm sorry."

"Great," he said, shutting down the laptop. "Shouldn't we be getting back home or make another stab at the Sea View? I have work to do in L.A., so the sooner we get this family reunion over with, the happier I'll be."

His overnight bag was already packed and standing at the door. If it weren't for the fact that they had driven down here together, he might have just left her there, she thought.

"Honey, come here," she said in a voice that at other times might have convinced him to let her lousy behavior slide and climb back into bed with her.

"Get dressed," he said, picking up his bag and leaving the room.

All the way back to the Sea View, while Dahlia drove, Seth had the computer open on his lap as he played solitaire silently.

"I'm just going to say good-bye to her," Dahlia said. "I want to give her my phone number. Tell her if she ever needs anything, she can give me a call." It was ten o'clock in the morning, but the day was already uncomfortably hot. The air-conditioning in the van was pushing out all the cold air it could muster, but it wasn't much. Dahlia felt sticky and cranky.

"You're not going over there to say good-bye," Seth said. "You're going to try one more time to get a signature out of her." Dahlia wanted to pull over to the side of the road and tell him to get the hell out of her van for not believing her, for continuing to characterize her as some hard-hearted, callous bitch. But she didn't, because the truth of the matter was that this time there was no doubt he was right.

Nobody was sitting on the porch of the Sea View as Dahlia pulled up at the curb across the street. "I'm gonna go take a walk," Seth said. "I spotted a bookstore and a camera store on the main drag, so I'll come back in a little while and get you." He was angry, Dahlia could tell. And he was probably justified in being angry. She'd been bitchy to him. But she would apologize on the ride home, and he'd get over it. Meanwhile this was her last crack at getting Sunny to sign the contract, and she wasn't going to let Seth's mood get in her way.

As she moved slowly up the steps of the Sea View, she could hear the sound of somebody's too-loud radio coming from somewhere, and she wondered if the drugged-out denizens of the board-and-care even noticed irritants like loud music. It sounded as if it was one of those religious music stations, because the choir of voices was harmonizing to something that sounded like a spiritual, rising in intonation, now changing keys, and then stopping abruptly.

As Dahlia moved past the kitchen and the stairs toward a little hallway leading to an outside door, she realized that the singing had come from live voices. It was a group of the people who lived here, and now they were gabbing and laughing outside in the tiny backyard of the big old house. Most of them were from the group Dahlia had seen the other day, among them Sunny, who was chatting with Santa Claus. She was wearing overalls and a bright pink T-shirt. Santa seemed to be the conductor of the group, because he stood in front of the others with his back toward the door.

None of them seemed to notice Dahlia, who remained behind the screen door watching them. Sunny was pulling some sheets of paper from a folder and passing them out to each member of the group. The black man who had driven the car yesterday studied the piece of paper she handed him, and the short, stocky woman took a pair of glasses out of her pocket and put them on so she could peer more closely at the sheet.

"Is everyone ready?" Dahlia heard Santa ask them. "How many remember that we talked about this song last time before we worked on it?" Nobody answered, but Santa went on. "It used to be a song of prayer. A Nigerian folk tune. And what the people were really singing was 'Come by here, Lord.' Asking God to visit them no matter how humble they were. I guess little by little over the years the three words got pushed into one, and now people call this song 'Cumbayah.' But I like to sing it in the original way."

The white-haired woman who chattered to herself was gesturing and talking to some inward person the whole time Santa spoke. The man who always tapped continued to tap repeatedly on his thigh, Sunny stared into space, a curly-haired woman Dahlia hadn't seen yesterday gazed intensely at the lyrics, and the short, stocky woman rose on her toes, then back down onto her whole foot as she listened.

Santa blew into a little pitch pipe, and somehow, at that moment, as if the sound of the pipe held magical powers, all of them mobilized. There was no more tapping, no talking, except from the black man who drove the car yesterday and who now sat glumly on a beat-up old Adirondack chair.

"I'm gonna sing from here," he said.

"Eddie," Santa commanded, "get up!"

"Too tired," Eddie replied.

"Can't do it if you don't stand up. You need to use your diaphragm, and it doesn't work as well sitting down," Santa said, "and we're not starting until you get up." It was an order, and after a moment Eddie sighed and stood and took his place. Then Santa blew the pitch pipe again, and they all focused on him. He raised his hands conductor-like, and they responded in song.

"Come by here, Lord. Come by here," they sang in a blended four-part harmony that surprised Dahlia with its quality. "Come by here, Lord. Come by here. Come by here, Lord. Come by here. Oh, Lord, come by here."

Dahlia was transfixed by what she was seeing and hearing, astonished at the way the act of singing completely transformed each one of them, making their formerly expressionless eyes look as if they were lit from within. The sound of their song was angelic and their concentration unbroken as they watched Santa Claus and stood with lifted chins and straight backs and glowing faces.

"Someone's cryin', Lord. Come by here," their voices rang out.

Sunny, who had been slack-jawed earlier as she passed out the song sheets to the others, now looked both angelic and powerful, and for the first time Dahlia saw in her expression a real suggestion of the cousin she had lost long ago.

"Someone's cryin', Lord. Come by here. Oh, Lord. Come by here."

As they reached the end of the song, Santa Claus, who had been waving his arms enthusiastically, now lifted them in a grand gesture, bidding the singers to hold the last three notes. Come by here!!!

And then, as quickly as they had become the able and powerful choir, just after Santa called out "Thank you" to signify the end of their meeting, Dahlia was fascinated to watch the retrogression of each of them as their postures sank back, their focus seemed to shift inward again, and one by one they shuffled back toward the house.

"Thanks, Bill," Dahlia heard a few of them say.

It was the short, stocky woman who noticed Dahlia first and poked Santa hard on the arm and nodded toward the door. He turned, and when he saw Dahlia, he said, "Company," in a voice that sounded as if he were warning the others. When Sunny looked up to spot Dahlia standing in the doorway, she didn't seem surprised. In fact, she didn't react at all, just trudged past Dahlia, making no sign of recognition, and pushed the screen door open to go inside, letting it slam behind her.

"Did you like our choral group?" Santa asked Dahlia. The two of them were the only ones left in the Sea View's spartan backyard.

"I loved your choral group."

"We don't get together very often, and Sunny, she's my partner. She and I go over to the library and find music, and they let us run it off at a quarter a copy, so it's not too bad. Then we have fun with it."

"I could see that," Dahlia said.

"There's something about music that nothing else can quite equal," Santa said as he and Dahlia moved into the house, where she could see some of the others filling the chairs that were parked in front of the TV. But Sunny wasn't one of that group. The medicine man was nowhere in sight to stop her, so Dahlia decided to make her way upstairs.

The upstairs hallway smelled of Old Spice aftershave, and a door was open, revealing a messy bathroom with towels on the floor. Most of the doors were closed, but at the end of the hall there was one more open door, and Dahlia approached it. Through the door she could see Sunny sitting on the fuchsia chenille bedspread playing solitaire. Dahlia watched her from a few feet away and saw Sunny's brow furrow as she moved the cards from one row to another. "Sunny?" Dahlia said softly, and Sunny looked up blankly, as if she'd expected to see Dahlia there. As if she'd known all along someone was standing there watching her.

"I came to say good-bye," Dahlia said. "And I was so glad I got to hear the choral group. You're all wonderful."

"Yeah," Sunny said, returning her attention to the cards as she continued the game. Red six on black seven. Black four on red five.

"I remember you taught me how to play solitaire when I was seven," Dahlia said, hearing her voice sound as tinny and hollow and insecure as it had with Marty Melman's receptionist. It was that shaky sound, the one that said, You have something I need, so I'm nervous when I'm around you. How could she have that feeling with her own cousin, a mental patient?

"Now I play solitaire on the computer. With virtual cards. My boyfriend's addicted to it," Dahlia went on as she walked to the window in Sunny's room to look down at the van, praying Seth was back and she would have a reason to say a quick good-bye, bolt out of there, and head home. But the street was empty, and Seth wasn't anywhere in sight. "If you want to see the computer, I can run down and get it and bring it back."

Sunny nodded. "I want to," she said, sounding like a child.

"Don't move," Dahlia said, and she raced down the

stairs to the front door. The others all sat zoned out again, staring at the TV. At the van Dahlia climbed into the way-back where Seth had piled the computer on top of their duffel bags. Then she looked up at the Sea View, and when her eyes traveled to the second-story windows, she saw Sunny in one of them looking down at her. She grabbed the computer, held it up to show Sunny, and made her way back into the house and up again to Sunny's room.

"Here it is," Dahlia said, coming breathlessly into the room and setting the computer down on Sunny's bed. "You see, the reason I have that van is because I'm a masseuse," she continued, opening the computer and turning it on. Sunny was deadpan. "Do you know what a masseuse is?" Why in the world would Sunny know what that was? And how would Dahlia describe it to her? People take off all their clothes, and I rub their bodies? Well, maybe Sunny knew what a masseuse did. Mental patients watched a lot of TV. Somebody on one of those glamorous daytime soaps must get massages. Somebody in one of those tacky stories they stared at probably fell in love with the hot little masseuse and left his wife for her.

"So I need a roomy vehicle to carry a table and sometimes oils and sometimes sheets and blankets and heating pads." Sunny had no interest in the story Dahlia was telling. All she cared about was the magic silver box Dahlia was clicking away at while she spoke.

"Okay," Dahlia said, "here's how you play solitaire on the computer. I'll show you." She sat on the bed next to Sunny and pulled up the solitaire game on the screen. Then she slid the computer onto Sunny's lap. Sunny looked at the screen and studied the little cards for a long time, then shook her head as if to say she couldn't understand what Dahlia was trying to teach her.

"Now what?" she asked, clearly flummoxed by the whole idea that a machine could play cards.

"Here's what you do." Dahlia took Sunny's finger and placed it on the mouse, the way Sunny used to take hers and place it on middle C. "Click on the six of hearts, but hold the button down, then move it this way and put it there!"

Sunny did what Dahlia told her, and when she saw the result, her mouth opened in happy surprise. "Whoa!" she said.

"Now do that with the black eight and the red nine," Dahlia said.

It took Sunny a minute to find the right cards, and as she did, her right hand accidentally pushed the escape key, and when the screen morphed into the desktop with all the icons, her face crumbled. "I'm sorry, I'm sorry," she said, on the verge of tears.

"Hey, it's okay," Dahlia said, pulling the computer onto her own lap, clicking the solitaire icon, and getting the game screen back, then putting an arm around Sunny, who looked relieved. Soon she was moving the cards quickly around the screen and laughing a little spurt of a laugh when the ones she needed came up. By the time she played the third game, she beat the computer and she was elated.

"I love this," she said, looking deeply into her cousin's eyes, and for Dahlia, in that instant, it was as if no time, no electroconvulsive shock treatments, no antipsychotic medications powerful enough to knock out an entire nation had ever come between them.

"I knew you would," Dahlia said happily.

seven

Dahlia remembered the day she and Sunny had just finished playing and singing at another one of Aunt Ruthie's parties when Esther Greenspan cornered Aunt Ruthie in the kitchen. "Those girls are adorable. Those songs they write are amazing. I could put them to work every weekend on the women's-lunch circuit. They'd make a fortune." Esther was Aunt Ruthie's girlhood friend, and she'd shown up at one of the family parties and couldn't get over the girls and their songs. Both Aunt Ruthie and Dahlia's mother, Rose, shrugged. A fortune? They would need plenty of money for college, so why not let them?

Dahlia couldn't believe they were getting fifty dollars each for appearing at this luncheon and as many more luncheons as they felt like doing, according to Esther, who hovered over them before the show. Her oversprayed bouffant hairdo was so unmoving that

Sunny couldn't take her eyes off of it. The women at
the luncheon streamed into the room at the Sports-
man's Lodge, all of them dressed in fancy suits and
high heels with purses to match. They were the kind
of women Dahlia's mother wished out loud that she
could be.

"The chicken-salad ladies," Rose called them wist-
fully. Women who had money to buy seats at charity
luncheons and then spend more money to buy
brightly colored suits to wear to the luncheons. And
on top of that, every one of them even had her hair
and nails done, to be what Aunt Ruthie would call "all
dolled up."

The girls sat backstage peeking out to watch the assembled women who chattered and scurried from one
table to another hugging one another, then sitting to
eat and gossip over their chicken salad. Esther
Greenspan came back and took the girls' hands in
hers, which were icy cold. She seemed edgy, as if she
were the one who was about to go out there and sing
for a few hundred people. "Break a leg, you two," she
said. Then she hurried onto the platform, and someone at one of the tables tapped a knife against a water
glass to tell the women it was time to be quiet. Dahlia
was tense. Sunny looked beautiful, her hair wavy all
around her white skin, and she seemed to be enjoying
watching the parade of clothes and jewelry.

"Am I on?" Esther said into the microphone, and
then there was a loud squeal of feedback, and all the
women held their ears. "*Now* am I on?" Then she put
on little half reading glasses and read from her notes,
"Welcome, paid-up members of the Beth El Sister-

hood. I won't make a real speech until later. But right now you should welcome and enjoy these talented little girls, who are cousins. One writes the lyrics—Rose and Benny Gordon's daughter, Dahlia—and the other the music—Ruthie and Max Gordon's daughter, Sunny. So give them a big round of applause."

The women seemed to appreciate the songs. Once they applauded in the middle of a number, and the girls were elated. Sunny leaned into the piano and added a few more musical flourishes that surprised even Dahlia. And the huge ovation at the end made it clear that the women were impressed with the little half-hour presentation the girls had practiced in Aunt Ruthie's living room, on those days when Louie would sidle by and say things like, "With a little bit of effort, this could stink."

"Let's hear it for these talented young ladies," Esther said, coming back to the platform. She looked very pleased with herself that the show had been so well received. Some of the women were even yelling "Bravo." Esther gestured for Dahlia and Sunny to take a bow, and they held hands and blew kisses. That was when Dahlia glanced over at Sunny, sure she'd see happiness in her cousin's face, but Sunny's eyes were moving back and forth across the room nervously, and Dahlia felt a quickening in her stomach, knowing that the worst was about to happen. The wild look in Sunny's eyes was unmistakable, and Dahlia inched closer to her to hear what she was saying.

"Birds' nests," Sunny muttered so only Dahlia could hear her.

"Sunny, it's okay. Let's just take our bows and get out of here."

"No. No. It isn't okay. I hate when ladies' hairdos are so stiff and stuck in position that they look like birds' nests. And they keep birds in there waiting to fly out and peck us."

Oh, God. Dahlia was filled with a sense of impending doom. "Sunny, don't," she said, knowing how powerful the forces could be when Sunny started off on a tangent like this. She had to get her away from this place as fast as she could move her.

Esther was still at the podium. "Ladies," she said as the women continued to applaud, "aren't they great?" But Dahlia, still holding Sunny's hand, felt the agitation flow through her cousin just as Sunny let go, hurried away from her, and bounded down the steps to where the twenty tables of ten were filled with jabbering women. Then, from a tray a waiter had left on a side table, Sunny lifted a pitcher of ice water in each hand, rushed to the table closest to the stage, raised the pitchers high, and spilled torrents of ice water on the bouffant, puffy, sprayed hairdos of the women. After that she moved back to the tray, grabbing another pair of pitchers and rushing to another group of women to do it again. The women were too stunned to stop her, and Dahlia stood in horror on the stage, watching.

After a moment Esther Greenspan realized what was happening and shrieked into the microphone, "Stop her! Someone stop her! She's crazy!" But nobody stopped her. Women were screaming as if it were acid Sunny was pouring, and they were leaping to their feet to run out of the room, horrified to be seen with their flattened, sticky hairdos and runny makeup and soaking-wet silk suits. Sunny was heading back to the tray, and she had just reached for another pitcher when Dahlia threw herself in front of the tray to stop her. She could see a phalanx of waiters marching angrily in their direction as she grabbed Sunny's hand and tugged at her.

"Come on!" she screamed, and they bolted across the stage, knocking down a microphone and nearly tripping over the cord, racing out the back door of the hotel and down Coldwater Canyon before anyone could stop them. Running breathlessly to get away, until Dahlia looked back and saw that nobody was running after them, and finally they stopped and sat down on the curb to breathe. Dahlia felt like throwing up. Just thinking about all of those women melting down under the deluge of ice water made her feel sick.

Sunny was crying. "They had birds' nests, and there were birds hiding in them, Dahl. I could hear them. The whole time we were singing, the birds were singing, too. Their chirpy little songs."

"No, Sun. They weren't. You need to change your medicine," Dahlia said, putting an arm around her and feeling Sunny's whole body racked with sobs. She remembered thinking at that moment how much she loved her poor, tormented cousin, wondering if anyone could stop this terrible devolution into madness that seemed to be sucking Sunny further and further from any semblance of normalcy.

The day after the luncheon, partly to appease the women who were threatening to sue and partly because Sunny became more and more uncontrollable at home that night, Dahlia remembered Aunt Ruthie and

Uncle Max putting Sunny away in a hospital outside the city, hoping the doctors could find some kind of medication that would put an end to those outbursts forever.

Today, as Dahlia sat on Sunny's bed at the Sea View watching her play game after game of solitaire, she felt as if things were going well. Probably if there was ever a moment to take a shot at getting Sunny to sign the contract, this was it. She seemed peaceful, she seemed friendly, and right now, for all intents and purposes, Dahlia was simply the nice person who'd brought her this new toy she seemed to be enjoying so much. Dahlia felt afraid to broach the subject, but she knew Seth would probably show up soon, still angry with her about last night, wanting her to leave San Diego and come home, so she had to make a stab at this now.

"Sunny, listen. I tried to explain this to you yesterday, but let me try again. A very famous movie producer wants to buy our song, and we stand to make some money. We could make a lot of money from it. I have a real contract here. See this?" She pulled the four-page contract out of her purse and held it up, then riffled through it to page 4. "This line with the little x next to it is a place where if you signed your name, it would guarantee that we'd both get a lot of money. See where I wrote 'Dahlia Gordon'? All you have to do is write 'Sunny Gordon' underneath."

Sunny ran her finger over Dahlia's signature, then nodded. "Okay," she said.

She said okay. Dahlia sat frozen, afraid that if she

blinked, Sunny would change her mind. Sunny said okay, and now she was smiling.

"Only you have to leave the room while I do," she added.

"Why?" Dahlia asked, barely breathing.

"Just because."

Just because. Okay. Sunny obviously had some fear of being watched, some problem with shyness, some need for control. Dahlia didn't care what the reason was. Why apply reason to this situation? She was about to get what she wanted. Sunny would sign the contract, so who cared why she wanted Dahlia to leave the room? Dahlia would do it gladly. Hell, she'd hang by her toes from the shower-curtain pole for that signature. In a few minutes she'd leave this depressing place with a signed contract in her hand.

"Yeah. Sure. I'll leave the room. You mean you want me to wait in the hall for a minute or two?" she asked, and Sunny nodded. Done deal. Hello, Grammys, Dahlia thought.

"See you in two minutes," Dahlia said, trying to keep the giddiness out of her voice as she walked into the hall. The strains of the theme music from some daytime soap wafted up the steps. Fantasies of the recording session danced through her brain. She'd wear a black turtleneck and black jeans. She and Jennifer Lopez would become instant friends.

"I love this song so much," J.Lo would say. "You must have a few more in your trunk that I can record."

"Oh, let me thumb through them and see what I can find," Dahlia would reply. Once you made contact with people like that, they looked to you for material.

Stars liked working with people they trusted. God, it was taking a long time for Sunny just to sign her name, she thought. Maybe she ought to holler in to her and remind her that even though the contract was four pages long, all she had to deal with was that little *x* on the last page. Surely she wasn't reading the damned thing. Dahlia had only skimmed it herself, and she was sane. Sunny could never wade through all that legal garbage.

Somewhere a toilet flushed, and from somewhere else Dahlia heard the moaning lady moan. This was taking way too long. Maybe Sunny didn't realize that Dahlia was just out in the hallway. Maybe she thought she'd gone back downstairs.

"Sunny," she said quietly, tapping lightly on the door.

"Yessss?" Sunny sang out.

"Are you ready?" Dahlia asked.

"I am," Sunny said.

Dahlia sighed with relief and pushed the door open to see Sunny, stone-faced, sitting at the little chair next to her desk. Spread out across the bed were the four pages of the contract, but something had been written on them in what, for an instant, Dahlia was certain had to be blood. Sunny's blood, like the time she dribbled it over the potato salad at the family picnic.

"What did you do!?" Dahlia shrieked. Then she looked back at Sunny, who was holding a small bottle of fiery red nail polish. The crimson letters she'd painted across the pages of the contract said: FUCK SIGNING, FUCK YOU, punctuated with little round faces with frowning eyes and downturned mouths.

"Why did you do that to my contract?" Dahlia

screamed. "Why?" This was a truly crazy person. The real question was why she had left the crazy person's room thinking something sane was going to happen.

"I'm not ever writing my name on anything again," Sunny told her. "My mother used to get me to sign those papers, too, because after I wasn't a kid anymore, I had to agree to stay in some of those hellholes where she put me. If I signed, I couldn't leave. Signing means you're trapped. No signing. 'Come on, honey,' she'd tell me. 'You know this is best for you.' No signing." Now she looked menacingly at Dahlia. "Get out of here. No signing."

"This was about a song," Dahlia said, trembling and knowing there was no way she could reason with this inflamed woman who was now red in the face and holding up the sheets of the contract, which had red polish dripping off them onto the floor. Dahlia snatched the laptop from the bed and turned to leave. "I'm sorry," she said to Sunny. "I'm sorry I never came to see you before, and I'm sorry I asked you to sign this, and I'm sorry I was stupid enough to think this could work."

Sunny was tearing at her own hair, repeating loudly, "No signing anything." As Dahlia hurried down the hall and down the stairs and out of the building she could hear her repeating, "No signing anything. No signing anything." In relief Dahlia stopped at the van, slid the door open, and put the laptop into the back, then glanced up to see Sunny standing in the window of her room, glaring down at her. Dahlia walked the few blocks up to the main street in town to look for Seth.

eight

Seth was in the bookstore sitting on the floor in a back aisle, reading a Tom Clancy novel. When Dahlia came around the corner and saw him there, she had a rush of longing to leap on him and cover him with kisses. Instead she slid down and sat next to him, and after a moment she rested her head on his shoulder. He didn't look up but took her hand.

"That was fast," he said. "What happened?"

"You won't believe this," she said, and told him the story. When he saw how rattled she was, he hugged her and didn't sigh his "Oh, Dahlia, you jerk" sigh. She loved him for holding on to her hand as he paid for the book, and as they walked back toward the van, he kept his arm around her and pulled her close.

"So here's what you do," he said. "Tomorrow you call Melman's office, say you misplaced the contract and you need to come by and pick up a new one. It won't be a big deal. It's probably some boilerplate thing you can get at the stationery store. Then you go to Louie, who probably has some power of attorney anyway, and you make it clear that closing this deal will get enough money for him to pay whatever expenses of Sunny's he has to pay. Believe me, he'll welcome you and Marty Melman's dough with open arms. So if you want to get your half, you'll have to eat a little crow and be nice to Louie for a few minutes. You can handle it. It's probably the way you should have gone to begin with."

"Yeah, I guess," she said. Seth opened the passenger door of the van for her, but before she got in, she looked up at the window of Sunny's room. "I just had this last spark of hope today that—"

"That what? You were gonna get her to take this seriously? She doesn't live in our world, Dahl. To people in her condition, a hit song doesn't mean a thing. Neither does a hot career or all the toys and troubles that go with having those things you crave so feverishly."

It annoyed Dahlia that he always made her ambition sound evil. She climbed into the passenger seat. "Actually, I was going to say I had a spark of hope that maybe there was some way to bring her back to being well. So many years have passed. Medical science has to have come up with something better than the stuff that guy is giving them from those little plastic cups. But how the hell would she ever be able to find out what it is? She's too drugged on the bad stuff to have any motivation to go looking for the good stuff. And that leaves that jerk Louie, who gave up on her a long time ago because he was afraid whatever she had was gonna rub off on his kids. So unless she has somebody to fight her battles for her, she's trapped in her own skin."

"You volunteering?" Seth asked, and she emitted a puff of air from her lips, scoffing.

"Yeah, right. Nurse Dahlia. As it is, you don't think I'd do it for you—and *you're* making love to me."

Seth grinned.

"And, by the way, not often enough," she teased.

Seth put his hand on her knee. "I'll catch you tonight," he said, and she was relieved that it was okay between them, at least for now. Of course it couldn't last. Because the truth about her adorable boy lover was that he was floundering around in the world just like she was. She had traveled all those miles to see a long-lost relative who didn't even want to see her, and she'd done it because she was afraid she had no spark left. She felt as dulled out as those people at the Sea View who were taking those little cups off the cart.

The loud blast of a car horn made her turn her head as Seth moved the van onto the 405 freeway. The driver was a pretty blonde in a black Mercedes convertible, cutting brazenly in front of the van. She had the top down, and Dahlia could see her yellow ponytail flying out of the back of a baseball cap. The Mercedes was shiny and new. The 430 convertible. Her favorite. Once Dahlia thought she'd be driving a car like that, but then she put those first big bucks she'd earned into that tiny house in Laurel Canyon, certain that after her first song was out in the world, she'd be on the map, sell song after hit song, and the dough would be rolling in. But that hadn't happened.

Now the damned house was falling apart, and she didn't even have enough cash to give it a decent paint job or to replace this van that creaked and complained at freeway speeds. It was a falling-apart rattletrap, and she knew she was going to have to get rid of it soon, but unless she made some kind of deal with Louie, there was no chance she'd be getting her hands on any serious money soon.

"Some people are meant to be rich, and some are meant to be worker bees," she remembered her mother saying when her father came home from putting in long hours at the furniture store, on a day when Rose could tell without asking her husband that not one single customer had crossed the threshold to come in to browse around, let alone buy so much as a lamp. And Dahlia's unhappy father stood on his tired feet all day, trying to look busy by dusting, by sweeping, by filing brochures, to justify the small salary that his rich Uncle Bernie, who owned the store, was paying him.

At least in the dental office where her mother worked, there were always the male patients who flirted with Rose, the woman patients who confided in her, and the handsome Dr. Raphael, who relied on her and who everyone thought looked like James Coburn, the movie actor. Every day her mother made small talk while she scheduled appointments and handed out mini–toothpaste tubes and toothbrushes with Dr. Raphael's name on them, and most days she felt very important. But at the end of the week, one look at her take-home pay reminded her that she was simply a worker bee, too.

No, Dahlia thought as Seth changed lanes now and she spotted the Mercedes again in the distance, I can't keep calling the bank and hearing the automatic teller report that I have no money. I have got to find a way to stop being a worker bee. Tomorrow she had to do eight massages in a row, and just the thought of it made her back ache. But she had to take advantage of the eight requests—because sometimes she'd only have eight appointments spread over two weeks.

"Hungry?" Seth asked. They were just fifteen minutes from home now, but she *was* feeling hungry, and some fast-food joint would do for dinner.

"Sure," she said.

He pulled the van off the freeway and into the parking lot at Carl's Junior next to a red pickup truck that had a pretty Alaskan husky sitting in the back.

"You want the drive-through, or should we live the high life and go in?" Seth asked her.

"I want to hobnob with the rich and famous. Let's go in."

While they stood in line, Dahlia watched an addled young mother surrounded by three screaming kids sitting in a booth by the far window. The young woman was stuffing a falling-apart burger into her mouth at the same time she hollered reprimands at her kids, one of whom was sitting on the table facing her with his feet in her lap. This is the quality of the places I get to dine, Dahlia thought, unless I put myself in hock like I did last night at that beautiful hotel, with elegant rooms and perfect lighting and soft sheets. I want that all the time. Not this. And Louie, that little weasel, is my ticket. What a joke! She looked up at the menu, and suddenly every choice made her queasy.

"Fries and a Coke." It was all she thought she could digest.

"Cheap date," Seth said, ordering a messy saucy burger for himself and getting a flirtatious smile from the cashier.

Sliding into a booth, Dahlia watched Seth looking out the window, watching a group of small children jump out of a car and rush gleefully toward the elaborate play structure next to the restaurant. There was another bunch of children inside the primary-colored maze, squealing noisily as they jumped on the trampolines, laughing as they crawled on their stomachs through the plastic tunnels, shrieking as they vaulted from the monkey bars.

Seth watched them with a longing look, as if he wished he could be out there playing with them. He was nuts about children. Dahlia thought they were cute from a distance, but motherhood would never be for her. It was a subject that could get them into heated discussions about how they could possibly have a future together. Not that there was a chance Seth would ever get custody of his daughter away from his ex-wife and the pediatrician, but he devoted an awful lot of time and attention to that kid. He'd come back from being with her and tell Dahlia all about the games they played and the things Lolly liked to do.

"She likes to pretend she's putting on a fashion show. She says, 'Daddy, you sit here,' and then she rushes into her mom's room and gets old scarves and earrings and her mother's shoes, and she comes out and spins around and shows me her dress-up outfits."

"Cute," Dahlia would say. Maybe she couldn't get too enthusiastic about Lolly because it was clear the kid didn't like her at all. She was only four, and she already had a determined stance and eyebrows that moved together and a forehead that furrowed when she looked at anyone who appeared suspicious to her. It was the expression she wore every time she was stuck with Dahlia during those outings when Seth tried to get them together.

"The kid hates me," Dahlia would say after they dropped Lolly off.

"She doesn't hate you. She has a negative feeling about you because you're a woman I care about who isn't her mother," Seth explained gently.

"Then why doesn't she hate Dr. Shapiro, the dashing pediatrician who stole her mother out of your arms?"

Seth had no reply.

Dahlia nibbled on a Carl's Junior fry and was sliding another one through the ketchup when she heard the screams. They were coming from the children's play area, and now she saw one of the young mothers pounding on the window of the restaurant and a man who must be her husband catching sight of her and leaving the line where he'd been waiting for food to rush out the door and help with some emergency. A few other parents were gathered around the play structure now, tugging their little ones out of the tunnels and lifting them down from the bars.

"Call the police!" a skinny, red-haired woman yelled into the restaurant.

"Oh, my God!" Seth said, his face flushing as he stood to get a better look at something that made his eyes open wide. Dahlia followed his gaze into the play structure, and she stood, too.

The parents were tearing the children away from the sight of Sunny, pushing them into the restaurant as Dahlia and Seth rushed out the door. Inside the structure Dahlia could see the completely naked Sunny bouncing around on the trampoline and shrieking happily, her breasts flying up, her eyes wild with glee.

"How did she get here?" Dahlia said as they hurried toward her, but then they passed the van and saw that the doors were flung open and Sunny's overalls and T-shirt were lying on top of their duffel bags. The laptop was open, with the solitaire game on the screen. By now all the children had been removed, and only a bouncing, laughing Sunny was left to play there.

"She fell in love with the solitaire game. I saw her watching me out the window when I put the computer back in the van. I forgot to lock the door, so she must have opened it and climbed in looking for it."

"But she didn't make a sound for hours."

"The van's so damn loud she could have been screaming her lungs out and we wouldn't have heard her."

Now they were at the play structure, and when Sunny saw them, she waved and laughed as if she'd been expecting them and was glad to see them. Seth took off his jacket and climbed onto the trampoline with her, causing him and Sunny to bounce together as he moved toward her and did what he could to cover her nakedness with the jacket. Then he crouched next to her and spoke gently.

"I'm Dahlia's friend," he said. "You have to come with us now and do it fast. I heard someone say they were calling the police, so they might be on their way."

Sunny's eyes darted rapidly back and forth between the two of them. "Are the police coming because of the little cards?" she asked, her face filled with fear. "I didn't steal them. I just wanted to play with the little cards and move them around." Her brow creased, and her voice was thick, as if she were about to cry.

"I know you didn't steal them," Seth said, slowly leading her forward.

"I'm cold," Sunny said. Dahlia could see that she was shivering.

It didn't look as if Sunny had a purse or a bag with her, which meant she didn't have her medication or a change of clothes. Somehow they had to get her back to San Diego now or in the morning. Tomorrow Dahlia had a busy workday, and she couldn't miss it.

"Let's go to the van," Dahlia said, and she and Seth helped Sunny rock forward so she could step out of the play structure. Dahlia took off her own jacket, and with Seth covering Sunny's front and Dahlia her back, they moved her toward the van. Dahlia hoped nobody in Carl's Junior was writing down her license number. Seth pulled out onto the street, and Sunny pulled her clothes on in the backseat as he moved the van toward the freeway.

"Should we go home or back to the Sea View?" Seth asked.

"We're almost home," Dahlia said. "We'd better go there and think this through."

Seth had just pulled the van onto the 405 when they heard the police sirens approaching Carl's Junior.

nine

"Indecent exposure." Those words flashed on and off in Dahlia's mind like a neon sign all the way home. Blessedly, when they reached the Laurel Canyon exit, the police were nowhere to be seen, and she took her first deep breath in an hour. Now she remembered, as Seth steered the van up the winding little street toward the house, that she'd forgotten to leave any lights on, and for a moment she was relieved, thinking that with no lights on, Sunny wouldn't see the chipped paint.

But when she glanced back at the bleary-eyed Sunny, she remembered this was not someone who was in a state of mind to notice paint, chipped or otherwise. All the way from Carl's Junior, Sunny hadn't said a word, just clicked away at the computer's mouse, still mesmerized by the solitaire game. She was breathing heavily and every now and then, emitting a little harumph, probably at the hand the computer had dealt her. It took both Dahlia and Seth to help her out of the van and onto the driveway by the carport.

"This is my house," Dahlia said. The stone path leading to the front porch was dark, and the two cousins moved ahead slowly, Dahlia guiding Sunny by the elbow. "When we get inside, I'll make you something to eat. Are you hungry?"

"I want the little cards," Sunny said.

"Seth's bringing the cards."

"I had a boyfriend once," Sunny said. "Norm."

"You had lots of boyfriends," Dahlia said.

"But Norm was the one who looked like someone famous. Did you know Norm?"

"I did," Dahlia said, fidgeting with the keys.

"Who did he look like?" Sunny asked.

"Arthur Miller," Dahlia said. She was pleased to hear that Louie had been wrong about Sunny. She actually did remember certain things. She remembered every note and word of "Stay by My Side," and Dahlia wasn't surprised that one of the things that remained in her mind was her romance with Norman. Norman had been the love of Sunny's life. It was good to know that certain people lived on in our hearts no matter what happened to our brains. Dahlia found the right key, inserted and turned it, and opened the door. Then, from the inside switch, she flipped on the porch light.

Sunny was dressed again, but she was disheveled and trembling. Maybe she never did take her medication that day, which could mean that she was dangerous. Dahlia moved through the small living room filled with the shabby furniture that had once been in her parents' house in the Valley. The couch that had sat for all those years in her parents' living room needed to be reupholstered. It was fraying at the arms, and on one of them the welting had come loose from the fabric and was showing through.

Of course, nobody who came by noticed the living room furniture anyway, because the piano took up most of the room. It was the Steinway baby grand that Aunt Ruthie had left to Dahlia when she died, which was the same one Dahlia and Sunny had played as kids. A piano that would have gone to Sunny, if things had been otherwise. But Sunny's future had looked so hopeless at the time Aunt Ruthie died that she never imagined her poor daughter would ever be well enough to play it again. And sentimental Aunt Ruthie, who wanted to keep the beautiful old instrument in the family, knew that Louie would sell it before her body was cold, so even though Louie was not happy about it, the piano went to Dahlia. Now she wondered if Sunny would recognize it.

In the dark she felt around for the switch and turned on the light in the little office that had been used as a second bedroom for the people who lived in the house before her. The office had a bathroom with an old Jacuzzi tub with jets that were so loud that, on those rare occasions when Dahlia used it, it sounded as if the whole house were an airplane about to take off. Dahlia remembered how she'd been so sure when she moved in that she'd be able to fix the place up and "make it her own," an expression the pushy real estate lady used repeatedly during the sales pitch. But here she was, still living with all of the same falling-apart furniture she had when she moved in.

"Gotta pee, fast," Sunny said. Dahlia walked her to the bathroom, wondering if it was okay to leave her alone in there, but too tired to care. She was about to show her where the light switch was when Sunny closed the door in her face, and a quick glance at the space under the door told Dahlia that Sunny hadn't even turned on the light to use the bathroom.

Seth was on the phone in the living room. "The Sea View," she heard him say. "It's a halfway house on Cormorant Drive."

"What are you doing?" Dahlia asked.

"Trying to get the number and call that place. Maybe somebody from down there will come up and get her." But then he frowned and shook his head. "They're not listed," he said, hanging up the phone. "Looks like we have a houseguest for tonight."

Dahlia was exhausted to the bone, aching and wanting to get to sleep. Not wanting to do what she knew she'd have to do next, which was to go into the kitchen and make a meal for Sunny and then cancel all her clients for the next day so that first thing in the morning she could climb back into the van from hell and drive back to San Diego.

"Maybe if you're nice to Sunny tonight, when Melman sends over another contract tomorrow, you can get her to sign it," Seth said. He was trying to be cute, but Dahlia wasn't in the mood.

"Not funny," she said, going into the kitchen to make scrambled eggs. When Sunny emerged from the bathroom, they put her in front of the TV and turned it on. *Third Rock from the Sun* was on. It was a sitcom about aliens, all of whom looked more human than Sunny did with her blindingly bright orange hair sticking up wildly.

"I have three meetings in a row tomorrow that I can't miss," Seth said after sliding some bread into the toaster. "So you're going to have to take her back alone. You better get on the phone to your clients and tell them you have to cancel."

From the kitchen phone, Dahlia left a message for Marty Melman and another one for Helene Shephard saying she had to cancel their appointments so she could take care of a relative in need. Then she called Leroy Berk's house and left the same message for him. Seth sliced tomatoes and buttered some toast, but as they walked into the living room to bring Sunny the food on a tray, they stopped. She was sound asleep on the sofa, snoring loudly as the sitcom laughter rose from the television.

Dahlia studied her slack-jawed, worn-out face and soft, chunky body for a moment, remembering the days when the two of them shared the big bed in Aunt Ruthie's house and she would lie awake at night studying Sunny's radiant beauty. Now she felt as if she must be having a nightmare. How could this possibly be that same person?

"Leave it there, and let's go to sleep," she said. Seth set the tray carefully on the coffee table in front of Sunny, and Dahlia covered her gently with the afghan she always kept over the arm of the sofa, then looked at her again and sighed.

"My lousy luck," she said. "She had to decide to find her way into my van, and now it's cost me a whole day's pay."

Seth was looking at Sunny, too. "Dahl," he said, "when you see that poor woman lying there and think about where she's been and what she has to look forward to, isn't it hard for you to start a sentence with the words 'my lousy luck'?"

"You know what I mean," she said, huffing into the bedroom, half wishing he would get his holier-than-thou self out of there, but afraid to be alone with Sunny who might do God only knew what in the middle of the night. In the tiny bathroom, Dahlia took off her clothes and turned on the shower, wondering if Seth would follow her and join her, the way he sometimes did.

She was soapy, and her hair was full of lathery shampoo, and her eyes were closed when the bathroom door opened and she felt the breeze as Seth pulled the shower curtain back. "I hope it's you and not Norman Bates's mother," she said, feeling him step in behind her.

"Not unless the old broad likes to do this," he said, sliding his hands onto her breasts and rubbing the creamy white soap all over her body. Okay, so this was one of the reasons she didn't let their fights go too far. He was sweet to her even when she was cranky, logical even when she flared irrationally. And then there were all those times he was sexy and hot, and when he turned her to him and kissed her, his kiss tasted like chocolate-chip cookies no matter what time of day or night.

"You ever gonna make my daughter a flower girl and become Mrs. Seth Meyers?" he asked, using the hand shower to rinse Dahlia's hair.

"When I can afford you," she joked, knowing this was alligator country for her, far too dangerous a discussion for her to get into now. Marriage, in her mind, was going to be elegant and filled with travel, living in a real house with lots of help and having one room with just a piano in it, maybe overlooking the ocean. Not continuing to live in this shabby little place that was all the two of them combined could afford.

In bed she curled up close to him as he fell asleep, wishing she could love him more than she did. Wishing that she were capable of fawning and fussing over him the way a good man like him deserved to be loved and adored, revered for all of the qualities he did have and not resented for the ones he didn't. Through the open bedroom door, she could hear Sunny's snores filling the night, and she worried that she'd never fall asleep, but soon she did. And in her dream she was at a black-tie party with Marvin Hamlisch and Itzhak Perlman and Kermit the Frog. All of them were at conductors' podiums, conducting her as she sat at the piano playing the song that she and Sunny wrote, "Stay by My Side."

Her playing in the dream got louder and louder, and the conducting became more frantic, until she stirred and realized she wasn't playing at all and that the music she heard was wafting in from the living room. She grabbed her robe from the bottom of the bed and walked to the door of the bedroom to see Sunny, sitting at the piano she had played throughout her childhood, the piano that would have been left to her if things were otherwise. She was naked with the moon lighting her white back as she played the last bars of "Stay by My Side."

Dahlia stood quietly as Sunny segued into a beautiful, lilting ballad, sexy and romantic, and she didn't move as Sunny played another one that Dahlia had never heard before. These had to be the songs Santa Claus at the Sea View had described to Dahlia. Better than the Beatles, he'd said. He called Sunny the Goddess of Music. Dahlia slid quietly to the floor, where she sat for a long time, listening to the nocturnal concert without making her presence known.

Tune after tune came out of Sunny's fingers, and all of them were fresh and lyrical, each one filled with emotion, whimsy, style, balance, and originality. They were Sunny's own melodies, songs from her poor abused brain, and probably over all these years nobody had heard them except a bunch of mental patients who were watching *All My Children* at the same time.

Now Sunny was humming softly. When she got to the musical hook of the song, she sang it out: "What's happened to me?" The song was so well composed and put together that it made tears come to Dahlia's eyes. They were tears of admiration, along with an incalculable sorrow too overwhelming to name. A sorrow about all the years that had gone by between those long-ago days when she sat admiring Sunny as a child and now. Sunny had been playing for quite a while when the beeping of Seth's alarm clock startled her. When she turned toward the sound, she spotted a wet-eyed Dahlia sitting there.

"Good songs?" Sunny asked, deadpan.

"Great songs," Dahlia said, hearing Seth shut off the alarm and make his way to the bathroom. "Will you show me the changes on that one where you sang 'What's happened to me?' What were the chords you played just before the bridge?" Sunny turned back to the keyboard as Dahlia sat down next to her, ignoring Sunny's nakedness, watching her play those chords and learning how to play the marvelous songs herself.

God, it was just as good as Dahlia remembered it. Maybe better.

"Do you have lyrics for it?"

"Just the title," Sunny said. " 'What's Happened to Me?' "

"It's so good," Dahlia said. A breeze swept in through the open living room window, and Sunny shivered, and Dahlia walked back to the sofa and got the afghan to wrap around her cousin's shoulders. "I especially loved hearing you sing the one we wrote together. 'Stay by My Side.' Wouldn't you like to let them use that in a movie? Do you ever go to the movies? You probably rent movies all the time at the Sea View. Wouldn't it be fun to see one of them that had your song in it?" Sunny's mouth screwed up, and she sighed and walked over to the sofa to gather up the pile of clothes she had strewn across it.

"It's time for me to go back," she said, completely ignoring Dahlia's question. "I'll get dressed."

She may be crazy but she's not stupid, Dahlia

thought as she watched Sunny go into the second bedroom and close the door. Seth hurried through and
gave her a peck on the cheek.

"You gonna take her back this morning?" he asked.

"Yep."

"At least she didn't kill us in our sleep. Tell her I
said good-bye," he said, and he was out the door just
as the phone rang. Dahlia grabbed it.

"Ms. Gordon?"

"Yes."

"I have Marty Melman." There was a silence and
then a click.

"You canceled me for today?" she heard Marty say.

"I have a family emergency, Marty."

"Well, shit, I got a fucking emergency, too. My
fucking back is killing me. Tell your family to go fuck
itself."

"By the way, Marty," she said, embarrassed to have
to say it, "I'm glad you called, because somehow I
must have misplaced the contract you sent me for the
song, and I need another copy." She wasn't going to
give this up. Somehow she'd find a way around
Sunny's reluctance. "Maybe you could send another
one over. I'm real sorry."

There was a beat of silence. "Uh . . . whoa! Didn't
Pepper call you?"

"What do you mean?" Dahlia asked. Something
was wrong. She could tell by the sound of his voice.

"About your song? What was the name of it again?"
Marty asked.

" 'Stay by My Side,' same as the title of your movie.
Remember? Why?"

"Ahhh, jeez. I told Pepper to call you yesterday to
tell you. We had a meeting with the studio suits yesterday, and we decided to change the title of the
movie, so we don't need that song anymore. Now it's
called *Hurry, Tomorrow*, and we've got Bob Dylan
recording on Friday."

No! Goddamn this business. How could this happen? Marty said he loved her song. Twenty-four
hours ago it was perfect. Now even Louie couldn't
make this deal work for her. And she would be back
to massaging obnoxious men like Marty, probably
forever. Not to mention the fact that it was because of
the damned song that she'd gone through this nightmare with Sunny, who was already dressed and had
gone into the kitchen, where she was taking everything out of the pantry and making random piles of
groceries on the kitchen floor for some inexplicable
reason.

"So, kiddo, now that you're out of the music business,
am I gonna see you tonight or not?" Marty whined. "I
can't handle working with people who cancel."

"This is the first time I've canceled in three years."

"Yeah, but still . . ."

"Look, Marty, I have to take my sick cousin down to
San Diego," she said, realizing the absurdity of looking
for sympathy from the devil himself. Now Sunny was
pulling paper bags out of the recycling bin and putting
the cans she'd pulled out of the pantry into them,
singing "Stay by My Side" at the top of her voice.

"Yeah, well, you'd better drive back by eight tonight, or I'm finding a new masseuse," Marty said,
slamming down the phone.

Getting back by eight meant she'd have to leave right away, and she wasn't even dressed. "Sunny, step on it, and I'll take you out for breakfast."

"I want to take a shower," Sunny said out of nowhere.

"No time. Besides, you're already dressed."

"I need a shower."

Dahlia looked at Sunny standing there in front of what were now three bags of groceries, wearing the same clothes from yesterday, hair flying, and she wanted to cry.

"What are you doing with the groceries, Sun?"

"Giving them to poor people," Sunny said. "But first I have to take a shower. I take one every morning. Sometimes I take one with Mr. Belzer."

More than I wanted to know, Dahlia thought.

"He lives at the Sea View, too. And we agree it's important to be clean." This was it. No reason to keep Sunny here. The song they'd written together could go back into a drawer somewhere now that Marty Melman didn't need it anymore, and Dahlia would take Sunny back to that dive in San Diego, where she'd continue to create brilliant songs that nobody would ever hear.

At least, Dahlia thought, I should give the poor woman a nice send-off. If Sunny wanted a shower, Dahlia should bring her a fresh, clean towel and some shower gel and let her luxuriate till Dahlia was ready to leave. She remembered the long baths and showers Sunny had always loved as a girl, in the high-ceilinged bathroom where little Dahlia sat on the lid of the toilet to keep her company, while Sunny, taking advantage of the acoustics of the echoey old room would sing Leiber and Stoller songs and songs by Dahlia and Sunny in her big-belt voice until there was no hot water left.

"Want a Jacuzzi?" Dahlia asked her now, not even sure if the old plumbing in the big tub still worked.

"What do they taste like?" Sunny asked, looking at her seriously.

"It's not food. It's a kind of bathtub. You sit in water and it bubbles. I have a real old one that the people who lived here before put into the other bathroom, and it sounds like we're grinding wheat when you turn it on."

Sunny's eyes filled with light, and she let out a chuckle. It was the first time Dahlia had heard her laugh since they were kids. It wasn't nearly that big belly laugh she used to have, but there was something about the sound of it now, coming out of this version of Sunny, that sent a rush of feeling through Dahlia. Screw Marty Melman. I don't know if I'll ever see this woman again, but she is my flesh and blood. She has suffered so much in her life, and I have this brief window of time where I can introduce her to something she'll love, so what the hell.

"I'll run the tub," Dahlia said.

In the bathroom she spilled a little bath gel into the water, checked the temperature, and turned to find a naked Sunny grinning behind her. "Here you go," Dahlia said, and she held Sunny's arm to help her in. "Now I'm going to switch on the jets. Ready?" Dahlia asked.

"Ready."

Sunny shrieked happily as the unearthly racket of the Jacuzzi kicked in. And Dahlia went and took the clothes from the top of the hamper where Sunny had dropped them. Underwear, overalls, a T-shirt—she put them into the washing machine and turned it on. She had left the bathroom door open, and now she walked past to see the bubbles rising all around a happy Sunny, who was singing "la, la, la," to the tune of that great song "What's Happened to Me?" But not just singing it. Wailing it in an eat-your-heart-out belting voice.

While Dahlia waited, surrounded by the clatter of the washing machine in one room and the roar of the Jacuzzi in another, she sat at the piano, playing the song the way she saw Sunny play it. Then, picking up her pen, she jotted down some lyrics, and after a few minutes, she felt a sensation come over her that she hadn't had in far too long, the feeling that she was taking dictation and some greater force was guiding her hand as she wrote lyrics to Sunny's tune. The lyrics were about losing control and falling apart, a kind of inner monologue she imagined Sunny must have had with herself at some point.

Dahlia was sure as she wrote them down hastily that the words were poignant and emotional and could have been mistaken for a love song about the way love can drive you mad. She was glad the sound of the Jacuzzi was so loud, because after she finished her first pass at the lyric, she played Sunny's tune softly, singing her lyrics along with it. And she already knew, as she heard herself sing it through for the first time, that it was good and smart and strong.

Of course, unless something changed drastically to get Sunny to change her mind, it was another song she'd never be able to sell.

Denny's on Ventura Boulevard looked the same as it did in the days when Dahlia had gone there with her parents as a little girl. If she was going to stop somewhere for breakfast, looking as wiped out as she did, it was the perfect place, since there was no chance she'd bump into anyone she knew. Yes, she thought, sliding into one side of a booth and watching Sunny slide into the other, it was the same old funky Denny's, and nobody looked twice at Sunny, because at least half the people in there looked as scorched as she did. Sunny was starting to get a little wild-eyed and couldn't seem to focus on the menu. Her jaw was moving back and forth, and every now and then, she would turn her neck in a funny way so Dahlia could hear it crack.

"You need your meds, don't you?" Dahlia asked her.

"Hate my meds," she said, picking up a salt shaker, pouring salt in her hand, and then licking it up.

"You hungry?"

"Need cigarettes. Need a smoke so bad."

"Have to smoke outside," a waitress with baggy eyes and yellow hair said as she stopped to put a glass of water at each of their places.

"Don't have any cigarettes," Sunny said nervously.

The waitress produced a pack from under her apron and held it out to her. Sunny pulled out three cigarettes, and for a second Dahlia worried that she was going to put all three in her mouth, but she slid two into the front pocket of her overalls and jabbed the third one into her mouth. Then the waitress gave her a book of matches.

"You can keep 'em," she said.

"Okay if we order before you go outside?" Dahlia asked as Sunny stood.

But Sunny didn't answer, just moved toward the outside door, so Dahlia asked the waitress to bring two orders of scrambled eggs with hash browns.

Nightmare, nightmare, nightmare, Dahlia thought watching Sunny through the window, afraid she could pull another stunt like yesterday's episode in the jungle gym. But so far she seemed okay out there puffing away, watching the traffic go by.

"Is that Dahlia Gordon, the foxy babe of my dreams?" she heard someone say, and she turned quickly, wondering who in the hell she knew who could possibly be in Denny's in the middle of the morning. No! she thought when she saw who it was, and she made a quick move with her hand to straighten her hair. Grinning down at her was Harry Brenner, the arranger who had worked on her song for Naomi Judd. Dahlia stood to get a big, warm hug from long, lean Harry, whose bright blue eyes gleamed at her from a tired face. "Where you been, good-lookin'?" he asked.

"Oh, I'm around," she said, praying Sunny would stay outside sucking on that cigarette for a long time, maybe even move on to the other two cigarettes so she wouldn't walk in here and embarrass Dahlia in the middle of this moment with Harry. Dahlia could never tell Harry what she was doing now. He was still working all the time, on big stuff. She saw his name on lots of CDs by major performers.

"Got any more songs as good as the one I worked on with you?"

"Oh, probably. I mean, I've got a few new ones I'm working on."

"So send 'em to me, gorgeous! I'm out there every day conducting and arranging," he said. "I know Faith Hill is cutting a new CD. Needs a big, soaring song. Bring me something, babe. Here's my number," he said, extracting a card from his wallet and handing it to her. Then he hugged her again, and when he walked away, she was still engulfed with the scent of his cologne, one of those long-ago scents her dad used to wear. Maybe it was Aqua Velva.

As Harry reached the door, she watched him hold it open for the person who was entering, and it was Sunny. Harry didn't even blink at the sight of the way her Day-Glo hair stuck up all over her head. Why would he? He was in the music business, he'd seen it all, Dahlia thought, chuckling to herself. Faith Hill, she thought. What song did she have for Faith Hill?

The smell of cigarettes wafted from Sunny's clothes and hair as she sat back down in the booth. "Hungry," she said as she opened a sugar packet and poured a little pile of sugar onto the table, then opened another and poured that out, and then another, creating a small white mountain range across the table, until their eggs arrived. By the time Dahlia had poured a puddle of ketchup on to her own plate, Sunny's plate was practically empty.

"Need another smoke," she said, standing and hurrying back outside. Dahlia was glad to have a minute alone to go off on her fantasy of what it would be like to bring Harry Brenner some of her songs. She remembered the recording studio Brenner owned out in Van Nuys and the other one that he'd built right at his own house. Maybe that's where they would meet when she brought him her songs. She'd sit down at the piano and play him some of her new stuff. "Don't Make Me Laugh"—of course, she had to finish that— and maybe . . . what else? She'd spend tomorrow at the piano, and by the end of the day she'd call him, just be kind of casual and offhanded, and say, "Hey, maybe I'll pop by."

The waitress was standing over her with the check.

"That woman your sister?" she asked Dahlia, gesturing with a nod in the direction of Sunny, who was still outside the window puffing away.

"Cousin," Dahlia said.

The waitress shook her head and grimaced. "I have a sister like her," she said. "Not that it's for me to judge—only God can do that—but sometimes I think gals like them would be better off dead. No point to their lives. She's got as much going for her as those potatoes you just ate. Only at least somebody enjoyed the potatoes."

Sunny, with a last puff of smoke still coming out of her mouth, pushed open the door to the restaurant and entered as the waitress walked away with a sigh. Dahlia left enough cash on the table to cover the check and the tip. Then she headed toward Sunny, and together they exited, walking in the hot morning sun toward the van. Dahlia opened the passenger door for Sunny and boosted her into the seat, feeling a wave of relief that this was about to be the end of this dumb situation she'd created for herself. She'd return Sunny to the Sea View, hurry back to massage the obnoxious Marty, and starting tomorrow she'd concentrate on her songs.

Parked next to her van was a shiny black Lincoln Town Car with black windows. As she opened the door on the driver's side of the van to get in, she heard the hiss of the window rolling down on the Lincoln. It was Harry Brenner. He was sitting in the back of the big shiny car, obviously having been driven by a chauffeur to Denny's. He was holding a cell phone to his ear, into which Dahlia heard him say, "Hang a sec, will ya?" Then he leaned out the window and smiled at Dahlia, who tried frantically to think of an excuse to give him about why she was driving this embarrassing old junker.

"Dahlia, sweetie," he said, smiling a big smile that showed off a row of newly porcelain-veneered teeth. "Don't forget to call me."

Forget to call him? What a joke. How could she even face him after he saw her looking so badly, then climbing into this crummy vehicle. In Hollywood the car you drove told people everything they needed to know about your life. It was way more important than clothes. If you walked around in jeans and a T-shirt, it might be because that was your fashion statement, meaning you were too cool to think about clothes. But a bad car was a dead giveaway about who you were in the business, and this trash-can-on-wheels had just given *her* away. Now Harry would know she was desperate and feel sorry for her. That gave her even more reason to have to dazzle him with her songs.

ten

$\mathcal{D}$ ahlia liked to drive with the radio on a jazz station, and today Sunny hummed along with the
songs. "Love jazz," she muttered every now and then.
"Need Marlboros," she said loudly when Dahlia
stopped for gas. After Dahlia put the gasoline hose in
the tank of the van, she ran into the convenience store
and bought a few packs of Marlboros and a throwaway lighter and eyed the Hershey's Kisses. Aunt
Ruthie always had a bowl of Hershey's Kisses on the
piano in her house. Sunny used to say, "Have some
Kisses," and then pelt Dahlia with them.

"Better than those wet ones you give all the guys,"
Dahlia would say, devouring the little pointed candies.

"Got you these," Dahlia said, handing Sunny a bag
of the Kisses and the cigarettes, hoping to see a flicker
of remembrance on Sunny's face about their old joke,
but there wasn't one. Dahlia couldn't stand the smell

of cigarette smoke and the way it tainted the air in the van, but she had to do anything she could to keep Sunny calm. The poor woman had been without her medication for a whole day, and maybe more if she'd pocketed that dose Grover was dispensing yesterday. Okay, Dahlia thought, I'll keep my mouth shut about the cigarettes.

Leaving the windows open in the van was the only way she could handle the smoke, but when she drove on the freeway, the hot ashes flew off the cigarettes and all around their faces as Sunny puffed. After a while Dahlia gave up and closed the windows and pushed a button on the dashboard, which was supposed to pull in fresh air, but it wasn't working properly, and within seconds she was overwhelmed by the smoke.

By the time they arrived at the Sea View, she was nauseous and depressed. She wanted to lean against the steering wheel and sob. It had all gone so horribly. She should have listened to that little creep Louie. Now she looked over at Sunny, who toyed with the cigarette box that was already nearly empty.

"I'll walk you up," Dahlia said as she slid out the door of the van and hurried around to help Sunny down from the passenger seat. Sunny moved quickly up the steps of the Sea View, and Dahlia followed. In the living room, some of the residents sat in front of the TV watching what looked like an A&E biography of Princess Diana. None of them even glanced over at Sunny or Dahlia when they came in. Zombie time, Dahlia thought. Grover the zombie maker must have just left. In her head she had rehearsed what she was going to say to Sunny when they parted, and she hurried to the stairs, where Sunny, not interested in formalities, already had her foot on the bottom step when Dahlia stopped her.

"Sunny," she said, and Sunny turned. "I'm glad I finally had a chance to see you again. I hope you'll take good care of yourself. I'll go by the hardware store and see Louie and tell him how well you seem to be doing, and if you'd like me to, I'll come back and see you again soon." That made her feel better about just dumping Sunny back here. They'd both had a nice, albeit brief, reunion. No harm, no foul is what Seth would say here. And maybe Dahlia actually would find herself in San Diego some time in the future and pop in to see Sunny. Sunny showed no emotion, just turned and walked up the steps.

Dahlia sighed a sigh of finality and turned to go, wondering why, after making that very thoughtful speech, she had that odd feeling of tightness in her throat. Maybe it was because while she was standing there making the speech, all of those times she and Sunny had been forced to say good-bye to one another as kids flashed through her mind, and she remembered how she always used to feel so helpless when the adults tore Sunny away to put her in one mental hospital or another. No, not now, she thought, knowing she couldn't let herself go all sappy and fall apart. She needed to get out of there as fast as she could. She turned toward the door and nearly collided with Santa Claus. He smiled a friendly smile, then clucked his tongue.

"You know you shouldn't say things like that to

her," he said. No, she couldn't handle this. Who in the hell was this guy to tell her what to do, with that all-knowing look on his face?

"Like what?" Dahlia asked, annoyed that he was making any of this his business.

"That you'll come back soon."

Dahlia forced a tight smile and walked past him, but he followed her to the door. "I mean, the reality is that more than likely you're not going to come back, and certainly not soon. But once you tell someone like her that kind of thing, she'll live on it. She'll spend the next year chewing our ears off about what she's gonna wear the day you come and where you're gonna take her that day and how close you are to her and how she's holding on to the hope that maybe you'll take her out of here forever. And then none of us will get any rest, because it's all she'll talk about. I know because that's what happened when her brother came—what was it? Four years ago? Maybe just three. Brought his kids and everything. Left here telling her that once a month they were coming back. But they never did. Not even once. She remembers, though, and she's still waiting. I think she marks the days off on her calendar."

"I'm not like her brother," Dahlia said. "I'll be back."

Santa Claus smiled patronizingly. "I've been through it with my own family," he said, "and I know how it works."

She was relieved at the sound of the ringing door-bell and the sight of the UPS man in the doorway holding a package.

"Need a signature for this," he said to Santa Claus, who signed his name to a form on a clipboard as Dahlia hurried out the door and down the steps to her van.

Driving back to L.A., she couldn't stop thinking about Sunny sitting at the piano that morning. All the tunes were great, but the one she called "What's Happened to Me?" was a drop-dead hit if Dahlia had ever heard one. Now Dahlia sang the lyrics that she wrote while Sunny was in the Jacuzzi, using Sunny's hook that was so perfectly right for the tune.

Outside Marty Melman's house, she took a deep breath. What she wanted to do was run in and scream at Victor the houseman to tell Mr. Melman to go to hell and then to jump back into the van and floor it out of there. But she was desperate for the check. The hundred bucks meant too much to her meager budget, so she'd have to put on her I'm-just-here-to-serve face and get it over with.

As she hurried through the kitchen past the usual starlet apprentices who were chopping red and green peppers in Marty's kitchen, she could smell onions sautéing. Upstairs she opened the bedroom door and headed straight for the closet to take out the massage table so she could get this over with. Somehow tonight the table seemed heavier than ever. After she tugged it, pulled it into the room, and set it up, spreading out the Porthault sheets that Marty's maid always left for her to use under and over Marty, she walked into his bathroom to wash her hands.

My God, I need to get myself together, she thought, stopping to peer at her face. It looked unusually puffy in the mirror, suddenly making the family resemblance to Sunny very apparent. What's happened to me? The lyric danced through her mind again as she heard a closet door open and close, and after a minute she heard Marty padding toward the bathroom.

"Hey," he said, as he walked in naked, getting a devilish little grin on his big fat face. Then he sashayed over to where Dahlia was standing at the sink and stood very close behind her, rubbing his naked front against her back.

"Marty . . ." she said, starting to protest, when he screwed up his face.

"Ugh. You stink of cigarettes," he said. "When'd you start smoking?"

"I didn't. My cousin was in my car for two and a half hours, and she was smoking."

"You're not touchin' *me* smelling like that. Either strip down and take a shower or go home."

Good-bye, hundred bucks. There was no chance she was getting into his shower, and even if she did, her clothes still reeked of cigarettes. He was the one who'd insisted she rush right over to massage him after San Diego. Of course, reminding him of that wasn't going to make him give her the hundred dollars she needed so badly. He'd send her away without paying her and not think twice about it.

"Hey, I got an idea," Marty said, leering. "Why don't you take a nice hot shower, then massage me naked?" Dahlia walked out of the bathroom, down the hall, and through the kitchen to where Victor was chatting and laughing with two pretty young girls.

"That was fast," Victor said as Dahlia walked out

the door to the van. When she opened it, the thick smell of stale cigarettes still hung inside.

In the van she finally allowed the tears of frustration to roll down her face. What in the hell was she going to do for money? She couldn't even count on Seth for anything extra. By the time he made his hefty child-support payments, he was in the same sinking boat. She wiped her eyes and blew her nose and drove out of Marty's driveway and down to Sunset, where she stopped for the red light at Hilgard, trying not to scream. Finally she promised herself out loud, "I will sell my songs this month. I will call Harry Brenner in the morning, and I will make an appointment, and I will stay up all night tonight and every night pushing ahead on my songs until I get them to work, and I will sell those fucking songs." Then she realized she had left the windows open in order to air the car out, and a bald man in a BMW convertible with the top down was looking up at her and smiling.

"Good luck," he said, just before the light changed and he drove away.

When she pulled into the carport and didn't see Seth's car, she remembered he was working late, and she was relieved. It would be a nice, quiet time for her to get some work done. No conversations. No television, no interruptions, no editorial comments like the ones he sometimes made. Remarks like, "That tune sounds like a steal from Barry Manilow" or "I don't get where the melody is in that one." After she'd been working on some tune all day, she didn't need him or anyone making judgments on her work.

She wasn't hungry, but knew she should eat something, so she went to the freezer and pulled out a tropical-flavor Popsicle, strawberry-banana, took a few bites while she sat on the piano bench, and looked over the music she'd written out. Finally she set the unfinished Popsicle on a coaster and played her song "Don't Make Me Laugh." Not bad, she thought after she breezed through it. The bridge was a little clunky, but she could smooth it out. Maybe. It was a love song about the way she always fell for men who were funny and how a man should be aware that he risked having her fall for him if he made her laugh.

Okay, so it was a little more of a cabaret song than a pop song. Somebody like Billy Joel could get away with it, not an unknown like her. But maybe Harry Brenner could think of a singer who would record it. It had an offbeat melody she liked a lot. It was definitely one of the songs she would play for Harry, and he would know exactly the right singer for it. What other songs of hers would he like?

"What's Happened to Me?" Her inner DJ was playing Sunny's melody along with Dahlia's lyric in her brain. "No," she said out loud. Too bad that's Sunny's tune, she thought, shuffling through her own unfinished songs and scrawling changes on them, trying and retrying the melodies, reworking lines of lyrics that hadn't worked for her earlier.

"What's Happened to Me?" That soaring bridge. That wailing tune. She wished it would stop haunting her. After a while she pulled out the rhyming dictionary and worked on "Don't Make Me Laugh," changing some of the rhymes that felt stilted. It was work she should have done a long time ago but never could get into. Now her own songs were finally starting to come together. Now they really worked.

The jangling of the phone made her look up for the first time and realize that it was dark outside, and for an instant she was startled. Then she smiled. These songs she'd written were going to put her back into the business. When she heard Seth's voice on the phone, she babbled at him excitedly.

"I did it. I sat here for hours, and I finished. I actually finished, and the songs are really good."

"Great, honey," he said. Then, after a short beat, he asked, "Any messages for me?" There was no excitement in his voice, just his usual, even, everyday tone. Completely lacking the giddiness she hoped he'd share. She had imagined he'd give her the big reaction she wanted, full of the possibility that maybe this meeting where she'd bring these songs to Harry Brenner would be the one that would change her life.

She knew that Seth's even tone meant he wanted her to understand that he was going to stay grounded and not get caught up in one of her foolish dreams of glory again. That he was the same if she had a hit song and became some big-deal songwriter or stayed a masseuse eternally. Screw him. She'd call Harry Brenner first thing in the morning.

"No messages," she told him.

"I'll be home late," he said.

"Don't wake me," she said, and placed the phone in the cradle.

eleven

"So what's shakin', good-lookin'?" Harry Brenner asked, showing her in, and right away she felt that soaring sense of being surrounded by luxury in Harry's high-ceilinged Mediterranean-style house. Harry's two golden retrievers sniffed her until he said, "Boys!" And then they moved away through an open glass door, toward the pool.

Harry had to be past sixty by now, but Dahlia saw him checking out her body with a leer. A housekeeper appeared and asked if she wanted something to drink, but she was afraid she was too nervous to hold a glass, so she refused. Having Harry Brenner falling for one of her songs could be a life changer. Last night she'd made a list of all of the things she could do with the money, and the first one was to fix up her house.

Now she was chattering away, trying to make small talk with Harry as they walked across the tile floor toward the glass doors, then outside past the pool area, but it wasn't coming easily. It was one thing to chitchat with some half-asleep, naked client under a sheet who was paying her for a massage. But this was a music-business hotshot who could decide to push a little business her way that could make or break her career.

"You ever get married all these years?" Harry asked her.

"Not yet," Dahlia answered. Her stomach hurt. Just one hour, she told herself. For one hour you have to give this everything.

"Me neither," Harry said

A couple of months earlier, Seth had bought her a book on creativity, and even though she was sure it was worthless, she read it one night when she couldn't fall asleep just because it was the one that was sitting on her night table. The author said it was a good thing to repeat the words "Turn on the power" to yourself before you started to work or before you were about to go into an important meeting. The book said that we all walk around every day on low voltage, but saying "Turn on the power" to ourselves would remind us to turn it up and get the dynamic forces to kick in.

Dahlia had said those words today, screamed them all the way over to Harry's house as the van careened around the bends on Mulholland Drive, but she was still a basket case. Especially when she followed Harry across the pool area into the building he had converted from a guesthouse into a studio, and she saw what she now remembered had been so intimidating the last time. It was that wall of gold records and the dozens of photos everywhere of Harry standing with his arm around every star in the music business.

"Well, I hope you have something as good as that one we worked on together. What was the title? Something about kids?"

" 'My Kids Are My Life,' " Dahlia said.

"Great little song. Long time ago, though. When was it?"

"Eight years," she said, avoiding his eyes, because she was afraid hers would show that for the last eight years she'd been out of the business and miserable.

"Let's cut to the chase," Harry said. "Whaddya got?"

She was at the piano now, trying to get comfortable with its touch, with the play of the keys, but her hands felt cold and a little stiff. She pulled out a lead sheet and took a deep breath. "This first one is called, 'Don't Make Me Laugh.' It's kind of a mellow, bittersweet—"

"Pass," she thought she heard Harry say. But he couldn't have said that already, without even hearing it. Or could he? She felt an aching in her chest, and she was afraid to look at him, but she made herself turn, and when she did, she saw that his mouth was set in a deep frown.

"No one gives a shit about mellow and bittersweet these days. What else?"

"But it's so—"

"What else?" he asked, and the harassed expression on his face made her sure that what she'd suspected when she called him yesterday was true. That when she bumped into him at Denny's and he urged her to call him and bring him songs, it was nothing more than a Hollywood invitation. Meaningless, not intended to be taken seriously. He never imagined she would take him up on it, and that was why, when she'd called, he'd sounded stuck, trapped, foiled by his own phoniness. And that was how he looked now. Trapped and wanting the meeting to be over.

She tried out a little jazzy tune on him called "Dude." It was an update of a song she'd written about Seth when they'd first started dating. Harry sighed, said "Fun," when she sang it, but leaned on the piano and yawned a huge yawn right at her. She tried a rock tune she loved, one she'd written within the last year called "You Get Me," but Harry was expressionless when she finished, and she could feel heartburn creeping into her esophagus. She only had two songs left now: "Images" and "Hang In." Halfway through "Images," the studio phone rang, and while she was singing the bridge, Harry answered it and talked animatedly to somebody on the other end with his back to her.

All that was left for her now was to figure out how she was going to keep from falling apart in front of him. To find a way she could stop herself from sobbing right here at the way this had gone. After all the investment she had in its going well, how could this happen? After she'd finally managed to get a shred of confidence back in her work. Look at me sitting here, she thought. Doomed to be a masseuse until my hands break off because I can't sell another song.

She thought of Sunny's song and the lyrics she'd written for it. "What's Happened to Me?" What *has* happened to me? she wondered. Why am I falling apart like this? Now Sunny's tune and her own lyrics repeated again in her head, and she started to play it softly just to avoid standing up and walking toward the door, because she knew if she did, she would cry in front of Harry. So instead she sang softly. "I keep getting in my own way, unable to change. Everybody sees it, and they say I'm acting strange."

The tune was coming out of her hands just the way Sunny played it and the way Dahlia had learned it by watching her play it, and she was singing it through quietly. Then, without looking at him, she felt Harry Brenner shift his weight and turn to face her, and she could tell he was leaning in to listen, and she sang it out, louder, going with it, getting bigger, and then wailing it. Copying Sunny's biggest voice, and she sounded pretty damn good for someone who hadn't sung in front of anyone but her boyfriend in a long, long time.

She didn't have to see Harry Brenner's face to be able to tell that he loved the song. She could hear it in his breathing, tell by the way he kept moving closer to the piano. And after she belted out the final plaintive line—"What's happened to me?"—she hesitated for a minute before she looked at him, just to postpone the moment that she already knew was inevitable.

"Now, *that* is a great fucking song! You wrote that? That's got to be your best tune. That'll be the next Faith Hill hit. I have got to get it to her, because she will slay them with that song. And you were saving it for *last*? Sweetheart, you ought to open with that one. As I'm standing here, I swear to you, this is going right to number one." He was spinning out, already humming Sunny's marvelous tune. "The day I saw you in Denny's was the luckiest day of both of our lives. Ay, ay, ay. Let me take you to lunch, let me take you wherever you want to go. I'm telling you, cuteface, that is some drop-dead song. And believe me, I don't have to say this. I could say, 'Let's get it out there, let's see what people say, let's take a shot with it,' but I am swearing to you like I know my name—this is a hit. Where's the lead sheet? You got lead sheets?"

"No lead sheets," she said numbly. Now she had to tell him.

"You got this on a CD?"

"Uh . . . no. I don't have it on CD." And I didn't write the music, just the lyrics, and I can't sell it to anyone, was what she thought. But she couldn't say that now.

"A tape?"

"I don't." Okay, this is when I'll tell him. I'll say, Sorry to break it to you, Harry, but I can't let you have this song.

"So let's do this. You take five while I set up the mike, and then we can lay it down with you and the piano. Then at least I'll have it when I see Faith Hill's people. Will you do that for me? Your old buddy Harry? You wrote that melody? That is like the old days of the Beatles."

This song *would* be incredible for Faith Hill. It could be huge. It could make the songwriter very, very rich. Her heart was pounding in her ears, and she couldn't look at him.

"What? You got something more important to do?" he asked.

"No, but, Harry . . ." What was the point? Sunny wouldn't sign a contract to sell this one either, because Sunny thought it was okay just to sit in the cuckoo farm and play songs for the other zombies. And here was this biggie from the music business wanting to turn one of her songs into a megahit. This wasn't going to fall apart like the Marty Melman deal. This had a million possibilities.

I'll do this for Sunny, Dahlia thought. Of course. I'm doing it for her. When it's the biggest song since "Happy Birthday," I'll say I had to do it this way so she could have the money she needs. To do what? Oh, I'll think of something. She'll agree if I tell her that the money is going to find new ways to make people with mental illness get well. Great idea. We'll name a pavilion after her at some mental hospital.

Harry was hurrying around the studio, into a back closet, emerging with a microphone and a headset, pulling a mike close to the piano.

"Sing it just like you did for me. Start out slow with that kind of soft, reflective quality, then start putting the emotion into it, and then build into that kind of caterwaul sound, 'cause that will really get the message across, and that's where it really starts to rock out," Harry said, looking around to make sure everything was in place in the studio, then backing out and closing the door with a hiss, leaving her to look out at him through the glass.

Dahlia's insides were trembling, and she had a

queasy feeling in her chest and an aching around her shoulders. This was either the worst crime in the world or the smartest move she'd ever made. Either way, just doing it made her feel so sick to her stomach that she was trying to remember if she'd seen a bathroom anywhere on the way in to the studio, because she was sure she wasn't going to make it through this recording in the middle of this lie. Oh, c'mon. It's only half a lie, her rationalizing self told her, as if lies could be fractionalized. You did write half of this, so you're only half a thief.

"Okay, babe. Want to sing a few bars so I can get a level?" Harry's voice from the booth startled her. He wanted her to sing the song now. The song that Sunny created. Well, this was it. This was when she had to tell him. Harry, this isn't just my song. This is a song idea that belongs to my cousin, who also wrote the tune, who doesn't even know my lyrics for it exist, and who will never sign a deal with you or anyone.

This is a song by a woman who would smear nail polish on a contract and play the song for her drug-filled gang of mental patients before she'd ever let you have it, so I'm sorry if you misunderstood my singing it as my having written it alone. In fact I didn't even think of the hook. That was hers, too. So your falling for this song would really be a problem, since there's no way you can sell it to Faith or anybody else. That was what she was going to tell him now.

"Uh, Harry . . . ," she said.

"Let's hear it, good-lookin'!" Harry said.

Dahlia took a deep breath, which made her feel a little dizzy, and then, instead of telling Harry the truth, she let herself play the opening chords of "What's Happened to Me?"

"Sounds good," Harry said, interrupting her. "Don't waste it. Let's lay one down just for openers. We're rolling, so start anytime."

"I keep getting in my own way, unable to change. Everybody sees it, and they say I'm acting strange." Sick, I am sick, she thought, and weak and spineless, and Seth is right about me. I am such a jerk with my big dreams of glory that I won't give up, to the point that I am stealing my poor cousin's tune and her idea, and I can't stop myself. But I don't have the guts to admit it, and I don't know how to get out of it, and I should be running out the door right now.

"What's happened to me?" she sang, full of anger at herself. And, when she finished, Harry's voice came over the speaker into the studio.

"Wow!" he said. "We got it, and it is to die, babe! I'm not letting you outta here until you make me a lead sheet."

"Look, Harry . . . ," she protested.

"Trust me, sweetheart," Harry said. "Invest another half hour in putting this into my computer, it'll pop out a lead sheet, and you'll be naming all your rich children Harry, after the guy who made you famous."

By the time Dahlia got back to her van, Harry Brenner was opening the door for her and helping her in gingerly, only now he was handling her as if she were a precious commodity.

"Sweetheart," he said, "I can guaran-fuckin'-tee you that this piece-of-shit vehicle of yours is history as of this moment. In fact, if I were you, I'd stop in at the

Ferrari dealership on your way home and ask if they'll give you a trade-in." Then he laughed and reached into the car and took her face in his two hands, so close that his too-sweet cologne gave her an instant headache.

"I want you back here in one week to play me everything you've got that sounds as good as this last one, so I can get you a big deal somewhere. Then all you have to do is churn them out, and I'll be your manager." He kissed her on each cheek, gave her a thumbs-up, and backed away so she could leave. Dear God, she thought, let this pitiful trash-can-on-wheels start, so I can make a decent exit.

She was amused at how dramatically different Harry's good-bye look was from his impatient, let's-get-this-over-with hello look. The expression on his face as he watched her drive away said that he adored her madly, that she could trust him, that they were a team who would knock the music business on its ass. My God, she thought, if he only knew.

❧

twelve

$\mathcal{H}$ ere's how it feels to massage Margie Kane: really weird, Dahlia thought, because everything about her was fake. Implants, inserts, nips, tucks, lifts, add-ons, remodels. Some of the scars were new, and Dahlia had to massage gingerly around them. Margie had tiny scars here and there, all of them dead giveaways of her numerous plastic surgeries. Not that Margie cared if Dahlia saw the scars. Who in the hell was Dahlia? The masseuse. Please. That's why Margie never once apologized about always being at least a half hour late for Dahlia, who came in, set up the table, and then read whatever book Margie had on her bedroom coffee table that week. Usually it was something by Danielle Steel.

Most of the time, Margie came sweeping into the bedroom, rushed into her bathroom, took a long shower, and then made a few phone calls, while

Dahlia read in the little seating area adjacent to the vast bedroom, waiting for her. When Margie finally emerged, she would be chatting away on the cordless phone, which she liked to hold in her hand even as she climbed onto the table via a small antique wooden step stool she kept next to it. She always made sure Dahlia positioned the step stool just so, because climbing onto the table improperly might jar some of her most recent stitches.

Margie would continue to talk on the phone throughout the entire massage, interrupting her conversation now and then only to bark "That's too hard" or "Dig in deeper." Dahlia couldn't remember ever having one actual conversation with Margie since her secretary had hired her a year ago to massage Ms. Kane, as the secretary called her. Probably because Margie was always on the phone. The telephone chats Margie had during her massages weren't business-related, as far as Dahlia could tell. Most of them sounded gossipy, about what certain people wore and how good or bad they'd looked at some event or other.

"Freddy always says—and he's right—" was how Margie began a lot of her sentences, and Dahlia figured Freddy must be the Frederic Kane of Marjorie and Frederic Kane, which were the names on the check she was paid every week, already made out and waiting in the kitchen by the back door. Freddy was a plastic surgeon in Beverly Hills. Dahlia had seen him mentioned in articles in beauty magazines.

Today, when Dahlia came in, Margie was already on the table, and remarkably, she was not talking on the phone. She was sitting up, and she held a small towel in front of her.

"Hi, Dahl," she said softly, as if they were and always had been chummy. "I need to talk to you. I mean, I need to talk to someone, and you're here, so I guess it's going to be you."

"Why don't you lie down, Margie, and I'll start on your back while we talk?"

"I don't think I can stand for anyone to touch me. I mean, my skin is crawling. I found out last night that Freddy's been banging his nurse, doing it in the surgery room at night when everybody's gone. The fucking nurse called and told me, because she wants him to leave me. It's kind of like Marla Maples and Ivana Trump. But don't worry about me. I'm going to emerge like Ivana did. Triumphant." She smiled weakly, and then a tear fell, and a terrible realization seemed to come over her, because her eyes got very wide. "Oh, my God. What if I don't? What if he takes everything away from me?"

If Margie didn't look so pitiful, with that big poofy hair and that overcollagened face, Dahlia would have laughed. Now her flow of tears made her too-thick mascara muddy up, then track slowly down her face, past her implanted cheekbones.

"That's really sad, Margie," Dahlia said, wishing Margie would lie down so she could get this over with. "I had no idea things were—"

"Me neither, honey. He was still ripping my clothes off every night, too. How do I live with that? Who knows what kind of horrible diseases she's been passing on to me? And now he's saying he's not going to give me any money because I was a lousy wife. My God. I could end up having to work. I could have to get a job at Saks, selling clothes I won't be able to afford anymore to women who used to come to my house for dinner. How do people live?" She looked imploringly at Dahlia. "How do *you* live? How much does someone like you make a month? Maybe I could do that. I could go to massage school."

Now she was off the table, pacing nervously.

"But then I'd have to massage people who had themselves done by Freddy. Unless I move somewhere else. That's it. I'll do massages in Maine. Where *is* Maine? Oh, my God. What if Freddy takes my car? What kinds of cars do people drive who give massages?" Margie hurried to the window, looking down at the huge circular driveway, where the rusting and dilapidated van stood waiting for Dahlia.

There was a long moment while Margie took in the van from end to end. "You have got to be joking!" she said, laughing a bitter laugh. "That's it? Hah! That's what it comes to? Well, I'd say that just about does it, then. I'm slashing my wrists," she announced, and she marched into her bathroom and slammed the door. Dahlia could hear her loud sobs punctuated with moans of "Ohhh, my God."

Another seventy-five bucks shot to shit, Dahlia thought, picking up her duffel bag of oils and candles and heading downstairs. In the kitchen a dour older woman in a white uniform stood at the sink, rinsing some dishes.

"I think Mrs. Kane needs some help upstairs," Dahlia said. "You'd better look in on her right away."

Then she pushed open the back door and made her way to the van. Inside she pulled the rearview mirror toward her face and looked into it. Pitiful, she said to herself, you should at least have told her she had to pay you for coming all the way over here. You are pitiful.

"Do you ever think I'm pitiful?" Dahlia had asked Sunny one morning. Dahlia was eleven, and she was sitting on the closed lid of the toilet seat, doing her homework, listening to Sunny sing in the shower. She was in the sixth grade, and Sunny had been spending the year working at the furniture store and taking a few music classes at Cal State Northridge in the evening. Her doctors told Aunt Ruthie and Uncle Max that a few classes were all she could handle with her on-again, off-again hospital stays and her unstable behavior patterns.

"Why on earth would you ask me that?" Sunny said, sticking her head out from behind the shower curtain. Her long white hair was matted against her head. "Hand me one of those little towels for my hair," she said, turning off the water and stepping out onto the terry-cloth mat as Dahlia handed her a small towel.

"Because I heard two girls at my school say I was a pitiful nerd with no friends and that's why I hang around with my cousin." Arthur the dog sidled over and licked the dripping water from Sunny's legs as she made a turban for her hair with the smaller towel, then dried off with the larger one.

"They said that? My God, they're so wrong. You're fabulous. Let's ask the studio audience."

"Who?"

"The ones who watch my show."

"You've got a show?"

Sunny nodded. "And you're in it." Then she wiped the steam off the mirror and looked at her naked reflection. "And this is the porno part," she said, and then she shimmied sexily, her big white boobs knocking back and forth. Then she winked into the mirror. "They love that," she laughed.

"Who do I play in your show?" Dahlia asked.

"You play the part of my little cuz," Sunny answered. "But your part will get bigger as you get older and more interesting. Right, folks?" she said into the mirror. "They like you and think those girls at your school are dumb," Sunny said.

The studio audience. That was the day Sunny told Dahlia that she was always being watched by people who were on the other side of a two-way mirror. Sunny also believed that every mirror in the world was two-way and the studio audience was on the other side of every one of them, which meant that anywhere there was a mirror, the studio audience was watching you. Like in those hospitals where Sunny went to try to get well, and the doctors sat on the other side of a two-way glass watching the way she and the other mental patients behaved. Many of the patients didn't know what that big window was for. But Sunny always knew and played to it. Once in a therapy group, she stood and pulled her pants down and flashed the two-way mirror.

"They're everywhere, Dahl," she said. "In department stores there are millions of them, in the beauty shop, at the dressmaker's, behind the lunch counter at Hirsch's Drugstore. In the car, of course, and in everybody's house. Have you ever been in somebody's house who doesn't have at least one mirror? Of course you haven't, and that's the way they want it, so they can watch every move we make. Compacts are part of it, too. The minute you open your compact and look into it, they're out there looking back and watching you powder your nose."

"I never powder my nose," Dahlia told her.

"Smart," Sunny said. "Very smart."

Dahlia stayed at Aunt Ruthie's every weekend, just to be near Sunny. Even when Sunny went out on dates, Dahlia would lie awake reading in the big double bed, waiting for Sunny to get home to tell her if the date was an HT, meaning the date was a heartthrob, or an NFM, meaning the date fell into the reject pile known as "not for me." Late one night when Sunny came home from her date, she threw her purse onto the bed with a thunk, waking Dahlia, who could smell the alcohol on her breath.

"Oh, shit!" Sunny cried, and she fell onto the bed, lying down with her coat still on. "The studio audience must be very depressed," she said slushily.

"Why?" Dahlia asked, sitting up, though part of her was still enveloped in her dream. The room was lit by the full moon as the light poured through the attic-bedroom window.

"Because they saw what I did tonight. The room had mirrors everywhere," Sunny said, her face flushed as she pointed at the mirror above the chest of drawers across from the bed. Then she took her high heel off and threw it at the mirror. "I hate them!" she hollered. The impact didn't break the glass, but it did make the big wood-framed mirror swing back and forth. The second shoe fell short and hit the floor in front of the dresser. "The studio audience saw the whole ugly thing," she told Dahlia. Then she got up, pulled her lipstick out of her purse, climbed up onto the dresser, and slowly and painstakingly drew letters in lipstick on the mirror.

"Stop it, Sunny. Your mother's going to kill you," Dahlia warned as Sunny scrawled the printed backward letters deliberately and carefully. "Sunny, don't. They'll send you back to the hospital."

ꟻᴜᴄᴋ ʏᴏᴜ. ɢᴏ ᴛᴏ ʜᴇʟʟ. She was writing a note to the studio audience. Writing it backward so they could read it on the other side of the mirror. She seemed to feel better when she climbed down, but she left her coat on when she got into bed and fell into a drunken sleep. Dahlia lay there for a long time listening to Sunny breathe, knowing in the morning Uncle Max would see the lipstick on the mirror and call the hospital, and Dahlia would have to see Sunny's terrified eyes begging her to find a way to stop them from taking her away again.

After she was sure Sunny was sleeping deeply, she climbed out of the bed and tiptoed down to the laundry room, opening cupboards and drawers as quietly as she could until she found some Windex and rags among the cleaning supplies. She came back up and climbed onto the dresser. Then, using the Windex, the rag, and her fingernails, she stayed up cleaning the mirror until it was perfect.

* * *

Dahlia remembered that night, as she turned the rearview mirror away from her own exhausted face and piloted the van home from Margie Kane's. Another night of going out to work and coming home without a cent. The studio audience at my show, she thought, inching along in the van in the heavy traffic up Laurel Canyon, is definitely depressed.

Seth's car was in the carport, and she couldn't decide if she was hoping he'd tell her that Harry Brenner had called or if she wanted Harry Brenner to be like Marty Melman, so flaky he'd already forgotten about her and her stolen song. She grabbed her duffel bag and slid out of the van. This pitiful down-at-the-heels house. Once she'd thought that by now she would have built a second story on it, put the bedroom up there among the trees, and turned her current bedroom into a music room. But now it was starting to look seedy. If she sold just one song, she could hire a painter.

Seth's daughter, Lolly, was sitting on the living room floor, engrossed in an episode of the *Powerpuff Girls* on television. She was wearing red stick-on earrings and a purple turban and flip-flops with big plastic flowers on them.

"Hello, Lolly," Dahlia said, trying to sound friendly and warm.

Lolly didn't bother to answer or look up.

"Harry Brenner called," Seth hollered out from the bedroom. "I left the message on the machine so you could play it back."

Guilt. Dahlia was sick to her stomach with guilt.

What if Faith Hill loved the song? Then it would really be too late to tell Harry, because then he'd have to be embarrassed and tell Faith that she couldn't have the song after all. Dahlia walked to the TV and turned it down.

"Hey!" Lolly yelled. "I was watching that! Dad! Tell her!"

"I'm just turning it down for a second," Dahlia said as Lolly stormed into the kitchen. Dahlia heard her say, "Let's get out of here, Dad!" Dahlia pushed the play button on the answering machine, and there was Harry's voice.

"Hey, doll. Harry here. Faith Hill wasn't feeling well, so she didn't show up last night, but not to worry. The fucking song is brilliant, and believe me, I don't say that a lot. So when the time is right, I'll get it to her. Meanwhile pull some more songs together and let me hear those, too. This is your manager," he sang in a cute little voice, "signing off."

"That man said a bad word," Lolly piped up.

Harry was calling himself her manager. Based on what? A song she didn't have the nerve to tell him she didn't own? One minute before she'd played that song for him, Sunny's song, Harry had been ready to throw her out.

"Nice message," Seth said coming back into the kitchen. "Was that a joke about Faith Hill?" He was smiling when he said it, and his eyes got wide when Dahlia shook her head and bristled.

"Why would you think it was a joke?" she asked, trying not to sound as indignant as she felt.

"He said your song was brilliant! Which song?" he

asked, and Dahlia thought there was something in his too-surprised question that implied that he thought it was funny that Harry Brenner thought one of Dahlia's songs could possibly be brilliant. And of course she couldn't tell him which one, since the song Harry thought was brilliant wasn't exactly hers.

"Oh, he liked them all. I don't know which one he wanted for Faith," she said, trying too hard to sound casual and hurrying into the bedroom to avoid Seth's eyes, which knew her well enough to detect a lie. Okay, she thought, Faith's not feeling well was God's way of telling her she still had time to confess the truth to Harry. Harry. My God, he wanted her to bring him more songs. As good as "What's Happened to Me?" She had to sit down and start working now. Shining up her old ones, coming up with new ones so Harry would think she was worthy of a publishing deal where they'd expect her to turn out song after song.

"Want to go out for a bite with us?" Seth asked, turning off the TV and gathering Lolly's backpack, which was a koala bear with a zipper in its stomach. Lolly held on to her father's sleeve and made a point of avoiding eye contact with Dahlia.

"No thanks," Dahlia said. "I need to work on some more stuff for Harry."

"Yesss," Lolly hissed triumphantly, thrilled to have Seth to herself.

By the time Seth's car pulled out of the driveway, Dahlia was sitting on the piano bench with her pencil, her big pink eraser, and her music paper, feeling nervous but determined to come up with something new and fresh to give to Harry. No wonder Harry hadn't warmed up to the stuff she'd written alone. It was old-fashioned and kind of low-key. But she could write something good, as good as "What's Happened to Me?" Couldn't she? All she had to do was come up with a strong hook, the way Sunny had done with "What's Happened to Me?" She needed the beginning of a lyric, and that would get her moving.

One songwriting book she read had a whole chapter called "Brainstorming." The book said to relax and let random thoughts float through your brain and make those thoughts into song titles. "I Could Be Homeless by Christmas." A cheerful holiday tune, she thought, laughing to herself. Those can always be counted on to bring in some steady income. "My Carpet Needs Shampooing." Probably not a candidate for the top of the charts. "I'm Hungry." "I Hate My Life." "All Men Are Jerks." Not a decent title in the bunch.

Her eyelids were getting heavy, and she thought about taking a nap, but she couldn't stop now. She had to come up with more songs for Harry. This was not like all the other times when she'd sat there for a while and eventually given up. Harry could turn her life around, so there would be no going to do her laundry or cleaning the kitchen until she knocked out some songs.

She had to do this. If Harry could get her a music-publishing deal, she could hire someone to do the laundry and clean the kitchen *for* her. And of course, once she brought him a few great ones of her own and he was dying to see them all, then maybe she'd be able to gently break the news that she had to take back "What's Happened to Me?"

She toyed with a few bars of something she'd written years ago, and it was lame. Now she was staring at the clock on the bookshelf. And she'd only been sitting here for ten minutes. She'd never noticed before how loudly that clock ticked, and she even tried playing a tune that used the clock tick as a metronome beat. But it sounded like the theme for a Saturday-morning cartoon show. Really stupid!

She drifted, she sighed, she went into the kitchen and made a cup of coffee, pouring boiling water through the filter and over the muddy little pile of ground coffee, hoping that the caffeine would give her a jolt, but it didn't. Harry was expecting her to show up in a few days and dazzle him with more songs, and she had to have something to give him. She tried the brainstorming technique again, but all that came out was "Help, I'm Dying Here, and I Have Nowhere to Turn." Maybe that one would work. No. She had to admit that nothing was happening. Nothing. Finally she walked to the phone and dialed Seth's cell-phone number. She didn't know what she was calling to say to him until she heard him pick up.

"Seth Meyers."

"Hey," she said.

"Whassup?" Seth asked.

"I'm going out of town tomorrow morning," she said.

"Yeah? How come?"

"I probably won't be back for the next few days."

"Where're you going?"

"Back down to San Diego to be with my cousin." There was a long silence.

"For days? You're going there for days? Is this a joke? You couldn't wait to get rid of her! Honey, do you have a lover you aren't telling me about, and is the crazy cousin visit a cover to be with him?"

"No lovers. She's my flesh and blood. We were close. I loved her when we were kids, and I kind of feel as if I owe her something. You know what I'm saying?"

"I don't," Seth said. "I mean, not that it isn't a noble idea to go and hold her hand, but . . . ?"

"But what?"

"Honestly? It just isn't like you, so it makes me wonder. And worry."

Dahlia felt anger rush into her chest. "You mean, because it sounds like something a *nice* person would do?"

"Oh, come on," he said. "Don't get pissy with me, honey. You know you've never been altruistic. So why would I believe you'd start being that way now?"

Anger coursed through her, and she couldn't stop herself from saying, "Seth, why don't you do us both a favor and clear your stuff out of this house while I'm gone? I can't handle your negative attitude about me."

Seth's voice was even, but she could tell he was rattled. "What you can't handle is that I'm on to you. You're busted for being the brat you are, and you don't like that. I guess if you don't want someone around who really knows you to the core and still loves you anyway, then you're right. I better move my stuff out of the house. And I'll do it tomorrow after you leave. But I want to go on record as betting everything I own that this has to do with her music and how you're going to exploit her and not a damn thing to do with your great and deep commitment to her."

Dahlia flared. "Well, bet away, friend, since you don't own a goddamned thing anyway!" she said before slamming down the phone. Then she went into her room, threw some clothes into her duffel bag, and prayed the van would make it back down to San Diego.

thirteen

*I*t was a few months before Dahlia's twelfth birth-day, and she was spending the weekend, as usual, at Sunny's house, getting to sleep in the same big double bed with Sunny, where she always slept, but that night she couldn't fall asleep because the stinky smell of nail polish was keeping her awake. Sunny had told her a million times that things would change dramatically for her when she grew up and that eventually she would love all the things Sunny loved already, because Sunny was five years older, but Dahlia found it hard to believe she'd ever like those sickening perfumes and lotions and oils that lined Sunny's dressing table.

And sex. Dahlia was sure she could never possibly like sex the way Sunny did. Sunny talked about sex much too much and way too often. And not the facts of life or the birds and the bees or the things an older cousin is supposed to tell a younger one. But details, gory details. "I'm only sorry," she said one night out of nowhere, "that there's no candlestick maker around here."

Dahlia had just started to drift off to sleep, so all she offered was a groggy "Mmmm-hmmm," even though she knew that when Sunny said something like that, it was her cue to ask, "What do you mean?" But Sunny kept on talking as if Dahlia had asked the question anyway.

"Because I've already had Mr. Waldman the butcher and Girard Perreau over at the bakery. So a candlestick maker would have been very poetic," she said, and then she laughed. She was polishing her toenails. There was a wad of cotton between each toe to keep them spread apart, making her feet look wide and weird.

Now Dahlia was wide awake. Not just because of the awful, acrid smell of the polish but because anytime Sunny got that certain twinkle in her eye, it meant she was going to share personal stories, and Dahlia had to hear every word of them.

"Why do you do that?" Dahlia asked, sitting up and trying to spread her own toes wide without the cotton. "Why do you think it's okay to sleep with anyone who looks at you?"

Sunny thought about her answer for only a second. "It's the *way* they look at me that makes me want to," she replied, and she had a serious expression on her face as if it were Johnny Carson or Dick Cavett asking the question. "When I see in their eyes how much they want me, I think how much fun it would be to give them what they want. To see that fabulously wild look they get when I take off my blouse. It's a riot. They turn into these bright red devils, all stiff and hard and tense and panting. And they come at me so feverishly I can't refuse. It's so much fun to say, 'Yes, yes, let's do it!' "

"Ugh," Dahlia said, hoping Sunny was finished describing those awful men and that she wouldn't say any more. But if there was more, of course Dahlia wanted to hear it.

"That's when you get to know who they really are," Sunny said, "underneath the apron or that dopey blue mailman suit."

"The mailman, too?" Dahlia tried to remember what the mailman looked like who came to Sunny's house. But Sunny didn't answer. She was expounding on her theories about sex now, and she didn't want to be interrupted by questions.

"That's when you see the primitive them, without the act they put on for the world, and I live to see that. The minute I know a man has to have me, lusts after me madly, I have to give myself to him."

"Yechhh." Dahlia put the pillow over her head, hoping it would block out the image of Mr. Waldman, the fat old butcher, and Sunny doing with him whatever people did in bed.

"You'll see." Sunny patted the pillow with her pretty white hand with the fuchsia polish on every shapely fingernail, which was now matched by every perfect fuchsia toenail. "You'll grow up and your hormones will kick in, and you'll see. You get this sense of power and surrender all in one. And it's not just the best feeling in the world, it's the *only* feeling in the world. Men fight wars because of it. They need that big, powerful rush you get, and all war really makes them feel is sexy.

"My theory is that if every man in the world were getting enough sex, there would never be another war again. But not just hooker sex. That doesn't count. Because they know they're paying for that. Or grudging-wife sex, where the wife says to herself, 'Okay, I'd better do this or he won't pay the bills.' That doesn't count either. I mean, if every man had sex with somebody who was dying to have sex with them, the way I am when I see that look on a man's face, the world would be perfect. So the way I see it is, the biggest problem in the world is that there's just not enough of me to go around."

Dahlia lifted the pillow from her head and looked at her cousin. There was something about the way Sunny said that last part about there not being enough of her to go around that struck them both so funny it made them laugh hysterically. Sunny's unrestrained laughter always got to Dahlia, and soon she was overcome by the same full-out belly laugh. Still laughing, Sunny took Dahlia by the shoulders and, from the bed, turned her so she could see herself in the mirror.

"Look how pretty you are. You'll be the best-looking girl in the world when you grow up. And the studio audience agrees. Don't you, folks?" She stopped to listen. "They're cheering. Hear them? They're roaring. They love you!" Then she stood on the bed and pulled

Dahlia up, and the two of them jumped on the bed until they collapsed from exhaustion.

How can I be so lucky, Dahlia remembered thinking, to be so close to the magical Sunny? Everything she says is wise, and everything she does is funny, and everything she wears is so beautiful, not because it's fancy or expensive but because of the way she wears it. She tosses a shawl around herself so it drapes perfectly and doesn't sag or fall. She puts colors together fearlessly, like purple and red, and on her they don't clash—they set off her white-blond curls in a way that makes me have to stare at her and want to copy her and be her.

And steal her songs? a voice inside her asked, breaking into her reverie as she drove back to San Diego.

Her plan was to get Sunny to pack and come home with her for a week or so, which meant that she had to get to the Sea View in time to talk about Sunny's medication needs with that man who came to deliver the daily dose to each of the house's residents. Dahlia had a vague recollection that he had shown up at around the lunch hour last time, so if there wasn't too much traffic on the 405, she could make it.

It was a perfect idea. She'd tell the medicine man she was going to take Sunny to vacation at her house for a few weeks. Then she'd ask him to give her a supply of Sunny's medications to last that long. Then, on the days when Sunny did want to take the pills, Dahlia could make sure she had food and a nice, quiet place to sit and watch TV or play solitaire with the computer. And on those days when she didn't want to take the pills, Sunny could be near the piano, creating those wonderful tunes. Dahlia would write words to the tunes, and somehow she'd convince Sunny to let her try to sell the songs for both of them. Once Sunny was staying in her house and feeling relaxed, she'd relent.

There must have been an accident in Orange County, because now the traffic was stopped and the damned van was clanking out a song all its own, and suddenly the plan didn't seem so great anymore. She had a strong impulse to turn around and go home. Maybe she would even call Seth and take back what she'd said about his moving out and hope he'd forgive her. But then the traffic started to move again, and she knew she couldn't turn back. As long as she stayed with Seth, she'd be trapped forever in nothingness— nothing with him, nothing for herself, nothing to bring to Harry Brenner. No, she had to forge ahead, because whatever happened as a result of this plan had to be better than what was happening now.

The traffic was moving well again when it started to rain, and her wiper blades were smearing the windshield so she could barely see. The blades seemed to be beating out the rhythm of another one of Sunny's songs, one that was almost as good as "What's Happened to Me?" Dahlia would call this one "Isn't It Sad?" once Sunny told her she could take the tunes and run with them.

It was still raining when she pulled up outside the Sea View. As crummy as the place had looked the first few times she saw it, on this gloomy day with rain dripping from its gutters, the old converted house looked even more shabby and depressing. "Ohhhkay," she said out loud, "here goes nothin'." Then she opened the van door and ran up the steps, her tennis shoes sloshing in the puddles. None of the regulars were on the porch, and the wind rocked the rocking chairs. Dahlia could hear the television blasting from inside. The door opened easily, and immediately she was face-to-face with Grover the medicine man. Perfect, she thought. Just the man I want to see. In the room to the left, the television group was gathered around watching Maury Povich, whose guests looked as if they were a group of transvestites. Sunny wasn't watching TV.

"Hello there," Dahlia said to the medicine man, putting on her best warm face and hoping he would buy her in this role of concerned relative. "We've met before. I'm Sunny's cousin. And I'm glad I caught you." Grover raised an eyebrow as she went on. "I'm planning to take Sunny to vacation for a week or two at my house. So I figured I'll need to take a supply of her medication to bring with us, and I was hoping you could give it to me so I could be sure she takes it every day."

"Sunny really shouldn't go anywhere," the man said, shaking his head. "She doesn't operate too well in the real world as it is. And even with me coming in here every day, she rarely takes her medication. That's why she is the way she is. So I ought to tell you from the get-go that the chances of her taking the pills for you are slim and none. And when she doesn't take them . . . you don't want to handle her."

Dahlia stiffened. She probably should have anticipated that somebody from within the system would give her a hard time. No, she wouldn't take that as an answer. This jerk had no power over Sunny, and she wasn't going to let him interfere.

"Well, maybe being with a family member who cares about her will make her feel better," she tried, smiling and hoping she looked confident. "Or maybe we can find her a medicine she likes, and then she'll be more willing to take it." The medicine man narrowed his eyes and clucked his tongue derisively.

"A medicine she likes? You mean strawberry-flavored?" He laughed a strained laugh. "Look, sweetie," he said, "this isn't child's play. And it's nothing to me personally whatever you decide. But I can promise you that even though you think you know what you're doing, you can trust me—you don't. People like Sunny need a routine. To eat and sleep and take their meds at the same time every day. To do their personal-hygiene regimen every day, to have their grooming and medical appointments at regular times. Well-meaning relatives take them home and screw them up. It's what always happens."

Don't get rattled, Dahlia said to herself. "I'm surprised," she said. "I'd think it would be good to get them out of here now and then. Very healing for them to spend time in a normal word. All they seem to do around here is stare at the TV all day, sleep, and eat," she said.

Grover shook his head scornfully. "Is that what you think? Well, isn't it amazing how the drop-in do-gooder relatives know all the answers about people they haven't seen in a million years? Great! Give us your knowledgeable opinions and meddle a little, and freak out about how drugged up your relatives are. And soon you'll do the same thing as the rest of them: bring her back here, make some phony good-bye speech, then rush out to your car, go back to your nice life, and forget about her. So save the bleeding-heart spiel, 'cause I've heard them all. Next time we see you after that is the day you come to claim the body. If you even do that. And by the way, that room of hers? If she's not back in it again by the end of three weeks, we give it away. There's a waiting list a mile long for these rooms. People are dying to get in here."

"I believe that's what they say about the cemetery," Dahlia said.

Grover sighed, took out an envelope and poured pills into it, then handed them to her. "The doctors wanted to put her on clozapine a long time ago, but they told her she'd have to take a blood test regularly, and she refused to do it. I remember her saying, 'No needles in me. No, sir.' As if some little needle stick was gonna be worse than the hell she's lived through. So they left her on Haldol. She's been on that one and a few others over the years, and none of them ever did a damn thing, and she knows it.

"So if you decide to keep her, you can just call down and have them change the address where they send her check. And that's what you need to know. Doesn't get much disability except enough to keep her in cigarettes and Coca-Cola. I've watched her and all the rest of them for ten years. I don't know how they still walk around. I'm moving to Florida next month to work in a retirement home. The guy who hired me said, 'These

old people down here are just waiting to die.' I said,
'The people here are, too, only they're younger so they
have a longer wait.' If you can give her some semblance of a life, you'll be a saint. My guess is, by the
time she's through with you, you'll be looking to get
into the hatch yourself."

"Thanks," Dahlia said. Then she watched him pack
up the rest of his things and exit, and as soon as she
was sure he was gone, she hurried up the stairs. Some
of the doors to the bedrooms were open, so she could
see a few of the residents sitting on their beds staring
out the window at the rain. Sunny's door was open,
and she was sitting on her bed playing solitaire.

He's probably right, Dahlia thought, letting doubt
fall over her. There are a million traps in this plan. She
knew she hadn't really thought it all through carefully
enough, and she'd have to figure it out on the fly. But
so what? Who was going to fault her for coming here
to free her cousin from a loony bin? She could say it
was a debt she'd owed Sunny for years. Even to get her
out of this place temporarily was a damn good deed.

"Sunny," Dahlia said softly. Sunny didn't look up
even when Dahlia moved into the room and sat on the
bed two feet from her. Her only movement was her
arm reaching down to place another card, then another. "How *are* you?" Dahlia tried, but there was no
reply. Today must have been a day that Sunny had
downed the contents of the cup.

"Me?" Sunny asked, still not looking up. The rain
was pounding hard against the small window. Dahlia
saw Sunny's jaw moving involuntarily back and forth,
back and forth.

"Listen, I had an idea," Dahlia said.

"Did you bring the little cards?" Sunny said. Of course Dahlia had brought the computer, because she knew it was a great way to get Sunny's interest.

"I did bring them. And you can play with them, but first I thought I'd ask you a very important question." There was a long silence. As Sunny continued to play, Dahlia looked down and realized that the rows of cards Sunny was laying out made no sense. There were reds on reds and blacks on blacks and bigger numbers underneath smaller numbers, but still Sunny methodically placed them where she wanted them to go, conforming to some system in her head, the tip of her tongue jutting out of the side of her mouth the way children's tongues did when the children were concentrating hard.

"How would you like to come and stay at my house for a while?"

"What about your boyfriend?" Sunny asked, suddenly sounding very lucid.

"I broke up with him," Dahlia said, and Sunny looked at her and emitted a mocking laugh.

"And they say *I'm* crazy," she said, and her laughter shook the bed. "How'd you let that studmuffin out of your sight?" For an instant she was the lusty, leering Sunny that Dahlia remembered, and they laughed together, and Dahlia saw a flash of the old light in Sunny's eyes.

"Well, now there's more room in my house for *you*," Dahlia said in a voice that was trying to sound positive and cheerful.

" 'Well, now there's more room in my house for *you*,' " Sunny said, mocking Dahlia's phony voice, as if even in her hazy state she could see through Dahlia. The rain was coming down hard outside, and a big wind blew a branch of a nearby tree against Sunny's window.

"I'm afraid of rain," Sunny said, shuddering now as she gazed out.

"It can't hurt you," Dahlia said, trying to sound comforting. Rain or no rain, she was not walking out of this place without Sunny. I'm like Jack and the Beanstalk coming to capture the goose that laid the golden eggs, she thought. And I am not leaving without that goose.

"I could turn the little office at my house into a very nice bedroom, and you could stay for a while and we could . . . I don't know. Hang out? Reminisce about the old days? Maybe even write songs together?"

Sunny didn't answer. Just continued playing her mad version of solitaire.

"I mean, you're an adult. You're here voluntarily, right? So you can just leave whenever you want, right?"

"Yeah," Sunny muttered. "Voluntarily."

"I already asked for a few weeks' worth of your meds, and I could help you pack and . . ." Dahlia opened the door of Sunny's closet. There were only three hangers of clothes. One held the overalls and T-shirt she'd worn the other day, a second held the red parachute-fabric jogging suit, and the third held a flowery print muumuu. "Guess you don't have a bag," Dahlia said.

"Yeah, I do," Sunny told her. She got up, walked to a drawer, and pulled out a Macy's shopping bag.

"So do you want to leave?" Dahlia asked.

Sunny shrugged and offered what might be construed as a nod.

Within a minute Dahlia had the items in the closet folded and stacked in the Macy's bag, after which she helped Sunny open the three drawers and empty their meager contents—underwear from the first, T-shirts from the second, and some Elvis CDs from the third—into the bag, too. It had taken less than three minutes to pack Sunny's things. Dahlia wondered how many days it would have taken her to pack all her own belongings if she had to move out of her house.

"If I come with you, can I play with the little cards?" Sunny asked.

"The little cards are waiting in the van," Dahlia said as they headed down the steps.

She's right, Dahlia thought. I am the one who's crazy. I don't have any idea when she's due for her next dose of medication or what happens if she doesn't get it. She could be violent, she could have seizures, and I'm taking her home as if she were a stray puppy I found in the street. How desperate am I?

At the bottom of the steps, she helped Sunny into the van. "Here are the little cards," she said, opening the computer on Sunny's lap, turning it on, and pulling up the solitaire game.

"So how was your day so far?" she asked Sunny as she pulled the van away from the curb, trying to sound casual. It seemed like a good way to start. Sunny clicked at the laptop's keyboard. "Did you take your morning meds?" Dahlia tried.

"Well, I took them, but I didn't take them, if you know what I mean," Sunny said.

"No, I don't know what you mean," Dahlia said.

"I mean, I took them from Grover but . . ." Sunny shoved her hand into the pocket of the jogging jacket she wore, then extracted it and held it out to Dahlia. There were a dozen or so of the same kind of pills Grover had put into the envelope he'd given Dahlia.

"I put 'em in there every other day, or on days when I don't feel like being a zombie, or on days that have the letter *d* in them," she said, and then she laughed a machine gun of a laugh. "Get it?"

"I get it," Dahlia said with a strained smile. The rain had stopped, and the sun was breaking through. It was so bright that Dahlia reached into her purse to get out her dark glasses and then pulled down the visor to shield her eyes.

"But don't worry," Sunny said, "because I don't need the pills. I'm okay without them." Then she squinted against a ray of sun that blasted into her eyes, and as she pulled down the visor on the passenger side, she gasped, then bellowed, "Fucking bastards! Don't you follow me here, or I'll kill you!"

She was holding her hand up to cover the mirror in the visor on the passenger side. Car horns screamed as Dahlia accidentally veered across a lane while she reached to flip up the visor on Sunny's side.

"Sunny, you're okay. Nobody is there."

Sunny whimpered as Dahlia drove nervously.

"Well," Dahlia said, searching her brain for something to say, "maybe this is good. That you're coming home with me, I mean. Maybe I can help you find a medicine that doesn't make you feel groggy but helps you not see people in the mirror."

"How can I *not* see them when they're *there*?" Sunny asked in a shrill voice. "No meds!" she shouted, rolling down the window of the van. Then she pulled one of her large, braless breasts out of her now-zipped-open jacket and waved it out the window at a truck driver, who honked his loud horn in reply.

Oh, God, Dahlia thought, finding herself in that inexplicable limbo between wanting to laugh and wanting to cry. This was not the way she'd imagined it would be to collect Sunny. All the way back to the house, Sunny stared out the window, and Dahlia felt her insides shaking.

The house was quiet as Dahlia put the key in the door, and she remembered now that Seth's things would be gone from the closet. As soon as they were inside, Sunny plopped herself down on the piano bench and Dahlia went into the bedroom and opened the tiny closet she and Seth had shared. Two empty hangers, the wire ones with paper covers that had the logo of Owl Cleaners on them, were all that was left of him.

On the desk he'd left behind two large piles of the magazines he always read every week so he could check on which of his company's clients were mentioned. *People, Us, Vanity Fair*. New ones, old ones he probably left there because he knew Dahlia loved to leaf through them and see which glamorous Hollywood personality was wearing what to the fancy parties she longed to attend.

Dahlia fought the impulse to rush to the phone,

track him down, and beg him to come back. Sunny was at the piano playing some boogie-woogie chords, and then she launched into a hot, sexy melody and hummed along. That's a tune I could work with, Dahlia thought. But when she walked into the living room and looked at Sunny with her head thrown back and her eyes closed, off in the world of her tunes, she knew that this was a really bad idea and that she would regret it. What have I done? she thought. What in the hell have I done?

fourteen

The sound of a siren screaming down Laurel Canyon woke Dahlia, and she opened one eye to look at the clock. It was already ten. She had to do a massage at noon, so she knew she'd better crawl out of bed and get dressed. Sunny. What was she going to do with Sunny while she worked? She hadn't even thought that far ahead, hadn't figured out the part about what their days would be like when she would have to go off to work and leave Sunny alone in the house.

Well, she wouldn't worry too much, because Sunny certainly wasn't a kid, Dahlia thought, making her way groggily toward the bathroom. This wasn't like the time Seth left Lolly with Dahlia for a few hours when he had an emergency meeting and nobody to watch her. That whole day Dahlia had to keep reminding herself not to leave the kid in the car when she went into the market or the cleaners. Sunny was a grown woman, for God's sake. A crazy grown woman, granted, but she certainly knew how to take care of herself, and Dahlia ought to be able to find things for her to do.

She was still half asleep when she walked into the bathroom, but what she saw there woke her like a slap in the face. Those big letters that filled her bathroom mirror grabbed her attention. GO TO HELL. Oh, no. Her ears rang with fear. Sunny's studio audience was still out there for her, without her medication. They lived in every mirror and watched Sunny's every move. And after all these years, Sunny was still writing her backward messages on the mirror, telling her demons to go to hell, just the way she had when she was a girl.

Dahlia hurried into the living room. It was quiet, and Sunny's room was empty. Where could she have gone? There was no place to walk in these hills around the house. When she stepped outside the front door, the sun was shining and the air had the clear, brisk feeling that always came on the morning after a rain. A bluebird was washing and preening at a puddle in the driveway, and something must have fallen out of Dahlia's car last night, because next to the bird she saw the flash of a shiny object. She walked over to see what it was.

"Oh, no," she said in dismay as she knelt to pick up the rearview mirror from the van. It had been torn from the center of the front windshield. Next to it lay the side mirrors from both the right and left of her car. Seth would have known what to do now. He would have calmed her and told her to think logically about where Sunny would be. Dahlia's head hurt as she walked back to the house and into the kitchen to make some coffee.

It was through the kitchen window that she spotted Sunny lying spread-eagled in the leaves and the grass on the hill behind the house. Her first thought was panic. Maybe Sunny was dead. Her eyes were closed, and her face was tilted up toward the sun. But there was an ecstatic smile on her face. Dahlia opened the back screen door and let it slam behind her so Sunny would hear her coming.

"You okay?" she called out, and Sunny waved a little wave of her fingers without opening her eyes. She had her head thrown back like a sunbather in a commercial, and the Day-Glo hair matched the orange of the scattered California poppies growing wild near the spot where she was lying on the grassy hill. When she felt Dahlia's shadow fall over her, she smiled.

"When I don't take my meds, the jackass doctor in San Diego says, 'Sunny, you're rejecting sanity.' But when I do take them, I stare, I drool, I limp, I sleep, I bloat, I get acne, and I twitch. So if I never take them, even though the studio audience watches every move I make, at least I *can* make moves. And I can lie in the sun and feel the heat on my skin." She lifted her head now to look at Dahlia. "Would you take a pill that didn't let you feel?"

"Sunny, you broke all the mirrors on my van," Dahlia said.

"Well, I had to do that," Sunny said, sitting up. "To protect your life from their snooping. They plot against us. The studio audience judges us and decides who's fat and who's thin and who's successful and who isn't. But if they can't see you, they can't judge you or make decisions for you. So when there are no mirrors, they are foiled. Foiled! Ha. A funny word, because you can see yourself in foil, too, and they are on the other side of it. Never use foil. Only Saran Wrap."

This was bad. Dahlia looked at her watch. She would go inside and cover all the mirrors with sheets and towels until she could get Sunny to a doctor someplace, but right this minute she had to get to her appointment. She had to work and get her hands on some money.

"Sunny, I have a client now, and I have to go to work," she said. "I'll just be gone for a few hours. Is it okay for me to leave you? Will you be okay if I do?"

"Oh, don't worry about me," Sunny said. "I have plenty to do around here."

Dahlia was afraid to ask what that meant. She walked back to her bathroom and took a fast shower, and since she didn't have time to remove the backward letters on her mirror, she managed to dry her hair and put on makeup by peering through them. Sunny was at the piano picking out some new tunes as Dahlia drove away in the van. She needed to find Sunny a doctor. Helene would know a good doctor. Dahlia would ask her what to do when she got out there.

Once, Dahlia remembered, after a lengthy hospitalization, the visit Sunny was making back home wasn't supposed to be a visit. It was meant to be her triumphant return from the land of the lost, proof that she had turned the corner, shaken off the pesky illness, and triumphed the way people always do in movies. In retrospect Dahlia realized how the whole idea of the return had contained far too much hope and set up too many unrealistic expectations for it not to fail. But Dahlia had been a child then and Sunny's ardent fan, so she became an eager party to the fiction. She was excited to help Uncle Max take down the mirror in Sunny's bedroom and to hold an end of the new bedspread and help Aunt Ruthie spruce up the newly refurbished room that would welcome Sunny home to what Aunt Ruthie called "a fresh new life."

Neighbors were arriving with cakes and cookies, eager to get a look at someone who had just spent six months in a mental hospital. Just the fact that Aunt Ruthie and Uncle Max threw a party to welcome Sunny made it clear, only in looking back, that they had no understanding of her condition. "Not exactly a party," Dahlia heard Aunt Ruthie say a little apologetically, "just a few friends dropping over is all."

But somehow, though it was Sunny's first day of looking out of windows that didn't have bars on them and her first day of dressing up in pretty new clothes that Aunt Ruthie had spent weeks buying and then laying out all over the new bedspread as a surprise, Sunny seemed to need no period of adjustment. She stood receiving the friends and neighbors in her mother's living room like a visiting movie star. Dahlia remembered when she walked into her aunt's living room, which was filled with cigarette smoke and chatter, and saw Sunny in a corner, how gorgeous her cousin looked in a sleeveless, low-cut white dress. She held a cigarette in one hand and a Coca-Cola can in the other, and she was smiling up at a slim, dark-haired man. She looked astonishingly beautiful.

"Oh, my God!" Sunny had said, dropping the butt of her cigarette into the Coke can, which she handed to the man. Then she rushed to throw her arms around Dahlia, who could feel as she was held in a very tight embrace that Sunny's body was emitting a low-frequency tremble. "My little baby cuz!" Sunny gushed, squeezing Dahlia harder. "You're so woman-ish!" Sunny pulled away from the hug and looked right at Dahlia's breasts, then put an arm around Dahlia's shoulders and walked her toward the kitchen.

"Did you see him?" she asked Dahlia between clenched teeth, as though, if her lips didn't move, no-body could hear her voice.

"The tall guy?" Dahlia asked giddily, smitten with Sunny's beauty and flattered as she always was that somebody as brassy and exciting as Sunny was so fo-cused on her.

"He's Rita Horn's nephew from Florida, Norman Burns. Well, he burns me, baby. And vice versa. Be-lieve me, Rita didn't bring him here to meet Ruthie Gordon's nutcase daughter—they were just stopping in on their way to dinner. But that boy is drooling into his cream soda. He already asked me if I'd join them at dinner, and when I said I couldn't leave the party, he asked me out for tomorrow night. Out of the booby hatch for four hours and already back in circulation," she said, grinning. Dahlia knew that grin meant

Sunny would be naked with Rita Horn's nephew before the weekend.

But she wasn't. Because, in spite of all of the sexy patter, the medication that was making Sunny seem well enough for her doctors to allow her to come home also made her completely uninterested in sex. Yet somehow, despite her lack of interest, or maybe because of it, the brooding Norman Burns continued to be so wild about her that he took a summer job in L.A., just to be near her. And while he worked in a music store in Westwood by day, he spent every evening with Sunny, and they fell deeply in love.

"His favorite plays are by Tennessee Williams. He reads them to me and plays all the parts. He acts as if he's all of those funny southern ladies with their insane ideas about the world. They're not supposed to be funny, but they make me hysterical, and we both laugh," she said. "The way I feel about him is the way you're supposed to feel when you fall in love. I'm sure of it."

Dahlia liked to be at the house when Norman came to pick Sunny up for a date, because she loved to watch his eyes take Sunny in each time he saw her wearing what was another new dress that Aunt Ruthie had bought her and altered that day. The tight yellow one, the off-the-shoulder gauzy white one. His eyes would squint in that way that said, I am devouring this glorious vision.

"I guess I'll do it with him anyway, even though I don't feel like it," Sunny told Dahlia one night. Sunny was cleaning out her closet, which one of Sunny's doctors had told Aunt Ruthie was a very good sign, since one of the symptoms of schizophrenia was disorganization, and tackling the sorting of clothes was a sign that the illness was under control. "Girls do it all the time. I mean, they pretend it's okay with them even if they don't really feel sexy, and guys don't even notice or care whether we like it or not. As long as we do it whenever they want. So I can just pretend I like it. I mean, that's how women work it who are married. Right?"

She realized that Dahlia didn't know the answer to that question, but she wasn't really talking to Dahlia. She was trying hard to figure out a way to get Norman to ask her to marry him. And she was afraid if she resisted his advances much longer, he'd go back to Florida. She had his photos everywhere in her room and stroked them as if they were voodoo dolls, hoping that when she touched them, Norman could feel the strokes at work.

"He calls me Marilyn Monroe, and I call him Arthur Miller because he thinks I'm that beautiful, and he's always so brainy and so gentle with me. He knows me like nobody ever has, and I know him. I can't even explain the way we're connected. It's so exquisite and so powerful. I want to marry him, Dahl. I'll bet if I could just cut back on the medication for a while . . . Or just, I don't know, stop it for a few days . . .

"I mean, it's great to be able to function almost like a real person, but I miss myself. Not just my sexy self but my funny self and my musical self. I've walked past the piano in the living room every day since I got here, and I haven't sat down to play it once. This new medicine may let me walk without halting and talk without drooling, but I miss the rush, the heat, the 'ooohhh, baby' feeling that I used to get when I was crazy. Imagine! I long to be crazy again." Then she laughed and said, "That's got to be a song title."

Dahlia remembered regretting what she asked Sunny next, which was "Does Norman know about you?" She could tell when Sunny scowled and dropped the armful of blouses she'd been holding on to the bed with a thud that it had been a mistake.

"What's to know? That I take a lot of pills? That I used to have a problem but now it's okay? That's all there is to know, Dahlia," she said, in a way that made it clear the family wanted to convey the message to Norman that that silly old illness was a thing of the past. They were banding together to tell that story.

"Yeah. Okay," Dahlia said, realizing that she was supposed to go along with this, too. Then one morning about a month later, when she stayed over in Sunny's room, she was awakened by the sound of Sunny vomiting in the toilet, and that same day she found herself left out of several whispered conversations, and one day when she came over to bring Sunny some new lyrics she'd written, she was told that Sunny was out of town for a few days, but nobody would tell her where.

Later that same day, when her mother was making dinner and her father was helping in the kitchen, she overheard her mother saying, "What's the point of telling him? Even if he did marry her, a baby would have probably come out deformed because of all the medication. When I was carrying Dahlia, I didn't even take an aspirin. Remember?"

"I remember."

"Who's having a baby?" Dahlia asked as she came in and washed her hands at the kitchen sink just to have an excuse to be in the kitchen.

"Nobody," both of her parents said in unison.

Within a week of Sunny's returning from wherever it was she'd gone, she was found naked on a bus heading north in the San Fernando Valley. When the bus driver tried to help her, she pulled out a pair of sewing scissors she had taken from Aunt Ruthie's sewing box and stabbed the driver in the penis. The police called Uncle Max, who went to bail her out, and since she'd left her own clothes behind on the bus, the police officers had given her a light blue shirt and some socks to wear home.

At home she seemed confused and embarrassed, and Dahlia heard Uncle Max tell her to get dressed so he could take her back to the hospital. Dahlia watched Sunny's eyes get wide and fiery and saw her throw anything she could get her hands on in the kitchen at her father's head, including a mayonnaise jar and a pot that still had beans in it from lunch. She missed him both times, and when he moved toward her, she dodged him and ran out the front door, but Uncle Max was too fast, and he grabbed the back of the blue shirt.

Sunny pulled hard to get away from him, but he was too strong for her. Her makeup was smeared, and she was screaming angrily, punching at him.

"Fucking bastard, no hospital! I'm saner than all of you! Fucking bastard!" she screamed and raged. Finally she tore away from him and was about to make a break for it when he tackled her, just as Norman and his Aunt Rita pulled up to take her to dinner. Uncle Max ignored the approaching car and lifted Sunny to her feet and deposited her into his car. Norman and his aunt watched from their car, and Dahlia stood on the front porch watching, too. Dahlia was numb. The window to Norman's car was open, and Dahlia could hear the appalled voice of Norman's aunt.

"Honey, don't look, don't make eye contact, don't feel guilty. I told you all the stories about how she was a deeply disturbed individual. Just make a U-turn and get out of here before she even sees you." But Norman opened the car door, which made the aunt even more shrill and insistent. "Can't you see that Max is obviously taking her back to the mental hospital? Do not get out of this car!" she ordered Norman.

Norman never looked at his aunt. He stepped out of the car and walked slowly over to Uncle Max's car, where Uncle Max sat in the driver's seat and Sunny sat hunched up in the passenger seat, almost unrecognizable as the beautiful girl Norman adored. Sunny's window was open, and Dahlia watched Norman reach his large hand inside and rest it on her face. Dahlia held her breath, afraid Sunny might bite him or scream for him not to touch her. But Sunny, who had been wild-eyed and raging only a moment before, screaming and protesting against her father's efforts to get her to the car, now looked up at Norman and into his eyes. Dahlia wanted to avert her own eyes then, because, even at her young age, she saw in the look that passed between them their sad realization of all of the things that were never going to be.

"Get better, Marilyn Monroe," Norman said, and he leaned in and kissed her gently on the cheek.

"Will you wait until I do?" Dahlia thought she heard Sunny ask in a choked voice. When Norman was silent in reply, Uncle Max started the car. As a bleary-eyed, blotchy-faced Sunny looked longingly out the window, still beautiful even in that state, he pulled away. Dahlia watched as Norman, his face a mask of sadness, walked slowly back to his aunt's car and got in.

"I told you," she heard Norman's Aunt Rita say. "I told you a million times—she's not stable. Now you see why I swore on my life to your mother that I would put you in a witness-protection program to hide you from that insane girl, and never would I condone a wedding between the two of you. A wedding? Over my dead body!" And then they were gone.

A little over a year later, playing canasta with Rita Horn, Dahlia's mother heard that Norman Burns had gotten married in Florida to the daughter of a cardiologist. After Rose told Dahlia the news at the dinner table, Dahlia went up to her room, lay facedown on her bed, and sobbed. After a while Rose came up to her daughter's room and sat on the bed next to her.

"I know," she said to Dahlia's heaving back. "I always had the same fantasy, that he would wait."

Helene Shephard lived so far out in the San Fernando Valley that one day Seth mentioned to Dahlia that the cost of the gasoline just to get out there was cutting into any profit she made massaging the sweet old woman. Dahlia joked that Helene was so thin that what she saved on massage oil made up for the cost of the gas, but the truth was that she hated the drive, and she continued to see Helene only because she was a longtime client who had started getting massages when she lived in Brentwood and had stuck with Dahlia all these years.

Today, as Dahlia drove in bumper-to-bumper traffic over Beverly Glen and then down Van Nuys Boulevard onto the ramp to the freeway, without any side or rearview mirrors on her car, she wondered why she was bothering. But she knew the shabby reason and was embarrassed by it. Not *very* embarrassed, but it was something she'd never tell anyone or hated to admit even to herself—and that was her secret hope that Helene was going to leave her some money someday.

The old broad really seemed to like her. She asked Dahlia's advice about everything, including what to do about problems she had with her adult children. And always, after the massage, she made it very clear that she needed Dahlia to stay and chat. Now and then Dahlia would decline and pack up the massage table that she brought with her, because Helene didn't have one. But sometimes Helene lured her into staying, and they'd have a long chat, and from time to time Helene would make some joke like "After I'm gone, you'll find something special waiting for you."

Helene had a few married children and some nieces and nephews somewhere, but in all the stories she told Dahlia, it sounded as if she didn't like them very much, so maybe there actually could be a little tidbit in her last will and testament for the nice masseuse who drove so far every week out of the goodness of her heart. Today, by the time Dahlia turned the mirrorless van onto Helene's cul-de-sac in Northridge, she was feeling grumpy. Maybe her blood sugar was low because she hadn't eaten, and she was ten minutes late, and now she was annoyed to see there wasn't even a place to park. There were four cars in Helene's driveway, and every spot on the street was taken, and for some reason the front door to the house was wide open.

Helene must be giving a party, Dahlia thought, and it was probably a brunch. She had obviously forgotten Dahlia was coming, and she'd scheduled a party at her massage time. Well, Dahlia thought irritably, she'd better pay me anyway when she realizes she screwed up. I am not going to be able to make my mortgage payment this month with Margie Kane trying to kill herself and Marty throwing me out because of Sunny's cigarettes. And now there wasn't even Seth, who used to kick in half.

Goddamn it. I am going to march in there and tell Helene she can't do this to me, she thought as she double-parked the van next to a shiny black Lexus. She'd walk in the door, and Helene would see her and be mortified about forgetting. Well, she'd better be mortified enough to give me a check for driving all the way out here, Dahlia thought. Through the open door, she could see a few dozen people standing around holding wineglasses.

Nobody looked over at her as she walked through the living room toward the kitchen, where she and Helene usually sat after the massage and had a cup of tea. There was a big group laughing and chatting in the kitchen, and a dark-haired woman was carefully placing deviled eggs on a platter. There was another woman dressed in a black sweater and white pants. She was filling wineglasses on a tray.

"Uh, hi . . ." Dahlia said to the dark-haired woman. "Is Helene around?"

"Pardon?"

"Helene. We had a twelve o'clock appointment. She obviously forgot to tell me she was having a party. Is she around?"

"Oh, good heavens. Are you Dahlia?"

"Yeah."

"Oh, Dahlia. I am so sad to be the bearer of bad tidings, but my mother died on Thursday. She had a heart attack, and I couldn't find a phone number for you. We buried her this morning, and this is her wake! I'm so glad you came by. You were in her will. Thank you for being here. Want a deviled egg?"

I was in her will, Dahlia thought. Oh, yes! I was in her will. Thank you, God. Thank you, Helene! It was worth all those hours of listening to those endless stories you told me, Dahlia thought, reeling with happiness. God bless you, I'm in your will. I can pay the mortgage this month. "I love deviled eggs," Dahlia said, devouring one and then another, thinking how much better deviled eggs tasted when you were solvent and eating them at your benefactor's wake than when they were all you could afford.

God, she thought, I hope her children don't hate me, a stranger, for being in the will. I mean, they were never around, and I was around once a week. And there *is* that old expression—"You snooze, you lose," kids. An interloper gets her share for being accessible and understanding. Wow! I'm beginning to see a real spot in heaven for myself here. First I rescue my crazy cousin, a major good deed for which there have to be some brownie points offered. Right? And now I find out that I meant so much to this woman who had several children but still put *me* in her last will and testament.

This was amazing. Dahlia wondered how soon she could ask how much Helene was leaving her without sounding too callous. The bad news was that she had to go home without her seventy-five-dollar check. After all, she couldn't exactly say to these folks, Hey, I'm sorry your mother died, but I had her in my appointment book, and I got here at the scheduled time, so cough up the dough she would have paid me for the massage. The good news was that Dahlia was about to get a nice payday and never have to drive out here again, she thought, thrilled that she never followed the impulse she often had to call Helene and tell her to find a masseuse who lived in the Valley.

"Hey, everybody! Whose van is blocking my Lexus?" she heard a voice call out. It was a heavyset man in his fifties with gray hair and a bushy gray beard.

"That's mine," Dahlia said, a rush of excitement passing through her as she wondered if what Helene left her could cover the down payment on a new car or maybe even pay for the whole car. "I'll let him out and move into his spot," she told Helene's daughter. She felt giddy. Full of hope for the first time in so long.

She would go home, figure out what to do about Sunny, then sit down and pay all her bills, knowing that for once they'd be covered. And if the money Helene left her was a lot, maybe she'd even admit the truth to Harry Brenner. Tell him the song was never hers to sell and that if he didn't like any of the ones she was going to play him, the ones she'd written by herself, then tough.

"Great," Helene's daughter said. "I'll go and get you the box."

"Box?"

"Of sweaters. That's what Mother left you. All her old sweaters. She said you really needed them, so my brother and I boxed them up. I can put the box right in your car now. Wasn't that amazingly sweet of her? Some of these sweaters are so old-fashioned you'll crack up when you see them. But I always believe it's the thought that counts. Don't you?"

"I do," Dahlia said, trying to keep the smile plastered on her face, hoping she could wait until she was in her van before she fell apart. She was getting old sweaters—and she was *not* getting seventy-five bucks for the massage. How could she say anything to the daughter about the seventy-five bucks? Give me the dough for your dead mother's massage? Helene had always thought Dahlia's clothes were shabby. This was her nice way of trying to dress up poor pitiful me, Dahlia thought.

The daughter left the room, and Dahlia ate a few more deviled eggs. This house. The children would sell this house on a corner in Northridge, and it was probably worth a million bucks. If Helene felt so sorry for her, why couldn't she have left her a chunk of that instead of a bunch of old sweaters?

"Here they are," Helene's daughter said, returning with a cardboard book box, one flap of which she opened to show Dahlia that it was filled with a pile of brightly colored wool sweaters. The smell of mothballs wafted out of the box. At the curb, after Dahlia put the sweaters in the back of the van and thanked Helene's daughter, she sat at the wheel looking at the stub that was all that was left of her rearview mirror and the rod where the passenger visor had once been. A new car. I thought it was going to be money. Enough money to buy me a new car. I broke up with my boyfriend and moved an insane woman into my life, and now I've lost another client. I can't afford to keep my house. I don't know what I'm going to do.

The bearded man with the Lexus was standing next to the open window looking in at her downcast face with big, sympathetic eyes. "I feel the same way," he said. "She was my aunt, and I was nuts about her." Dahlia nodded and started the van. The guy was obviously waiting for her to pull away so he could get out of his parking spot. "I took care of her during her depression, and she was always a pleasure, even when she was feeling blue," he said.

Yeah, yeah, yeah, Dahlia thought. He probably got the money that could have gone to me. Well, she sure as hell didn't feel like making small talk with him. Besides, she had to get out of there and hurry home to her kidnap victim and her stack of unpaid bills and her empty bed. The guy smiled broadly enough to make his beard lift up to his ears. "Well, sorry to make you move your car, but I have to get back to my office to return some calls. When you do what I do, there's always somebody out there needing to check in," he said.

He was obviously trying to be friendly, hoping she'd jump into a conversation with him, but all Dahlia wanted to say was, Get out of my way or I'll run you over, pal. Now she looked at him coldly.

"Hey, I can tell that you're real upset about losing Helene," he said. "Here's my card. The death of a treasured friend can trigger lots of old feelings in each of us, and I'm here to help if you ever need to talk to someone who specializes in all kinds of emotional-distress syndromes." This had to be a joke. This guy was like some ambulance-chasing lawyer who showed up at the scene of an accident to pass out his card to the victims.

Dahlia glanced at the card, spotted that the guy was some kind of -ologist according to what it said there, and then she stuffed it into the vast black hole that was her purse. Real low-class move, she thought. Soliciting business from the bereaved. The guy smiled a saccharine smile that Dahlia knew had to be the same kind of smile he gave his Aunt Helene to convince her to leave him the money instead of Dahlia.

In an instant she peeled the rattletrap van out noisily and headed home, trying to figure out how in the hell she was going to pay her bills.

fifteen

She could already see there was something wrong as she drove up to her carport. The front windows of the house had swirls and *x*s drawn all over them in some slimy substance, and as she opened the door, she saw that the TV screen in the living room had been defaced the same way.

"Sunny?" she called out, and the angry edge in her voice reminded her of the way Sunny's parents used to call out to her after she'd committed some destructive act as a teenager. The door from the kitchen into the backyard was open, and when Dahlia walked through the kitchen to close it, she saw that the black glass door of the microwave had the *x*s and swirls drawn on it, too. She touched the marks and realized that the *x*s were made with soap, in the same way schoolkids used to soap up people's windows on Halloween. Dahlia rubbed her fingers on the flaky substance, then held them to her nose. Yes, it was soap. Through the back door, she could see Sunny holding a shovel and standing by a mound of dirt in the garden, and she hurried out there.

Sunny spoke without looking at her. "Natalie Wood used to look at her own face and then fix her makeup in the blade of a knife," she said as Dahlia approached. "So I buried all the knives, too."

"Sunny . . ."

Sunny spun on Dahlia now, her eyes wild. "That's why she died! Because they were making the rules about who lives and who dies, and they saw her in the knife blade. They were on the other side of it. You don't have to worry, because I saved you by putting all the knives in the ground."

"You buried my knives?"

"Spoons, too. You can see yourself in both sides of the spoon. Ever notice if you look at yourself on the inside, you're upside down? That's so they can disorient you."

"Sunny, I need that flatware. I can't afford to—"

"Get plastic. It's the only way, and it's also the reason they use it in hospitals. And if you've ever seen your reflection in the microwave, it's because they're there too, so I took care of that. The basic rule is this: If you can see yourself, they can see you. Oh, my God, give me your purse! Right now!"

Dahlia clutched her purse to her chest. What in the hell was Sunny going to do now? It would take days to get the house cleaned. And who knew what this poor woman was capable of doing next? No. Dahlia had to correct the mistake of bringing Sunny back here. Fast. She was destroying the house and everything in it and threatening to get worse.

Sunny's face was blotched with red and her eyes were full of fire as she pulled the purse out of Dahlia's grasp. Dahlia watched wordlessly as Sunny shook the purse madly, dumping the contents on the ground, then ferreted through everything until she found what she wanted. A compact and a lipstick. She opened the compact and, using the lipstick, drew little circles and xs on the compact mirror. Then she broke the mirror off of the compact and threw it in the air. It landed in the bushes. Dahlia, who had been frozen, knew she had to do something to stop this.

"Sunny, listen to me," she said, and as she grabbed her cousin's shoulders, she felt Sunny trembling. "I made a mistake. I brought you here because I thought I could help you and because I thought you needed a break from being in that place in San Diego, but this is not working. You need to be in a place where you can have your medicine controlled, have a more regimented life, be among people who are like you. I was wrong thinking I could handle this. You have to go back. So here's what we'll do—"

Just then the doorbell rang. Who in the hell could it be? Dahlia hurried through the house to the front door and pulled it open to a blast of purple and fuchsia in a breathtaking bouquet of flowers held by a hollow-eyed deliveryman.

"You Miss Gordon?" he asked, and Dahlia nodded, taking the flowers and putting them on the coffee table. Flowers? Who on earth would be sending her flowers? Seth. Maybe Seth wanting to make up, she thought, tugging at the little plastic pitchfork that was strategically placed among the splashy-colored flowers. She removed it and the card it held. "Hang for one second," Dahlia said to the deliveryman, and as she walked, she opened the envelope to pull out the card. *Faith loves your song. It's going to be on her next CD. You've got a sure hit. Contracts to follow. Harry.*

A hit. With a stolen song. A song that came from that lunatic in her yard who was burying her silverware. Someone who didn't give a goddamn about having a hit. She was more interested in ripping apart the contents of Dahlia's purse, which Dahlia hurried outside and knelt to retrieve now, so she could get some money out of her wallet to tip the deliveryman. And as she gathered up her checkbook and her keys and her makeup, a business card landed at her feet. It was the card Helene's nephew, the guy with the beard, had given her an hour before. It said *Joe Diamond, psychopharmacologist.*

As Dahlia handed the deliveryman a few dollars, she could hear Sunny rummaging through kitchen drawers, probably moving on to soaping up cake cutters, metal spatulas, and serving spoons. Now Dahlia was feeling panicky. Maybe she should call this Joe Diamond. Call anyone who might be able to help. In desperation she hurried to the phone and dialed the number on the card.

She didn't have any idea how she'd pay a doctor, how Sunny paid for anything, but the kitchen drawers were all pulled out, her chrome teakettle was soaped up, the house was under siege, and she had to call somebody fast. After three rings she heard what she recognized as Dr. Diamond's gentle voice on his answering machine promising to return the call as soon as possible, and then there was a beep.

"Dr. Diamond, I'm Dahlia Gordon," she heard her own voice quaver as she tried not to cry. She could hear Sunny moving into the bedroom. "We met at Helene Shephard's. I'm the one with the Toyota van. Please call me. I have a real emergency on my hands." From the clattering sounds, she guessed that Sunny was now going through Dahlia's makeup drawer.

"Try to see through *this*, you lousy sons of bitches!" Dahlia heard Sunny say as she put the phone down. Now she rushed to the door of her bedroom to find Sunny digging into every possible cosmetic container that had a mirror and smearing it frantically. Dahlia watched her take a small travel mirror into her bare hands, break it, then throw the pieces into the wastebasket. Dahlia couldn't remember feeling this afraid since she was a child. The tears rose in her eyes, and she sat down on the bed.

"Sunny," she said. "Listen to me. I am going to help you find someone who will get you into some shape to make the trip back to San Diego. You can't do this to me anymore. Or to yourself."

"You're right. I can't do it anymore. But it isn't me." Sunny ripped the lid off a pretty little leather lipstick case and flung it over her head. "This isn't me," she said, making a pronouncement as she looked in Dahlia's eyes in a way that made her almost seem lucid. As if she were telling Dahlia that the drugs and the shock treatments and the years of institutionalization had taken away every shred of who she once was.

But then Dahlia realized that wasn't what she meant at all when she lowered her voice and whispered, "It's the studio fucking audience."

In a stucco building on a corner of Encino, in a small third-floor office, Joe Diamond watched Sunny, whose eyes darted all around the office looking everywhere but at him. Dahlia had just finished telling him everything she knew about Sunny's condition, information that she was embarrassed to admit had a twenty-five-year gap in the middle. Sunny would correct her from time to time and then stand up and pace. Now the affable doctor turned all his attention to Sunny, his eyes following her everywhere she walked.

"You take yourself off the medications because you hate the side effects. Is that right?" he asked. No answer. "Sunny, can you tell me the reason for your non-compliance? Why do you stop taking the meds?"

"Um, could you possibly get rid of those framed photos on the shelves?" Sunny asked, looking down at the floor now. "I can see myself reflected in them, and you know what that means."

Joe Diamond walked over to the shelf, which held several photos of his family, and one at a time he laid each of them facedown.

"Better?"

"Better," Sunny said. She was trembling visibly.

"Ever try just lowering the dose?" he asked.

"Doesn't work. I even smell those pills and I'm a zombie," she said.

"What if I offer you a medication that might let you

play your songs and not see the studio audience?" he asked.

"Wouldn't work that way," she said. "Never works. Doesn't work. Pills do not work, and I won't take them. I am an adult. Not a guinea pig. I have a right not to take medication."

"That's absolutely correct. You do have that right. But with rights come responsibilities. If you don't take medication and you hurt yourself or anyone else, there are consequences. Do you understand that?"

"I understand that you have chrome knobs on your cabinets and if I get close to them I'll be able to see my reflection in them, and you know what that means."

The doctor turned to Dahlia. "I'm going to tell you what I think is going on with her, but you may not want to hear it."

All Dahlia wanted to hear was that the doctor could and would give Sunny some knockout pill that would make her docile so Dahlia could deliver her back to the Sea View. The medicine man had been right. This was way more than she'd bargained for.

Joe Diamond went on. "The only patients I've seen who have symptoms this severe and make it are the ones who have a strong advocate, a partner in their daily progress who acts as a touchstone for them. This disease is a monster, and nobody should have to fight a monster alone."

Dahlia was afraid of where he was going with this, and she felt edgy and uncomfortable as he looked at Sunny now, thought about what he was going to say, and then asked her, "Sunny, what if I gave you some-

thing new to try and the three of us were a team—
you, me, and your cousin? She'd be the captain, and
she'd make sure that you took the new medication for
just a period of weeks so we could begin to get some
kind of an accurate picture of how you respond to it."

"Whoa! The captain?" Dahlia said, her eyes wide. "I
don't even have a plant in my house. I've never even
had a cat. I can't be the captain. I mean, I'm all for her
getting better, but . . . I'm an out-of-work songwriter
trying to survive as a masseuse, and I'm just in your
office today because I made a mistake and took her
out of the place in San Diego. She needs someone like
the nice guy down there with the little cups who
shows up every day and passes out the drugs."

There, she thought. That made my position pretty
clear. But the doctor seemed to ignore what she'd said,
and he never took his eyes from Sunny.

"Sunny, why don't we all talk about putting you on
a new antipsychotic for a month or six weeks, just
enough time to get an idea if it's effective, and then re-
group, with Dahlia not necessarily supervising but
helping." Now he was backpedaling a little, playing
both of them to get the desired result, Dahlia thought.
Pretty smart of him to make it sound as if Dahlia's job
wouldn't be that big after she told him she couldn't
and wouldn't handle it. But there was no way on the
planet she was going to get sucked into being Sunny's
nurse, especially now that she'd seen what kind of
damage Sunny could do. Songs or no songs.

"I'm not taking anything new, with her or without
her," Sunny said, and Dahlia almost cheered "Amen."

There you go, Doc, she thought. She just gave you the big "No way, José."

Joe Diamond sighed. "Sunny, do you know what meds you were taking when you stopped?"

"Navane, Haldol, Thorazine, Stelazine. Take the cup, suck it up, lose your brain, get pimply and quiet, drool and limp. I've been in shock therapy, rock therapy, dance therapy, and one very cute attendant in one of the hospitals even gave me fuck therapy. I liked it," she said, laughing, "but he got fired when they found out he was giving it to everyone. Girls *and* boys."

"Would you let me prescribe a drug I think might help?" Joe Diamond said. Whoa, Dahlia thought. This guy won't quit.

"No."

"Sunny," Joe Diamond said, and then he waited until she looked at him before he went on. "Let me ask you this: If you were locked in a room that only had one door and I gave you a key ring with hundreds of keys, wouldn't you try every key until you found the one that worked so you could escape?" he asked quietly. Sunny didn't answer. Nice one, Dahlia thought. That key-ring analogy was pretty good.

"You would," the doctor said softly, "and I'm willing to give you the key ring to get you out of the prison you're in. The first key may not work, but if we keep trying, maybe we can get you to a place where you can play your songs and not see those people on the other side of every mirror."

"Ha!" Sunny said. "They're there no matter what I take. I have never *not* seen them. Just because they don't bother you and you may not see them doesn't mean they didn't do away with Natalie Wood and Marilyn Monroe and Grace Kelly and Princess Di. Beautiful women who looked in the mirror a lot."

"What if I told you the drug might make those people on the other side of mirrors disappear?" he asked. His voice was kind.

"I don't need it. If I play my songs loud enough and sing along, I don't need any meds. And anyway, I have to pee," she said. She looked over at Dahlia with her hand raised as if she were a child and Dahlia were the teacher.

"I'll get you the key," the doctor said, getting up and walking to the door of his office, "but I have to warn you, there are mirrors in the ladies' room."

"Dahlia will come with me, and she won't let me look."

The doctor looked at Dahlia, and she nodded reluctantly and sighed. How in the hell did this happen? Now she even had to take the patient to the bathroom. The key was on a large round metal ring, and Dahlia took Sunny's shaky arm and walked her out the door of Joe Diamond's office and across the hall.

"I'm afraid they'll see me," Sunny said.

"Don't look," Dahlia told her.

"It's not me looking at them. It's them looking at us, and I need a cigarette."

Dahlia turned the key and pushed open the door to the institutional ladies' room. There were four rectangular mirrors above a bank of four sinks.

"I can't do it," Sunny said. "I'll pee in my pants instead. You tell them to leave me alone."

"Here, go into this cubicle right now," Dahlia said, turning Sunny away from the mirrors and propelling her into a stall with a toilet.

"No."

"Sunny, go in. Close the door so they can't see you. I'll keep them busy."

After Sunny hurried into the cubicle and slammed the door and Dahlia heard the lock click shut, she walked over to the mirrors. She was bleary-eyed, and she had to get Sunny something to calm her and take her back to the house to sleep, because she had a massage to do in less than an hour. I'm trapped. How could I think this was a good idea? She could hear Sunny in the cubicle fumbling with her clothes.

"You have to be tough with them," Sunny shouted out loudly to Dahlia. "Tell them you know what they're trying to do."

Now Sunny would come out and have to wash her hands. How was she going to stand at the sink and wash her hands without looking in the mirror above the sink? Dahlia wondered.

"Tell them!" Sunny hollered now.

Dahlia pulled the lever on the paper towel machine three times. She wet and soaped the first piece of paper towel, saturated the second with warm water, and left the third one dry.

"Goddamn you, Dahlia, tell them!" Sunny shouted from the cubicle.

"What do you want me to say?" Dahlia asked her.

"You should say, 'I know you are up to no good, and when people are evil, they always pay the price. So don't think you can get away with anything, because

God can see you, and he has ways of making sure the devil gets his due.' Say it."

Dahlia looked at her own weary face in the mirror, and as Sunny repeated the message, Dahlia delivered it into the mirror line by line, and the irony of the situation that was making her deliver those words into the mirror at herself didn't escape her. "I know you are up to no good, and when people are evil, they always pay the price. So don't think you can get away with anything, because God can see you, and he has ways of making sure the devil gets his due." It was true, she thought, and she was already paying the price for her greed.

Sunny emerged smiling from the cubicle, and a queasy Dahlia whisked her toward the bathroom door, as far away from the mirrors as possible. Then she washed, rinsed, and dried her cousin's hands the way she remembered her mother washing and drying her hands and Sunny's after they'd played all day at the beach.

"I can't make her take it," Joe Diamond told Dahlia as they stood in the foyer of his office. "I can give you six weeks' worth of a drug I think she ought to try and hope that you can convince her to do it. It's not going to be a quick fix. There's no such thing with this illness. It may not even work at all. There may be times when she seems even more agitated than she was before she started taking it. But by the end of four weeks, you could see some subtle changes."

"Four weeks?" Dahlia emitted a nervous laugh. "Oh, believe me, she's not staying in L.A. that long," she told him. "First of all, she'll lose her spot in the board-and-care if she does. She has to go back to San Diego or to a hospital or something. It's going to take me a month just to clean my house after what she did to it."

Joe Diamond went on talking quietly to Dahlia, as if she were the one who was the mental patient, in a voice that let her know he was completely disregarding what she had just said and instead was forging ahead with his plan. "There are plenty of what we call atypical antipsychotics for her to try, drugs that might bring her around to feeling a lot more like herself. New ones that have very high success ratios. But like they say in the twelve-step programs, 'It only works if you work it.' Somebody has to watch over her.

"Unfortunately," he continued, "at those board-and-care places, nobody is going to monitor her or worry about how compliant she is, or pay attention to how the crossover to a new drug is working, how to find an effective dose, how to monitor the side effects versus the benefits. I don't blame you if you don't want to do it. It's fraught with relapse and disappointment. Like the myth of Sisyphus, the rock rolls back, and it requires really big shoulders to keep pushing it up that hill." He was trying to sell Dahlia, and she wasn't going to buy it.

"I don't have big shoulders," she said, thinking how much her own shoulders ached right now. She shook her head at Joe Diamond as he handed Sunny a bag of samples.

"Then I guess you'd better take her back to San Diego," he said, patting Sunny gently on the arm.

"I have no clients on Saturday," Dahlia said. "I'll drive her back then."

"Okay," Sunny said, staring at her feet.

Dahlia hated the look of disappointment she saw on Joe Diamond's face, and all the way home she told herself that no songs were worth what she'd have to put up with to keep Sunny around for another month. On the way down to the van, she'd seen Sunny pause and freeze for an instant as she stared at a building on Ventura Boulevard two doors from the one they had just exited. It was a tall modern building that glistened brightly as the large panes of reflecting blue glass mirrored back the passing cars and trucks and people in the street.

"That must be their headquarters," Sunny had said under her breath as Dahlia turned her and moved her toward the van.

On Friday morning she took Sunny to Nordstrom in Westwood and let her choose three new outfits, the prices of which added up to two hundred dollars. While Dahlia put the charges on her already overburdened Visa card, Sunny watched a man in a tuxedo sit at a baby grand piano on the first floor and play old standards to entertain the shoppers. Okay, Dahlia thought, looking over at her cousin as Sunny watched the man, fascinated. I am about to get rid of her and I'm feeling guilty, so I'm buying her the clothes I can't afford. I don't need a therapist to tell me that.

On Friday evening, after Dahlia massaged Leroy Berk and then his sister who was visiting from New York, she massaged Margie Kane and then Risa

Braverman. Then she came home and made burritos for Sunny, which were Sunny's favorite dinner, and while she was washing the dishes, she heard Sunny talking to someone out in the backyard. Dahlia sighed. What had she mistakenly left out there that had a reflective surface? But as she approached the door, she could tell that the conversation Sunny was having was a quiet and tender one. Not hostile and raging like the ones she had with mirrors.

"You'll be okay. I love you, and I'll make sure nothing bad will happen to you, I promise. Maybe when I go away, Dahlia will take over for me. I'll ask her tonight before we go to sleep." Sunny was sitting under a tree talking gently into her hand when she spotted Dahlia. Her eyes were red, and her face was tear-stained as she slowly lifted her hand to show Dahlia what was in it.

"This little squirrel must have hurt itself, because it was stuck in some ivy just outside the window of my room, so I've been taking care of her. I'm so worried about leaving her. Because I see her getting a bit stronger, and it warms my heart. Look at her little face, and her sweet brown eyes. I've been feeding her with this dropper you had in the medicine cabinet in my bathroom. You'd be amazed at how much better she is already. And I'm afraid if I leave her she could . . ." Sunny's lip trembled as if she might cry. "I mean, I named her and everything, and she really seems to perk up when I'm there. Will you take care of her when I leave?"

No shot I am taking care of any damn squirrel, Dahlia thought. The minute Sunny's out of here, I send that nasty rodent to the SPCA.

"What'd you name her?" Dahlia asked, trying to sidestep making any promises.

"Rose. After your mom. She has that sweet nature that reminded me of Aunt Rose. Look how frail she is. Even her tiny chirping sounds are so faint. When I go back to the Sea View, promise you'll take care of her?"

"I don't think so, Sun, but maybe you could take her with you."

"Oh, I couldn't do that. She needs to be near her family who live in the trees around here. Don't you remember how our mothers always told us about the importance of family?" Sunny asked.

"Yeah," Dahlia said. "I remember." Then she walked closer to get a better look at the squirrel. Cute little thing, she thought, if you like rodents. And then she listened as Sunny, trying to calm the damned thing, hummed a gorgeous lullaby she was improvising on the spot.

sixteen

*H*ere's how it feels to massage Risa Braverman: frightening, Dahlia thought. Rubbing tenderly, carefully, and trying not to shudder visibly when your hands slide over the number on her arm that evokes images of what Dahlia knew could never be as frightening as the nightmare Risa had survived in Auschwitz. Dahlia had read enough about the horrors of the Jews in Eastern Europe that when she found herself complaining about her problems to Risa, she stopped short, realizing how inane they were. Today she heard herself going on and on about Sunny and was just ready to apologize when Risa laughed a bubble of a laugh.

"So you let her stay? Because of the squirrel? And now she's actually been living in the house with you—and the squirrel, too?" Risa asked, her face down in the faceplate as Dahlia worked on her back.

"Just for the time being," Dahlia said. For a woman in her eighties, Risa was unusually muscular and lithe, and she was always eager for conversation, usually questioning Dahlia about her life. "I mean, first I let her stay because I couldn't tear her away from this baby squirrel, which is now getting really active and has just about healed. It's kind of amazing how she cured it. And brilliantly enough, she named it Rose, after my late mother, so I'm sure that's what must have made me get all mushy about the damn thing. Then, all of a sudden, my massage business picked up a lot, and I was too busy to realize she's been at my house for nearly three weeks. But I have to do something, or she's going to lose her place in that board-and-care in San Diego, and that would be a huge problem."

"You are a good person. In the old country, we always had the families living with us. The meek and the halt and the lame. And in my family . . . that was everybody," Risa said, and she let out a laugh at her own joke. "It is the way it was supposed to be. You take care, you are responsible for others. But nowadays nobody does it, because they don't have such a good heart like you."

A good heart. A flare of shame rose through Dahlia. A good heart had nothing to do with it. Her motive had been to get the music out of Sunny.

"Oh, I agree. I think we were meant to take care of one another in this world," Dahlia said.

Risa lifted her head and looked hard at Dahlia. "We had a woman in my barracks named Leah who had only one possession left." Dahlia sat on the bed. Risa rarely told her stories about the Holocaust, and Dahlia wasn't going to rush her or interrupt her. "Somehow she had managed to keep from the Nazis her mother's wedding ring. She knew someone who worked in the kitchen, and she traded that ring to him for bread. Then she shared the bread with the rest of us. She didn't have to share, but she did. When a working woman like you takes the time to go and get a person like your cousin who needs you so badly, and then lets her live in her home, it is a mitzvah. You know what is a mitzvah? A wonderful deed."

It was time for Risa to turn over, and when she sat up she grabbed tightly on to Dahlia's arm with her veiny, skinny hand. "You are a righteous human being, and I am proud of you," Risa said intensely. Dahlia couldn't look into her eyes, certain that a woman who had witnessed as much evil as Risa had would see right through her ruse.

Sunny had okay days and bad ones. She was still refusing to take any medication, but on the whole she seemed slightly less agitated, relieved to be in what were, compared to the life she'd been leading before Dahlia came for her, idyllic surroundings. And when Dahlia looked at her little "tree house," as Sunny called it, through Sunny's eyes, her tiny place took on a kind of rustic beauty, nestled there among all the greenery. Maybe it did need a paint job, but it was cozy and quaint. And now that Dahlia had removed the soap from all the places where Sunny had smeared it, the house was back to normal.

Happily, Sunny hadn't made any more attempts to destroy anything. She played solitaire on the computer and watched TV. Her worst times were at night, when she would pace for a while, then put herself down in front of the piano and create the most amazing tunes. Dahlia would sit up in bed, not wanting to walk out there and distract her, but she listened carefully and marveled at how consistently haunting and melodic all the songs were. And often she would write lyrics for them, lyrics she would never show Sunny but instead put aside in the hope that someday Sunny would change her mind about selling the songs.

"Sunny," she said to her one night when the song Sunny played was so soulful that Dahlia had to go into the living room to get closer so she could watch her cousin's hands on the keys to see how she was playing it, "that song is so special. What are you going to do with it?" she asked.

"Hold it in my heart," Sunny said as she got up from the piano bench and walked into her bedroom.

The Jet Delivery truck rattled to a stop next to Dahlia's carport, and the chunky woman in the white shorts and black shirt pounded on the door. Dahlia opened the door and sighed when she saw the big envelope from Harry Brenner. She felt rattled when she opened it to find a stack of papers with a note on top printed on stationery that had a G clef next to Harry's name: *Hey, doll. Sign here and make some big bucks. Faith is gonna do your song, but you have to get these contracts back to me ASAP. Your manager, Harry.*

She could hear Sunny rummaging around in the kitchen, and the papers felt hot in her hand. She was holding a contract that said Dahlia had written the music and the lyrics to the song "What's Happened to Me?" and another contract saying that Harry, as her manager, would take 15 percent of Dahlia's earnings on this and every other song she wrote and sold hereafter. Then there were some other papers she didn't understand, papers that, if she'd received them under ordinary circumstances, she would probably have run by a lawyer. But how could she ask a lawyer if these papers were okay? They were a lie. She shouldn't send them back to Harry. She should burn them and tell him the truth. This was her last chance to get out of it. Last chance to be honest.

"Hey, Dahl, aren't you supposed to be doing another massage soon?" Sunny called out. Dahlia's heart was pounding, and she suddenly had a nagging headache. *You are a righteous human being, and I am proud of you.* She could still see the look in Risa's eyes when she'd said that. And now she was going to send this contract off with a lie. Maybe it wasn't too late to change her mind. Of course Harry Brenner would laugh her out of any chance she ever had to be in the business if she called him and told him she was withdrawing the song. And if she told him Sunny wrote it, Sunny would have to sign it over so Faith Hill could sing it, and there was no way in the world Sunny would ever do that.

Unless maybe there was some chance that Dahlia could make her change her mind. Sunny did seem a little more stable this last week or so. Rose, the squirrel, was hopping around in the backyard every morning, and that seemed to have a positive effect on her. Dahlia had to take another shot at making Sunny understand what a big deal selling this song could be. She wouldn't have to mention that she had passed off the song as her own. She could just say she'd penciled in some lyrics that seemed to fit and had happened to play it for Harry and that he liked it, and then she'd mentioned to him that her cousin might be interested in the two of them selling it.

"Just on my way out," she called back to Sunny.

She couldn't wait. Harry had made it clear that she had to do something right away about these papers. That meant she had to send them back to him accompanied by a letter that said "Here is my signature" or "Here is the signature of the person who actually wrote the song" or "I am withdrawing the song because I didn't write it by myself and don't have the right to sell it." No. That would be a mistake. Dahlia shuffled through the papers again and again. These days the music business was so screwy that selling a song, unless you were a known insider, was nearly impossible. A huge star wanted to record this one. To hold it back would be really dumb.

Sunny came into the room carrying a stack of Seth's old magazines. She loved sitting for hours turning all the glossy colorful pages of the ones that still arrived in the mailbox daily because Seth had never bothered to send in his change of address. Now she collapsed on the sofa, and Dahlia wandered over to sit across from her until she looked up.

"Feeling okay today?" Dahlia asked.

Sunny nodded. She was thumbing through Us magazine. "I'm always a little better during the day. Not so great at night. But I make it through by coming in here and playing songs."

"Your songs are awesome," Dahlia said, thinking that was a good segue into the subject and hoping she didn't sound as phony as she felt.

"Thanks," Sunny said innocently. "You always liked my songs." Dahlia saw Sunny stop to look closely at a photo in *People* of Jennifer Aniston. "Can I tear this out?" she asked, holding it up.

"Sure," Dahlia said, wondering why on earth Sunny wanted a picture of Jennifer Aniston. She steered the subject back to the songs. "I am a thousand percent sure the world will like your songs, too. You could probably sell them for a lot of money."

Sunny put the magazine down and looked her cousin in the eye. "Dahlia . . . I don't want a lot of money," she said evenly. "I want something that no money in the world is ever going to buy me. I want my brain to be still. I want my world to not be badgered by demons. I want peace. But my music is a part of me, and I am going to keep it that way. I don't want to give it away or sell it. I won't let someone else have a piece of me, because to me it's like giving away my arm or my leg.

"I write songs for me because I need to. Because they flow out of me. I don't write them for the world. You like sharing yourself with the world. You sold a song because that meant something different to you than it does to me. You sell your services to go and touch naked people. That's you, not me. I couldn't do that. I'm not selling. I write songs for the same reason I breathe: because I'm supposed to. I may not have much, but I'm keeping what I have inside me. When we were kids, I did those shows for other people, and I always hated it. So please stop trying to get me to do it."

Dahlia held in the torrent of words that rushed through her mind. I touch naked bodies because I have to eat, and I couldn't sell my songs. But you can and you should, because you could buy the mental hospital and all the doctors in the world to help you if you did. In the meantime I can't afford you. I can't feed you and let you live here forever. I need to pay for this life, and you could pitch in and buy us both a better life with your songs, especially if you'd let me write them with you. But instead of saying any of that, she went into the kitchen and made them both lunch.

After lunch Sunny went outside and lay on her back in the grass, her arms spread and her head arched up to get as much sun as she could on her face.

"Back later," Dahlia called out. No, no, no, she said to herself as she walked out of the house toward the van. It's ridiculous for Sunny to hold these fabulous songs in her heart. I will sell this song in spite of her. And I won't worry about it until the check comes and it's such a big one that she has a tax problem. She may not think she needs money, but she does, and when she gets it, she'll love the feeling of having it so much that she'll want to write more songs, and I'll write the lyrics, and we'll be as famous as her precious Leiber and Stoller. She doesn't know what she's talking about.

I am doing the right thing, Dahlia told herself again and again as she put the signed contracts on the passenger seat of the van and drove down the hill to drop them at a FedEx box. Besides, she thought, there was always a chance, a good chance, that nothing would happen with the song. But she couldn't let this opportunity pass. Even as she held the FedEx envelope up to the slot in the drop box, she felt afraid, knowing that this was a crime, not sure what the worst part of the crime was. Tricking Sunny? Lying to Harry? Surely Harry didn't give a damn, as long as he owned a piece of the song. Sick, I am sick, Dahlia thought. Why don't I just go home and write my own songs?

She knew how fickle artists could be. One minute they loved something, and the next minute they hated it. Sometimes a song could get recorded by the artist and still never make it to the CD after the producer and the artist listened to the way it sounded up against all of the other songs. Maybe, after all of Dahlia's raging guilt, there wouldn't be anything to worry about. Maybe Faith Hill would change her mind.

Certainly Dahlia was not about to tell her massage clients that she wasn't going to be a masseuse anymore so she could go back to the music business. Her massage business was actually starting to pick up even more. Margie Kane had left her cheating plastic-surgeon husband and, contrary to her fears, had moved into a beautiful condo in a high-rise on Wilshire and was calling Dahlia twice a week to come and give massages to her and to her new boyfriend, a yoga teacher. And since Marty Melman had hurt his back, he needed Dahlia to come in to work on him several times a week, so he was being a little bit nicer to her, and the money was good.

That evening she steered the mirrorless van up Marty's driveway, promising herself no matter how obnoxious he was to her, she'd ignore it. She'd breathe deeply and not let him rattle her. *"You sell your services to go and touch naked people."* Imagine Sunny saying that to her! How about *healing* naked people? That's what she did. Sunny was getting on her nerves. It was definitely time to get her back to the Sea View.

Dahlia jammed on the brakes when she saw Marty's Rolls-Royce backing out of the garage with a tanned and dressed-up Marty at the wheel, and angrily she pulled up behind him to block his exit. He's leaving. He's going out on a date, he's completely forgotten about me, the son of a bitch. When Marty saw it was Dahlia's van that was in the way of his backing the Rolls into the driveway, he leaned on the horn, and it blared loudly. Dahlia jumped out of the van and ran around to the driver's side of Marty's elegant silver automobile. She could smell his aftershave wafting toward her.

"Forget about me?" she asked. Hoping at least there would be the hint of chagrin on his face.

"Not at all," he said, looking at her chest. "How could I ever forget about you, you hot little tootsie? But I have a screening in ten minutes, so you'd better move that blight you drive out of my way. You still get to oil up a naked guy, because I offered your services to my houseguest, who's hoping you'll throw in a blow job."

Dahlia didn't laugh at his feeble joke. "You mean, he's there now?"

"Yeah. He owns an ad agency in New York. Grew up in my old neighborhood, so move the van before I call a tow truck, and then go inside and make him happy."

Great. Now he was trading her services off to a friend without even asking her if it was okay. She got into the van and parked it as Marty drove the Rolls off into the dusk.

"Mr. Kroll is in the shower," Victor told her. "I can hear the water running, but he'll be out soon. I already set up the table for you in the guest room."

Dahlia made her way through the upstairs hallway, passing the photos she sometimes stared at when Marty was late. Marty with Warren Beatty and Annette Bening, Marty with Sidney Poitier, Marty with Julia Roberts. In the pretty green guest room, she sat on the bed, then jumped to her feet when the bathroom door opened and there stood Danny Kroll. He was a vision of a man, slim and dark-haired and tan, wrapped in a white terry-cloth bathrobe, hair wet and flyaway, and his beautiful brown eyes were taking her in.

"Lily, right?" he asked.

"Dahlia," she corrected him, and he grinned a white-toothed grin.

"I knew it was some flower, but I don't know from flowers. I grew up in New York City. I'm Danny. Nice to meet you." He was a strikingly handsome man in his late forties. "So you have the pleasure of massaging Melman every week? Gee, there's a dubious honor. I hope you charge him by the pound," he said, and they both laughed as he unself-consciously dropped his robe on a nearby chair.

He was perfect-looking, and Dahlia found her heart running a little too fast. She loved the expression on his face, the self-assured way he sat on the table, pulled up the sheet, and grinned at her. She felt as uncomfortable as a teenager, with that rattled feeling of rushing hormones. Oil, where had she put the oil? Danny was lying on his stomach now, and she pulled the sheet up over his fantastic rear end and started working on his left leg.

"Marty tells me you're a songwriter," she heard him say with his face down on the faceplate. Now, there was a surprise. She figured Marty would have told him something sleazy about her. "Said he felt bad about not using your song in his new picture."

She was rubbing the back of his left calf. He must be a runner, she thought dreamily, imagining him jogging in Central Park with his pretty wife, and then she glanced up at his left hand lying outside the sheet and smiled to herself when she saw he wasn't wearing a ring.

"He changed the title of the movie. My song was the same as the original title of the film. That's why I brought it to him in the first place," she said.

"What was it?"

" 'Stay by My Side.' "

"How does it go? Can you sing it?"

Dahlia's heart fluttered, and her old shyness took over. "Oh, it's kind of a sweet little melody. Nothing profound. It's catchy, though."

Maybe she should shut up now. Usually men clients

didn't like to talk or be talked to during their massages. Most of the women clients blabbed away from the minute they got onto the table until the minute they got off. Sometimes the men would shush her even if she were just asking them a question that could help her know how to adjust her touch.

"That firm enough?" she asked Danny.

"Perfect," he said. "So go on and sing it for me. I use jingles every day in my business. If it's catchy enough, maybe I can use it in a commercial."

"Oh, that's nice of you but—"

"C'mon!"

"My voice is—"

"Hey, Barry Manilow got his start writing jingles for commercials. Don't sneer at it."

"Oh, I'm not, it's just that—"

"No excuses," Danny said, lifting himself up onto his forearms to look at her. God, he was handsome. Dahlia flushed. "I insist."

She cleared her throat. "Stay by my side forever. Stay by my side, my friend. . . ." She sang the whole song for him, hearing her own voice sound nearly as childlike as it had on those tapes when she was eleven, probably because she was so taken by this amazing-looking man that she felt like a child. When she finished, he sat up to applaud.

"It's perfect," he said grinning. "I'll bet I can find ten clients who'd love that. A pet food, a kid's teddy bear, a Band-Aid commercial. The song is just right for my uses. I'll be over at Marty's office tomorrow and get him to give me the CD you gave him."

Dahlia started to say, "Oh, no, you can't," but then

she stopped herself. What was the point in telling him that the song was written with a partner who wanted to keep her music to herself? He was probably just being polite anyway, and once she walked out of here, she'd never see him again. Danny rolled over onto his stomach, and Dahlia was sure it was just another phony showbiz promise that he'd use the song, so why bother to go into all the complications?

"Now," he said, "let's have some more massaging and then dinner." Dinner. He said dinner, and Dahlia felt herself hoping he meant with her. "I want you to tell me all about the rest of the songs and the rest of your life, and then I can tell you what Marty was like when we were little kids—which was the same nasty, obnoxious jerk he is right now."

Dahlia giggled. He *did* mean dinner with her. He was taking her to dinner. Or maybe just downstairs, where the chopping girls and Victor would fix them something. Then Marty would come home and find them together and pee in his yellow underpants to see that Dahlia, the masseuse, was his buddy's date. Of course she'd have to bring a doggy bag home for Sunny, because Sunny was waiting for her to come home and make dinner.

Dahlia felt so good thinking ahead to their date that she gave Danny Kroll a brilliant massage, her hands and the oil kneading and manipulating, soothing and caressing, warming and coaxing and calming his body until, by the end of the hour, he'd fallen into a deep sleep. She decided not to wake him. Instead she'd leave her business card on his chest with her phone number on it and run home to shower and change so she'd look great when she joined the gorgeous Danny for dinner.

All the way home, she imagined herself at a candlelit dinner, gazing across the table at Danny Kroll. She probably should have shaken him awake to tell him she was leaving. No, this was better. Stopping at home would give her a chance to make herself look good. She'd rummage through her old jewelry box full of fake and funky earrings, the box that used to belong to her mother, and dig out some sexy bauble. In her mind she ran through the possible outfits she would wear, as she hurried into Domino's and ordered a medium pizza with pepperoni for Sunny, then placed the box on the passenger seat and propelled the van up Laurel Canyon.

Sunny was asleep in her room with the door open just a crack. Dahlia could hear her snoring. The phone was ringing, so she grabbed it.

"H'lo?"

"Stay by my side forever. Stay by my side, my friend." It was Danny's voice singing to her. "See how catchy it is? I know it already. I'm going to find a spot for it, pretty Dahlia, and make you rich." He thought she was pretty. "Why didn't you wake me? Should we meet in a little while for a bite?" He liked her. This was the kind of man she should have been with all along. "How 'bout if I come over? Tell me where you are. I know my way around L.A. I used to live here."

"Not possible for you to come over," she said as Sunny's snores erupted in a series of loud spurts.

"Aha! You have a husband? A boyfriend? A few children?" he guessed.

An insane cousin probably wasn't going to come up on the list he was running by her. "A sleeping relative," she offered.

"I won't wake him or her. I'm a stealth lover," he pressed. A kind of heat rushed through her that she hadn't felt since the early days with Seth. This sexy man seemed to have all the qualities she craved in a mate. All the qualities that Seth didn't have. And somehow, even though she'd come in through the back door of his friend's mansion, he still seemed to take her seriously. Didn't talk to her in the condescending way Marty did and didn't leer at her. The first thing he'd asked her about was her music. No wonder she liked him.

"Do you know where Laurel Canyon is? I live on a little street off Laurel Canyon. Here's how you get here," she heard herself say. Mistake, she thought, this is a terrible mistake for a million reasons. But she was so lonely and so in need of treating herself to some pleasure that she allowed herself to say yes. Sunny was a heavy sleeper. Maybe Danny could come over for a drink and they could just talk, and Sunny would sleep through the whole visit.

After she showered, she opened the turquoise silk jewelry box that used to sit on her mother's dresser. It was filled with the odds and ends of costume jewelry her mother had always loved. Black jet-bead earrings, a cloisonné butterfly pin, crystal and silver bangle bracelets that looked as if the beads came from a hobby shop, a string of fake pearls, brightly jeweled rings, so fake their bands could be squeezed or expanded to fit any size finger, a jeweled choker made of paste stones, and a pair of gold hoop earrings.

As she touched each of them, she silently asked her mother to help her choose the bauble that would transform her into the kind of woman Danny Kroll could fall for. In the end she settled for crystal clip earrings with pearls hanging from them that her mother adored, and for a flash, as she leaned in to the mirror to check the angle of the earring on her earlobe, she thought how much she looked like her mother.

"Rose and Dahlia. Two flowers together in the vase," Rose Gordon would say to her as she pulled her little girl onto her lap. And Rose even smelled like a flower, always dusting herself with Shalimar bath powder and then using the cologne, too. Rose and Dahlia never argued, and Dahlia never got tired of her mother's hugs or had the thoughts she heard coming from teenage girls at school who referred to "my bitch mother." Maybe, Dahlia thought later, it was because Rose was always so busy at work and not waiting at the house for her daughter to bring home triumphs at school so she could live vicariously. Maybe it was because Dahlia was an only child, so prized that everything she did was perfect in Rose's eyes.

Mommy, Dahlia thought, look down and make this man appreciate me. Then she heard Danny's car driving up to the carport.

When he stepped inside the front door, he took her into his arms for what began as a friendly hug, but then, unexpectedly, he kissed her. His kiss tasted like mint mouthwash. It was a deep, searching, earth-shattering, knees-turn-to-jelly kiss, and then, as if he'd been in the house before, he began moving her toward the bedroom.

"That massage was so incredible, I thought I ought to return the favor," he said.

Dahlia let herself be led, delighted that it was dark and the house was in shadows, so everything looked quaint rather than dilapidated. And then he was removing her sweater, fondling her, and kissing her everywhere, moving her gently onto the bed. Dropping his own clothes to the floor, gracefully extracting a condom from his pocket, and placing the car keys he still had in his hand and the sunglasses he removed from the top of his head on her bedside table.

"Dahlia, you're so beautiful." He was exquisitely expert, so smooth, so sure of every move. His hands pressing and touching her seemed practiced and part of a routine he knew very well. But she didn't care if this was a con. She wanted it to work, needed to be swept away, so she relaxed and soon felt herself sinking into that other world where all that mattered were his hands, his breath on her, his taste. With Seth it took her so much longer to get to this fever pitch, maybe because he was so tender and this man was so aggressive, coming at her, moving with her, and she had a fleeting worry that their sounds would wake Sunny.

But in an instant Sunny was forgotten, and Dahlia exploded in a blaze in Danny's arms, and he collapsed on top of her. She wanted to say something but had no idea what. Maybe now he would put on his clothes and leave. She wasn't sure what was supposed to happen now. Seth was the only man she'd been with in years. Seth. What a funny time to miss him. She was already feeling the regret creeping through her that she'd tried not to think about earlier. Why had she allowed this stranger to come over here? And then she remembered Sunny telling her, so long ago, that she was too young to understand what it meant, that the best way to really get to know a man underneath his façade was to have sex with him.

"That's when you see the primitive them, without the act they put on for the world, and I live to see that. . . . They turn into these bright red devils, all stiff and hard and tense and panting," she'd said many times. But though Danny had been stiff and hard and panting, he wasn't at all primitive. His lovemaking had been methodical, orderly, systematic, and now that it was over, it made her long for Seth. Seth who always fell asleep wrapped around her, kissing her back and the back of her neck and her hair as she drifted off. Danny rolled to the other side of the bed, grabbed the pillow that was Seth's favorite, and was asleep in a minute.

Dahlia, feeling sad and very lonely, pulled the comforter up over herself and set the alarm for six so she could wake him and shoo him out the door before Sunny got up in the morning. At dawn, when she remembered in a dream that he was next to her, she opened her eyes to check the clock and gasped in horror when she looked right into the eyes of Sunny.

"Oh, baby!" Sunny hollered. She was in the bed, between Dahlia and Danny, completely naked and grinning in Dahlia's face.

"You had sex with a stranger!" Sunny said, then let out a loud peal of laughter. Dahlia sat up and looked over at Danny, who sat up and looked at Sunny and then over at Dahlia. "The best kind!" Sunny shrieked out. Then she sang to some improvised tune. "Sex with a stranger. The very best kind . . ." so loudly that Danny's face filled with horror at this lunatic in the bed next to him. "When you were little, you used to think that sex was going to be yucky. Ooooh, weren't you wrong? He's sooo cute."

"Sunny, get out of here and go to your room," Dahlia said through clenched teeth. Danny was out of the bed now, pulling on his clothes from the floor and hurrying into them like a character in a bedroom comedy who's just been caught with the wrong woman.

"She's my cousin," Dahlia said. "I'm taking care of her. She's got problems."

Danny smiled a forced smile and tried to avert his eyes from Sunny's nakedness. He was partly dressed, and a very bright morning sun was pouring in through the bedroom window. That was probably why he chose that moment to put on his mirrored sunglasses. As he did, Sunny looked into them, saw her reflection, and let out what sounded like a war whoop as she lunged for Danny.

"Get out of this house! We know what you want and what you're doing! You're the devil!" she screamed as she tore the glasses from his terrified face. Then she snapped them in half and threw them at the wall as Danny ran for the front door. In a minute Dahlia could hear his car start and hear Sunny laughing wildly as she ran into her room and slammed the door behind her.

"Sunny!" Dahlia screamed so hard it made her throat hurt. "Goddamn it, that's the end! I am giving you two choices, and here they are." Dahlia wrapped herself in the top sheet and, holding it around herself, headed for Sunny's room. "You are either going to start taking the pills from Joe Diamond right away— and I will personally stand there and watch you put those little suckers in your mouth and check with a dental probe to make sure you're not storing the things in your cheeks like Rose, the fucking squirrel, who I hope is not carrying bubonic plague, which is something I recently read ground squirrels can do— or you are going back to the Sea View or some other facility where if you don't take the pills nobody gives a shit!"

The last was said with a barefoot kick to the partially open door to Sunny's room. To which, when she saw it now, Dahlia realized she hadn't paid a visit in a very long time, because it must have taken ages for Sunny to create what was there. Every large surface—the ceiling, the floor, and all of the walls— was covered with pictures cut out of magazines of the faces of beautiful women. Glossy shots of movie stars, models, high-profile actresses torn from the pages of Seth's magazines, taped, glued, and pushpinned everywhere.

"Movie stars, models, and princesses," Sunny said, following Dahlia's gaze. "Those on that wall are the dead ones. Princess Di, Marilyn Monroe, Grace of

Monaco, Selena, Natalie Wood. And that whole wall over there is covered with ones who are in the most danger as we speak. Gwyneth, Courtney, Jennifer Aniston. Now do you understand why Dolores Hart became a nun? And why I let myself go? And why I always do my own hair? Because the hairdressers and the makeup artists in those salons? They're in on it, too. They make you look in all those mirrors. But if the studio audience sees you looking too good, they will claim you. The way they did each one of them. They were murdered, Dahlia. And it was covered up by the police."

"Sunny, none of those deaths are connected in any way."

"Really?" Sunny said scornfully. "And how is it that you know so much about it? Does anybody really know about those deaths? Aren't they suspiciously shrouded by mystery? All of them?"

"Sun, you need to find the right medication," Dahlia said quietly.

"There are no medications for this," Sunny said, flaring.

"Don't you understand that you think that because of the illness?" Dahlia asked her.

"No," she insisted. "Because if you look at the evidence, you will see that beautiful women die all the time at the hands of the studio audience."

A breeze from behind Dahlia made the pictures on the wall flutter, and she looked at her cousin standing among them, and the scene was more than a nightmare. Eventually these terrible delusions would have to do Sunny in. Now she was just pasting pictures on the wall, but what if the studio audience, those people on the other side of the mirrors, told her to do away with herself?

"Please, won't you try taking the medication that Dr. Diamond gave you?"

"No. I won't be a zombie ever again."

"Maybe this pill will be different. Don't you remember what he said about trying all the keys to the door?"

"I remember. But he's not the one who has to walk around feeling the way I do when I take them. I won't be helpless. No."

"Sunny, if a psychopharmacologist who prescribes pills to people like you every day says there's even a remote chance that you might get to the point where you can make your music and not see the studio audience, won't it be worth the struggle? Please go and find the bag that Joe Diamond gave you with the pills in it."

"It can't work," Sunny said.

"We have to try," Dahlia insisted.

"No."

Dahlia sighed. "I'm out of energy, I'm out of ideas, I'm out of money, and I don't know what to do next. I'm going to go sit out there and work on the songs I wrote and see if I can get them into some shape for Harry Brenner to hear. I probably should try to get a room back for you, if not at the Sea View, then at someplace like it. And understand, I don't say that as a threat but because it's the only real way for you to go on."

Sunny was wearing an old pink bathrobe of

Dahlia's, and her face was almost as pink as the terry cloth. Dahlia turned to go back to her own room. She hated herself for a million reasons. For stealing the song, for fucking a stranger, for losing Seth, for ever thinking that Helene would leave her money and then being pissed when she didn't. She wanted to get back into bed and pull the covers up and stay there until she died. She was just at the door of her room when she heard Sunny call out, "Please. Don't desert me," so she turned back.

Sunny stood stiffly as she said the next, as if she were summoning up all her courage to say it. "Don't you think I want to be okay? Don't you think I'd take even the tiniest glimmer of hope just to be able to get through one day feeling the way you do every day? Even with your boyfriend problems and money problems and career problems, you have a choice every day to be able to function without seeing monsters everywhere you look. I would give up all my musical ability to trade problems with you for one hour.

"No, I take that back, not trade with you, because I wouldn't wish this on you or anyone. Dahlia, for some reason you decided to bring me this far. To let me be in your house, where you could feed me and take care of me, so I want you to see you made the right choice. I'm not sure if this will do a damn thing, and I suspect it won't, but . . ." Sunny pulled her hand from behind her back, and in it was what Dahlia recognized as the bag Joe Diamond had given her containing the pills. Then Sunny reached into the bag, pulled out a card of pills, and pushed one out of the sample bubble pack.

"I'll give it a few weeks," she said. "And not be-

cause I'm afraid you'll take me back to the Sea View.
I'm not afraid of that compared to some of the places
I've been and things I've seen. I'm doing it because I
desperately want anything resembling the old me
back again, the person I know I am when my brain
isn't fried."

The two cousins walked into the kitchen, where
Dahlia poured a glass of apple juice for Sunny to help
her swallow her first new pill.

"Ooookay," Sunny said, holding the pill up to her
mouth. "Here goes nothin'."

⤜✦⤛

seventeen

$\mathcal{D}$ahlia agonized for hours over her monthly stack of bills. She had so little money left that every time she sat at her desk, she had to decide which ones she could pay part of and which ones she could postpone paying for another month. The money she earned as a masseuse covered her expenses some months and other months amounted to too little. And she hadn't heard a word from Harry Brenner. Another Hollywood con job, she thought. Faith loves your song. It had to have all been another Hollywood lie. But then how could she expect Harry to be honest with her when she hadn't been honest with him?

She had no skills, so it wouldn't be long before she'd have to try to get a job waiting tables, if anybody would even hire someone like her, who didn't have a minute's experience doing anything. At four o'clock in the morning, always the time in the dark night when she'd find herself wide awake obsessing about something, she'd lie in bed picturing herself in a piano bar playing requests to earn the few dollars that the drunken patrons shoved into a brandy snifter.

Every time the phone rang, she hoped it would be a new massage client. Today when it rang, she'd been looking at the coupon for her mortgage payment, thinking she would definitely have to sell something to get the money to pay it, but the only thing she owned that was worth selling was the piano, and she couldn't part with that.

"H'lo."

"Miss Gordon? This is Louise. I work for Leroy Berk. Leroy asked that I call to tell you he's been traded to a team in Boston, so he's moving, and he won't need your services anymore. He said to send you his best."

"I understand," Dahlia said, sighing. "Tell him I wish him the best, too." They were dropping like flies. She had some clients left, but she was afraid those few were iffy. Risa Braverman was talking about moving to New York to be closer to her children, and Margie Kane and her yoga-teacher lover had been cooing over the idea of buying property in Santa Cruz and opening a yoga school there. Unless Harry Brenner came through with a miracle, Dahlia would have to figure out a way to scare up some new clients.

She took a handful of her business cards out of her desk drawer and tried to think of places she could post them where some potential client might see them and respond. She couldn't even afford to take out an ad in any of the throwaway papers. When Seth was around, he always kicked in more than his share during her lean times. Now there was no Seth to rescue her. And keeping Sunny around was costing a fortune in food, not to mention how much energy it took to care for her.

Sunny's room was still a mess, and the movie-star, model, and princess photos seemed to be increasing in number. Now they were taped to the windows and the lampshades, too, haphazardly stuck on every available surface. After the last three weeks of standing over Sunny each day, presenting her with a glass of juice and watching her take her pill, Dahlia was sure the new medication was never going to work.

She bought a little timer with a beeping alarm to remind herself to remind Sunny to take the pill. Then she took the calendar she'd gotten as a gift from the Owl Dry Cleaners at the beginning of the year and made an *x* on it every day as soon as she saw Sunny swallow the pill. Once a day she made Sunny get out of the house with her to take a long walk around Sherman Oaks Park, and Sunny seemed to be feeling stronger physically.

In a journal next to Dahlia's bed, which she kept there in case she had any late-night ideas for lyrics, she made sure to include a sentence or two before she fell asleep about Sunny's mood. When she called Joe Diamond to tell him Sunny had finally agreed to take the pills, he seemed pleased but cautious.

"You have to be patient," he told Dahlia. "We need to determine if the dose is appropriate, and we really won't be able to assess the efficacy for certain until she's been on it for three months."

Dahlia grunted into the phone and said something about how she was sure that at the end of three months, *she* would be the mad one. The doctor called in a refill prescription, and Dahlia picked up the new supply of pills and kept them in her own bathroom, continuing the rituals. But she wasn't hopeful. Most days Sunny seemed to be getting worse instead of better. Dahlia could hear her pacing the house every night and, after a while, pounding out songs on the piano.

Dahlia wondered how long she could continue to postpone listing the house? One morning she looked through the want ads, then called a telephone number that was in an ad placed by a talent agency looking for a receptionist. "Got computer skills?" the woman on the phone asked her, and Dahlia hung up.

By the end of the fourth week of Sunny's taking the new medication, she was sleeping through the night and making her bed in the morning. One day she took down all the movie-star, model, and princess photos. That same day at breakfast, she asked Dahlia if they could go to the movies in Westwood to see an Arnold Schwarzenegger movie she'd seen advertised on TV, and Dahlia agreed. Sunny loved going to the movies. She seemed to get as much pleasure from being among the people who were milling around in front of the theater and waiting in line to go in as she did from the movie itself.

At the multiplex in Westwood, Dahlia waited in line to buy a huge box of popcorn for them to share, and as she sank back into the soft seat in the air-conditioned theater, she was hoping to get caught up in the action of the film, but she couldn't stop her mind from racing with worry about money. Probably Harry Brenner's not calling her was the best thing that could happen regarding "What's Happened to Me?" If Faith Hill had changed her mind and didn't use the song, at least Dahlia wouldn't need to worry about having Sunny find out that she'd sold it as her own. Right, she said to herself, all I'd need to worry about instead is the small stuff, like how we're going to afford to eat.

Sunny loved the movie. She cheered and stomped and applauded at all the action scenes. Afterward, on the way to the parking lot, she took in Westwood Village hungrily with her eyes, looking with amusement at the crowds of people, clucking her tongue at the odd outfits or the spiked hairdos. "I feel as if I've just landed from some other galaxy," she said. "I mean, when I was at the Sea View, I went to the mall all the time, but I guess I never really noticed how strange some of the people were. Unless maybe they're stranger here than in San Diego."

Her mind is clearing, Dahlia thought. The great fog must be lifting, and that's why she's noticing details about people now. On the way home, Sunny babbled endlessly about which scenes she loved in the movie as Dahlia steered the wobbly van around Mulholland Drive. The curvy road that divided the city from the Valley was Dahlia's favorite route home. On clear days she liked to look out on each side at the bird's-eye views of the panoramas of L.A. and the San Fernando Valley.

Today it was bright and warm, and the windows of the van were open. The radio was on, and Sunny was pushing the buttons as impatiently as a child, listening to a song on one station for a few seconds, then turning to another and another until Dahlia wanted to scream for her to stop. And when she finally did stop to listen for a moment, she heard a haunting song.

"I keep getting in my own way, unable to change. Everybody sees it, and they say I'm acting strange." Holy shit, Dahlia thought. I wrote those words. It was all she could do not to pull over to the side of the road just to stop and drink it in. Her lyrics. Their song. She wanted to shriek with joy. It was Faith Hill's marvelous voice belting out Sunny's tune combined with Dahlia's lyrics, and there was a drop-dead arrangement behind her. But Dahlia was elated for only one instant, and then she was clutched with anxiety.

Every day for weeks, she had promised herself she would take care of this situation. She'd meant to break the news to Sunny before something like this could happen, but she'd postponed it again and again. Now her heart pounded, both from the exquisite excitement of hearing her lyrics sung by a big star and because she knew that the time had come when Sunny would discover her crime, and she didn't know what she was going to say about it.

Her first instinct was to reach over and change the station in the hope that Sunny wouldn't realize what was happening. But she thought again and let it play, deciding that maybe it was good for Sunny to hear it this way. She was counting on the idea that the thrill of hearing that wonderful singer selling her song could be so exciting for Sunny that she'd forget her ridiculous rules about keeping the songs to herself.

That's it, Dahlia thought, reaching to turn it up louder, but as she did, Sunny grabbed her wrist hard and stopped her.

"My God!" Sunny said. "My God! That's my song! Isn't that my song? Do you hear it, too? That's not something *like* my song—that's my very song. With my hook. And somebody must have written lyrics to it. My God, who stole my song?"

The song sounded so good and so powerful. Dahlia felt ashamed and afraid and elated at the same time, and she had no idea what to say. Cars behind her were honking and then peeling around and past the van. There was a buzzing in her ears, and her cheeks were hot. She was caught. She had to confess. This should be a thrilling moment for her. The fact that the song was on the air meant that now the checks would pour in. Big checks. But she wasn't happy. She was sick and guilty and horrified at her own greed.

"How did this happen?" Sunny wondered, her hands clutching her hair and pulling at it frantically. "Dahlia," she said, turning to her cousin with panic in her eyes. "Am I creating this? Is this a delusion? Do you hear this, too?" Sunny saw Dahlia hesitate, and she took her hesitation to mean she didn't understand the problem. "I can hear Faith Hill singing lyrics to my song," she wailed, her face contorted in pain. Now she reached over and turned up the volume. "Oh, God! I hear that, and I know it can't really be there. And I thought the pills were working so well. But this is just another hallucination."

Now the music swelled, and Faith was singing the bridge. What an awesome moment this should be for both of us, Dahlia thought. Now, at last, she had to tell the truth.

"Sunny, it isn't a hallucination," Dahlia said, hoping Sunny would be able to handle the news. "It *is* Faith Hill singing your song. Those are my lyrics, and I sold it to her. I mean, I lied to my friend the arranger and told him that I wrote both the lyrics and the music, and he took it to her, and she wanted to sing it because it's so good. So I said it was okay."

Maybe it *will* be okay, Dahlia prayed for an instant. Maybe she'll be glad now that she realizes she isn't hallucinating. Maybe now that she knows she wrote a song a big star wanted to record, she'll be happy. But what had been fear in Sunny's eyes only a moment earlier was now blind rage.

"You what?" With a lunge toward Dahlia, she grabbed the wheel of the van and jerked at it, forcing the rickety vehicle to swerve and career crazily off the road, toward the edge of the cliff.

"No!" Dahlia cried out in terror, slamming on the brakes just in time to stop the van from plummeting into the valley, but now its front wheels jutted out perilously over the cliff. Dahlia elbowed Sunny hard, trying to regain control of the wheel, afraid the van was going to roll forward if she let go, but the much bigger Sunny held on tightly enough to make her knuckles white, all the while glaring furiously at Dahlia.

"You stole my song? You took credit for my music? You let somebody record it when you knew I didn't want that?" Sunny screamed while Dahlia, nauseated with terror that the van was going to go over the cliff with the two of them in it, cringed and whimpered apologies, to Sunny and to God. "You sold it without asking me?" Sunny's face was purple with rage. I'm going to die, Dahlia thought.

"I could kill us right now," Sunny said, as if she were reading Dahlia's thoughts. "I *should* kill *you*. You know I could do it and get off scot-free, because I'm a proven crazy person. What's the worst they could do to me? Put me in an insane asylum? They'd have a hard time finding one I don't know intimately. And so what? I'd be back in the lockup? At least there they tell me the truth! At least there they don't steal from me! How could you do this to me? I rocked your crib at night, and you would steal from me?"

"I did it to help you," Dahlia said, choking on her own lie. It was a desperate lie.

Faith was belting out the last few bars, and the song sounded spectacular. The powerful emotional finish was rising all around them. "I'm sorry." Dahlia's voice was thick with fear and guilt. "It started because I loved your melody so much, and then that lyric came to me, and I was singing it to myself while Harry was on the phone, and he overheard me." Sunny took her arm off the wheel, enabling Dahlia to throw the van into reverse. Miraculously, the back tires took hold and moved, and the van lurched back onto the dirt shoulder. Sunny pushed the door open, got out, and walked to the edge of the cliff, where she sat down with her face in her hands, but Dahlia could still hear what she was saying.

"All I have left is my music, and you took it without asking me. How could you do it?" She was right. She had one thing, her gift, and Dahlia had violated her by lifting it wholesale, and now Sunny was lucid enough to understand what had happened. Seth was the one who'd told Dahlia about Sunny's mind-set right from the beginning. "She doesn't want the same things you want. She wants to compose her songs and play them, but selling them to the world isn't part of the deal." Dahlia looked over at Sunny, then climbed out of the van and walked over to sit next to her.

Sunny didn't say anything for a long time. Fast cars whizzed by on the road behind them. Finally she spoke, staring straight ahead. "Did you know there used to be rumors that Irving Berlin didn't write his own melodies?" Sunny said, staring straight ahead. "That they were written by someone who people in those days called 'a little colored boy'? There were people who thought that the songs Irving Berlin wrote were too hot for some nice, staid, white Jewish boy to write. Maybe that same little colored boy, a long time later, worked for Leiber and Stoller, too. Because everyone wondered how two East Coast Jewish boys could write songs that were so filled with soul and sounded so black."

Dahlia was still shaking. All she wanted was to go home and for this to go away.

"Well, now I see that I'm just *your* little colored boy. Only I really exist, and I'm really writing the songs, and you're taking the credit for them, Dahlia. Could that possibly be true? It is true, isn't it? What were you thinking? I know. You thought I was so crazy that I wouldn't notice or that I wouldn't care. Well, I care. You money-grubbing, thieving, desperate con artist. I care." Now Sunny scrambled to her feet. "I don't want to be anywhere near you," she said, and walked toward the road.

"Sunny, where are you going?" It wasn't safe for her just to walk away in all this traffic.

"Maybe back to the Sea View," Sunny called back to her. "So what if people there are doped to the moon and pee in their pants and don't know who they are? At least they don't steal a part of your soul. My music is sacred to me. My work is sacred to me. I may be crazy to you, but I make music for me, and that's the way I want to keep it."

"I thought I was doing you a favor," Dahlia shouted, so desperate that she knew she was lying and she didn't care. "I was so positive the money could change your life for the better, that I did it even though I knew you'd be angry." Now she was following Sunny. "You have to know I meant well. For the first years after you left, all I wanted to do was come and save you. Not just wanted to. I mean, I dreamed about it the way kids dream about growing up to be baseball stars or Miss America. Wished on every set of birthday candles that I could grow up and have enough money to come and get you out of all of those horror-show places where I knew you were trapped. Ride up on my white horse, not in that stinking tin can of a van, and say, 'Gordon and Gordon are back together at last.' But after a while it started to look like I could barely save myself. I couldn't make it big. I tried. I'm still trying. I had to become a masseuse so I could eat and still write songs, so after a while I couldn't even think about the idea of saving you, because it was all I could do to save myself."

A dump truck clanked by loudly on Mulholland. Dahlia felt dizzy, and she hoped God wasn't going to strike her down on that very spot, but she had to get Sunny to stop and believe her. "Sun, even if you don't want to keep the money, if you have some big aversion to selling your songs, wouldn't it really be sacred if you gave your half of what we earn to charity? And we could write a million fabulous songs together, just like Leiber and Stoller. We could dedicate the Sunny Gordon Pavilion at the UCLA Center for Mental Health. And the two of us would be there to cut the ribbon and sing 'Stay by My Side.'"

Sunny stopped and looked at her and Dahlia held her breath watching her cousin's tense face, hoping that her message had penetrated. But after a moment Sunny shook her head. "You're rewriting history. You're trying to cover your ass and your full-out thievery by lying to me about saving me and everything else. Well, guess what? I may be crazy, but I see right through you. You're a selfish little con artist, and I don't want you in my life," Sunny said and walked away and this time she didn't turn back when Dahlia called out to her.

"Sunny, come home with me." Sunny kept walking. "We'll work this out." Cars were flying by, and there wasn't any pavement where Sunny was walking, so sometimes she'd have to move from the shoulder of the road onto the cement and be inches away from the traffic.

"Sunny, this is dangerous!" Dahlia called out, but Sunny ignored her. Dahlia turned and ran back to the van, started it, and pulled out onto Mulholland, slowly moving along across the road from where Sunny walked. "Sunny," she tried, "Rose can't make it without you. You have to come home and feed her."

Cars behind the van were honking as Dahlia inched it forward, hoping Sunny would change her mind. The light was green at Beverly Glen, and she crossed the intersection, then pulled up at the curb with her hazard lights on so that cars whizzing by could see her and there was a chance that Sunny could see her, realize how perilous it was to walk around there, and come back to the van and get in.

Dahlia turned to look behind her, and sure enough she could see Sunny, now reaching the corner of Beverly Glen, taking an instant to think about it, then making a right turn and disappearing down the hill.

eighteen

$\mathcal{D}$ahlia was a senior in high school when her mother bought herself the black silk high-heeled shoes to go with the new black beaded peau de soie dress she was going to wear to Rita and Gary Horn's twenty-fifth anniversary party. Dahlia watched her mother carefully remove the party dress from the closet, the price tag still hanging from it, then smooth it out on her bed and go to her pretty turquoise Chinese silk jewelry box, where she pulled out several pairs of earrings before she chose two pairs of crystal and jet beads and laid them on the bed next to the dress. Then she stepped back and looked the picture over as if she were observing a piece of art, to see which glittery jet-bead-and-crystal combination would look best.

Dahlia had never seen her mother wear either of those particular pairs of earrings, but when she asked her if they were new, Rose said, "Oh, I've had them for years." Dahlia imagined that she'd worn them when she and Dahlia's father were dating, at a time when she was still trying to look pretty, before she let herself become the frumpy wife who rushed out the door to work with wet hair and not a drop of makeup.

"It's going to be the bash of the year," Rose Gordon said animatedly, now pushing her dark hair behind her ears, holding up the glittery earrings next to her face, and moving close to the mirror. "There's the party and a party before the party and a brunch the day after the party. Rita and Gary's relatives are all coming in from everywhere."

Later that afternoon Dahlia was in Hirsch's Drug-store trying to decide which shampoo to buy when she looked past the vitamins toward the aspirin shelf and spotted a man standing there who seemed famil-iar to her. She remembered what her mother had told her earlier and was confident when she walked up to him and said, "Norman?"

The man was unquestionably Norman Burns, Sunny's Arthur Miller. Dahlia hadn't seen him since she was eleven, and his now craggy face and graying hair made him look even more like the famous play-wright than he had when he and Sunny were dating. Norman squinted as he took Dahlia in without a trace of recognition, and she realized that the last time he'd seen her, she'd been a little girl of eleven.

"Dahlia Gordon," she said, putting out a hand to shake. Then she watched as the name registered and he smiled warmly.

"Oh, my! Dahlia . . . all grown up. How are you?"

He walked toward her, the smile brightening, but when they touched hands and looked into each other's eyes, a bolt of enormous sadness passed between them.

"You must be here for your aunt's party," Dahlia said, and Norman nodded, his eyes never leaving hers, as if he were looking for some message from her. Then his face became melancholy, and he spoke quietly so that nobody else in the drugstore could hear him.

"I still dream about her all the time," he said.

Dahlia was moved and speechless. But she knew she had to say something. She could see his eyes begging her to say something.

"I'll bet she still dreams about you, too," she said, hoping that was enough.

"We had so much together. I should have married her, even though she had all those terrible problems. I know the problems seemed insurmountable in those days. But I could have helped her through them, and at least we would have been together. I always believed God meant for us to be together. But I was young and stupid, and I let my parents tell me what to do.

"Don't get me wrong, Dahlia, my wife and I have two kids—a nice life. But Sunny . . . oh, that Sunny," he said, shaking his head. "She was something more to me, we were—" Norman couldn't go on. Tears welled, and he pulled a handkerchief from the pocket of his khaki trousers and dabbed underneath his glasses at his eyes. "Forgive me," he said. "I had no idea this was still so loaded for me. But seeing you brought it all back."

Dahlia knew that at that very moment Sunny was in

Camarillo State Hospital having regular sessions of shock therapy, but she kept that information to herself, hoping Norman's memories of Sunny were still of the Marilyn Monroe look-alike.

"If you ever see her—and I'm assuming you do, because you were like a little sister to her—please tell her I send her Godspeed and that she is never out of my thoughts for a day." Dahlia remembered promising him that she would relay that message, but she was afraid she would probably never see Sunny again. And in fact she didn't, until that first day at the Sea View.

Every time Dahlia thought about the horrified look that came over Sunny when they heard Faith Hill sing the song, it made her feel sick. Now, in her living room, she couldn't get over the sound of Faith Hill's big voice singing her words. What an arrangement. Not overproduced, not too subtle, but perfect and hot and memorable. In the kitchen she took the cordless phone out of its holder and slipped it into the pocket of her sweatshirt so she wouldn't have far to go to answer it when it rang. If it rang. She'd been crazy to let Sunny go. She should get back into the van and go and look for her now. But where would she look?

She felt a gnawing in her stomach, reminding her that she hadn't had anything to eat all day except the popcorn at the movies, but when she opened the refrigerator to see what there was, nothing appealed to her. "Please let her be okay," she said out loud. "Let her call and tell me she's okay." She probably could call the police and ask them to go and look for Sunny, explain her history, and then hope they wouldn't say that Sunny had to be missing for a certain number of days before they could do anything. She tried to remember from the television cop shows she watched what the rules were about that. She wondered what the chances were of tracking down an unhappy forty-two-year-old woman in Los Angeles. Weren't there too many residents who fit that description?

For a while she sat at the piano trying to work on some of her tunes, but soon sleep tugged at her, so she curled up on the sofa, holding the cordless phone in her hand as she fell asleep. It was four-thirty in the morning when the ringing jarred her awake, and she answered it with her eyes still closed.

"Mmmmm?" was all she could manage to say into the phone.

"Yeah. Is this Delilah Gordon?"

"Dahlia."

"John Mulcahey over here at the mall on Westwood and Pico Boulevard. I'm the night watchman here. I was just walking around in Nordstrom's, and I found someone here you ought to come and get."

"What?" Dahlia asked, sitting up.

"I'll tell you the truth," the voice on the phone went on, "I didn't have the heart to call the cops on her. I don't even know how she got into the store, but I found her sittin' there in the altogether down on the first floor playing the piano. Now, I happen to be a big music fan, and she was so out of this world, I'll tell you the truth—not because of her nakedness, believe me. I'm an old married man with three daughters, I've seen it all. But the way she can tickle those ivories, filled the whole place with that music of hers, and her singing was so gorgeous it made me want to cry. I'm tellin' you, this girl could be a big star, just like— what's that R-E-S-P-E-C-T lady's name? Aretha. That's it. She's better than that Aretha."

"How did she get in there?" Dahlia wanted to know.

"I think she might have walked part of the way and hitched part of the way. Then she came into the store and just stayed till they closed up around her. I came in and was doing my rounds and I heard music, so I followed the sound, and there she was, naked as a jay-bird playing tunes on that big old piano they've got down there on the first floor. Now, that's a first for me. And she didn't want to steal anything. Nothing like that. All she wanted was to play that piano. If this is her mom, I'd like to offer a suggestion. You ought to get this gal a piano of her own so she doesn't have to break into stores to do it. Oh, and on your way down here . . . come to the exit off of Westwood Boulevard. She's all dressed and ready now, so if you could get over here real soon, we'll be waiting for you in the parking lot out back. I'd bring her home to you, but I can't exactly leave the place."

"I'll get there as soon as I can."

Sunny and Mr. Mulcahey, the night watchman, a short, red-faced man wearing a uniform with a walkie-talkie hanging on his belt, were chatting in the empty parking lot at Nordstrom as Dahlia pulled the van into a parking spot. Mr. Mulcahey smiled as she got out of the van. Sunny was expressionless.

"Thanks," Dahlia said to him, "for taking such good care of her." It was dawn, and the morning air was brisk, and Sunny shivered as she climbed into the passenger seat of the van. Dahlia started it and waved good-bye to the night watchman. She wasn't sure what to expect from Sunny now. More rage, or maybe an apology for the middle-of-the-night call.

"Thanks for coming, Dahl," Sunny said as Dahlia pulled the van out of the lot.

Dahlia grunted an annoyed version of "You're welcome."

"I got a ride down Beverly Glen Canyon in a truck with some pool man," she said quietly, "but a lot of the time I was walking, so I had ages to think about my song. Our song. I couldn't stop thinking about how there we were just driving along and we heard it. I mean, that really did happen, didn't it?"

"It did. And I should have asked you if it was okay. I'm sorry I didn't," Dahlia said. But she wasn't sure if she meant it.

Sunny looked straight ahead out the window. It was still dark, and there was only an occasional car driving past them. "I was also thinking about my mom and dad and all the grief I caused them and wondering what it would have been like if they were still around to hear that on the radio today." Dahlia turned onto Pico Boulevard and drove east. "And I realized that they would have loved that. They would have been the most proud, and isn't it about time, after all they suffered over me, that I did something to make them proud?"

Dahlia wondered where this story was going. She

was exhausted and irritable and not wanting to listen to anything Sunny said, and what made it all worse was that Sunny didn't seem to be the least bit chagrined at making her come out to get her at this hour. Now she was going on and on about her parents. "Can you imagine how many nights they said to each other, 'What are we going to do with her?' The times my mother must have cried and prayed, wishing she could fix me? Those poor people."

"They loved you," Dahlia said, "and they always handled it."

"Yesterday I was watching *Oprah*, and Dr. Phil was the guest. Do you know who he is?" Sunny asked.

Dahlia nodded. She knew he was some shrink who gave advice to people in books and on Oprah Winfrey's show.

"He was telling the audience that every parent can only be as happy as his or her saddest child." Sunny shook her head and pressed her lips together until they were white. "I realize for the first time how much sadness I brought my mother and father for so many years.

"Not only the days I went mad when I lived in their house, but when other mothers and fathers were going to visit their daughters at colleges, they were coming to the mental ward, sitting in those awful rooms waiting for me to shuffle in, seeing all the other pitiful people wander around. Having to deal with their baby living like that. God, it breaks my heart to think about those forced cheerful faces they would try so valiantly to put on for my sake. I knew they did it out of love, and all those years I wanted to respond to them, to thank them for being so devoted, for never missing a visit, but I was so drugged I couldn't get past the wall of medication to get the words out.

"They never had a chance to see me grow into my music, and they were the ones who deserved to see it most of all," she said, and then she was silent. When Dahlia stopped for a red light and looked at Sunny, she saw that Sunny was crying. "After all the waiting rooms they sat in," she said, "don't you think I ought to dedicate the Ruth and Max Gordon Waiting Room in every nuthouse in the nation?"

"That would be nice," Dahlia said. "But I think probably giving money to research schizophrenia would be better."

Sunny wiped away a tear with her sleeve and nodded. "So I was thinking about what you said, and I'm ready to go along with it under certain conditions."

"What I said about what?"

"About us being the girl Leiber and Stoller. Writing songs together again like when we were kids, and then if we make money doing it, your half of it can go to you for buying all the useless stuff you think you can't live without, and my half can go to build new places for other people like me. To take the place of the too-much-medication places and the sit-and-stare-at-TV places. They could be clean and have good food and real doctors who come and check on the people and somebody whose only job is to say nice things to the people who live there. Wouldn't that be awesome?"

"Awesome," Dahlia said, suddenly awake and alert and afraid she might be dreaming. If she could harness Sunny's gift, write lyrics to Sunny's music, get

Sunny to be really productive, if they could be Gordon and Gordon back together at last, the partnership had the potential to be a gold mine. Okay, nobody *really* knew who was going to make it in show business and who wasn't, there were no guarantees, but at least this was a shot now that they already had one great song on a Faith Hill CD.

"And I forgive you, Dahl," Sunny said, sniffing as more tears fell, "because I understand you were desperate and had to do something. But my wish for you is that you would get once and for all that all money does is complicate people's lives and make them think they never have enough, when they ought to know there's nothing important that money can get you. Look how unhappy wanting money has made you. So if I do this, you're gonna be okay if I give away my half completely. Except for rent and food. Right?"

"Right!" Dahlia said.

"And someday when you feel more secure and you're not so desperate about it, you can give your money away, too," Sunny said, but Dahlia only half heard that part. In her fantasy she was all dressed up and at the Grammys because some killer song of theirs had been nominated, and she and Sunny were walking up together to get their award.

"Stay by my side forever," Sunny sang. "Stay by my side, my friend."

Dahlia made a right onto Wilshire Boulevard and was heading east when the dawn broke, and she harmonized with Sunny all the way home.

nineteen

"Tell me all the song hooks you have in your head, and I'll tell you which ones grab me and which ones don't," Sunny said as Dahlia scraped a bright yellow mound of scrambled eggs onto her cousin's plate. Then the toast popped, and Dahlia hurried over to try to extract the two pieces from the toaster without burning her fingers.

After breakfast they took a hike up through the hills around Dahlia's house, talking over the songs Dahlia had been trying to make work and the ideas that Sunny wanted to try. Sunny was never more lucid than when she was talking about songs.

"When it comes to lyrics, you have to deliver ideas that are from so far inside you that you need to wear one of those hats with the lights on it to go in and find them. You get what I mean? The ones you're giving me now are cute, they're fun, but they're not from where you hurt. Great songs come from you really, truly telling your story, and if you tell your story, you tell everyone else's story, too. Because in the end people are all the same."

Dahlia wasn't so sure that was true, but Sunny was right when she said that the ideas Dahlia was coming up with were from some surface level she'd always shown to the world. Certainly it was the level she'd shown her clients, the friendly, chatty, nice girl. Maybe the only person who had ever mined beyond that level, insisted she give more, was Seth, and she'd sent him away. Sunny had never learned the worldly art of faking it, so what she showed the world was always genuine.

"Yeah, maybe," Dahlia said grudgingly.

"Well, don't do that anymore," Sunny said, as if it could be so easy for Dahlia to drop the artifice of a lifetime. "I think you need to make a point of dredging up ideas you don't want to tell anyone. And then sharpen your pencil and tell them to the world. Not that I'm an expert. But I think that's the secret." They walked for about a mile before Sunny spoke again. "So with that in mind, try coming up with some message for Seth," Sunny said. "Not anything cutesy."

Dahlia sighed. Seth. God, she missed him. "I want you back so much I ache," Dahlia tried.

"That's a very feeble start," Sunny told her, and they both laughed.

"If I get you back, I'll never let you go again."

"Better put on your miner's hat," Sunny joked. "It's a long way down."

By the time they got to the piano every morning,

they were excited by most of their combined ideas and afraid they'd forget all the potential song hooks they'd come up with if they didn't start writing them down in some form. They laughed over some of Dahlia's bad rhymes and talked about which old songs were their favorites and which songs they wished they'd written. Then Sunny pulled melodies she wanted to try for Dahlia right out of the air, melodies that would work with whichever of Dahlia's hooks she liked best.

Within minutes she could take musical riffs that sounded at first as if she were primitively banging them out and work them into a lush tune. The cousins' collective energy was as high as it had been when they were girls, and they tossed the ideas back and forth excitedly. Many days they never even stopped for food, and suddenly they'd realize they'd worked without a break and it was five o'clock in the afternoon.

"I'd better get to the market," Dahlia said, searching for the keys to the van, "or we'll starve to death for our art."

"I could use a little starvation," Sunny said, patting her own hips.

"You look gorgeous," Dahila told her, and it was true. Sunny's cheeks were rosy, and her eyes were bright, and she was looking more and more like a weathered version of her young, beautiful self. And Dahlia was surprised at how easy it was to have her around all the time. Except for those early years of Dahlia's life when she'd spent nearly all her time with Sunny, Dahlia thought of herself as a music nerd, interested in doing only the minimum required academic work to get to the next music class and then hurry home to practice or to write her songs, hardly ever socializing with kids her age. Even in her few years of college and after, the men she allowed into her life were always the type who were too busy to cling to her during the day, knowing instinctively they had to leave her alone to make her music. She had never been comfortable having another person around constantly.

Tonight she was planning to make the burritos Sunny especially loved, so she went to Whole Foods Market, even though it was expensive to shop there and she was down to the bottom of her checking account. She loved Whole Foods Market. The colors of the produce piled high along one entire wall and the cans of flowers and the bins of bulk grains looked so pretty and abundant and lush that just strolling through the aisles always felt like a luxury.

She'd been cooking dinner for Sunny nearly every night, explaining the basics of nutrition to her as if Sunny were a Martian. And, in the food department, she might as well have been a visitor from another planet. She'd spent too many years in hospitals where the food had been badly prepared, overcooked, too salty or too saucy, so she'd rarely had a well-prepared meal of fresh, wholesome foods.

Now she'd become a big fan of Dahlia's cooking. She watched the chopping and sautéing, as fascinated as a child, sneaking and nibbling the ingredients and then laughing when Dahlia caught her in the act. And as a result of all the healthy eating, she was looking very good. Her skin was radiant, and the orange hair had grown out so that now it was just orange at the tips, and her own white-blond color was back.

Today Dahlia was marketing alone. She had left Sunny at home in the backyard, feeding the squirrel. Her bag of groceries was filled with clusters of bright red tomatoes still on the stem, an assortment of lettuces, and pears she was going to put into a salad. A sourdough baguette and some sunflowers stuck out of the top of the bag as she made her way to the parking lot. But her walk to the van was stopped short by the sound of a scream as an old woman tripped over a parking barrier and toppled forward with a thud.

"Oh, nooo!" the woman wailed from the ground, her bag of groceries ripped and lemons and onions and cans and jars rolled out in all directions. Dahlia dropped her own bag at her feet, rushed to the old woman, and knelt to comfort her.

"You'll be okay," she said. "Let me help you." Then she jumped to her feet and put her hand up like a traffic cop to stop a Lexus that was just about to back out of a spot and run over the woman's bag. She helped the woman to her feet, slowly and carefully, and walked with an arm around her to a seat at one of the iron sidewalk tables, where a few oblivious people sipped coffee.

"My heart is racing so fast," the woman said, and Dahlia held her hand and told her to take long breaths and relax. As soon as she was calm, Dahlia hurried back to the parking lot, gathered up the groceries and the now torn paper shopping bag, and came back to comfort her.

"I'm fine, dear," the woman said, "and you're too kind. I guess I didn't see that cement guard sticking up there. I'm sorry to inconvenience you. You are my Good Samaritan."

"Are you sure you're okay?" Dahlia asked, gesturing at the same time for a bag boy to come over. "Would you mind rebagging these, please?" she asked him, and the boy took the woman's groceries back into the store. The woman gave Dahlia a thank-you hug, and Dahlia sighed, picked up her own bag, and was heading toward her car when she was surprised to see Seth and Lolly sitting on the hood of Seth's Jeep, applauding. She felt her face flush.

"Nicely done," Seth said. And Lolly was actually smiling at her. Seth looked so adorable wearing jeans and a washed-out blue work shirt that Dahlia thought about just throwing her arms around his neck and begging him to come back.

"You saved that lady," Lolly said, surprised. She was wearing a blue work shirt, too, and looked as cute as her daddy. "We were proud of you."

"Real proud," Seth added, and his eyes held Dahlia's for a long moment.

"Didn't know I had an audience, or I would have washed her bruises and carried her home," Dahlia joked. There was an awkward silence. "So where are you living now?" she asked.

"Got a little place in West Hollywood. You can come by anytime," he said, and she felt a surge in her solar plexus.

"Except when *I'm* there," Lolly added, and Seth grinned.

"Hey, wait a minute," he said. "Now that we know she saves little old ladies, maybe we'll let her come when you're there, too." He ruffled Lolly's hair.

"Maybe," she offered with a grudging nod.

"You can come to my house, too," Dahlia said. "My cousin Sunny lives with me now," she added. Dahlia watched with great satisfaction as surprise filled Seth's face. She knew that that was a statement he never thought he'd hear in a million years. Dahlia, the selfish bitch, was taking care of another human being. And a difficult one at that. "We're writing songs together, and one of them was just recorded."

"No kidding?" Seth said. "And Sunny actually lives there? How's she doing?"

"Okay. Good days. Bad days. We weather them. Just us and her pet squirrel." Seth raised an amused eyebrow at that mental picture.

"Whoa," Lolly said. "I want to see a pet squirrel. A real one?"

"Yep. It fell out of a tree, and we nursed it back to health," Dahlia said. Okay, that was pushing it. It was Sunny who had done everything for the chirpy little beast. Dahlia had never once lifted a finger for it. But she was on a roll here, looking like Lady Nice, so why not include herself in the credit for Rose's recovery? After all, wasn't *she* the one who was paying for the goddamned walnuts or whatever the hell else Sunny was feeding the freaking thing?

"Can we go see the squirrel, Dad?" Lolly asked Seth, tugging at his shirtsleeve.

Seth looked at Dahlia for a response. "Sure, come on," Dahlia said, and Seth and Lolly scurried off in the direction of the Jeep, climbed aboard, and followed Dahlia as she walked to her parking spot. She was pleased to be getting into the new Celica convertible she'd traded the van for last week. Okay, it wasn't the Mercedes yet, but that would be her next car.

"Must have been a good song," Seth said, rolling down the window as he watched her deposit her groceries in the trunk, then slide in and gesture for them to follow her. My God, she thought, he is so adorable it makes me weak. You're a jerk to do this, she told herself as they drove up Laurel Canyon and she looked at Seth in the rearview mirror. This is probably a giant mistake. Sunny could be naked in the garden or at the piano or doing God-knows-what bizarre thing a kid shouldn't see.

She heard the sobs as she unlocked the front door and turned to Seth and Lolly. Another Sunny incident was in progress, and it could be about anything.

"This might be a bad idea. Sounds as if we're in crisis mode here," she said softly.

"We'll be okay," Seth said. "We'll lay back while you check on her. If it's too big a problem, we'll leave."

Sunny was sitting on the ground out in the backyard looking up into the tree and crying. "It's Rose," she said when she saw Dahlia. "I took her out of her box so she could run around a little bit, and after a while she ran over to the tree and didn't even look back to say good-bye to me. Just zoomed right up there as if I were never a part of her life. And now she's so far up I can't even see her anymore. I can hear her singing to me. She's back in her world, Dahl."

"Sun, you knew someday she had to be on her own again," Dahlia said, silently thanking heaven the furry beast was gone and trying not to show it.

"But I miss her," Sunny said.

"And she'll miss you, but it's better for her to be on her own now. Aren't you glad for her? Like parents who send their kids off to college. Think of it as Rose going to college." Sunny laughed through her tears at that. "Besides, we have company who I think will cheer you up. Seth and his little girl are here."

"A little girl?" Sunny brightened. "I love little girls. Oh, if only Rose were here to meet her."

Seth and Lolly were still standing in the open doorway when Sunny and Dahlia came in from the yard. Dahlia tried to imagine how Sunny with her pink-trimmed white hair and her long shocking-pink nails looked to Lolly.

"Lolly, this is my cousin Sunny."

"Where's the squirrel?" Lolly asked, seemingly unfazed by Sunny's appearance.

"She went away to college," Sunny answered, and that made Lolly giggle. "But I can teach you how to play the piano. Want to learn how to play the piano?"

"Okay," Lolly said, and she hurried over and climbed up onto the piano bench as Sunny sat next to her, and Dahlia watched the lesson begin, with Sunny explaining very carefully which notes were which and then placing the little girl's fingers on the keys, just the way she used to do with Dahlia.

"This is called 'Chopsticks.' You put these two fingers on these two notes, and you play them like this."

"Guess we're not needed *here* anymore," Seth said to Dahlia.

"Want coffee?" she asked, loving the familiarity of having him follow her into the kitchen, remembering his touch, wanting to drop all the formal chitchat and put her arms around him, feeling genuinely sorry she had ever let him go for such stupid reasons. One of the songs she and Sunny had written recently was all about how Dahlia never appreciated Seth. Sunny said it was Dahlia's best lyric so far. It was called "Knowing What's Real." It played in her head now as she watched him walk to the freezer and take out a can of Yuban as naturally as if he still lived there.

"What is all this?" he asked, looking around at the toys Sunny had put out for Rose.

"Squirrel stuff," Dahlia explained.

"Squirrel stuff?" He laughed, filling the glass carafe of the coffeemaker with water. "I love it. I remember when you told me you wouldn't even buy a plant because you wouldn't have time to take care of it."

"I still say that. Believe me, nothing's changed. I didn't really take care of the squirrel. Sunny did. And every day we write songs together."

"So you got what you wanted," he said, and Dahlia's eyes tested his for any trace of malice in that statement, but there was none.

"I got much more than I bargained for," she said.

"Because you're responsible for her care now?"

"Not really. She's pretty independent. I made her go to a doctor who got her on a regimen of new meds.

That's all. I just make sure she takes them. No big deal."

Seth poured the water into the well of the coffeemaker as he smiled at Dahlia and clucked his tongue. "Still can't admit there's a soft part of you hidden under all that tough bullshit, can you?" he asked.

"Maybe a speck," she said, fighting her own smile and turning to get down some mugs from a kitchen cabinet. She could feel that Seth had moved precariously near her now, and when she turned again she was facing him, close enough to smell his chocolate chip-cookie deliciousness.

"I miss you," he said. "God knows why, you crabby little bitch, but I do."

Dahlia loved the twinkle in his eye when he said that, and she put her arms around his neck as the dissonant sound of "Chopsticks" rose from the living room. Lolly had her part down perfectly by now, and Sunny was improvising an elaborate duet around the childlike banging. The sound was lighthearted and bright, and Dahlia was sure that through the kitchen window she could hear Rose, the errant squirrel, chirping along to the rhythm. The music was so loud that, as Seth kissed her, she wasn't sure whether she actually heard the phone ringing or not, and she hated to move her mouth from his kiss that was so warm and sweet.

"Better get that," he whispered, breaking the kiss.

"Probably a neighbor who doesn't like the sound of 'Chopsticks,'" she said, kissing him again.

"Want me to get it?" he asked.

"Sure, but tell them I'm not home," Dahlia said as Seth grabbed the receiver.

"Hello," he said, holding a finger in the other ear to block out the pounding sound of "Chopsticks." "Yes, she is. May I say who's calling?" Then he looked at Dahlia. "Someone named Danny Kroll calling from New York."

Dahlia felt the flames rise in her chest and her cheeks. Her eyes couldn't meet Seth's as he handed her the phone.

"Stay by my side forever. Stay by my side, my friend." Danny Kroll's voice was singing on the other end of the call, and she knew Seth could tell she was flustered. Even with "Chopsticks" hammering away in the next room she could hear Danny Kroll's sexy voice say, "Hi, pretty Dahlia."

"Hold on. I'll take this in the bedroom," she said into the phone. Then she pushed the hold button, gave Seth a little squeeze on the arm to say she'd be right back, and hurried into her bedroom and closed the door. But before she put the phone to her ear again, she took a deep breath. She had seen in Seth's eyes that he knew this wasn't purely a business call. He knew her well enough to be able to tell by the way she'd avoided his eyes that she had feelings for this man on the phone. What was she going to say to him when she finished this call?

"Hello?"

"Dan Kroll here, Dahlia. Last time I saw you, we had a threesome with your insane relative."

Her brain was replaying Danny Kroll's departure the morning after their lovemaking, with a wild-eyed

Sunny in the bed shrieking, and then Sunny pulling off and breaking his reflector glasses, and she felt as embarrassed as she had that day. She'd tried very hard to put the incident out of her mind, never imagining in a million years that she'd ever hear from Danny again after that. And she wouldn't have blamed him for never calling again after the Sunny incident.

"I'm calling to ask if it would be okay for my agency to use your song 'Stay by My Side' in a commercial. We have a client who really wants to use it to sell their product, a health-care policy, and it could be a very big spot for the song. Can I send you some paperwork followed by some money? Or do you have an agent I can call?"

"No, no agent . . ." She was a little disappointed that the call was all business. Not even a "So how have you been?" Dahlia sat on the sagging bed feeling flustered and uncomfortable talking to this man for the first time since they'd been in the same bed together. And it was especially weird since Seth was in the other room now and she felt as if she'd betrayed him with Danny, even though she and Seth had been broken up at the time. Still, she felt as if, in a way, she'd cheated by being with some smooth operator.

Okay, put that out of your mind, she thought. This is a business call. There was barely a shred of any flirtation in it. All he wanted from her was the song. He was offering her another opportunity for the two cousins to sell the song from long ago. And now Sunny would probably agree to sell it. Only last week Dahlia had shown her an item in a magazine saying that the brilliant Lorenz Hart had left all his royalties from lyrics to songs he'd written with Richard Rodgers to the United Jewish Appeal. Hart wrote a thousand songs with Richard Rodgers, and every time one of them was sung or played publicly now, the royalties were used to care for the needy. Sunny had read the paragraph after Dahlia pointed it out to her, and when she finished reading it, she'd held the magazine to her chest as if she were hugging Lorenz Hart in thanks.

"I'm pretty sure it's a yes," Dahlia said to Danny, "but I'll have to discuss it with my partner."

"Long as your partner is saner than that crazy cousin of yours," Danny Kroll joked.

Dahlia smiled to herself. "As a matter of fact, my partner *is* that cousin. Call you later," she said, jotting down the number he gave her. When she turned to leave the bedroom, she noticed there was no more music coming from the living room. And when she opened the bedroom door, she saw that only Sunny was there sitting on the sofa, leafing through magazines.

"They left in a hurry," Sunny said. "Seth looked like something bad happened. Did it?" she asked.

Dahlia sighed, knowing she'd been right about Seth's guessing why the call had flustered her. And now he was gone. She should have told Danny she had company and called him back later. It was clear that Seth had wanted to find a way to reconcile before that phone call. But the call had meant a fortune to her and to Sunny.

"No," Dahlia said, refusing to let Seth's exit taint the moment. "Something wonderful happened, actually. I just found out that you're going to have even more money to give away. We're about to get what I expect will be a big windfall."

"Really?" Sunny asked, not looking up from an issue of *More* magazine. "Well, no windfall's gonna keep you as warm at night as that boy that just walked outta here."

Dahlia decided not to think about it. No. This was a time to celebrate, and her idea of celebrating was to go into the kitchen and look through the Yellow Pages for the phone numbers of house painters.

twenty

With the creative fees from the commercial, Dahlia jumped headlong into her project to redo the house. She decided that as long as the painters were coming to paint the outside, they really ought to paint the inside, too. And when they'd finished, the inside looked so fresh she decided that maybe instead of those old-fashioned fifties-style sliding doors in the living room, she ought to have somebody come and put in French doors leading to the backyard.

The new doors gave the formerly dull house a lot of charm, especially when they were thrown open to the backyard. But then the backyard looked shabby, so she decided to put a brick patio out there and maybe even a hot tub. And while the men were installing the new plumbing for the hot tub, she asked the plumber to take a look at Sunny's bathroom with the idea of putting in an updated Jacuzzi. The new tub in

Sunny's bathroom was so shiny and good-looking it made the other fixtures look dull by comparison, so Dahlia remodeled Sunny's bathroom and her own, and before the commercial was even on the air, Dahlia's share of the money from that check had dwindled dramatically.

But it was worth every penny to her, because the house had never looked better, and certainly, if the day ever came when she had to sell it, it wouldn't be an embarrassment to show. Of course, she couldn't let herself think that way, though. She had to stop any thoughts about having to sell the house. Things were on the upswing. She and Sunny were working hard and well together, and Harry Brenner called once a week to ask her how her new material was coming along. The last time he called, Dahlia bit the inside of her cheek nervously when he started talking about her performing at Highland Grounds. No, she thought. I will never do that.

"These record-company guys always say they don't go to these open-mike nights, but somebody tipped me off that on Wednesday night two of 'em are gonna be at Highland Grounds because some boy band they're hot to sign is closing the evening. So I figure you slide in there, they just happen on you, and they start thinking they're the big talent scouts and take the credit for discovering you. It's not the most sought-after gig in town, but if they see you there, it's way better than me sending them Faith's CD or making a demo of your stuff."

"Harry, you know I'm not a performer."

"Hey, we're not looking to make you a concert attraction, babe. We're looking to have them hear the songs, get you a publishing deal that means they pay you a weekly draw in exchange for turning out a certain number of songs every month. That would make you happy, wouldn't it?"

"Yeah, but I hate doing those showcase things."

"Hey, we all do stuff we hate."

"I'm working with a partner now, Harry."

"Yeah? So what? Bring her, too. Oh, and only do songs like that Faith song. None of that cute cabaret-style shit you played for me the day you came over here."

Dahlia hung up the phone and went outside, where Sunny was lying facedown on a lounge chair on the new patio, her white hair splayed in all directions.

"Maybe you should do this gig *with* me," Dahlia said. "I mean, I *am* going to sing one of the new songs we wrote together, and misery does love company."

"Not me," Sunny said. "I could play for the people at the Sea View because they knew me, but not for some real audience. At least I don't think I could ever feel okay about doing that again."

Sunny worked with Dahlia on the new song they'd written with Dahlia's lyrics for Seth, "Knowing What's Real." It was a love song, and the lyrics apologized for the cavalier way she'd handled their romance, asking him to see how she'd changed. He hadn't called since that day he'd followed her back to the house after seeing her at Whole Foods. One day she'd dialed his number, planning, when he picked up the phone, to fabricate some story about Danny Kroll's just being an advertising exec she'd met through her massage practice. Partially true. But when Seth's machine answered, she hung up and spared herself from offering up what really amounted to a lie.

She practiced singing the new song in every style, with a jazzy upbeat delivery, a country twang, a bluesy sadness, and finally she opted for a straight-ahead tell-a-story style, which Sunny said sounded best. But when the open-mike night rolled around, she felt very afraid.

"You're nervous? What're you nervous about? You got songs on big records. Compared to most of these people, you're big-time!" Harry could probably guess what Dahlia's state of mind was because as he sat at the table with her and Sunny, he watched Dahlia tear each match out of the matchbook that said "Highland Grounds" on it, light the match by the flame of the candle on the table, extinguish the match, and put it in the ashtray. Harry was shaking his head in disbelief as his eyes left the ashtray full of burned matches and scanned the room for what seemed like the millionth time.

Highland Grounds was a dark, noisy club on Highland Avenue near Melrose Avenue. The entry opened onto an outdoor seating area of picnic tables, and the door to the right led to a large room divided by a U-shaped bar with a small kitchen setup behind it. In the far right corner across from the bar in front of a screen, which concealed the door to the ladies' bathroom, was an upright piano. Dahlia was worried, knowing if she needed to bolt for the bathroom with a sick stomach, which felt imminent, or even if she just wanted to go there to splash cold water on her hot cheeks, everyone in the club would see her and know how panicky she felt.

She watched all the eager performers laughing and chatting excitedly with one another by the picnic tables, and she hated herself for being there. Sunny sat quietly eating a pizza, and the cheesy smell of it was making Dahlia even more nauseous. She was scheduled to be on after the next act, but she wished she could just run out the door and drive away. Anything but put herself up there in front of this hooting, booze-swilling audience.

Harry was drinking a beer when he spotted the two record-company executives the instant they walked in the door. They were dressed in expensive jeans and black T-shirts. One of them wore a black Armani blazer, the other a leather jacket. Dahlia watched them order mineral water, and one of them held an unlit cigar in his teeth. A few sycophants rushed over to fawn over them, but Harry, who'd said nothing to Sunny all evening, was playing it cool, acting as if he were actually watching the acts that were working.

The first one had been a singer/pianist who was an Elton John wannabe, wearing a sequined cape and singing in a whining voice about how he needed to tear down walls to make his relationship work. After he was finished, there'd been a brief setup for the next act, which was comprised of two teenage girls who looked like runaways, with hair dyed too black and bangs falling in their heavily lined eyes. They had pierced noses, into which they'd inserted a few gold studs. They were playing electric guitars and singing about dying for love.

On open-mike night, the rules were simple. The performers put their names in a hat, and then the manager of the club pulled out the names and posted a list of them on a bulletin board in the order of the draw. Each writer/performer was allowed to sing two songs, and that was it. In return for the performance, the artists were able to hear a live audience respond to their material. Sometimes there was polite applause, sometimes loud cheering, and often the act was so boring that the audience talked loudly through the entire performance.

"Those two guys at that table," Harry said, elbowing Dahlia. "They already like you. They heard your cut on Faith's CD, so you're in hot shape." Tonight, somehow, she'd find a way to tell Harry who the genius was behind the song.

"Hot blooooood," the two grungy girls sang as they strummed their guitars. "I got such hoooot blood."

"My *mother* could follow them and look good," Harry said through his teeth. Dahlia needed to breathe some fresh air before she went on, so she got up nervously, walked out past the picnic tables, and stood at the open archway of the front entrance facing busy Highland Avenue. Across the wide street she could see the shiny Celica convertible gleaming under a streetlight.

The checks were coming in, and she was living it up. The same day she'd bought the car, Sunny, who had spent a little bit of her newfound money on a few inexpensive jogging suits, repaid Dahlia for some of the cost of living there and then donated a huge chunk of her share of the money to Step Up on Second, a rehab center in Santa Monica she'd read about, that provided support for adults recovering from mental illnesses.

I'd better get inside, Dahlia thought, I'm next. She started to turn back to the entrance as a Jeep Cherokee pulled up across the street behind the Celica. Some crummy driver might get too close to her hot new car, so she'd better watch. It wasn't until the lights of the Jeep went out and the door swung open that she realized the driver was Seth, who was waving to her as he crossed toward the club.

"Support your local songwriter," he said, grinning. "That's what I always say. What do *you* always say?" he asked as he hugged her.

"A good man is hard to find," she said, pulling him close and inhaling his sweet scent.

"Sunny called me this morning and said I had to be here," he said into her hair.

"Next, please welcome Dahlia Gordon. She'll be singing a song she wrote with Sunny Gordon called 'Knowing What's Real.'" Dahlia rushed back inside and made her way through the tables toward the piano. Deep breath. Here goes nothin', she thought as she sat in front of the keyboard, and after a moment she watched her hands play the first few chords of the tune. The club grew still right away, and then the only sound in the room was her childlike voice singing the new song she and Sunny had written, and she was pleased with the way she sounded singing it.

After the first chorus, she could tell that the song was getting to the crowd. She could feel them settle into their chairs, hear their grunts of approval at her sentiments in the lyrics, and when she actually allowed herself to look out at their faces, she saw they were rapt as they watched her, even the record-company executives. Across the room she spotted Seth, who was smiling a heartfelt smile at her as she sang the words she'd written from her deepest feelings about him. Now she leaned in to play the last chorus, and all her stage fright was gone.

The applause rose, and she was about to launch into another new song when she felt a hand on her shoulder. She turned to look into Sunny's eyes. For an instant she thought Sunny just wanted to congratulate her on doing a good job, but it was clear from the way she squeezed Dahlia's shoulder and nodded that she wanted to join her on the bench. Dahlia understood why and took the microphone in her hand.

"This is my partner and my cousin, Sunny Gordon," she said into it. Then she drew in a deep breath and took her cue from Sunny's expression. "We're going to sing a song that was her wonderful idea and her awesome tune, to which I had the good fortune to write the lyrics, and I'm grateful." Dahlia's eyes didn't leave Sunny's as she said the rest, "A song that Faith Hill recently recorded. It's called 'What's Happened to Me?' "

Dahlia looked over at Harry and saw his eyebrows screw up in confusion as Sunny played the intro and the two cousins' voices rose in song. Their blended voices filled the room, and as they went along, they improvised harmonies. Dahlia could feel the energy in the room crackling with excitement and admiration for Sunny's breathtaking musical style. Sunny improvised a piano interlude, always looking shyly at the keys while she played and never at the crowd, but her impassioned playing of her blockbuster tune was soaring. She and Dahlia joined together to sing the last verse, and before they belted out the final powerful notes, all the people in the crowded club leaped to their feet, and one of the barmaids jumped onto the bar, and all of them were stomping and whistling and cheering for Dahlia and Sunny and their glorious song.

They held their arms up in triumph and took one bow and then another, flushed with happiness. Then Dahlia worked her way back through the crowd to the table and sat between Seth and Harry as Sunny was being stopped at every table by her new fans. Harry leaned close to Dahlia's ear so she could hear him above the din.

"*She* wrote the music?" he said, looking confused. Dahlia felt Seth watching her as she looked back at Harry and nodded. "I thought you said *you* wrote the lyrics *and* the music. I have a contract that says *you* wrote this," Harry said, looking pale.

"It was a lie, Harry," Dahlia said, and out of the corner of her eye, she saw Seth grin. "But you can relax. Sunny says you can be her manager, too."

"I'm gonna be her manager, too? No kidding? She's a killer!"

Sunny was getting high fives and hugs of congratulations from everyone in her path. Finally at the table, she looked at Dahlia, then leaned over to hug her. She was sweating, her hair matted against her face, and she hurried to pull Dahlia to her feet and hug her and cry into her cousin's shoulder. Then she tugged her outside.

"Don't be mad at me for calling Seth and telling him

you were appearing here tonight. He told me that the day he and Lolly came over and Danny called, he could tell by the look on your face that you had something going with Danny, and he just couldn't bear that idea. But I told him you never stopped loving him. Was I lying?"

"No," Dahlia said.

"Then you better tell him that tonight, too," Sunny said, and they walked back into the club with their arms around each other's waists. Sunny was still flying from their triumph, looking around the room at the people gazing at her with admiring eyes. It was intermission, and the two record-company executives were heading for their table. Dahlia watched Harry jump to his feet nervously to greet them. She stood nearby with Sunny, trying to overhear the men's conversation.

"So whaddya think of my two clients?" Harry asked. "Dahlia had a song a while back that was recorded by Naomi Judd, and the other girl—"

"The other girl . . ." the older one of the record company executives said, shaking his head. "Man, she delivers. I haven't seen anyone like her since Laura Nyro. What's her name again?"

Dahlia heard the panic in Harry's voice. "Uh . . . yeah . . . she is kind of like Laura Nyro and she . . ." He didn't have a clue what Sunny's name was. Didn't remember it even though Dahlia had announced it.

"Sunny," Dahlia said, stepping into the circle of men. "Sunny Gordon. I'm Dahlia Gordon," she said, shaking the hands of the two men as Harry sighed with relief.

"Great stuff, great tunes," one of the men said, barely looking at her. "You know how to find me,

Harry. I'm very interested in these girls. Get me some of their latest songs, and maybe we can make a deal." Then the two men left, and Harry ordered a scotch from a passing waitress to calm himself down.

Seth hugged Dahlia in congratulations, and while Harry and Sunny chatted about the demo he planned to make of Dahlia and Sunny's songs and how he wanted to arrange some of them, Dahlia relaxed in her chair and held tightly to Seth's hand.

"I guess it would be stupid to think you could ever come back and live in Laurel Canyon with two crazy women," she said hopefully, but Seth smiled at her sadly and shook his head.

"Can't do it," he said.

"Didn't think so," Dahlia said, embarrassed that she'd even mentioned it. It must have been the high of the moment that made her think she could get away with something so impossible.

"I mean if I did, it would end up being me and *three* crazy women, because I just got full-time custody of Lolly last week." Dahlia saw the sad smile on his face, and she realized that Seth's having Lolly to himself must mean something bad had happened. "My ex broke up with the pediatrician, or, more accurately, he left her, and she was so depressed she decided to go live in Maui and become a reflexologist, but she didn't want to take Lolly with her there or anywhere else. So she moved her into my place last week and got on the next flight out."

"I'm sorry for Lolly," Dahlia said. "Poor kid. Abandoned like that. She must be very sad."

"She's completely blown away," he said. His voice

was even, but Dahlia could see the worry in his eyes. "And that's why I promised myself that the next time I live with a woman, she'll be my wife and someone who really wants to be a mother to my daughter."

Dahlia didn't know what to say to that. There was no chance he or anyone else would ever believe her if she said she could take on the job of being a good mother to a little girl. And worse yet, she probably wouldn't believe it herself.

"Okay, you two," Harry said, patting both Sunny and Dahlia proprietarily on their backs. "First thing Monday morning, at my place, we start working on the demo. Gotta use this momentum to get it made and out there to the guys that matter."

"Sounds like fun. You happy, Dahl?" Sunny asked.

"Very happy," Dahlia said, looking at Seth, who knew she was lying. "Very, very happy."

It took two seven-day-a-week workweeks plus evenings to pull the demo together, even though there were only four songs on it. Some of the instrumentals were created by Harry's synthesizer, and some of them were done by live musicians who came into the studio and played along with Sunny.

Sunny did all the vocals and rerecorded each one of them at least twenty-five times. Harry was a perfectionist, but Sunny was worse, needing to be certain every note of every song was flawless, every lyric clear and comprehensible. Dahlia would rewrite lyrics on the spot and change them again and again until they sounded good to Harry's ear. In the end Harry and his engineer, Dave, pieced together a line from one verse, with two lines from another, a chorus from yet another take, until they had a perfect and completed version of each song.

Every night after their grueling day at Harry's, Dahlia and Sunny drove home to the cozy, pretty Laurel Canyon house, still singing the songs, and when they arrived, they were elated but too exhausted to do anything except collapse on the sofa and watch television. On several of the nights when Dahlia didn't have the heart to wake her, Sunny slept through until morning on the sofa in her clothes. One night on a re-run of *The View*, they watched four teenage girls having "prom makeovers" where they showed the girls in their "before" states, then had all the young women appearing live after they'd been made over by studio hair and makeup artists. Every time one of the redone teenagers walked onto the stage, the audience gasped and cheered.

"I need a makeover," Sunny muttered at the end of the segment.

"Me, too," Dahlia said. "So let's get them. As soon as we finish the demo, let's make ourselves appointments and go get them."

Sunny didn't respond, and when Dahlia looked at her cousin, she saw the trepidation in her eyes.

"Oh, sorry. I forgot," Dahlia said, realizing.

"Forgot what?" Sunny asked, even though she knew what Dahlia was thinking, because she was thinking it, too.

"There are mirrors, big mirrors in every salon. Lots of them. Sometimes wall to wall. We've been avoiding mirrors everywhere we go. Has that changed?"

Sunny thought about the question for a while, then looked at Dahlia and shrugged. "I'd like to try to do it," is what she said.

It was at least eighty degrees outside, but Sunny was shivering a little as they rode up in the elevator. The Beverly Hills salon was big and brightly lit, and each station was out in the open so Dahlia and Sunny could see every one of the other women who were having their hair styled.

"We don't have to do this," Dahlia said, looking at Sunny's expression as she took in the room, standing far enough away from all the mirrors so she wouldn't have to see her reflection yet.

"We do," Sunny told her. "We're in the music business now. We have to look a lot cooler than we do, or nobody will believe us."

Dahlia laughed at that. "How do you *know* how you look? You never get near a mirror."

"Believe me, I can tell," Sunny answered.

The giant mirrors over each station had strips of lights over them, and Sunny froze in the middle of the room. From where the two of them stood, their images were re-created dozens of times all around them. Dahlia felt afraid for an instant as Sunny made a 360-degree turn to see all of the Sunnys everywhere, even the distorted ones in the chrome domes of the hair dryers. Dahlia held her breath, knowing Sunny could fall apart at any moment, but she seemed very even.

One of the hairstylists was away from his station, so the mirror above his counter wasn't blocked by anybody. Sunny noticed that and headed toward it cautiously. Dear God, Dahlia thought, let this be okay for her, and she crossed her fingers the way she used to as a kid, hoping for Sunny's well-being.

Sunny moved closer and closer to her own image, seeing herself, looking at the reflection of herself probably for the first time in years. She was still a radiantly beautiful woman, with pink skin and that naturally white-blond hair, and her body was curvy and well proportioned. Today she wore a pair of black jeans Dahlia had ordered for her from a catalog and a scoop-necked black T-shirt that set off the whiteness of her skin and hair.

Now she was in perfect range to examine herself, and after a moment when she took herself in at last, Dahlia exhaled. Yes, she thought. Yes, thank you, because she could tell by the upturned corners of Sunny's mouth as she studied every inch of herself that she was pleased with what she saw and that the intruders in her life, the ones through the looking glass, were either gone or benign for the moment. And then she lifted her arms over her head and tossed her head back, victorious, as she spun around in a circle joyously and rushed over to tell Dahlia the news.

"I'm free, I'm free! The audience's seats are still there, but they're empty. At least for the moment, I'm free!" The two cousins embraced with joy.

"Which one of you is Gordon?" the pretty brunette hairstylist asked.

"We both are!"

"Sunny?" she asked, referring to a piece of paper in her hand.

"That's me."

"Come on, darlin', you're next."

A color specialist put a toner in Sunny's hair to brighten its whiteness, and then she put reddish highlights in Dahlia's dark hair. While the cousins sat waiting for the colors to set, with Sunny's hair in a turban and Dahlia's sticking out in every direction wrapped in pieces of aluminum foil, they had manicures and signed up to get pedicures. It was while their feet were soaking in water in adjacent tubs that they heard the music coming from the countertop TV that one of the hairdressers was watching. The music was part of a commercial in which an older, white-haired couple was walking hand in hand.

"Stay by my side forever. Stay by my side, my friend . . ."

"Sun, it's our commercial!" Dahlia shouted, and she was so excited she stood up in the tub of hot water and hollered out across the salon. "Turn it up! Please turn it up!"

The hairdresser with the TV hurried to turn the volume louder.

"I hear it," Sunny said, and she stood also. Dahlia was too fired up to stand still, and she jumped out of her tub and grabbed Sunny out of hers, and they twirled in circles, getting soapy water everywhere, dancing to the song they'd written more than twenty-five years before as it played behind a commercial. Dahlia left wet, soapy footprints as she hurried to the TV and turned up the volume even more, and they cheered for their song with everyone in the salon looking over at them.

❦

twenty-one

It wasn't until a few weeks after Louie Gordon saw the commercial on TV that Dahlia heard the whole story. Louie had been getting ready to leave for work in the morning. Just doing what he did every weekday at 8:00 A.M., pouring coffee into his thermos so he'd have a few extra cups at the store while he was opening up and putting the merchandise on the sidewalk. The coffeemaker in Louie's pretty Valley house was on the same counter where he and Penny kept the portable TV, because Louie liked to watch the *Today* show every morning, and on that particular morning, just after Katie Couric said, "We'll be right back," a commercial came on.

Ordinarily Louie pushed the mute button during the endless commercial breaks, but that morning he didn't remember where he'd put the remote and the coffee was only halfway into the thermos, so he was stuck watching this commercial for whatever the hell it was . . . health insurance or something like that. There was a cute little old couple with white hair holding hands and walking in a park. And the song that some really syrupy singer was singing in the background was one that Louie recognized instantly. But for a minute he couldn't remember from where. So familiar. From a long time ago.

"Stay by my side forever. Stay by my side, my friend." Jesus Christ! Louie whirled around and stared at the TV.

"My sister wrote that song," he said out loud to nobody. "But how did it get on TV?" Now the announcer was saying something about some insurance policy for old folks, and the little white-haired couple was on a golf course together yucking it up. And then there were a few more bars of the song again, and the commercial ended and Louie went to his little leather phone book to look up the number of that weird halfway house in San Diego, even though he knew he didn't have a prayer that anyone there would ever answer.

After he finally found the number and dialed the place, he let it ring twenty times, but something told him he didn't have to go all the way down to San Diego to look for Sunny. No. Not at all. Louie was pretty sure he knew where to find her instead.

"Louie, what a surprise. I've owned this house for eight years, and you've never once dropped in on me before. How come I get the pleasure today?" Dahlia asked, trying to look calm, even though she knew that Louie's being there had to mean trouble.

"Yeah, yeah, yeah. Don't get cute with me, Dahlia," an irate Louie said. "You got my sister here?"

"What's the problem, Louie? You look as if some disaster happened."

"Some disaster did happen, Dahlia, and it's you! You took her outta that place in San Diego without asking me."

"You're right, Louie, but I did ask Sunny, and she said yes, and she's an adult, so that was enough."

"She's a retarded, mental-case, dangerous-to-the-world adult. And you have her out walking the streets. She's liable to hurt somebody, and they could come after my ass for not keeping her in a safe place. I'm her next of kin, Dahlia. Not you. That means I'm responsible for her and I should decide when she's in a fruit-cake factory and when she's not."

"Louie, if you decided that she was better off in that falling-apart home where they overdrug people and call it taking care of them instead of her living with me, then you're the one who ought to be locked up. And she isn't going to hurt a fly."

"How do you know? *What* do you know? You're the big expert?"

"Louie, what do you want?"

"I want to talk to her."

"Yeah? Well, I'll ask her if she wants to talk to you."

"Oh, right. As if she's capable of making that decision."

"She's not only capable. She's in a really good place

right now emotionally. And she's on her way to being real successful. Have you seen the commercial for—"

"Yeah, I've seen it. How much did she get for it, Dahlia? And what's she doing with the money? Do I need to send in my accountant to make sure you're not taking more than your share?"

"Louie, get your nasty little face out of here," Dahlia heard a voice behind her say, and Louie stepped back at the overwhelming sight of the way his sister looked standing in that doorway. How could this possibly be the woman he saw last time at that stinking place in San Diego where she'd been so scary-looking that his kids had gotten sick just meeting her? Now her hair was its natural white, and she had it cut in a very trendy spiky haircut. She was far from Hollywood skinny, but her slick black parachute outfit was as shiny as leather and made her look very show-business cool.

Dahlia loved the expression in Louie's eyes, somewhere between awe and terror. Later she told Seth it was like Ebenezer Scrooge must have looked when he saw Marley's ghost. Louie's first impulse was to laugh, but then his face twitched—maybe just holding back tears of joy made him blink that way. Whatever the emotion that came with that look in his eyes, he seemed genuinely stunned to realize that this pulled-together woman in the doorway was the once-tragic figure Sunny.

"My sister. You're my kid sister, and you're okay," Louie said, shaking his head and clucking his tongue. "It's a miracle. This is some kind of miracle."

Sunny exchanged a look of disdain with Dahlia. "Believe me, it's no miracle, Louie," Sunny said. "It's hard work, but I'm doing it, and Dahlia's helping. Now, what are you doing here?"

Louie put his hand on Sunny's face, and Dahlia watched her try not to recoil, just gentle his hand away. "All I can think of is Mom and Dad and how happy they'd be to see you like this," he said. "When I think of all the years they wished for this." His words sounded as stiff as if he were reading lines from a TelePrompTer. "I take my kids to the cemetery every year because I want Mom and Dad to know how big they're getting. Hey! Maybe you should come with us. We always go on Mom's birthday, and it's next week."

Dahlia remembered that Aunt Ruthie's birthday was in March, and this was September. "You're not taking her anywhere, Louie," she said as Louie put on an insulted face.

"Hey, this woman happens to be my children's aunt," he said. "The only aunt they'll ever have, and they don't even know her," he said, reaching into his back pocket and taking out his wallet. "Sun, look," he said, opening it and pulling out three school pictures, which he thrust at Sunny. "Here's Kassie, and here's Robin, and here's Michael. Look how much he looks like Daddy."

Sunny held the pictures and looked closely at each of the children's faces as Dahlia watched her.

"My God, he does look so much like Daddy," she said, shaking her head in amazement. "And Kassie is so pretty with that white-blond hair."

Louie grinned. "And who does she look like to a tee?" he asked. "Her Aunt Sunny. Do you know how many times I've called her Sunny by mistake?"

"Really?" Sunny looked at him, and her eyes were so filled with hope that Dahlia knew this was all heading in a dangerous direction.

"Sun," Louie said, knowing that his appeal to her was working, "she couldn't look more like you if she were your own daughter. And she plays the piano like an angel. Of course, we don't have the baby grand, because Ma left it in her will to her," he said with a roll of his eyeballs toward Dahlia. "But Kassie could make a broken-down spinet sound like a Steinway in Carnegie Hall, just like you. And look at my little Robin. She plays, too, and writes songs that the two of them sing. Listen, the kids hear stories about you night and day. And that time I brought the older two to see you? They don't even remember that. They idolize you."

Sunny was going for it hook, line, and sinker. Flushed and smiling and holding the pictures to her chest and misting up.

"They're so adorable," she said.

"Sun, I'm not kiddin'. These are the daughters you never had, these are your surrogate children. They want to be with you. Dahlia doesn't understand because she's an only child, so she can only imagine the way aunts and uncles feel about the children who look up to them. The way you have to be connected to these children who are your blood."

Dahlia leaned on the doorjamb waiting for Louie to finish. Sunny was probably thinking about how sad it was that she had missed the early childhood years of these children, but Dahlia couldn't believe that Louie, that little rat, wanted Sunny to be with his children for anything other than the most selfish reasons. Now Louie was taking Sunny's hand and holding it tightly as he went on.

"Hey! Want to be spontaneous? Throw some stuff in a bag and come to my house for a few days! These kids will be all over you. They'll put on a show for you, and you'll think you're watching yourself. They need you in their lives, and you need them. These three kids are carrying the genes of our mother and father into the future. Long after we're gone, who's gonna talk about their Aunt Sunny who fought her way back from mental problems and had her songs sung in commercials? And probably had her great songs being sung in other places, too."

Sunny nodded proudly, and Louie brightened.

"For example . . . what other places can I tell them about?" he asked. No, Dahlia thought. Please don't tell him. Don't give him fodder for his nasty, greedy plot. But Sunny already had the words on her tongue.

"Well, Faith Hill has a song of ours on her new CD."

"Faith Hill?" Louie said, wide-eyed. His breathing had changed to a pant. "By the way, Dahlia," he said, turning to her, "would it be too much to ask if I stepped inside your cute little house instead of standing out here like I've got cooties or something? I mean, I know you always hated me, but some courtesy . . ."

"I never hated you, Louie," she lied, knowing there was a force at work between the two siblings that she was powerless to counteract. "And of course you can come in," she said as Louie backed her and Sunny into the room, then strolled over to the piano and looked at it covetously.

"You know, Sun, Ma left this to Dahlia because I didn't play and she was afraid you were so hopeless you'd never come back from your hell, and now here you are, doing so well. You really have to come and be with my kids. The girls will both be dying to hang around with you. I have a gorgeous house with a pool. You'll think you're at a luxury hotel."

"Louie, Dahlia and I write songs together every day," Sunny said, but it was a halfhearted attempt, and now Louie was on a mission.

"So? You'll write them at *my* house. It's a hotbed of creativity over there. And nobody's home all day. Dahlia can come to my house. I'll let her in. I'll even offer her a cold drink, unlike the way she is currently treating me."

"I'll be glad to give you a cold drink, Louie, and Sunny doesn't want to come to your house," Dahlia said, but when she looked at Sunny, hoping for a nod of agreement, she saw the wistful look on Sunny's face that made it clear Louie had gotten to her. "I've been keeping her on a schedule. I'm the one who makes sure she takes her pills every day," Dahlia tried.

"Dahlia, don't make me laugh," Louie said scornfully. "I run a highly profitable business that everyone said wouldn't last because big hardware chains were opening all around me, and you think I'm not capable of making sure my baby sis takes one stinking pill every day?"

Sunny let out a little giggle at hearing him call her his baby sis, and Louie picked up on that. "Remember how I used to call you baby sis?" She laughed a big laugh now. "When you were a toddler and you called me—"

"Woowee," Sunny said, remembering.

"My God, she remembers!" Louie said, running his hairy arm against his eyes to remove a crocodile tear. "My kids know that about their Aunt Sunny. How she used to call me Woowee before she could pronounce her Ls. You didn't know that, Dahlia."

"I wasn't born yet, Louie," Dahlia said, wanting to strangle him for this obvious con job he was pulling on Sunny. If his sister didn't have money pouring in, Dahlia was sure he wouldn't even be here.

"I rest my case," he said. "I'm the one who has a lifelong history with her. I went to the hospital, and my dad lifted me up so I could look into the nursery window when she was born, and I said, 'Let's take her home and love and hug her forever, Daddy.'"

"You never said that or did that, because they didn't even let little kids into hospitals in those days, Woowee," Dahlia said disdainfully.

"What do you know? Get your toothbrush, Sun."

"Hold on there, Louie. When does she come back?" Dahlia asked, watching Sunny turn to go to her room.

"Whenever she feels like it," Louie said, "but don't hold your breath. We've got a lot of catching up to do, and besides, I don't owe you any explanation. She could decide to come and be at my house for good. And I could become her manager."

"She has a manager. Someone who really knows the music business."

"Those guys are all sharks. How do I know if he's looking out for her best interests? What about a financial planner? What's she investing her money in?"

"She's giving it to charity," Dahlia said, and Louie gasped and clutched his chest.

"What?" he said, glaring at Dahlia with fire in his eyes. "What charity?"

"Board-and-care places. Places that specialize in taking care of people like her."

"Oh, my God. Who told her *that* was a good idea? And your share? Don't tell me you're giving your share away, too. *That* I will never believe." Dahlia didn't say a word. "Oh, I get the whole picture now. You went to get her out of that nut palace because you needed her music 'cause you're burned out. I saw a movie like this. It was called *Death Trap*, about a playwright who lost his talent so he kills a young writer and pretends he wrote the young writer's play."

"That's not the story. The older writer and the younger writer were lovers, and they were trying to kill the older writer's wife," Dahlia said.

"Whatever," Louie said, his eyes glowing. "In tonight's performance the part of the has-been writer is played by you."

"You're nuts, Louie."

"Oh, am I? From now on I'm making sure her interests are taken care of by a business expert. Me! You want to work with her? You call me, and I'll let you know if she's available," he said. Then he marched past her to where he'd seen Sunny disappear, and within a few seconds he hustled Sunny out of the room toward the door. Sunny was carrying the same Macy's shopping bag she'd brought to Dahlia's, and it was filled with a lot of clothes.

"Bye, Dahl," Sunny said. "I'll call you." And she never looked back as Louie escorted her to his car.

twenty-two

For the next week, every time Dahlia called Louie's house, which she did at least twice a day, the answering machine picked up. By now she had the damned message memorized. "This is Kassie, this is Robin, and this is Michael," the children said individually in their cute little singsong voices. Then in a chorus they said, "We're not here right now, but leave us a message and we'll call ya back as soon as we can. Bye-bye."

"Bye-bye," Dahlia said along with them, trying to keep the annoyance out of her voice as she left another message.

"Uh, hi . . . this is Dahlia calling again to speak to Sunny. Please ask her to call me," she said, knowing that it was futile.

Louie had to be the one who played the messages back at the end of the day and then never even mentioned to Sunny that Dahlia had called. Some things never changed. Here it was all these years later, and Louie was still jealous of his sister's relationship with Dahlia.

Harry Brenner called her every day to tell her that he and the engineer were mixing the tracks, which sounded great, and to describe his plans for the demo. He knew exactly where he was planning to send it and who the music business biggies were that he was planning to assault with phone calls after he was sure they'd received the demos. He was confident about how much they were going to love the music. But Dahlia barely heard a word he said. Her house was empty, and she felt lonelier than she ever had before she'd met Seth, and long before Sunny came back into her life.

It was the eighth day of no return call from Sunny. Every day Dahlia tried working on a few new songs but couldn't seem to finish any of them. Yesterday at the market, she threw a package of tortillas into her basket because Sunny's favorite dinner was burritos. She was all the way at the checkout line when she remembered she wasn't cooking for Sunny anymore, and sadly she wheeled the cart back to the tortilla section and tossed them back into the case.

Today she was sitting at the piano with the French doors open to the brick patio, and she heard an odd chirpy sound and looked outside. On the small glass end table next to one of the patio chairs sat a creature that had to be Rose, the squirrel, looking right back at her.

"I know," Dahlia said. "I miss her, too."

Then she played "Stay by My Side" at a melancholy tempo, and it sounded like a dirge. She decided to focus on the newspaper, so she turned the pages until she found what she was looking for. The astrological forecast. Then she moved her finger down the column to her astrological sign, Pisces. Her horoscope today read *Getting together with family members will cheer you.*

"Ha! I *would* if they'd pick up the freaking phone," she said out loud sadly to the newspaper. Then she dumped cornflakes into a bowl and poured some milk on top of them, realizing, when she looked at the contents of the bowl that she hated cornflakes. She was thinking about making some toast when she stopped and listened, trying to figure out what that insistent little tweeting sound was that she heard repeating itself again and again. Then she walked in the direction of the bedroom, because it sounded as if it were coming from there.

Of course! It was that silly plastic timer she'd bought to remind her every morning to make sure Sunny took her pill. She hadn't seen it since Sunny left and hadn't bothered to look for it, but now it had gone off for some unknown reason and it wouldn't stop beeping until she pushed the off button. She marched into the bedroom following the sound, which seemed to be coming from somewhere in her dresser, but she couldn't tell where.

"Damn it," she said aloud as she tore open each drawer and pawed through it. First the underwear drawer, then the T-shirt drawer, until she finally spotted the stupid timer under the dresser, where it must have fallen. With a sigh she stooped, grabbed for it, and pushed the off button, then sat on the floor holding the timer in her hand and let herself cry.

Lolly stood at the door of the apartment. The babysitter was standing a few feet behind her. "Who *is* it, Lol?" she asked.

"Nobody," Lolly said, and her reply was so obviously intended as an insult that Dahlia had to stop herself from laughing. "My dad's not here," Lolly seemed pleased to be able to report to Dahlia.

"Didn't come to see him," Dahlia said.

"Try his office," Lolly said, and she started to close the door, but Dahlia stopped it with her foot.

"I came to bring something for you."

"Oh, right," Lolly said, scowling in disbelief.

"I was cleaning my apartment, and I came across some things I don't use anymore. I thought you'd like to have them."

Lolly's eyes looked tired. The expression in them was a cynicism far too developed for someone her age. She folded her arms in front of her chest and pursed her lips, waiting to hear what Dahlia would say next.

"Okay, what is it?" she asked.

Dahlia reached behind her back and produced the turquoise Chinese silk box that had been her mother's and then hers. That morning she had sifted through it and removed a few of the best pieces and transferred those to a shoe box, but what was left inside was a treasure trove of glittering baubles, dozens of costume pieces she knew she would never wear.

Lolly stood silently as Dahlia opened the box, and when she saw all the sparkling necklaces and bracelets and rings piled inside like pirates' treasure, she grinned a grin much bigger than any Dahlia had seen on her face before.

"Where'd you get these?" Lolly asked.

"From my mother."

"Wow! And how come you brought them over here?"

"Because I never wear them, and I said to myself, 'Who do I know who likes sparkly stuff?' And I remembered that your dad told me you like to play dress-up. So I thought . . ."

Lolly was touching the long strand of pearls and slowly extracting them from the box, then hanging them around her neck, looking down to see that the strand was so long on her that it nearly touched the floor.

"Ooooh," she said. "You're giving this stuff to me?"

Dahlia nodded. "The box, too," she said.

"Lolly," Dahlia heard the baby-sitter call from inside, and then the woman was standing in the doorway. A middle-aged blonde wearing a green hooded sweatshirt and jeans.

"It's okay, Mary," Lolly said. "She's my dad's old girlfriend, and she wanted to bring me some stuff."

The sitter smiled and went back inside, and Lolly came out and sat on the front step so she could go through the contents of the box. "Awesome," she said. "I love this," and she tried to clip a jet-bead earring onto her tiny lobe but couldn't do it. "Will you help me?" she asked, and Dahlia did, while Lolly fished around in the box for the earring's mate.

This poor little girl, Dahlia thought. Her mother

walked out on her. She'll probably never get over that. She'll always wonder what she did to make that happen. She'll always hurt when she sees girls who are close to their mothers. She'll have to limp along without that mentor in her corner to give her the kind of audience only mothers can give.

Dahlia and Rose. Two flowers in the vase. Remembering her mother made her want to pull Lolly onto her lap and give her a reassuring hug. But she knew she hadn't earned that right with this child, and she felt sorry for all the times she could have been warm to her instead of distant. But she'd been afraid to let herself get too close, because she was so sure that she and Seth wouldn't last, and then she'd have to part with not just him but the kid, too.

Now the sitter was back in the doorway.

"Lolly, you have to come and get cleaned up for ballet," she said. "I'm going to take you, and Daddy's going to pick you up."

"Mary, look what Dahlia gave me!" Lolly said, standing and turning her head to show off the earrings and the long pearls.

"Very nice," Mary said in one of those voices adults use to humor kids. "Now, say good-bye and come along."

"Bye," Lolly said as she picked up the jewelry box and headed inside, but she turned back to see Dahlia still standing there and added, "Thanks a lot."

"You're welcome," Dahlia said, watching the door close and then walking slowly back to her car, wondering if what she'd just done was stupid or maybe even desperate. When Lolly saw Seth that night, would she tell him that Dahlia had brought her jewelry, and would he think, Too little too late, babe! Forget trying to worm your way back through the kid.

Somewhere among Dahlia's old photos there was a yellowing picture her mother used to have in a frame in the living room. It was a still shot her father had taken when Rose was trying to teach the seven-year-old Dahlia to ride a bike. She was afraid but determined to learn, and that particular day she'd been nervously wobbling along on the tiny old two-wheeler that had once been Sunny's, with Rose holding on to the back and running along to keep the bike balanced.

"Don't let go yet, don't let go yet!" Dahlia would shout, and Rose didn't. She held tightly until the moment she was certain by the feeling in her hands that Dahlia had the balance on her own, that Dahlia had finally incorporated the feeling into her own body, the sense of how she had to sit and move and tip to go it alone. And at the very instant she felt it, Rose lifted her arms joyously to the sky, Dahlia felt the ecstasy of her independence, which registered clearly on her face, and her father was there with the camera capturing the moment.

That was what being a parent meant. That's what being a valuable adult to a child was about. That kind of moment, not bringing her junk jewelry. Seth would probably laugh at the whole idea of Dahlia's showing up with that stuff. But never mind. At least she'd made the kid smile for a change.

* * *

"Dahl, it's me."

"Sun? Are you okay! I've tried to call you a million times."

"Really? Nobody around here mentioned it. I've been so busy with these children—and, Dahl, they are amazingly fabulous. You have to get to know them. They're everything we wanted to be and more. Yesterday was their school fair, and Penny had to stay home and cook for this party she's having, so I helped Kassie out in the face-painting booth. I'm really good at that! Maybe from all those years of nail polish," she said, laughing.

"Anyway, I'm calling to tell you that there's a big party here tomorrow night. Louie says he wants to show me off, so he's invited a million people—some are in show business and some are just wholesale-hardware people—but I said I'd sing for them. The kids have never heard our songs, and Louie's pushing it, so I thought . . ." Then there was silence on the line between them until Sunny said, "Dahl, I know you won't like this, but I'm thinking about letting Louie manage me. I mean, he says he's the only one I can trust. So I figure what he doesn't have in experience, he makes up for in being on my side. And he says business is business. He's convinced that if he can sell hardware, he can sell me. He says it's okay with him if you use Harry to manage your half of the act, and I'll use Louie for mine."

"Louie's wrong," Dahlia said, her heart sinking, knowing that the battle lines were being drawn. The music business was hard enough without having to fight Louie from getting in the way of their success. "It's not the same as selling a bicycle lock."

"We'll talk about it more when I see you," Sunny said. "My mother used to say when there was a big decision that has to be made, 'Hide and watch, and something will happen to tell you what to do.' And I know it's last-minute, but I really want you here for the party. Will you come?"

"Sure," Dahlia said, certain that Louie would bristle when he saw her, but hoping that once she and Sunny were in the same room, she'd be able to convince her not only to come back but that Louie was a louse.

"I'll see you here at five?" Sunny said.

"Yep."

Dahlia hadn't been to Louie's house in years, but she remembered the tree-lined street where his small, pretty bungalow sat at the very middle of the cul-de-sac. A cute young valet-parking guy in a red vest said, "I love your car," as he drove off to park it. Dahlia was perspiring as she rang the bell, and it wasn't a very hot day. She could hear the piano and the voices of the crowd inside, and after a while a woman opened the door. It was Penny, Louie's round little wife who matched him in size and shape as if they were salt and pepper shakers, except for their hair. Louie was balding, and Penny had a big pouf of red curls. The last time Dahlia had seen her, she was wearing her hair straightened and sprayed into a bouffant, but now the curls were natural and flyaway around her face.

"Penny? It's Dahlia."

Penny smiled and opened the door, then gave her a perfunctory hug and said, "Dahlia, it's been far too long," in an icy voice that made Dahlia know it was only because of Sunny's coercing that she'd been invited here at all.

The house was in a much better neighborhood than the one where Dahlia and Sunny and Louie had grown up, but the crowded living room, filled with people holding drinks in plastic cups and the buffet platter with cold cuts and paper plates and plastic utensils and large bottles of cola on it, made it look so much like a throwback to the way her parents and Sunny's parents used to set up every party that Dahlia felt as if she were back in the past. A hired piano player wearing a white shirt and a bow tie sat at the upright piano in Louie's family room playing "Moon River."

Louie was out by the pool. Dahlia could see him through the glass doors talking and laughing with a few of the men. He was wearing jeans and an open denim shirt, and even from that distance, she could see he was wearing a thick gold chain around his neck. His dark Ray-Ban glasses were perched on his head, and he wore soft black leather loafers without socks. Wow, Dahlia thought. Give a guy his first showbiz management client and he goes Hollywood.

When Louie spotted Dahlia, he broke away from the men and headed toward her with what she could see was a tight smile on his face. A smile she knew was strictly for the benefit of the company. As soon as he was close enough to her so that she was the only one who could hear him over the surrounding din, he put his hand on her arm and squeezed. "Let's be clear that from now on I'm in charge of every aspect of her career." Then he held out his pudgy hand and enumerated his ideas about Sunny in a speech he'd obviously been rehearsing.

"Number one," he said, extending one finger: "She works alone. She gets up and sings the songs without you. Elton John doesn't have Tim Rice on the stage with him when he performs. Tim Rice is in the audience or watching Elton on TV. That's where you'll be. Number two: She gets two-thirds of the money, not half, because she's the composer/performer. You're just the lyrics. Number three: When we start making our album, I got ideas for the titles, and Harry whatever-his-name-is bows to my creative input or we find someone else to do the arrangements, et cetera. Our first album should be called *On the Sunny Side of the Street*. With a gorgeous picture of her on the cover. I've been talking to photographers all week about how to make her look skinnier."

"Louie, you're an idiot," Dahlia said. "But that's good, because it proves to me that some things never change."

"Hey, you want to be a smart-ass? I happen to know that there are plenty of lyricists out of work who would die to work with her once they hear her incredible tunes."

Dahlia shook her head. "You don't have a clue," she told him.

"What *you* don't have a clue about is that there is no bond stronger than the one between a sister and a brother, since your parents decided to stop having children after you were born—which I don't blame them for doing." It was the same na-na-na-na-na voice he'd used when they were kids.

"Louie, why are you turning this good thing, your sister's getting well, into something so bad?"

"Because some people only want to take advantage of her getting well for their own personal gain."

"Boy, are you right! And I'm talking to one of those people right now," Dahlia told him as she turned away. She could see Penny chatting with a woman who looked familiar, but she couldn't remember why. Maybe it was because the woman was an old card-playing friend of her mother's, but she couldn't call up a name for her until Penny introduced her.

"You remember my Aunt Rita?" Penny asked Dahlia as the tight-lipped woman offered a bony hand. And as Dahlia looked into the woman's eyes, she remembered Rita Horn too well, and all the bad memories suddenly flooded through her head. This was Norman Burns's aunt. The one who'd hated the idea that Norman was wild for Sunny. Dahlia had forgotten until that moment that Louie's wife, Penny, was the first cousin of Norman Burns. Arthur Miller, the love of Sunny's life.

"I used to play canasta with your mother," the old bitch said, and Dahlia felt her heart race as she remembered the way this woman had disapproved so powerfully of Norman's relationship with Sunny. She wondered if Sunny retained any memory of the influence this nasty woman had probably had on her life. Dahlia's stomach rumbled, and she headed toward the buffet table.

"She's here!" Sunny called out happily, spotting Dahlia and running toward her to hug her. "Wait until you see them, Dahl." Then she called out, "Kassie. Robin. Come out here."

Dahlia recognized the two little girls immediately from the pictures Louie had shown her. Now, as they emerged from a back bedroom, she could see that the white-haired one looked eerily like Sunny had as a child, and the other one was tiny and dark-haired and pale by comparison. "This is your cousin Dahlia," Sunny announced, and the two girls walked to Dahlia and gave her one of those uncomfortable hugs children give when they're forced into it.

"Okay!" Louie yelled out now, silencing the buzz of the crowd. "For those of you who haven't ever heard my sister, Sunny, perform her songs, you're in for a treat. She's verging on the brink of major stardom, and now she's gonna thrill you with a few of her fabulous tunes, so gather 'round."

Dahlia was worried. Sunny was flushed, and her white bangs were wet and matted against her face. She smiled at the people around the piano, who cleared a path for her, and she sat down at the piano bench, staring at the keys for a long time. Dahlia felt engulfed by that same fear she used to have when they were kids, a panicky terror that Sunny might suddenly cave in and fall apart, but then Sunny played the opening chords of "What's Happened to Me?"

"I wrote this song with my cousin Dahlia," she said as she played, "who has been my collaborator since we were kids." She sang the first few lines, and then they heard the screams.

"Ohhh, God! Help me! Ohhh!" There was a gurgling cry of pain from a far corner of the room and then a loud thud, and Penny cried out, "Quick! Louie! Call the paramedics!" Sunny grabbed the girls from where they stood near the piano bench and ushered them into a back bedroom. Louie was on the telephone shouting his address into it. Dahlia stood at a distance from where Penny leaned over her Aunt Rita, trying to give the older woman CPR.

But by the time the paramedics arrived, Rita Horn was dead. Penny wept, and Louie made sure the girls and Sunny stayed out of the room until the paramedics removed the body. When she returned, Sunny looked panicky and on edge. She begged Dahlia, before she left for home, to promise she'd come to Rita Horn's funeral with her, and even though Dahlia loathed the woman and certainly would never have gone otherwise, she promised, because she knew that if Sunny was going, she ought to be with her to get her through it.

The guests all clucked their tongues and hugged Penny sympathetically as they filed out the door, and when Penny was out of earshot, Dahlia heard Louie joke to one of the waiters who was just leaving, "Hey, didn't I say my sister was gonna knock 'em dead?"

Mount Sinai Memorial Park glimmered in the bright California day. Sunny was babbling nervously as they walked toward the sanctuary. "This is my first funeral. I'm scared," she said. "Will I have to do anything?"

"Yeah," Louie said. "All the first-time people have to kiss the dead body."

"Honey, quit scaring her," Penny said. "No, you

don't have to do anything, Sun. Louie's gonna be a pallbearer. Those are the men who carry the box in and out of the hearse. That's all. You'll just sit with me and Dahlia."

"Looks like we're late," Dahlia said.

The sanctuary was filled with friends and family of the deceased, and by the time the four of them were inside searching for seats, the rabbi was already standing at the podium eulogizing Rita Horn. She was an exceptional mother, aunt, grandmother, philanthropist, blah, blah, blah. Dahlia felt herself nodding off and trying hard to stay awake.

In the row just in front of the one in which she and Louie and Penny and Sunny sat, Dahlia spotted an older couple who had been friends with her parents. The man used to play poker with her dad. A number of people had nodded at Louie or shook his hand as he walked in, and Dahlia heard him whisper to Penny that they were customers of his from the hardware store. Now one of Rita's daughters came to the podium to read a poem about her mother, and then another daughter told a few stories about her. The rabbi came back to the podium and recited some prayers in Hebrew, and then everyone stood and said the prayers in unison.

It all seemed to take forever, and Dahlia wasn't even sure why she was here. Now a man from the mortuary stepped up to the podium, holding a three-by-five card from which he read, "Will the following gentlemen please remain after the others exit?" Dahlia was sorry she hadn't come in her own car. Since Louie was a pallbearer, he'd have to go to the grave site, and this would have been a great opportunity for her to slip out and go home.

"Brad Freeman, Sam Forbes, Lenny Kendall, Norman Burns . . ." read the man.

Sunny clutched Dahlia's arm. "He's here! Oh, my God, he's here," she whispered. "And I look so fat."

Dahlia, whose mind had been drifting, didn't understand why Sunny was frozen in her spot as the others started to move out of their row and head toward the exit.

"What?"

"He's here! Norman is here, and he's a pallbearer. That means we'll see him." She nodded toward the front of the funeral home, and both cousins craned their necks to look toward the coffin where the men were gathering, and there he was in the first row. Arthur Miller.

"Oh, God. We should sneak out and not let him see how fat I am," Sunny whispered.

"You look great, Sun," Dahlia whispered back. "And we can't leave. Penny's her niece, and Louie's going to be a—"

"Louis Gordon," said the man from the mortuary.

"See?" Dahlia said. "We're stuck."

"Maybe I can hide in the crowd," Sunny said. There were beads of sweat on her forehead. She was wearing a black suit that Penny had lent her, and except for the top button on the skirt, which was open under the jacket, it fit her amazingly well, since she was much taller and slimmer than Penny. She looked beautiful.

"My luck, I'll say hello and my skirt will fall down,"

she joked in a whisper as they walked up the aisle to the door.

"That'll make him like you even more," Dahlia said, and they both stifled giggles.

Now all the mourners stood outside on the grass in front of the sanctuary, and, in a moment, through the door came the serious-faced men bearing the coffin. Louie was in the front, and Norman was in the rear. He looked elegant in a black suit and a red tie, much more elegant than Dahlia remembered. Slowly and carefully the men slid the box containing Rita's dead body into the hearse and dispersed to walk to the grave site. Norman, oblivious to Sunny's tearful, longing gaze, walked a few yards ahead of them now, chatting with some of the other men.

Dahlia could feel Sunny vibrating with tension next to her. Surely this would have to turn out badly. He was a married man with grown children. He knew her history. What on earth could possibly happen today, all these years later?

"He didn't see me," Sunny said softly. "Or maybe he did see me and he can't imagine that this fat old hag could be me, so it hasn't clicked."

"Will you stop talking about yourself that way?" Dahlia said as Penny caught up with the two of them. She was blowing her nose, and her eyes were swollen from crying. Well, *somebody* liked the old bitch, Dahlia thought.

"What a sad day," Penny said. "I'm glad that so many people turned out for her. Everyone on my mother's side. Even from out of town. I mean, I haven't seen my cousin Normie in ten years," she said. "Since his wife died and I went to Florida for her funeral. Isn't it sad that we only see family at funerals?"

Sunny grabbed Dahlia's arm and turned pale. "His wife died," she mouthed, and Dahlia nodded as Penny walked ahead and called out, "Normie?"

Norman Burns stopped and turned, and when he saw it was his cousin Penny calling him, he smiled warmly and walked over to hug her. As he did, he looked at Dahlia and smiled at her over Penny's shoulder. Then he took his arms from around Penny and stood transfixed when he looked next to Dahlia and saw Sunny. Later, when she talked about it, Dahlia told Sunny she was certain that at that moment the earth stopped turning.

When Norman's eyes met Sunny's eyes, Dahlia saw expressions on both of their faces that said that all the years and the pain and the distance and the misery had melted away, and all that mattered was that they were in the same place at the same time, at last. And best of all, Dahlia said later, it was over Rita Horn's dead body, exactly as she had requested those many years ago. The two star-crossed lovers gazed at each other for the first time in more than twenty-five years and fell into each other's arms making sounds so primitive and joyous that Dahlia and Penny knew it would be good for the two of them to keep walking and allow Sunny and Norman to be alone with their moment.

Minutes later, when Dahlia and Penny had gotten close to the grave site, and the driver of the hearse had parked, and Louie and the other pallbearers were in position to remove the coffin, Dahlia looked back to where Sunny and Norman stood, and they were still embracing. Dahlia could see Norman whispering into Sunny's hair as he held her tightly. His eyes were closed, but tears were falling from them onto her, and it wasn't until later that Sunny told Dahlia what he'd been repeating over and over:

"I will never let you go again. Never, never let you go again."

I guess Louie was wrong, Dahlia mused to herself, grinning. There *is* a bond stronger than the one between sister and brother. The other pallbearers managed the coffin without Norman, because now he and Sunny were walking hand in hand, completely oblivious to where they were. And Penny and Dahlia stood very still, trying to overhear the bits of conversation that floated by them.

"After Celia died, I kept working in the practice I inherited from her father in Boca Raton, Florida. My girls are in college. I love golf. Ever played golf?" he asked her.

"You may not believe this," Dahlia heard Sunny say, "but very few mental institutions have golf courses." Then they both laughed.

"Maybe you'll learn. You don't have to play golf. What would you like to do if you could just do anything you wanted?" he asked.

"Be with you," Dahlia heard her say.

Norman's voice was choked with tears when he put his arm around her again and said, "We'll make up for lost time."

twenty-three

"Meetings, meetings, meetings," Harry Brenner said. "I've got them hot and ready for the two of you all over town. Let's get those cute tushes moving and start making some real dough. I even sent the demo over to Céline Dion's people, and they're interested in two of the songs. What in the hell are we waiting for?"

"Uh . . . that's great news, Harry. We just need to get a few more songs finished," Dahlia said, wondering how much longer she could go on stalling him while Sunny and Norman celebrated their reunion by seeing each other every night and burning up the phone lines between Louie's house and Norman's hotel room. Sunny didn't care if Harry sent the demo to Céline Dion or Dion & the Belmonts. Norman was back in her life, and that was all she cared about, talked about, thought about.

Louie couldn't stand it that the once-postponed love affair now had the power and the forward motion of a freight train. He could see that his plans and dreams of grandeur were threatening to go up in smoke, and it made him so desperate he even called Dahlia to report on Sunny's behavior.

"You gotta help me here," he whined. Norman was taking her out to lunches and dinners and feeding her like there was no tomorrow, and if she didn't quit "porking out," she wouldn't be able to get into the slinky outfits Louie thought she should wear onstage. Sunny wanted to get her hair cut in some chic hairdo she'd seen in a magazine because she thought Norman would like the way it looked, but it was wrong for the image Louie wanted her to project on album covers.

"Last night she didn't get in until two o'clock," he said, sounding like some gossipy old biddy. "Do you know what that could do to her voice? *You're* gonna have to talk some sense into her. And the capper is that you'd think at that hour she'd go up to sleep, but frigging Arthur Miller hangs around in the living room, and I can hear them laughing until God knows when. I finally put my robe on and acted like I was going into the kitchen for a glass of water so maybe he'd get his ass out of my house, and he finally took the hint."

An hour after getting that phone call, Dahlia's doorbell rang, and she opened it to find Sunny holding the Macy's shopping bag, looking apologetic and asking, "Can I have my old room back?" There was a taxi waiting behind her. "I mean, I paid this guy, but he's waiting just in case you don't want me here." Dahlia looked at Sunny standing in the doorway, threw an arm around her, and walked her into the house.

Sunny looked shaky but happy. "Louie's gonna have a shit fit."

"We've survived Louie's shit fits before," Dahlia said, leading her into the kitchen, where she poured her a cup of coffee while Sunny chattered away nervously about Norman.

"He rented a Jaguar convertible from some rental place in Beverly Hills, and we drive around with the top down. He likes fancy restaurants, but I make him take me to Bob's Big Boy because that's where we used to go. You've got to help me with clothes. I need new clothes, and I never know what goes with what. I told him I was moving back in here, so he's picking me up here tonight." Then she sighed a happy sigh. "I love him, Dahl. I love him, and he loves me. Imagine."

"I'm imagining, Sun, and I'm so happy for you. But we have to talk about something else for a few minutes," Dahlia said, sitting at the table across from her. "It's important. Harry's been calling me every day. He says everyone in the music business wants us. He'd like us to come in and have a meeting with him on Wednesday at ten to strategize about our future." Sunny didn't react to that at all, except to avoid looking at Dahlia. "I'd be lying to you if I didn't say I want us to keep on writing songs together," Dahlia went on. "I mean, maybe we can keep doing it after you're married. Long distance or something."

Sunny looked into her coffee cup as if it were a fortune-telling eight ball and she were hoping some answer was going to surface from it. Then she sighed, a big, shoulder-shrugging sigh. "Dahl, life is full of twists and turns. Who could have ever imagined that all these years would go by and then you'd come looking for me, and we'd be back together with a hit song and a commercial? And best of all, in my wildest dreams I never thought I'd get Norman back, but I did. Remember how my mother always used to say, 'Man plans, God laughs'?"

Dahlia nodded. That used to be Aunt Ruthie's favorite expression.

"I guess what I'm saying is, I don't want to be Leiber and Stoller anymore. And I think the most fair thing for everyone is for me to retire before any more happens with us."

Dahlia folded and unfolded the paper napkin in front of her as Sunny went on, surprised at how calm she felt at the news she knew would be coming sooner or later. Sunny looked a little jittery, but Dahlia decided it must be because of the anxiety around rushing away from Louie's house. "I mean, as far as I'm concerned, you and Harry can do whatever you want with the songs we've written so far," Sunny said. "But my fantasy of how the perfect life should be is different than yours. Mine is me sitting at a phone dressed in a white uniform saying, 'Dr. Burns's office. Can I help you?'"

Sunny's fondest wish was coming true at last. The one she'd made on all those stars long ago. Dahlia knew that. With Sunny's retirement, her own dreams might never come true, so she was surprised that she felt a lighthearted gladness about it all. "You want me to tell Harry, or do you want to come to the meeting and tell him yourself?" she asked, pouring herself a cup of coffee, too.

"On Wednesday at ten, I'll be in Joe Diamond's office with Norm. Norm's going back to Boca on Wednesday afternoon, and he wants me to plan a wedding and get ready to come there with him. I told him there's so much about the way I am that he needs to understand before we get married, that he has to come with me to this appointment to meet the doctor who put me on this medication and let someone who knows about it explain it all to him. Dahl, I'm so afraid I'll never be a good wife. So afraid that one day I'll just lose it and not be able to handle life the way other people live it. Every day when I wake up, it's iffy that I'm even going to get through to dinnertime. I don't live one day at a time. I live one hour at a time. So it's a tentative proposition. I can barely handle most of the stuff you're so good at. Probably 'cause you're so fearless."

"Fearless?" Dahlia said, laughing and shaking her head.

"You are!" Sunny said.

"No way."

"What are you afraid of?" Sunny demanded to know.

Dahlia could barely say the next words. "That I can't write a decent song without you."

Sunny emitted a puff of air though her lips in disapproval. "That's completely wrong. You've done it. When I was still walking around drooling, you had a hit song," she said, putting her hand over Dahlia's.

Her nails were a shiny fuchsia. "But then you just lost your confidence for some dumb reason. Maybe it's because you got all turned around by the money and forgot you knew how to do the work. Dahl, when we were kids, there used to be a picture in your house of you learning how to ride my old bike."

Dahlia smiled in amazement. Wasn't it rich to have someone so close that you shared a history, shared a frame of reference down to something as specific as remembering an old family photograph? "Remember the one I mean?" Sunny asked.

"Of course," Dahlia said. "I was just thinking about it the other day."

"Remember how your adorable mother let you go so you could realize you had the stuff to balance the bike on your own? Well, that's all I'm doing. I'm letting go of the bike, Dahl. And I'm so happy to be doing it, because I have the confidence that you won't fall or crash. You have to go tell Harry that you're great with or without me."

Dahlia used the side of her right hand to push along a pile of crumbs that were still on the table from the toast she'd eaten at breakfast, and then she swept them into her left hand and stood to take them to the sink. But her sudden interest in the crumbs was just an excuse to walk away and not let Sunny see the tears she was fighting. Not that Sunny couldn't tell.

"Dahlia Gordon, this is your cousin speaking," Sunny went on. "Your first and best friend in the world. When everyone else gave up on me, you gave me a life. As far as I'm concerned, there isn't anything you can't do."

Dahlia turned, and now she said words she never thought she'd be able to utter. "I gave you a life for selfish reasons."

"I'll never believe that," Sunny said, walking to her. "I think you waited until you had the power to take care of me, and then you goddamn did it."

"No," Dahlia said. But Sunny put her hand up and gently covered Dahlia's mouth to stop any more objections.

"Yes," Sunny said. "Now, come and help me with my makeup. I can never quite get it right lately. I'll bring everything out here." Within minutes she'd created a makeshift dressing table with all her cosmetics set out across the coffee table.

"Let's do this," Sunny said. "You make me up tonight for my date. Just as if I were a movie star and you were my makeup lady. Teach me about eyeliner. I don't remember how to do it anymore."

Dahlia got into the game, doing Sunny's makeup the way she remembered Sunny liked to do it herself. She was using the eyeliner pencil and talking Sunny through the steps. "You need to keep the liner very sharp," Dahlia said. "And then come up like this from under the lashes, and that way the line becomes very thin and very close to the top of the lashes. Then try putting some loose powder on the lashes, and that'll give the mascara something to hold on to."

"You're wonderful," Sunny said, looking at Dahlia. "Thank you for doing this." But Dahlia couldn't help noticing that something was very wrong with the look on Sunny's face, a pallor that was unusual, and the blusher she applied couldn't conceal it.

When the makeup was finished, Sunny said she had to get dressed, and she swept up the bottles and jars and brushes and hurried into her room. Dahlia could hear her opening drawers and closet doors, probably unpacking and trying on outfit after outfit, like a teenager getting ready for her date. She didn't emerge until the doorbell rang and it was Norman. Dahlia watched Norman take her in the same way he had when they were dating twenty-five years before.

But Dahlia noticed there was something unsteady about Sunny's walk and something odd in the way her voice quavered when she called back, "Don't wait up," that made Dahlia worry. Louie had promised when Sunny came to live with him that he would be the pill monitor, making certain Sunny took a pill every morning. Surely, Dahlia thought, he must have given her one that morning.

After Dahlia heard Norman's car pull away, she sat down at the piano. Sunny was going to make a life with her great love at last. And Gordon and Gordon were through. "There isn't anything I can't do," Dahlia said aloud to the empty room. Then she composed the music and wrote the lyrics to a song she called "I Had the Secret All Along." And when she finished, she was sure it was the best song she'd ever written. Exhausted, she put on her pajamas and climbed into bed.

The shaky walk, Sunny's asking her to put on her makeup for her in the living room. There was only one reason for her to do that. She had never once looked in the mirror to check on what Dahlia was doing. She couldn't look in the mirror, because the studio audience was back. Sunny must have stopped taking the pills. After a while Dahlia fell asleep. She had a dream that she was back in school and sitting in a class where the professor was talking in a raised voice, but she opened her eyes to hear Norman's raised voice in her living room.

"What am I supposed to do? Pretend I didn't have a life?"

"No. Not pretend," Dahlia heard Sunny say in a choked voice. The bedroom door was ajar, and Dahlia slid into her robe and moved toward the door, standing just inside where she could barely see the two of them. Sunny was collapsed on the sofa, and Norman was pacing. Dahlia thought Sunny had stopped smoking, so she was surprised to see her puffing away on a cigarette.

"Not pretend." Sunny's lip was quivering, and her jaw was moving back and forth. "But when you always talk about my wife, my girls, my wife, my girls— and all I ever wanted from the day we met was to be your wife and have your children—it hurts me, Norman. So I can't help that it cuts through me and . . ."

"And what? I can't change that I had a wife, a life, two daughters."

"Yes, yes. I know. And I had nothing. Nobody. So every time you say that, it just emphasizes that I lost twenty-five years of everything—of loving, of feeling. But most of all twenty-five years of you being *my* husband, *my* lover, the father of *my children*."

"Sunny, I got cheated out of that, too. I never stopped wishing it were you. But after a while that kind of thinking can make you—"

"Crazy? Say it. Crazy!"

"Stop this. I didn't say that word. Sunny, I had to go on. I had to make it all right. It was more than all right. And I don't ever want to feel guilty that I created two amazing children."

"Three."

"Jennifer and Samantha."

"And the baby I had to get rid of, Norman. Because even though we loved each other and I wanted to tell you, my parents and my aunt and uncle decided that because of the medications I was taking, it might have been dangerous to have a baby, so they made me not tell you."

Dahlia could see Norman look as though she'd slapped his face, and after a moment he sank to the sofa next to Sunny.

"That was a mistake. Not telling me was a mistake. I could have gone with you," he said. "Or married you. Or . . ."

Dahlia remembered now, the little snatches of conversation she'd overheard from her parents, and she put the sleeve of her terry-cloth robe up to cover her eyes while she cried.

"I wanted to, but my mother said it would make you feel guilty, as if you owed me something or as if I planned it to trap you. And then, if you stayed with me out of guilt, you would hate me. I'm sorry I listened to her."

"We would have had a twenty-five-year-old together," Norman said. "You should have told me."

"I plead insanity," Sunny said. "I watch *Law & Order* on TV. People who are insane can get away with anything. And I'm not a *pretend* crazy person who puts it on to stay out of jail. I've got credentials. Full-out fruitcake aborts baby of man she loves more than she loves breathing. Doesn't that prove it? What are you doing here, Norman? Surely in Boca Raton, Florida, there are women standing in line waiting to be with a rich widower doctor like you. Why are you bothering with a schizophrenic songwriter who can barely make it through the day? If you have any self-respect, you'll open that door and run as far the fuck away from me as you can. And I guarantee you'll be married to some nice Florida matron—or better yet a young wife who can start a whole new family with you—any minute."

"Sunny . . ."

"You're a schmuck if you stay here for me. I could be the way I am right now forever. On the edge, never sure, fragile, so needy I'd suck every ounce of energy and joy out of every moment. Who needs that, Norman? Maybe I'm saying this because I love you so much. But given the life you'd have to look forward to with me, I believe you should go now and never look back."

Dahlia clutched the front of her robe together and said a silent prayer to her parents and Sunny's. Please, if you're up there looking down, don't let him listen to her and leave. Let this man be better than that, and make him stay. The silence was too long, and Dahlia was worried. An eternity passed until Norman spoke, so softly that Dahlia had to get closer to the door to hear him.

"Sunny, don't test me. Don't think you're going to get rid of me this time, because you never will. I'm back in your life to stay, until I die, and no matter what you do, I'm not leaving you. So just tell me the most important thing: Why did you stop taking the pills?"

"How do you know?" she asked.

"Look at you. You told me a doctor gave you pills that helped you hold it together. But you're trying to get me to leave you, and that's the craziest fucking thing I've ever heard."

"I don't know why," was what she said.

"You don't know?"

"That's how it works sometimes. You do stuff and you don't know why. But, Norman, honey, this is only the tip of the iceberg." That was when Dahlia stepped forward into the living room, just as Norman followed Sunny into her room. When he entered, he saw what Dahlia could now see, too—the magazine photos once again taped and clipped and pushpinned everywhere, of the movie stars, models, and princesses. It looked to Dahlia as if the collection had increased tenfold. That's what Sunny had been doing in there all those hours, taping and gluing and pinning them to the walls and ceilings.

"Who are all these people? Why are their pictures all around?" he asked gently, knowing already that the answer would have to come from Sunny's madness.

Dahlia leaned on the doorjamb for support. If Sunny went into her spiel, he would finally see how powerful her demons really were and find a reason to leave her after all, in spite of what he'd said. But Norman sat on the bed and listened to the whole thing about how the studio audience conspired in the death of beautiful women, about how they watched everyone in the world from the other side of mirrors, and how she was onto their evil. When she finished, he took her hand and gently pulled her onto his lap.

"Sunny," he said, "when did you take your last pill?"

"A few days ago," she said.

"Let's go and find them right now and give you one. Okay?"

"Okay," she said. She went to one of her dresser drawers, opened it, and produced a small vial, which she handed to Norman. Dahlia, now in the living room, watched him hold it far away from his face and squint to read the directions.

"I'll go get some juice," Dahlia said, and Norman turned.

"Thanks," he said.

≈✦≋

twenty-four

$\mathcal{D}$ ahlia sat nervously in Harry Brenner's living room, looking at her watch. When she saw that it was ten-fifteen, she tried to picture Sunny and Norman sitting with Joe Diamond. Before they parted that morning, Sunny had hugged her.

"We're both grabbing for what we want," she said. "What we each wished for on all those stars so long ago. I got my wish. You can get yours." Dahlia had worked the whole morning on the speech she was going to make to Harry.

First she'd tell him that Sunny was dropping out. That she had instructed Dahlia to tell Harry that all the songs she and Dahlia had written together were okay to sell if anybody wanted them, but Sunny didn't want to make an ongoing deal with anybody. She wasn't going to stay in L.A. and write songs. Maybe Dahlia would skip the part about Sunny's wanting only one thing, and that was to be a receptionist in her soon-to-be-husband's medical office.

Harry's housekeeper had shown Dahlia into the living room twenty minutes earlier, telling her that Harry was on a phone call in the studio and that he'd come and get her when he was ready. The wait was giving her more time to remind herself to "turn on the power" and to go over the new song in her mind so she could play it for him this morning.

"Hey, gorgeous, come on in." Harry opened the door from the pool and walked inside. "Sunny in the powder room?" he asked, looking around.

"She's not here, Harry."

"Oh, then let's wait. You want something to drink while we're waiting for her?"

"We're not waiting," Dahlia said. "She's not coming at all. Let's go out to the studio and start the meeting."

Harry looked disquieted. "Is there a problem?" he asked.

Dahlia didn't answer him until they were seated across from each other on the leather sofa in the air-conditioned studio. Turn on the power, she said to herself and sat up straight.

"Harry," Dahlia began, "I owe you an apology. Sunny and I agree that you can run with the songs on the demo or any other songs she and I have written together, and in terms of management, you can have me as a client on my own. But if that doesn't work for you, then we have no deal."

"Is this about that turkey Louie who keeps calling me? The brother who wants to manage her career out of his hardware store?" Harry asked.

"No," Dahlia said, "it's because Sunny is getting married and retiring from the music business. I'm the one who prodded her into working with me, but she doesn't really want it. She's glad Faith's song is climbing on the charts, she's happy if you can place the others, but she quits."

Dahlia watched the redness start in Harry's ears and spread to his face. "What *is* she, crazy or something?" he asked, shaking his head, as if Dahlia had been speaking to him in a language he'd never heard before. "Say this again? Doesn't really want it? This isn't a bid from the sorority we're talking about here. I'm getting offers up the wazoo for these songs, record deals where big-time labels want you two to write a song a week for them—and she doesn't want them anymore? That's completely fucked! Let the boyfriend wait a year or two! First you cash in on all the buzz about these frigging songs and become independently wealthy. Then she can get married and be the dentist's wife."

"Cardiologist," Dahlia said.

"Who gives a crap?" Harry screamed in her face. "You started this by lying to me about the authorship of the Faith song, then you told me I had the two of you, and now you're telling me I got you and not her? What *is* this?"

"You're right, and I apologize, but all I can offer is what exists," Dahlia said, surprised to find that seeing this hysterical side of Harry seemed funny to her and not threatening.

"Well, let me tell you something, doll." Harry stood, and Dahlia knew that whatever was coming next was not going to be nice. "You better see if you can buy that old van of yours back, because unless you got Sunny and her tunes in your corner, you're not gonna be able to cut it without her. You know what I'm saying to you?"

Dahlia bit her lip. "I know exactly what you're saying, Harry," she said, "so that pretty much ends our association." She walked out of his studio and over to the Celica that sat at the curb with the top down. After a minute she took a deep breath, started the car, and all the way back home she sang her new song at the top of her voice.

Norman was back in Florida. Sunny talked to him ten times a day, and she spent the rest of her time shopping with Penny for outfits for the children and a wedding dress for herself. This morning she was sitting in the kitchen reading the newspaper when Dahlia wandered in for breakfast. The paper was opened to the obituary page. Dahlia saw that Sunny had circled one of the obituaries she wanted her to see, but the name of the man whose obituary was circled wasn't familiar to her. Bill Gibbons of Santa Monica had died of heart failure in San Diego on Monday. Dahlia's eyes continued down the column to read that Mr. Gibbons, once the CEO at Rainbow Paper, had been living in San Diego for the past fifteen years. Sunny looked sad.

"I'll bet nobody will even have a memorial service for him," she said. "His family basically left him for dead. He broke down in his late forties and could never quite come back. He always loved music. Even when he was in big business, he had some of the guys at work with him form a barbershop quartet."

Dahlia looked at Sunny curiously. "Why are you showing this to me? Am I supposed to know who this is?" she asked.

Sunny nodded. "You *do* know him. It's my friend Bill. You met him. The big fellow with the white hair and beard. He was very successful in business here in L.A., but he had a breakdown years ago, and his whole family abandoned him. He was in and out of the mental-health system for years, and he finally seemed to find his only peace of mind at the Sea View, believe it or not. Conducting our choir was the thing that seemed to make him the happiest. I wonder if any of them will remember and do something for him."

Santa Claus. Dahlia remembered him now.

"I need to go down there. Will you take me?"

The Sea View looked the same to Dahlia, but she wasn't surprised to hear that to Sunny it was practically unrecognizable, probably because in a way she was seeing it with new eyes. "It looks so different," Sunny said. "I never realized what a dump it was."

The minute the car stopped, she opened the door and hurried toward the porch, with Dahlia behind her. Her pale blond hair caught the sun and sparkled as she moved. The four men on the porch puffed on their cigarettes and didn't look at the two women at all. Sunny stopped to look at them. "Hello," she said. Two of them glanced over, but there was no recognition in their eyes. She looked dramatically different than she had when she was a resident, so there was no reason why they should. One of them nodded.

Inside the front door, a woman in a nurse's uniform

was dispensing medications from a cart. "You ladies here to see someone?" she asked.

"I'm here to see everyone," Sunny proclaimed. The black woman who chattered to herself was just taking a cup from the cart. "Hello, Ella," Sunny said, and the woman looked at her blankly. "Do you remember me? I'm Sunny."

The woman studied Sunny's face for a long time before her eyes filled with recognition. "Why, of course I do," she finally said, and she opened her arms wide. Sunny hugged her warmly, then looked into the living room, where the usual group sat watching *Oprah*. "Hello, everyone," Sunny said loudly, but nobody turned to look.

"They don't pay much attention to strangers," the nurse said.

"I'm not a stranger," Sunny said. "I lived here for twelve years in room three."

"I'm in room three," a skinny woman with silver hair said. She had just reached the bottom step, and the nurse handed her a cup, but she didn't take it, just looked at Sunny nervously. "Did I do something wrong? I try so hard to do everything right, but accidents happen. It isn't my fault."

"You're fine, Grace," the nurse said. "This lady used to live in your room, but she moved away. That's all."

"Mind if I use this?" Sunny asked, picking up a bell that the nurse used to call everyone to medication and shaking it. It worked. Most of the TV watchers looked over.

"I'm Sunny. I used to live here," she said. The men who had been on the porch were standing in the doorway peering inside now. "I read in the newspaper that Bill Gibbons died." A few people nodded. "And I'm sure you must miss him. He was my friend when I lived here, so I thought maybe we could all get together and do something in his memory. He was so kind to all of us and so proud when we sang." She walked to the piano. "This was Bill's favorite song," she said. Then she repeatedly played a note to give them the pitch and said, "So why don't we sing it to help Bill's journey to the other side?"

Now the men came inside from the porch. Dahlia recognized the tapping man and the man named Eddie.

"Ella," Eddie said to the woman who chattered, "stand up! You have to use your diaphragm, and it isn't gonna work proper if you don't stand up."

"Everyone remember this? It's an easy one," Sunny said, "that Bill loved." Then, in her biggest voice, she sang the first line all alone. "Come by here, Lord. Come by here." The people moved closer to the piano, and one or two joined in haltingly, as if they had only a vague recollection of the song. "Come by here, Lord, come by here." By the end of that verse, a few more had joined in.

"Someone's praying, Lord. Come by here. Someone's praying, Lord. Come by here." Now more of them seemed to remember, and Dahlia watched the magic of the music envelop them, causing their postures to change while their voices rang out. It was such a simple song that even the ones who'd never sung it before were singing now. "Oh, Lord, come by here."

"Someone's crying, Lord. Come by here." Sunny's voice was the loudest of them all. "Someone's crying,

Lord. Come by here." Dahlia felt the tears rush into her face, and someone was definitely crying as she felt around in her purse for a tissue and sang along with all of them. "Someone's crying, Lord. Come by here."

"Oh, Lord. Please come by here," they all sang proudly. And at the end they applauded for themselves, and Sunny bowed her head and said, "Thank you, everyone, and thank you, Bill."

The chattering black woman and the short, stocky woman hugged Sunny, and so did the new woman, Grace.

"We all miss Bill so much," the black woman said.

"We're glad you came, Sunny," the man who tapped told her as he accepted her hug.

"Thank you for letting me do this," she said to everyone, including the nurse, who was wiping her eyes and blowing her nose as she told Sunny, "When Grover was prepping me to do this job, he said that none of them would ever say thank you to me. He said they were too zoned out. But he was wrong. They say lots of nice things all the time. His problem was, he couldn't really see them. He saw mental patients. I see individual people. You were good to come back. Gives them something to talk about, and the way you are gives them hope."

Sunny stood for a long time watching the others move back to their chairs and back onto the porch before she turned to Dahlia to say, "Thank you. I'm ready to move on."

ere's how it feels to massage your cousin on the night before her long-awaited wedding: impossible, Dahlia thought. She's so giddy she can't lie still, can't stop jabbering about the groom. She laughs for a while, and then the next minute she's in tears, because she wishes her parents could be around to see her joy. And then she sits up and wants to chat.

"Dahl, you have to promise you'll come to Boca every chance you get. Maybe once you get show business out of your system, you'll come and live there, and Norman will fix you up with his doctor friends, and you'll move in next door to us, and we'll be together all the time."

"Want to turn over on your back for the rest of the massage?" Dahlia asked her.

"I don't want any more massage. I want to get into my pajamas," Sunny said, sitting up on the table, "and look at my dress again and touch it, and look at the flowers Norm sent me today and the card."

Norman had taken a room for the cousins at the Hotel Bel-Aire, where the wedding would be held the next morning. In the room next door were his two daughters, Jennifer and Samantha, who seemed to take to Sunny right away, liking the romantic idea that she'd been their dad's girlfriend of long ago. They would be Sunny's bridesmaids. Kassie and Robin would be junior bridesmaids, and Louie's little son, Michael, would be the ring bearer. Louie was giving away the bride, and Dahlia was the maid of honor.

"How am I ever going to fall asleep?" Sunny asked, slipping into the rose-colored silk pajamas Penny had bought her as a pre-wedding gift.

"You will," Dahlia promised. "Eventually you'll close your eyes and drift away till morning."

Sunny sat on the turned-down twin bed leafing through a copy of *People* magazine, and by the time Dahlia had taken down the massage table, she was asleep with a smile on her face. For a long time, Dahlia gazed at her from the other twin bed, amazed at the circumstances that had brought them to this place tonight. Finally, with some wonderful ideas for a song that she wanted to write ringing through her brain, she fell asleep, too.

In the late morning, she opened her eyes to the sound of the blow-dryer to find that Sunny was already showered and wearing the slip she would wear under her wedding dress. Soon Penny and the children pounded on the door and filed in, all of them eager to see the bride and help her get ready. The girls were dressed in elegant lavender party dresses with pretty matching shoes, and Michael looked uncomfortable wearing a seersucker suit with short pants.

Dahlia didn't like herself in the lavender silk suit Sunny had chosen for her, and she couldn't believe she'd been talked into wearing the matching lavender shoes, but Sunny said she was afraid that if she left the decision to Dahlia, she would have worn jeans to the wedding. Oh, well, Dahlia thought, it's Sunny's wedding. I guess I don't mind looking stupid for her.

By the time Louie knocked impatiently on the door to say that the rabbi had arrived, Sunny had redone her hair three times. Penny wove sprigs of baby's breath into it, and then, leaving Sunny behind to do some last-minute touch-ups, the others marched out toward the garden, where Louie was waiting to give his sister away.

"I ought to sell her to this guy, not give her away," he joked in a too-loud voice. "Her friggin' royalties are gonna be worth a fortune."

A few of Norman's cousins were chattering to one another and to Penny. Joe Diamond was in the front row, and Dahlia felt panic and then embarrassment as she spotted Seth and Lolly sitting in the second row of white folding chairs facing the canopy. Lolly was wearing a long string of pearls from the jewelry box, wound around three times. As the rabbi took his place next to Norman, the guitarist Norman had hired began to play. Dahlia recognized the song as "Turn, Turn, Turn."

Penny seated herself in the front as the procession began with Norman's daughters, wearing matching lacy lavender dresses, moving slowly toward the canopy, flanking their kind-faced father. Then five-year-old Michael bounced down the grass, grinning as he carried the rings on a pillow. Then came Kassie and Robin in their froufrou dresses. And, after a fluttering stomach made her want to bolt, Dahlia tried to maintain an even pace as she moved slowly along, hoping Seth didn't think she looked dopey in that silk lavender cocktail suit.

Dahlia and Norman exchanged a smile when their eyes met, but behind his smile she saw the pain of all the intervening years that had gone by. She tried not to look at Seth and Lolly and Joe Diamond, but as she passed them, she thought she caught sight of Lolly clapping her hands together. Now everyone turned to look across the lawn in the direction from which Sunny, looking tall and stunning in her high heels, in contrast to her small round brother, clutched his arm as they made their way toward the canopy. She was a blinding and beautiful vision in her fitted white dress, with white pearls and a short white veil. Dahlia glanced at Norman and saw his eyes brimming with tears.

"Where you been all my life, gorgeous?" he asked softly as Sunny reached him. After everyone was in place, the rabbi began.

"Sometimes in this life, we have to take long and circuitous journeys simply to get back to where we began," he said, smiling at Norman and Sunny. "But in the end God's plan prevails, and what is *beshert*—which is a word that means 'something that was meant to be'—inevitably happens. Norman had a wonderful life with Celia, and their marriage blessed them with Jennifer and Samantha and many years of happiness. Then, after the painful and tragic loss of Celia, Norman feared he would never find a new love.

"Fortunately, God had a plan for him, and instead of finding a new love, he encountered his former love, who might not have been ready for a marriage to him all those years ago. But now, happily for both of them, after many of her own struggles, Sunny is ready and welcoming him to her side at last. All of us here are certain that this marriage of Norman and Sunny is not only blessed but was meant to happen at this time, at this moment, when all the other circumstances of their lives made them ready to be together at last.

"I believe that when two people love each other, the difficult moments are halved and the joyous events are doubled. So it will be for Norman and Sunny, who have turned a malediction into a benediction."

A cool breeze whispered through the trees around the lush green lawn, and Dalilia was surprised at how comforted she felt by what the rabbi said, how peaceful she felt, even with her own life in such a state of uncertainty. In the last week, she had put her house up for sale because she wanted to scale down her expenses, she'd met with several music agents to try to find a good one, and she continued to write her own songs, which seemed to be getting better over time. She was determined to market them and find a way to make a living in the music business, and selling the house and moving to a cheaper place would help her to stay afloat in case her new songs didn't find a deal.

Seeing Seth as she walked down the aisle had

thrown her. She didn't know Sunny had invited him, or what she would say to him once the ceremony was over and the group assembled for lunch. Now she watched Sunny and Norman as Michael stepped up to give them the rings.

"Do you, Norman, take Sunny to be your wife?"

"I most certainly and unequivocally and deliriously do," Norman said.

"That goes for me, too," Sunny said softly.

"You may kiss the bride," said the rabbi, and Norman lifted the veil from his beloved's face and took her in his arms, and they kissed.

It was a kiss that brought the whole group to its feet, applauding and cheering for the ecstatically happy couple. And their bliss made all the guests hug and congratulate one another. Dahlia hoped that the mascara Sunny made her wear wasn't running onto her face. She was about to search in the suit pocket for a tissue she'd placed there earlier, but she felt something sharp sting her on the leg, and she looked down. It was a paper airplane that had now fallen at her feet. She noticed as she bent down to pick it up that it had little flowers drawn on the wings in colored pencil.

"This is cute," she said as she looked around and saw Seth and Lolly still standing back by the chairs on the lawn, and she knew that the airplane had come from them.

"Thank you," she mouthed, nodding. Then Seth did some pantomime with his hands, trying to tell her something. But when she shrugged to tell him she didn't understand what he meant, Lolly called out, "Open it up!"

That was when she realized that inside the airplane was a note.

Dear Dahlia,

The note was written in a child's block printing.

You are much nicer than you used to be when you and my dad were roommates. Now you have Sunny who is your good cousin and if you marry my dad he says she will be my cousin too. That is one of the reasons I told my Dad it would be okay now to marry you, even though I used to didn't like you a lot. So here is a picture I made of our new family. Me, Sunny, my Dad, you, and Rose the Squirrel. Oh, also the guy Sunny is marrying. If this is okay with you, please tell my Dad and I will get a new dress for your wedding. To this wedding I wore an old one.

Lolly Meyers

Dahlia looked back at Seth and Lolly, and neither of them moved as they waited for her to reply in some way. They were holding hands, standing near the flowered canopy, both of them looking so beautiful to her that she could never possibly get a word out. So instead she walked toward them with her arms spread, and when they saw that gesture, they ran to her, and the three of them embraced and held one another tightly.

"Does this mean you'll marry us?" Lolly asked.

All Dahlia could do was nod and hug them again.

"And now," Sunny called out as everyone moved toward a private room for the luncheon, "my cousin has to keep a promise she made to me when we were little girls—actually, we made it to each other. That we would sing a certain song we wrote at one another's weddings."

As Dahlia's eyes adjusted to the dark, cool room, she saw that there was a small upright piano at one end of it, and she and Sunny sat down on the bench and played their song as they sang it together.

"Stay by my side forever. Stay by my side, my friend . . ."

And soon the rest of the group surrounded them, arms around one another, singing along.

"Our love's a perfect circle. That means it cannot end."

After Sunny and Norman left for their honeymoon in Norman's rental car, Seth and Lolly offered to help Dahlia get her things out of the hotel room. Together the three of them walked across the grounds of the elegant hotel, with Lolly in the middle holding their hands.

"This will only take a minute," Dahlia said. "I packed nearly everything this morning, and all I have to do is throw in a few last-minute things and I'll be right out."

When she opened the door to the room she and Sunny had shared the night before, a blast of air-conditioning made her feel chilled. As she walked back toward the bathroom to gather her toiletries, her step was light, but when she entered the pretty, white-tiled room, she was jolted by what she saw. Sunny must have done it before she and Norman departed. The words Sunny had written on the hotel bathroom mirror in lipstick were a reminder that her health would always be a work in progress. Dahlia shook her head and smiled to herself sadly, put her cosmetics in her bag, and took one last look at the message. It said, BYE-BYE FOR NOW, FOLKS!!